I0652626

PUZZLE
OF THE
PAST

PUZZLE
OF THE
PAST

(Trilogy - Part 2)

G. P. Schumacher

DISCLAIMER

This novel is a work of fiction. Names, characters, and events are products of the author's imagination. Any resemblance to real people, living or dead, and actual events is purely coincidental. Certain long-standing institutions, agencies, public offices, and places are mentioned in this novel, but the events happening and the characters involved are entirely imaginary.

Copyright © 2024 by Greta Schumacher

Title: Puzzle of the Past

ISBN: 979-8-89316-956-0 - eBook

ISBN: 979-8-89316-957-7 - paperback

Cover design by: Joice Panilagao

Book design by: Honeylette Pino

Line edits and proofreading by Motif Edits – www.motifedits.com

All rights reserved. No part of this publication may be reproduced, distributed or transmitted in any form or by any means, including photocopying, recording, or other electronic or mechanical methods, without the prior written permission of the publisher, except in the case of brief quotations embodied in critical reviews and certain other noncommercial uses permitted by copyright law.

Interested in learning more about the author?

Follow me on Facebook: G. P. Schumacher

Follow me on Instagram: author.g.p.schumacher

Find me on Pinterest: gpschumacherauthor

Email me at gpschumacher.author@gmail.com

To Ben—
the love of my life, my best friend,
my soul mate, my wonderful husband!

CHAPTER 1

The bruises on her face had only just begun to turn from red to purple, though the largest of them was covered by a big bandage the doctors had used to patch over the stitches on her forehead. Beside her, the soft, steady beeping of a vital signs monitor synced with the oscillating line on its screen, showing her heart rate and oxygen flow were stable. Every thirty minutes, a blood pressure cuff reinflated and took her blood pressure.

The beeping monitor and the occasional inflation and deflation of the cuff were the only sounds in the hospital room where Maria slept. The young patient might almost have seemed peaceful, if not for her eyelids fluttering as her closed eyes moved rapidly.

She must be dreaming. Trying to process the horrible things that happened to her. Elisabeth Collins suddenly couldn't help but sob loudly as she took in her long-lost daughter lying in the hospital bed. She felt a hand on her shoulder. *Oh, Brad.* She leaned into her ex-husband's warm embrace, then looked at Aaron. The young man was sitting on the other side of her daughter's hospital bed. He had stared at Elisabeth after her outburst but looked away when their gazes met.

She eyed him. The name tag on his blue Air Force uniform read "HEIKINNEN." The one golden bar beneath it was so dirty, so sandy. His light blue shirt was stained with blood—her daughter's blood. The fabric around the knees on his pants was crusted with twin crowns of muddy sand. His shiny black shoes were stained with seawater and had clumps of sand stuck to their soles. Dark circles were visible under his ocean-blue eyes.

Elisabeth now tilted her head to Brad, his arm around her. His arm in the green camouflaged Air Force uniform. The sand and bay water hadn't left much of an impression on his camo. She now eyed her own clothes; her summer dress was still stale from the previous wetness. Sand clung to it in clumps.

"We all look so terrible and dirty," she whispered.

Brad nodded. "Yeah, especially Lieutenant Heikinnen. He likely ruined his brand-new blues uniform."

Upon hearing his name, Aaron glanced up at the pair again. They hadn't spoken much with each other, not even in the car when they were following the ambulance.

"Please, just call me Aaron," he said. "And I don't care if my uniform is ruined. Most important is that Maria is okay."

"*Moana*," Elisabeth corrected him.

Aaron raised one eyebrow. "Well, Mrs. Collins, I know her as Maria, and I'm not sure I can bring myself to suddenly start calling her Moana."

"Well, that's her real name. Get used to it," Elisabeth said, her voice raised.

Aaron stared at her, his blue eyes now sparkling in anger. "*Well*, I don't think that's *your* choice. I think Maria should choose what she wants to be called from now on. And I wouldn't be surprised if she wants to be called Maria like she has been the past twenty years!"

"Excuse me, young man, she is *my* daughter and *I* named her Moana when she was born. It's her real name! Just because—"

"Elisabeth," Brad interrupted, "I agree with Aaron. We just found our daughter again, and she's all grown up. It should be her choice which name she goes by."

"What? You want our daughter to keep the name *her kidnapper* gave her? How dare you even say that out loud."

Elisabeth's face flushed, and she now stared directly into Brad's unique hazel eyes, each a mosaic of golden-and-green flecks orbiting a dark-brown center and encircled by a blue rim. She watched as they changed green, tears forming in front of them. Suddenly, her face took on softer lines. *My poor Brad. I don't want to fight with you. I just found you again. And together, we found her.*

Then Aaron said, "We don't even know yet if Martina kidnapped Maria," and Elisabeth's sternness returned.

"What? Of course we do!" She jumped up and looked down at Aaron, sitting there across the bed where her injured daughter was lying. "Martina Sullivan and her ex-husband are guilty. It's obvious! You saw it! He *just* kidnapped her again and tried to kill her. You saw it with your own pretty blue eyes."

Aaron stared back at Elisabeth. "Martina Sullivan wanted nothing to do with her ex-husband. She was afraid of him. Why would she partner with him to commit a crime five years after they'd divorced?"

Suddenly, a frantic beeping noise filled the room and Maria groaned, then started throwing her head from side to side. They all stared at the beeping vital signs monitor, which showed a spike in the squiggly line that measured Maria's heart rate.

"Shhh… Both of you," Brad said, his voice firm but calm. "Please stop fighting. You're stressing her out. Her heart rate is way up. Please don't wake her. She needs her rest so she can heal."

Aaron's face flushed in embarrassment, and Elisabeth watched him train his focus back on her daughter, who had stopped moving and was now sleeping soundly again. The beeping noise stopped. Elisabeth sat back down in the chair next to Brad. She took her daughter's hand and cupped it in hers. *My poor baby girl. Mein Engel, meine Süße.*

It was then she felt the ring on her daughter's hand, a beautiful round diamond in a cathedral setting. She inspected the golden ring more closely. *An engagement ring.* She sighed, then glanced over to the young man in the dirty blues uniform.

My daughter is engaged to that guy over there and I don't know anything about him. Or her, actually. She's been gone for twenty years. Tears formed in Elisabeth's eyes. *She's not a toddler anymore; she's an adult now. I need to get to know her.*

She cleared her throat. "Aaron?"

The young man in the blue Air Force uniform looked up, his face wary.

"Can you tell us about our daughter? What is she like? What does she do? How did you come to know her?"

Aaron broke out into a big smile and nodded. "Sure. Well, she's great. She's super smart, has a full-ride scholarship to Embry-Riddle University in Daytona Beach and just finished her junior year there. And—"

"What does she study?" Brad interrupted.

"Human Factors."

"Is that where you met? At the university?" Elisabeth asked.

"Yeah, we met there during my sophomore year. My friends Nick, Jim, and I were on the welcome committee for the freshman class and I noticed her right away 'cuz she's super-hot—" He bit his tongue and blushed. "H-happy, I mean. You know, happy, confident, very pretty."

Brad and Elisabeth grinned at each other. "She sure is pretty, isn't she?"

Aaron nodded, his face still bright red. "Yeah. She is. And she has this amazing laugh that's always contagious. She has a lot of empathy, deeply cares about others, and has a lot of friends. She's a real people person. Everyone likes her."

Brad and Elisabeth both smiled. "Can you tell us more about that?" Elisabeth said.

"Okay, sure. She's best friends with Keisha from Chicago and Brandy from Georgia. Maria and Keisha are studying Human Factors together, while Brandy is an engineering student like Nick, Jim, and I were. The six of us hung out all the time." He sighed. "But now us guys are all graduated and commissioned, meaning we're scattered all over the country."

"I see. And that's why you proposed to our daughter?" Brad said.

Aaron's eyes rested on Elisabeth, then his gaze turned to Brad. "Well, not just because I had to leave Embry-Riddle. I don't doubt we'd have been fine if we'd stuck to being boyfriend-girlfriend, but I thought it was good timing. Maria can finish up her studies, then we'll get married and she can look for a job around here. I mean, if she wants. Um, we could make long-distance work, I guess. But I was hoping to have her with me. She's my *wingwoman*. I always call her my wingwoman."

Brad gasped. "What did you say?"

"Well, sir, I said she's my—"

"—*wingwoman*. I heard," Brad said, the color leaving his face. "When and where did you propose?"

"Oh, at the ROTC ball about a month ago in downtown—"

"—Daytona Beach. Oh my gosh, the woman in the red dress at the water fountain," Brad whispered. He closed his eyes, then took both Elisabeth's and his daughter's hands into his.

Elisabeth turned to him. "What are you talking about?"

"I *met* her. I saw her there. At the ball. She irritated me. Goodness, I should've known! I should've recognized her." Tears started streaming down his face. "I failed again. I should've recognized her."

Elisabeth glanced over to Aaron, who shrugged his shoulders.

"At the ball," Brad mumbled through tears, then turned to address his sleeping daughter directly. "I should've recognized you."

"What the heck are you talking about, Brad?" Elisabeth pressed.

Aaron had already put one and one together. "General Collins was the guest speaker at our ROTC Ball in Daytona. He was there when I proposed."

Elisabeth's jaw dropped. "What? You were?"

Brad nodded, tears in his eyes. "I should've recognized her. I'm sorry, Elisabeth, I'm so sorry I failed again to bring her back. I met her right before I left that night, talked to her at the water fountain in the hallway."

Aaron stared at him. "She never told me she ran into you. It all makes even more sense now. She didn't just see you on stage—she actually met you? No wonder her dreams started right after that."

Brad used his bare hand to wipe his tears away. "Dreams?"

"Yeah, well, flashbacks, as we now know. She kept dreaming of drowning. And a dad in uniform. And German words."

"She did?" Tears started welling in Elisabeth's eyes.

"Yeah, she did. And when I found out I'd be stationed at Eglin Air Force Base, Maria—"

"*Moana*," Elisabeth interrupted.

Aaron stopped talking immediately. "With all due respect, ma'am, I already told you, I can't call her that. It's not who she is to me. For goodness' sake, I'm engaged to a Maria. I can't just start calling her by a different name."

Silence reigned in the room.

Aaron put his head in his hands. "If she wants me to use this other name, I'll try my best to honor her wishes. I'll do whatever she wants me to. Even then, it'll be hard, but I'll try. But until then, what you're requesting is too much to ask of me."

Elisabeth saw the young man look up at them, his eyes suddenly moist.

"You have no idea how hard these past few weeks were. And then tonight! Jeez, who would've thought that freakin' Jonathan Sullivan would attack her. I just didn't see it coming. I didn't." A tear escaped his ocean-blue eyes and ran down his nose. "And it's all my fault. I should've protected her. I should've, but I was so focused on finding her real parents that I—"

"Stop, Aaron," Brad said, and stood up. "Please, stop. It's not *your* fault! It's *my* fault!" Elisabeth and Aaron now stared at Brad as he went on: "*I* should've protected her. Back then. I should've never left our little one alone. I should've been more like you, Aaron!" Both of Brad's hands formed fists now.

"Like me?" Aaron asked, surprised. "What do you mean?"

"Look at yourself. You don't care about your uniform! You don't care if it's dirty or not. I shouldn't have cared either, but instead, I did, and went to the stupid laundromat long enough for her to be kidnapped." He plopped down into his chair, slammed his fists into his own two legs, then hunched over. "My gosh, it's all my fault. I'm so, so sorry."

Gently, Elisabeth took one of his fists and slowly unfolded his fingers to hold his hand. "No, Brad, no, it's not *just your* fault! It's not. It was *my* idea to wash your dirty uniform." She couldn't help herself and started crying. "*My* idea!"

"Yes, but *I* insisted on going with you to the laundromat. I did. And we just left her alone, right there in the TLF." Elisabeth and Brad hugged each other tightly.

"But you were on a secure military installation," Aaron said. "You had just moved to Eglin and couldn't have known anyone there, much less made any enemies."

Elisabeth stopped sobbing. "That's right."

Brad let go of her and looked at Aaron. "How do you know all that?"

"Well, I did my research. I read about it in newspaper articles I found online. About the 'accidental drowning of the toddler Moana Marie Collins.'"

Elisabeth raised her eyebrows. "You read about her case? Why? When?"

"Well, it all started when Maria…" Aaron stopped talking and glanced at Elisabeth.

She briefly smiled. "It's okay, Aaron, I understand now. Just call her Maria."

"Okay, thanks," Aaron mumbled, and continued. "Well, when Maria began having these weird dreams, these flashbacks, I started researching. It took me a while to figure it out. But when I put the pieces together, I knew she must be the missing toddler that had apparently drowned at Eglin twenty years ago! The daughter of General Collins and his German-born wife. *Your* daughter."

Elisabeth jumped up. "You knew? How long? Why the heck didn't you tell the police?"

Aaron's eyes rested on her. "Because I didn't have any proof. And I tried calling you, General, but got stonewalled by your exec."

"You *did*?"

"Yeah. He gave me enough to realize you were here in Florida. And then I learned you were having a work dinner at Compass Rose last night, so I brought Maria there. By that time, I was pretty sure she was your daughter. I knew for a fact that her birth certificate had been faked; my top secret security interviewers told me as much. And the night before my interview, Maria had this crazy flashback when we tried to stay at the TLF—she was spiraling, and I knew the best thing for her would be to meet you."

The Collinses stared at him. "But why didn't you tell the police?"

Aaron shrugged. "I told the interviewers and they contacted the police. Then, we went to see Chief Parlot who talked to Maria only. I didn't say anything about my assumption she might be your daughter as it was still all circumstantial. Guess I needed more proof. And I got it at the restaurant. Seeing you. *Both* of you, ironically. Didn't expect to see you at that restaurant, Mrs. Collins."

A quick smile lit up Elisabeth's face. "Well, I'm only here in Florida because my friend Sarah wanted me to fly back here to find closure. But then I contacted Brad and we decided to meet here and ask the police to open up the case again."

Aaron nodded, and they all went silent for a little bit.

"Why now?" Aaron asked.

"Because Moana... Maria... disappeared twenty years ago. And tomorrow"—Brad checked his watch—"actually, today, is her birthday."

Aaron stared at him. "Today?"

Both Elisabeth and Brad nodded. "Yes, on June second. She was born June second, 2001, in Utah."

Aaron let out a sigh. "This will be complicated. She'll have to choose a name *and* a birthday. We always celebrated in September."

"What? That lady even changed her birthdate?" Elisabeth squinted at Aaron again. "She kidnaps my child, gives her a new name, and changes her birthday?"

Aaron jumped up. "Mrs. Collins, I assure you that Martina Sullivan—"

"—is definitely guilty!" Elisabeth yelled, her face flushed.

Aaron rolled his eyes. "Please, think about it! That's what I thought at first, but I don't know if that's true anymore. I seriously doubt it."

"What?" Elisabeth yelped, ignoring Brad's gestures for her to quiet down.

"Why? Why do you doubt it, Aaron?" Brad asked. "*We* don't doubt it! Jonathan and Martina Sullivan obviously kidnapped her.... Their names are on the fake birth certificate."

"I know. But like I said before, it doesn't make sense that Martina would work together with her abusive ex-husband to kidnap a child. When it happened, she'd already divorced him, didn't want anything to do with him. And as far as I know, she's never left Miami."

Elisabeth and Brad looked at each other. "Miami?"

"Yes, Miami. Where she immigrated to from Venezuela. Where she runs her own store. Miami. Where her whole family lives. And where Maria grew up. They've never lived anywhere else and never ventured far from home, even for vacations. Why would she come to Eglin with her ex-husband five years after they divorced to kidnap a child?"

"She's always lived and worked in Miami? But didn't she work at Eglin? In Eglin's temporary lodging facilities? As a cleaning lady in the TLFs?" Elisabeth's mouth felt suddenly dry.

Aaron shook his head. "No, not as far as I know." He thought for a bit. Suddenly, his face lit up. "And I think I have proof that Maria was taken by a guy, by a man!"

15

"What?"

Aaron's eyes were wide. Elisabeth watched him search for his phone in his pants' pocket. His bright face abruptly lurched pale. "Damn it, I have proof. Proof that Martina is innocent. Totally forgot about it."

"What do you mean, Aaron?"

"I filmed Maria. I filmed her when she had that flashback at the TLF. Oh my gosh, I filmed her. She mentioned 'bad guys.' She said she was afraid of bad guys—emphasis on *guys*. It's all right here on video."

Elisabeth and Brad looked at each other. "Can we see it?"

Aaron nodded and walked over to the other side of Maria's bed to show them the recording on his phone. Silently, they all watched.

Elisabeth threw her hands over her mouth and started crying. *My poor baby girl. She remembers being at the TLF? She remembers being taken? Being kidnapped? By bad guys? Oh my gosh, what did they do to her?*

She glanced over to her sleeping daughter, now all grown-up, her face bruised, her forehead bandaged.

And how in the world did they get her off base? And how did she end up in Miami? With that woman who pretended to be her mom?

With Martina Sullivan.

CHAPTER 2

Martina Sullivan stared at the cold, bare wall. It was late, after midnight, she assumed. She just sat there on the uncomfortable concrete bed, waiting for time to go by. She still couldn't believe it. *I'm in jail. In this strange outfit. Jumpsuit. ¡Dios mío!*

Martina took in a deep breath. She felt like crying but knew that wouldn't lead anywhere or help at all. *I've done nothing wrong. I'm innocent. I didn't fake a document and I certainly didn't kidnap a child. What are they even talking about?*

She sighed and shivered. *Well, guess I lied about being Maria's mom. But I had no other choice. Had to protect her. Mija, my Maria. Definitely need to keep my beautiful girl safe. She's everything to me. This is absolutely crazy! What should I do?*

A lawyer. Maria's last text message told me to get a lawyer.

Before she could think about it any longer, she heard footsteps. Two policemen came and stopped in front of her cell.

"Mrs. Sullivan?" one of them said.

She got up and nodded.

"Back up against the far wall. We're gonna enter your cell now."

What? Enter my cell? Why?

She did as ordered and the two men unlocked her cell. She noticed they had her personal belongings and even her purse with them. *What, are they letting me go?* She smiled; her hopes were up. She took a few steps forward and pointed. "That's my purse. And my clothes."

The one police officer grinned at her. "No, not yours. This is *evidence!*"

What? Staring at this man in confusion, Martina didn't notice the other policeman walk around her until he was standing right behind her. Without warning, he grabbed her arms and crossed them behind her back.

"Aua," she yelled out in surprise as cold handcuffs bit down on her wrists. *What are they doing?*

"Martina Marie Sullivan, you're being transported to Niceville."

"What? Where? Why?" Without an answer, she was led out of the cell by the police officer carrying her belongings and purse as the other officer escorted her.

"Chief Parlot requested you be there for the interrogation," the chatty policeman informed her.

Interrogation? A real interrogation? ¡Dios mío! In Niceville? Where is that? She thought she'd heard of that town before but couldn't remember.

"It'll be a long trip. The drive will take about nine hours. The whole night."

"What? Why are we going so far? Why there?"

"None of your business. Chief Parlot needs you to be there, so you'll be there," the escorting officer barked, his voice low.

Martina shivered, glanced at both of the officers, then almost stumbled over her own two feet as she was led out of the police station toward a police car. The pair opened the door to the backseat.

"Watch your head," she was told as they pushed her inside. Before she knew it, she was buckled up, her hands still tied behind her back. She saw the one officer throw her purse, her clothes, and a file folder with her name on it onto the car's center console. The other policeman remained standing by her open door.

Martina shifted uncomfortably in her seat; her arms tied behind her back were fast losing circulation. "Please, can you take this off? The handcuffs are hurting me."

The officer at her door started laughing, an unfriendly rumble. "Take off the handcuffs? So you have a chance to escape when we open the door again? Yeah, right. Mrs. Sullivan, remember, you're still under arrest. We're not going to Niceville for a vacation. We're just transporting you. The handcuffs stay where they are. Now, enjoy your trip." He slammed the door shut and both police officers got into the front seats of the police car.

"Off we go to Niceville," she heard the chatty one say as he started the car.

Niceville. Where have I heard of that town? She felt the car move and suddenly remembered. *Maria told me they were looking at apartments in a city called Niceville. A city located right next to the Air Force base. Eglin, Aaron's new duty station. Eglin AFB. The place Maria and Aaron are at.*

She heard the car's blinker and noticed they were leaving the parking lot. She had no choice but to go along for the ride. *Don't want to leave Miami. Have never really left Miami. But at least I'll be close to Maria. Maybe I could even talk to her?*

She smiled, then her smile faded. *I will have to tell her. Tell her what I know. But can I? Is it safe? Jonathan will be furious if I do. If I make him mad, that's not safe for anyone.*

She sighed; her heart was beating fast. She quickly shifted her focus onto her daughter, the little one she had raised so lovingly. *She's all that matters right now. Maria. Her safety. Will she still love me when I tell her my secret?*

Martina stared out of the window as the car raced through the dark Florida night. She found herself deep in thought and realized she hadn't contemplated this for years—decades, actually—but now she couldn't help but think of it. Of that first moment when she had seen little Maria. Scared, intimidated, hungry-looking little Maria.

Tears sprang to her eyes. Her thoughts went back to that moment. The moment that had changed her life forever. A moment she wouldn't exchange for anything yet had handled all wrong.

She closed her eyes, and a scene formed in front of her, so clear, so real, as if she was watching it happen. A scene from a long-ago time.

It was the middle of the week, late at night, and Martina was finishing a work project she had taken home from the store. She felt safer at home, as she knew her ex didn't know the address to her little apartment. He did, however, know the address to her store. After the customers and other employees left and she was all alone, she never really felt safe there and often took work home to finish in her cozy little apartment.

The doorbell rang, startling her. Her body's involuntary jerk almost knocked over a glass of water on the coffee table, but she caught it at the last minute. *Phew. That was close. Almost spilled it on my customer's handmade dress.*

The doorbell rang again and startled her once more. *I'll ignore it. Definitely won't open the door. Not expecting anyone.*

She continued to work on the dress, but the doorbell rang again. She sighed. *Who could it be? I don't know any of my neighbors. I like keeping to myself and only interact with customers on a strictly professional basis. Nobody has a reason to come visit me—especially this late at night. How would they even know where I live?*

But the doorbell kept ringing and ringing. With a big sigh, she got up to go to the intercom at her door. She was a bit curious despite herself. "Hello?"

"Open up, Martina. I need to talk to you."

She froze. *I'd recognize that voice anywhere. My ex. He's here? In front of my apartment's door? How in the world does he know where I live? How did he find me?*

She stumbled backward in fear and ignored the ringing a few more times. *I can't open that door! I don't need to open that door. I have a restraining order against him and it's completely right to ignore him. I should call the police!*

Determined to tell him exactly that, she went back and activated the intercom. "Listen, Jonathan, you need to go, or else I will call—"

But then, she heard it: a whine. A soft whine, a little cry. Her heart stopped. *What is that? Sounds like something is scared, so very scared, scared to death.*

Over the intercom, she heard him trying to muffle the wailing. But he couldn't and the crying got louder. She heard him trying to shush that little thing, until finally he yelled, "Argh, shut the fuck up!"

A loud, long, sharp wail followed, then sobbing that got softer and muffled and finally stopped. *What is that? A baby? A child?* Martina's heart sank; her hands started sweating. *He's not capable of caring for a child. That man doesn't have a loving bone in his body.* Right away, she understood that this little child was in big trouble.

"Martina, open up! Please!"

Please? Since when does he use nice words? Her fingers were so sweaty they slipped off the intercom button. *Don't know what to do.* A big part of her wanted to send him away, call the police, and forget about this, but another part of her was worried for that little human being he must have with him.

The doorbell rang again. She put her fingers on the intercom to hear him speak. "Martina, please open up. I really need to talk to you."

She heard a soft yet constant whimpering that gnawed at her heart. "What's that noise? Who is with you?"

"A child. Baby girl. My child."

Martina stared at the door. *His child? What in the world?*

"Please, Martina. I need help. Well, *she* needs help, actually," she heard him say, his voice almost begging.

What am I supposed to do? Want to just send him away, but what about that little baby girl? The soft whimpering was clearly audible over the intercom. It swirled around in her ear, became too much for her to handle.

Without thinking, she pressed the button.

The buzzing that opened the door to the apartment complex shocked her. She listened to his footsteps as he walked up the flight of stairs and stopped right in front of her apartment door. Instead of ringing the doorbell now, he knocked on the door, a heavy pounding on the thin layer of wood that separated her from him.

What do I do now? I let him into the building. He's standing right here in front of my apartment that he should never have been able to find the address to. Her heart was pounding. She peeked through the hole in the door to see him.

His face was red, his greyish-blue eyes enraged. *I know that look. Too well. It's never good when he looks like this.*

On the third knock, Martina saw the little bundle in his arms. She was just able to make out a small little nose and small little cheeks. A small child, a little toddler. *Chubby cheeks? No, not these ones. These cheeks aren't round like they should be with a small child.*

The cheeks she saw were pale, almost greyish, the bones clearly defined. Her heart sank. *A starved child. He's holding a fragile, starved little child?*

She could also see wetness on the bony-looking cheeks. *Traces of tears.* Then she saw the bundle shiver. *It's not cold right now. It's a warm Miami night.* In her heart, she knew then and there that the shiver wasn't because the child was cold.

On the fourth angry knock, Martina saw the little living thing in his arm pull the dirty, scratchy-looking blanket over her little face. In fear. That moment, Martina changed her mind.

And when she opened the door, her whole life changed.

"Finally," he roared in his scary, deep voice and pushed her aside as he stepped into her apartment.

She watched helplessly as she let the predator in. For a second, she thought about running away from her apartment to call the police, but instead, she closed the door and shut herself in with him. With the lion that could pounce any minute.

Despite her fear, she remained focused on that little bundle in his arms. That shivering little bundle, barely visible. She was curious to see. And, of course, he noticed, and smiled.

"Nice, cozy little place you have here," he spat out, mocking her, making her feel little.

She had yet to move, still standing by the now-closed front door, just watching him as he inspected her apartment. Her safe space now violated. That safe space was gone now, touched by him. For a second, she got mad, but then saw the wiggle and heard the whining coming from the scratchy old blanket in his arms.

"Who is that?"

"Oh, this annoying little thing?" He laughed and violently shook the bundle. The whining got louder. "Gosh, just shut up, you fucking little thing."

He put his big fat hand over the little one's mouth. The whining stopped, and Martina could see the little blanket bulging as the small child struggled to breathe.

A sudden feeling of urgency to protect the child came over her. "Stop it! You're hurting her! Let go of her!"

With a nasty grin, he looked at Martina. "Let go of her? Sure, will do," he said, and bent at the knees.

And before Martina could say anything more, he threw the bundle high up into the air without any intention of catching it.

"Noooo!" Martina stumbled across the room, her eyes fixed on the bundle flying through the air, her feet moving fast. She tripped over the leg of her coffee table and fell, but somehow managed to catch the bundle with the little one in it, and, with motherly instinct, cradled it in her arms before she herself hit the ground with a loud thump.

His laughter filled the room as she lay on the ground, holding the shivering, sobbing bundle. And then something special happened.

The little child opened her eyes and looked at her, looked at her with unique hazel eyes, a mosaic of golden-and-emerald-green flecks with dark-brown centers, encircled by a blue rim. Martina's heart melted.

"Mi niña pequeña," she whispered, and found strength, a reason to stand up to this man, a reason to speak up.

Even though her whole body was aching from the fall, she managed to get up, tightly holding the little girl wrapped in that scratchy blanket and walked over to him. She looked him in the eye, her voice stern. "You will stop treating this little child like that. You will *stop!*"

She focused again on the little one in her arms and gently rocked her back and forth. Suddenly, she felt a little hand grab her shirt, and the child's little body cuddled up to her as if saying, *Protect me, please, protect me.* The next few moments would become a blur in her memory. Not because she was choked up, in tears over this first moment with her daughter, but because it was all so unexpected, so surreal.

"You like her?"

Martina nodded, felt the little one hold on tight to her shirt, the grip strong. The girl opened her pretty little eyes again and looked at Martina. *She looks so small, so helpless, so hungry. So neglected.*

Martina glanced at her ex and saw him smiling, his lips pursed up, and then he laughed out loud. "You like this little piece of shit? This fucking needy toddler?"

The way he talked about the little one made Martina cringe. She held her tighter, rocked her back and forth, sought to protect her.

"You wanna keep her? Want her as your own daughter?"

Irritated, Martina looked up at him. "What?"

"I can either take her back home or leave her here with you."

"Leave her?"

"Yeah, I don't want her. I don't fucking *want* her. She's a little brat, a little piece of shit, nothing but trouble."

Martina was confused. "What about her mom?"

She heard him laugh his loud, cruel laugh and felt the little one cuddle closer to her. "Her mom? Her fucking mom's gone! Ain't here no more! Just me and her now."

Martina swallowed hard. *¡Dios mío! He can't care for a child. Especially not by himself. No, the poor thing.*

"So, you want her?"

Martina nodded. "But how—"

"Shut up and listen, Martina!" He came close to her, his bloodshot eyes locked on hers. "It's all arranged. All you have to do is tell everyone she's your daughter—yours *and* mine. If anyone doubts it, show them this." He pulled out an official-looking paper and laid it on the coffee table. "And this." He put another small piece of paper on the table.

She glanced over the papers. *Looks like a birth certificate… and a social security card?* She focused on him again as he lurched even closer to her, until he was nose-to-nose with her.

"If you ever tell anyone she's not our daughter, I'll come back and fucking crush you. I'll come back and find you, and her, and it ain't gonna be pretty. You hear me?"

Martina nodded, smelled the alcohol on his breath, the warm breath that numbed her nostrils.

"Nobody will ever know. All you need are those papers over there and to pretend she's yours. Raise her as your own and I'll leave you alone. But if you disobey me, if you say anything about tonight to anyone, I *will* come back and destroy you. Destroy you and her."

He suddenly grabbed her neck with both his hands and squeezed it tight, so tight. Martina struggled to breathe. He leaned in further, his strong body threatening to crush the little one in between them.

"I have ways of finding you and will make sure you won't have any more words left to say if you ever mention tonight to anyone. You got that, Martina?"

He squeezed her neck so hard she couldn't even nod anymore. She gasped for air. The little one was wailing; Martina felt big wet tears on her shirt, the tightening grip of little fingers.

Suddenly, he let go of her neck and shoved her across the room. She did her best to protect the little toddler in her arms as they both crashed to the floor. Then the man was towering over them, looking down on them, ready to end both woman and little girl should the urge strike.

"If you ever tell anyone or even *think* about going to the police, you'll be sorry. I fucking swear to God that no one will be able to save you or that child then. You hear me, bitch?"

Martina nodded; the little one whimpered.

"Shut up," he yelled at the girl, and raised his hand, ready to hit her.

But Martina had found her strength and protected the child. Her own arm took the blow from him. He cursed the child again, then opened the door to the apartment.

"Bye, Martina." He laughed. "Here's to never seeing you again. Just do as I say and I promise you, you'll never have to see my face again. But if you slip up…"

He closed the door behind him, leaving Martina and the little child on the floor, crying and shivering.

She shivered and shook her head. The scene from long ago disappeared before her eyes. In place of huddled bodies, she saw outlines of palm trees flying past her window. Her hands, still tied behind her back, were hurting her. Her thoughts swirled.

Unbelievably, he kept his promise all these years. Up until the moment Maria went to see him in Jacksonville.

She sighed. *I so wish she didn't go to see him. ¡Naguará! But she did. And then he came back to renew his threats. Why did she go see him? He didn't even know what she looked like all grown up. But now he does.*

Martina sighed again. Then her eyes widened. *Wait, if they arrested me, did they arrest him too? How did they even find out the birth certificate was a fake? Does Jonathan know the police know?*

She started sweating and shifted in her seat.

"Getting uncomfortable?" a low voice said.

She looked through the wire barrier inside the police car at the officer sitting in the passenger seat.

"It'll be a while to Niceville. Better get used to it, lady—or should I say, señora?" He turned around and grinned at his partner, then eyed her again. "Sweating now, huh? Yeah, the guilty ones always do."

Martina stared at him. *¡Idiota! Rude racist!*

But she didn't say anything and just stared out of the window again to watch the trees fly by in the dark night, wondering if the police had already apprehended her ex, Jonathan Sullivan.

CHAPTER 3

"Jonathan Sullivan isn't ready to be interrogated yet, Chief," the nurse said.

Chief Parlot was disappointed. "I thought you said he'd regained consciousness?"

"Yes, he did, but he has a severe concussion and needs rest. His head wound was not as bad as it first looked, but he did suffer a significant blow to the head and needed stitches. We plan to keep him in the hospital for a few nights to observe. And to let him rest. That's the best thing for a severe concussion. And since rest is so important, he's certainly not ready for any visitors—let alone an interrogation."

"But, ma'am, we need to talk to him to figure out—"

"No, Chief," the nurse interrupted him and held out one of her hands. "We understand he's the main suspect in your case, but we have to care for him first, before he gives a statement. You of all people should know the law. Besides, if we do it too early, I doubt he'll be of any use for your investigation."

Chief Parlot sighed and nodded.

"I suggest you go home now, Chief. There's nothing else you can do here tonight. Both suspect and victim are being taken care of as we speak; they'll both have to get some rest before we consider any social visits."

"I understand, ma'am," Chief Parlot said, and looked at her, then saw her name tag. "Thanks again, Nurse Karen. Appreciate the updates."

She smiled at him. "You're welcome. If you need me, just ring the bell right here." She pointed to the red button on the wall. "Good night now." Nurse Karen disappeared behind the counter of the nursing station.

"Okay. Thank you. Good night," he called after her. He turned around to check his watch, then pulled out his work phone. A text message from his colleagues in Miami informed him that the suspect was on her way to Niceville and gave him an ETA. He quickly responded via text and thanked them for their cooperation.

He yawned. His body felt how late it was, but his brain was sharp and ready to go. *This is certainly the most confusing case I've ever worked on. Also the most exciting. Still can't believe that little toddler from back then is still alive. A grown woman, no less, reunited right here with her parents.*

He pulled out his work phone again. *Get parents' genetic test done,* he typed into his notes.

He idled near the empty nursing station, consumed by his thoughts. *The docs already got Maria's DNA sample last night, but still need to get the Collinses' tomorrow morning.* He chuckled. *Today, actually, but at a more decent hour. Not in the middle of the night. Yeah, genetic testing is the first thing that needs to be done. But I've no doubt she's their daughter.*

He sighed. *How could the police and the FBI have gotten this case so wrong? They considered it a 'closed case' reduced to a slip of paper shoved inside the back of some filing cabinet at the station.*

He shook his head and began a slow trek down the long hospital hallway.

There's certainly a real-life story behind every slip of paper. Real-life people who are more than affected by what the paper simply describes. And this specific slip of paper has become personal to me now also. Their story, their lives. It's hard not to feel for the people involved in such tragic cases.

Especially this one.

29

I feel so sad for the mom. Elisabeth Collins just found her long-lost daughter but has yet to learn just how long twenty years really is. Her little daughter has become an adult with her own thoughts and feelings.

I feel worst of all for the daughter—Maria, Moana, whatever they're calling her now—from what they've told me, she's been going through hell lately. And that's before she got attacked. By the guy who pretended to be her dad…. Ah, it still doesn't make any sense.

A loud voice tore him from his thoughts. "Chief Parlot, wait, wait up!"

He turned and saw Aaron running after him. He stopped and waited for the young man to catch up with him.

"Oh, good, you're still here," Aaron said.

"Yes, I am. What is it, Lieutenant Heikinnen? Is your fiancée okay?"

Aaron nodded. "Yes, she is. Still sleeping, resting. She's okay. But I have something to show you."

The chief peered at the young man in the dirty blue Air Force uniform. "What, Lieutenant?"

"Please call me Aaron, Chief. I'm not quite used to the rank yet."

Chief Parlot grinned. "Very well then, Aaron. What would you like to show me?"

"A video, Chief. I recorded Maria's reaction when we arrived at Eglin's TLF housing. I think it proves Martina Sullivan is innocent."

The chief raised his eyebrows. "Well, let's see it then, please."

Aaron nodded, and they both took a seat on a bench in the hospital hallway.

"Thank you for showing me this, Aaron," Chief Parlot said after the video was finished.

"So, will you let Martina Sullivan go?"

The chief patted Aaron on the back. "That's not for us to decide right now. She's already being transported here to be interrogated tomorrow. No matter what, we'll need to talk to her."

Aaron sighed, then looked down at the floor.

"Please understand, I'm glad you showed me this recording. It's promising and helpful. Please send it to me so that we can officially submit the recording as evidence."

Aaron looked up again, a faint smile on his lips. "Yes, sir, I will definitely send it to you."

The chief nodded. "Great, thank you, Aaron. Let's do this right now then. Just AirDrop it to me." Aaron did as he was told and soon enough, the recording was saved on Chief Parlot's work phone. "Wonderful, thank you, Aaron. And seeing this, I'm thinking we might want to bring in a trauma specialist to work with Maria. That might help her remember more."

"A trauma specialist?"

"Yes, a professional who knows how to navigate PTSD and childhood trauma."

Aaron nodded, then his intensely blue eyes rested on Chief Parlot. "Do you think we'll find out what really happened to her?"

"All I can promise you is that I'll do my best to help uncover the truth. It seems we have a bit of a puzzle on our hands, but I'll try to piece it together until we can see the full picture. To that end, if you have any other information, Aaron, it would be more than helpful to get it to me as soon as possible."

Aaron stared at the chief.

"Aaron, *do* you have any other information? I know you did some 'research' already. Please help me do my job and give me anything you might still have."

Aaron bit his lip. "Well, I don't know if it will be particularly helpful—"

"Trust me, whatever you have will be helpful."

Aaron sighed. "Well, I assume you'll want to take a look at Maria's notebook then."

"Notebook?"

"Yeah, the notebook she used to write down her dreams, which turned out to be memories of her early childhood. It's a bit confusing. We just wrote down the dreams each time she had them."

"That's okay, Aaron. We can make sense of it. Where's the notebook?"

Aaron jumped up. "Oh my gosh, I lost track of it. We had it at the restaurant and were just looking at it, trying to make sense of it, but then we saw the Collinses, and I don't know if we just left it on the table or—"

"It's okay, Aaron," Chief Parlot assured him. "My team took everything with them when we combed over the restaurant. We have Maria's purse as well. My team's competent enough that they likely put the notebook in it. What does it look like?"

"It's a regular notebook, a purple composition notebook labeled *My Past*."

The chief took out his work phone and noted that detail. "Okay, thank you. I'll look for it in her purse. Anything else I should know?"

Aaron shrugged his shoulders.

"Anything about Martina and Jonathan Sullivan? What do you know about them?"

"All I know is that Martina is a very loving mom. She loves Maria and they have a special bond. It was only her and Maria her whole life." Aaron stopped and cleared his throat. "Well, not her *whole* life, I guess, but ever since she was a toddler."

The chief nodded and continued taking notes on his phone.

"Maria didn't know anything about her dad. Finally saw his name on her birth certificate. But when we asked her mom about him, she refused to talk about him. All I know is that she has some sort of secret she's been hiding from us."

The chief glanced at Aaron and then back down, his fingers swiftly typing the info into his digital notebook.

Aaron finally noticed. "Wait, are you writing this down?"

"Yes, what you're telling me is important. I need a record of it."

"But… shouldn't I have a lawyer? Shouldn't you read me my rights first?"

The chief smirked. "Why? Did *you* commit a crime?"

Aaron shook his head. "No, of course not. But aren't I a key witness?"

"You are. Aren't you giving me this information willingly? Information that should help your fiancée?"

Aaron shrugged his shoulders. "Well, I guess I am."

"Good. So keep going. What do you know about Martina Sullivan's so-called secret?"

"Not much. She told everyone her ex was Maria's dad and that she left him when she was pregnant with Maria." Aaron snorted. "We sure know now that's not true."

The chief nodded.

"We figured it out ourselves a while ago. When we confronted Martina about it, she told us she met this guy in the Army with the same first name as her ex—Jonathan—and claimed she had a fling with him before he deployed. Said he was Maria's dad. Also not true."

The chief nodded again.

"Beyond that, I don't know. I have no idea how in the world Martina ended up with Maria. But I really doubt she kidnapped her from Eglin. Seriously doubt it."

"Why? Because of the video?"

"Yeah, there's that, but also because Martina is a *nice* person. She has a lot of empathy. I don't think she's capable of committing a crime like that, inflicting terrible harm by stealing someone's child."

"How do you know?"

"I don't know. I don't have proof, I just have a feeling."

The chief raised his eyebrows.

Without warning, Aaron broke out into laughter. "Oh my gosh, listen to me, Chief. I'm the one who loves facts and proof while Maria is all about knowing things because she has 'a feeling.' I've even made fun of her for that. And now *I'm* the one who suddenly has 'a feeling.' Ridiculous." His laugh turned into a sob. "I don't know, Chief, I just don't know."

Chief Parlot put a hand on Aaron's shoulder. "It's okay, Aaron, it's okay. It's a confusing case. Like a jigsaw puzzle. We'll figure it out, don't worry."

Aaron nodded and wiped his eyes and nose with his bare hands.

"What do you know about Jonathan Sullivan?" the chief asked.

"Not much. We've only seen him once."

"We? Once?"

"Yeah, Maria and I visited his plumbing store in Jacksonville. It didn't go well; he threw us out."

The chief took notes. "Why? Why did he throw you out?"

"Maria told him she thought he was her father, but he said he couldn't have been. Then she told him she knew he'd been abusive and that she thought he'd come back and, you know… taken advantage of her mom, and that's how he was her father."

"Interesting," Chief Parlot mumbled, and kept filling out his digital notes. "What happened then?"

"Nothing. He just threw us out. We drove away. Never saw him again."

The chief got up. "Thank you, Aaron. For everything you shared. I'd say we all need to get some rest now. Go back to your fiancée and keep me posted on when she wakes up. We still need to obtain a statement from her as well." He handed Aaron his business card and pointed to a cell phone number. "Use that number to reach me. Same number you AirDropped the video to."

"Okay, thanks," Aaron mumbled, and put the card into his pants' pocket. "Good night, Chief."

"Good night, Aaron." The chief waved to him and walked off down the long hallway, already deep in thought once more. *Yes, a lot of puzzle pieces to put in place....*

It was then he heard a peculiar noise. He stopped to look around for the source but didn't see anything. Now on alert, he resumed walking, kept looking around until he arrived at the elevators. He pressed the down-arrow button and waited.

Right as the elevator arrived, the noise sounded again, slight and little. The elevator doors opened but the chief held them, kept them from closing as he peered up and down the hallway. He still didn't see anyone. Finally, he entered the elevator.

He felt uneasy. *I should have someone guard the hospital.* He pressed the button for the hospital ground floor.

Right before the elevator doors fully closed, he saw a little flash of light. *What was that? Who's there? A journalist with a camera?* But it was too late to force the doors open to investigate; the elevator was on its way.

As the elevator went down, he picked up his phone and called the station. He ordered a couple police officers to guard the suspect's and victim's hospital room doors.

Just in case of reporters. Just in case anyone *tries to bother them. With a big case like this, you never know....*

The elevator doors opened with a chirp. A shudder ran down his spine as he walked out.

CHAPTER 4

"**W**alked out and drowned? No, we now know that little toddler Moana Marie Collins did not, in fact, just walk out and drown, despite the police and FBI concluding as much twenty years ago," the reporter said. "She's alive but *not* well—she got attacked last night, right here at the Compass Rose, a seafood eatery that's a local favorite in the area."

Sitting in his big leather chair behind his mahogany desk, the middle-aged man watched the breaking news. The twenty-year-old case of the missing toddler from Eglin AFB who had apparently drowned but now suddenly shown up in the very area she'd disappeared from was making headlines on all channels that morning.

He watched silently. He lifted a hand to scratch his face, leaving behind a sweaty handprint on his desk. *Holy shit. How did this happen? How did she end up back at Eglin? And both of the Collinses were there? I knew one would be back, but the German-born mom? Why is she there?*

He swallowed hard. *And how stupid of Sullivan to attack her. So fucking stupid!* He formed a fist and slammed it on his table. *Stupid guy!*

He barked a laugh. *Well, we all knew Sullivan was never the smartest. He wasn't. Perfect for the job, but not the smartest. No, he strikes me as freaking dumb to attack her like that. What was he thinking?*

He checked his watch. *Morning here on the East Coast, but not out there. Should I call him anyway? For advice?*

He decided to do so and used his office phone to call him. He knew his number by heart. It rang for a while, but then he heard him pick up.

"Hello? Who's this?" the voice said.

"It's Cliff."

"Cliff? Haven't heard from you in a while. How you doing, son? Been following your career. Impressive stuff, impressive. Proud of you. Always believed in you."

Cliff smiled. "Thanks. Appreciate your support. Yeah, it's been good. Real good."

He heard a content smile on the other end. "I knew it, son, just knew it. You always been a smart guy. But did you forget about the time difference? I'm still in bed. Was in the middle of a nice dream here."

"I'm sorry to wake you. But I need your advice."

"My advice? Well, love to give it to you, but why you need it so damn early this morning? Is it that urgent?"

Cliff sighed. "Yeah, I think so. Unfortunately."

"Well, spit it out. Do I need to get you outta trouble again?"

He sighed. "Probably."

"What? What happened?"

"Turn on the news," he told the man on the other end of the line. "I'll stay on until you see it for yourself."

He heard noises and shuffling coming from the other end of the line, then heard a TV turn on. "What the…" he heard the man say, and they both listened to the news for a while without saying a word to each other.

Finally, there came a gasp on the other end of the line, then a deep sigh. "This story again, son? I thought you were on a better path now. I'm real disappointed in you."

Cliff felt so small, like a child getting scolded. He hated feeling that way, absolutely hated it. "I'm sorry. Tried my best."

"Tried your best? *Really*. This will threaten your career—your very freedom."

"I know," Cliff whispered.

"And the girl is alive. Did you know?"

Cliff cleared his throat, then swallowed hard. His sweaty hand almost slipped off the phone he was holding up to his ear. "Well, I—"

"I'll ask you again, son: *did you know about this?*"

"Well, yeah, I guess...."

"You 'guess'? There's no guessing here, son. Last chance: did you know she was alive?"

Cliff nodded, then whispered, "Yeah."

"Huh. And you never told me about it? How can I give you advice if you lie to me? I can't do what's best for you, son, if you lie to me."

"I know. I'm sorry."

"So am I. Really disappointed in you."

"I'm sorry," he whispered.

"Me, too. I'm sorry, too, son. Not cool. You messed up. Thought you were done messing up your life."

Those words hit Cliff like a slap to the face. "I *am* done. And I've done well. Look how far I've come."

The line went silent.

"Yeah, fair enough, but now it's all going downhill. This might be the end for you, son."

"No, no, please, that's why I called. I need to figure out what to do now. Please, help me. I've come so far."

A sigh on the other end. "Yeah, you have. You really have. But I'm not sure how to get you outta this pickle now."

"I know, I mean—I don't know either. I was hoping we could come up with a plan together or... something."

"A plan? I'm not sure how to help you, son."

"You don't have any ideas? Please, think of something. I'll take any ideas."

Silence for a bit. "Well, maybe you know someone who could make your problem go away?"

Cliff thought for a moment. "Well, maybe. What about Bill? Maybe I could let him take care of it."

"Bill?"

"Yeah, you know. He's pretty easy to manipulate."

"Yeah. I'm listening, son. Keep going."

"I could, maybe... well, just thinking, I could tell Bill to shut Sully up?"

"And how would he accomplish that, son? Without it coming back around and you getting yourself in trouble?"

Cliff caught himself smiling. He would show him how good he had gotten. How smart he had gotten. He'd show him, make him proud. "Don't worry, I have an idea."

"Well, good for you, son, good."

"Thanks for helping me out again. Really appreciate it."

Cliff heard slight laughter on the other end. "Well, you're welcome. Just make sure you stay out of trouble—and keep out of this! This is serious business."

He smiled. "Yeah, I know. But I have a plan now. No worries, I'll take care of everything."

"Good, then, good. I'll take your word for it."

"Yeah. You have my word."

CHAPTER 5

"Word got out quickly." Brad sighed. He'd been watching the reporters crowding in around the hospital, jockeying for position. "I was looking forward to enjoying the sunrise with all of you, but I certainly don't want to see that mess."

He drew the blinds tighter and stepped away from the window to sit back down next to Elisabeth on their side of Maria's hospital bed.

"So, the press is outside? Reporters?" Aaron got up to peek through the blinds. "Holy cow, you weren't kidding. A bunch of them."

Elisabeth sighed, her hands forming a fist. "Yeah, I bet there's a lot. Swarming like flies. Just like twenty years ago. I just hate reporters, really hate them. They get all in your face!"

Aaron smirked. "Well, not with these heavy blinds drawn. They can't even see us up here. So I guess we're good?"

"Until we have to leave the hospital. Then they'll follow us everywhere. Trust me, Aaron, I've seen it all before." Elisabeth grimaced, then pointed to Brad. "*We've* seen it before."

Aaron nodded, then sat back down on his side of Maria's bed. He picked up the steaming cup of coffee he had gotten from the vending machine earlier and took a sip. Slowly sipping his coffee, he got lost in thought. *Guess this is bringing back bad memories for the Collinses, too. I feel bad for them. Must be so hard for them. This whole situation is crazy.*

"Aaron, does Maria drink coffee, too?" Elisabeth's question ripped him from his thoughts.

Aaron looked over to Elisabeth and saw her holding her own cup of coffee, filled to the rim with pure-black liquid. He then glanced at Brad holding a Styrofoam cup of plain black coffee as well.

He grinned. "Yeah, she does. But it appears she takes after her parents. No creamer. Black coffee only—unlike everyone else in her life."

The Collinses smiled and took a sip of their coffees.

Then Aaron saw Elisabeth's smile fade, her sternness returning. "Unlike everyone else? Does that include that… that… lady who took her?"

Aaron sighed. "I meant people in general. Pretty unusual for a college kid to drink straight-black coffee."

Elisabeth's facial lines softened. "Oh, I see. Yeah, I suppose."

Aaron's phone beeped. He picked it up and read the text message from his dad: *I'll be at the hospital soon. Bringing new clothes for everyone.*

He smiled. *Thank goodness. He'll be better at talking with the Collinses. It's been awkward. They get mad at everything I say.*

"Anything important?" Brad asked. He pointed at Aaron's phone.

"No, not really. That was just my dad texting that he'll be here soon."

Elisabeth and Brad nodded, silently sipping their coffees.

Oh no, are they mad? Do they not want my dad here? Aaron's face flushed. "Oh, I hope that's okay with both of you. Maybe I should've asked first if my dad could come by? I'm sorry."

"Don't worry, Aaron, it's okay. Your dad can certainly visit," Brad said.

Elisabeth nodded, but then her face turned sad. "Guess he knows our daughter pretty well, huh?"

Aaron shrugged his shoulders. "He's met her a few times. She came out to visit me and my family in Montana last summer. And they hung out with Maria when we were all in Daytona."

The Collinses nodded and looked back at their daughter, still sleeping. Elisabeth took her grown daughter's hand again and played with the beautiful ring on her finger. "Do you truly love her?"

Aaron almost choked on his coffee and had to cough. Then, he looked at Elisabeth, his fiancée's real mom. "Yes, I do. I truly do."

"That's good, that's real good," he heard Brad mumble, and both men took another sip of their coffees.

Elisabeth's gaze still rested on Aaron. "And she loves you?"

He chuckled. "I sure hope so."

"So, you're not sure?"

He now grinned. "I *am* sure. Yes, she loves me. Not only because she said yes to my proposal, but because we're like soulmates, great friends. We know each other well."

"That's good, real good," Brad mumbled again, repeating himself.

A phone rang loudly, interrupting the delicate conversation. Everyone flinched. Maria's eyelids fluttered, and she moved her head from side to side.

"Shoot, it's my phone," Brad realized. He searched for it in his pants' pocket, then picked up. "Hi, yes. Hi, Chief Parlot."

Elisabeth and Aaron listened in on Brad's part of the conversation.

"Yes, sure, we agree to do the genetic test." Pause. "Okay, sure. Glad they already got her sample." Pause. "Sure, we'll head straight down. Thanks, Chief." Pause. "No, not yet. Still asleep." Pause. "Yes, sure, will do. Thanks."

He hung up. Elisabeth's and Aaron's eyes rested on him.

"Well, that was Chief Parlot," Brad explained, and then turned to Elisabeth. "They want us to do the maternity and paternity tests right away this morning."

Elisabeth clung tight to Maria's hand. "I will not leave my daughter."

"You won't have to go far. They'll do it right here in the hospital. Should be quick, he said."

Elisabeth sighed. She stroked her daughter's hand one more time, then let go and grabbed Brad's instead. He pounded his coffee and threw away the cup; she left hers on the little table near their seats. "We will be right back. Please, let us know if she wakes up," she said.

Aaron nodded and waved goodbye, then fixed his attention to his injured fiancée.

Yeah, hope she wakes up soon. Luckily, the doctors said she's not seriously injured. Nothing broken. Just bruised. Badly bruised. He sighed as he looked over the purple staining her neck and face. *Her head wound was minimal. Mild concussion. Wonder how in the world Sullivan got hit so hard in the head that he went unconscious? Compared to him, Maria's head is fine. What happened last night?*

Why did he attack you, Maria?

He carefully pushed a few strands of hair away from her face, then gently stroked her cheek. He let out a deep sigh and took her hand into his, holding it, stroking it. Absent-minded, he sat there by the hospital bed, her hand in his, and had lost track of time when he suddenly felt a squeeze.

He looked up, then jumped up without letting go of her hand. "Maria! You're awake! Hi!" He smiled his biggest smile for her.

Her eyes slowly focused on him. She smiled a weak smile. "Hi, Aaron.... Where are we?"

"Well, Maria, it's a long story, but we're—"

"I had this really weird dream," she interrupted. "Not my childhood drowning one, but similar. I dreamed someone was pushing me underwater. Attacking me, like... trying to kill me or something."

She paused and moved her arm. "This is so uncomfortable. What am I wearing?" She eyed her nightgown, then looked at the bed, her arm, the IV attached to it. Abruptly, she sat up. The blood pressure cuff on her other arm began inflating; the monitor's frenzied beeps made it transparent just how fast her heart was beating. "Aaron? Where the heck are we?"

"We're in the hospital. And... what you experienced wasn't a dream. An attack did happen last night."

Maria now stared at him, then looked around her at the cluster of empty chairs. "Who else has been visiting? Your dad and... who else?"

Aaron shook his head, then took a deep breath in. "Not my dad. He hasn't been here yet. He's on his way right now." He followed Maria's gaze. "Um, those are the Collinses' chairs. As in, Brad and Elisabeth Collins. Your—"

The color washed away from her bruised face. "—*parents.*" She ended his sentence and then looked at him, her eyes now freakishly green again, wide open, moving quickly back and forth. "Oh my gosh. I just remembered what happened last night."

Aaron nodded. "Yes, you've been through a lot. But you need to stay calm, relax. We need you to be strong."

She nodded absentmindedly. He could tell she was still processing everything.

"The police still need to take a statement from you about last night. And then we need to—"

"Mamá! Where's Mamá?" she cried out.

"They're transporting her here so the Niceville police chief leading the investigation can interrogate her."

She flung her head around to look at him directly. "Interrogate? Did they start already? Did she get a lawyer? Oh my gosh, she needs a lawyer! I need to help her. I just know she didn't kidnap me. Don't know why, but I know. In my heart, I know it. Aaron, I need to help her."

She ripped her hand out of his, sat up fully, then swung her legs off the hospital bed to get up. "Aua, stupid IV." She touched the cord, ready to rip it out of her arm.

Aaron jumped up to stop her. "My goodness, Maria! Don't do that. Wait for the doctor. Maybe you can even be discharged today. But for now, let's stay calm. One step at a time."

Tears were welling in her eyes now. "But Mamá..."

"Please, don't worry about her right now, Maria. She's still en route. That gives us time to figure something out."

Maria's mind was racing. "She needs a good lawyer, she really does, you know. I think she's innocent and—"

"Why do you think that, Maria?"

"I'm not sure. I just have a feeling, you know, something I can't explain, but…" Aaron smirked; she saw it. She sighed, her eyes sad. "I know that's not evidence. Still, we need to figure out what happened and—"

Aaron put a finger to her swollen lips. "First of all, Maria, *we need you to get better*. To get healthy. Of course we need your help to figure this case out. But you can't help unless you're strong. So, I think our patient should lie back down and rest."

"Guess so," she mumbled, and did as she was told.

"And we better let everyone know you're awake. The nurses, the doctors, the chief, your parents, your whole family in Miami…."

She grimaced. "Well, not that they're family, are they?"

"But they love you, Maria. They're worried about you. I've already talked to them a few times since you were admitted."

"Really?"

He nodded and briefly filled her in on the conversations he'd had. "They're all very worried. All your relatives."

Maria snorted. "Ha, you say that, but they're not my relatives, are they? Everyone I grew up with and loved isn't related to me. My *own mother* isn't even related to me!" Her face turned red. "You know what, Aaron? I might still be fine calling Martina Sullivan my mother if she had just told me the truth about not giving birth to me."

Aaron raised his one eyebrow, the way only he could.

"Can't believe she hid that fact all these years. I even remember asking her about the night I was born, about when I was an infant, and guess what? She always had a story. A good story. A plausible story. Mamá always told me the story of how I was born on a stormy

September night. She told me every year on my birthday. A lie. All lies!"

Aaron stared at her. Her face red, her swollen lips pressed together, her eyes green. He cleared his throat. "Yeah, that was a lie. Turns out your real birthday is June second. Today."

"What?"

"Your parents just told me that. But Maria, let's take everything one step at a time. We'll find out what happened. Consider that your mamá might have had her reasons for telling you all those lies, all those things."

She sighed. "Maybe… but why? What reason could possibly justify those lies? And why did Jonathan Sullivan attack me?" She suddenly started sobbing. "Gosh, I can't remember, I just can't remember. I feel like there's something there, something he said.…"

"Maria," Aaron said, taking her hand, "you just woke up. Please, give it time. I bet your memory will come back. And maybe those memories might even help your mamá?"

"Yeah, maybe. I hope so," she said, tears dripping from her nose. "Because… because… you know, I *do* love her. I know that that woman with the freckles, the woman we saw in the restaurant, is the one who gave birth to me, but I have no other connection to her. I somehow recognized her, I think, but we have no real memories together, you know?"

Big tears ran down her face.

"That woman with the freckles wasn't there for my first scrape, first tears, first fears, first day of school, so many firsts. She wasn't there. But Mamá was, has always been there for me."

Aaron nodded and kept listening.

"So, who's the real mother? The one who gives birth to you, or the one who raises you?" Maria sobbed louder, tears streaming down her face.

"Well, maybe both?" Aaron said, his heart heavy. He gave her a kiss on the hand.

Maria shook her head. "I don't think so. I did a research project about adoptions once in high school. All the adopted kids were sure of one thing: their mother was the one who was always by their side, the one who raised them."

She sighed, silent tears running down her swollen face. "However, there's one big, huge difference here for me: the woman at the restaurant, my birth mom, didn't *decide* to give me up. It wasn't *her choice*. I understand now that somehow, *I was taken from her*."

Aaron nodded again. "Correct. You were kidnapped."

Maria's tears stopped flowing now as she stared at Aaron. "I was kidnapped. Oh my gosh. I was kidnapped! From Eglin AFB? From the TLFs? Why, Aaron, why? By whom? Jonathan Sullivan? Him and Mamá?"

"Well, that's what everyone's assuming right now, but we're not one hundred percent sure. I understand you seem to somehow know in your heart your mamá, well, Martina, is innocent, and I finally believe you, but you know I like—"

"—evidence, I know." Maria smiled, but her smile faded quickly. "Nothing makes sense to me right now. I need to remember, to think harder."

"Give it time. And just know that the whole Niceville police force is working to find out who kidnapped you."

Maria stared at him wide-eyed. "The *whole* police force?"

"Err, might as well be. I assume they're putting a big team together," Aaron said. "I bet it'll be a great team."

CHAPTER 6

A *great team. I need to find a great team.* Chief Parlot sighed. *Who can I trust most?*

Officer Sally Johnson came into the room. "Chief, the guards are all set at the hospital. The Collinses took the genetic test. I told the boys from Miami to pull into the station around back so those reporters don't scare Mrs. Sullivan."

"Good, Officer Johnson, thank you. That's all very good. Let's make sure no reporter bothers those at the hospital—the Collinses, Aaron Heikinnen, especially Maria. And they shouldn't get a glimpse of Martina Sullivan yet. We need to talk to her first."

"Agreed. No worries, everything's already been taken care of. By the way, the test results should be in soon."

"Good."

Chief Parlot looked over his young colleague. *I like her. She's a good person and a smart cookie. Lots to learn still... but maybe now's the time?*

And with that, he had decided on his team. "Hey, how about you and me work this mothballed missing toddler case together?"

Sally's face lit up. "Me? You want *me* to work the case?"

He grinned. "Yes, I do. And why not? If you're waiting to feel ready, you'll never pick up a case. None of us ever feels ready. All we can do is be ready to jump in and try. So, Officer, what do you say? Ready to jump?"

She looked at him for a while, then literally jumped up in the air in excitement. "Yes, yes, yes, I *am* ready! Hah, see that jump?"

They laughed and both walked down the long hallway to the back room with the extensive collection of file cabinets.

The light shining between the blinds of the window illuminated the room in the police office they had decided to use as their workroom. The rays fell upon an old, dusty file; the handwritten words scrawled across it read "Missing Toddler Moana Marie Collins—one year and eleven months old, missing since May 28, 2003."

"I still can't believe they found her alive," Sally said, and shook her head. "After all this time. Wow!"

Chief Parlot agreed. "Unbelievable that Eglin's military police, our people, and the FBI got it so wrong."

She glanced at the chief. "Speaking of the FBI and base police— don't we have to inform them?"

Chief Parlot sighed. "Yeah, I suppose." He grimaced. "But first, let's see if we can find anything in this old case file. I'll call them, I promise. Just want to get a head start."

Sally shot him another glance. "Isn't it against protocol not to let them know right away?"

He grunted. "Well, maybe, but you might say I hold a grudge. They stole the case from me way back when. The FBI swooped in and ripped it right out of my hands. Only the former chief was allowed to work in tandem on it, even though I was there when they first interrogated the parents. It wasn't fair."

"I see. They usually push the young ones out when things get serious, huh?"

Chief Parlot nodded.

Sally smiled. "Well, not this time. You asked me to help you figure out this case, Chief, and I will. I'll help you, and nobody will dare take this case away from you again."

He returned her smile. "Thanks, Sally. I promise to make sure no one does the same to you either."

She grinned. "Appreciate it, sir."

"Well, enough with the small talk, let's focus on our work before the Feds start trying to muck things up."

"Yes, sir. Just read the interview with the parents, Brad and Elisabeth Collins. Looks like they shared the same story, told it the same way over and over again no matter who did the interrogating, down to the last detail."

"And what did they say, Sally? Brief me."

She nodded. "It was the family's third night at Eglin AFB. They were in one of the TLFs down by the water. Row three, apartment four."

The chief took notes.

"The night of the disappearance, the parents went to the laundromat together and left their little girl in the TLF. They claimed they only wanted to quickly throw in a load of laundry and come back. Saw one other man in the laundry facility. They returned to their apartment about eight minutes later. Found the door slightly open and their daughter missing. Not in her bed where they'd left her."

Chief Parlot nodded.

"They were both sure they had shut the door tightly behind them and it was set to automatically lock when you walked out. They were both sure they hadn't seen or heard anything suspicious around their home before they left for the laundry facility. And they were both sure their little one had been fast asleep. Ah, I take back my earlier claim: they disagreed on one thing."

"And that is?"

"The mom was adamant their little one wouldn't have been capable of opening the door on her own. At her age, she apparently couldn't push down the door handle and pull at the same time. But the dad wasn't so sure. He said it was possible she might have learned how to open it without them realizing."

"Interesting. Any other minor disagreements?"

"Yes. The mom was convinced their little one would never have walked out without bringing along her favorite cuddle toy, a security blanket with a duck head they called Enti. The dad thought it was plausible their daughter woke up, panicked when she found herself alone, and left the TLF to find them, without her cuddle toy."

"I see."

"Though both parents agreed their daughter usually needed a moment to wake up from a deep sleep. They doubted there would have been enough time for her to wake up and walk out in the eight minutes they were gone."

"Thank you for the excellent summary, Sally." Chief Parlot paced the room, chewing on a pen. "Any witnesses?"

Sally searched through the file, quickly scanning one document after another. "Yes. The Airman at the laundry facility. He saw them walk in, throw in a load of laundry, and walk back out again. Said they were there maybe five minutes, a quick visit. Nobody else heard anything during the event. There weren't many guests rooming in the TLF at the time, and the few families that were there didn't hear anything."

"Okay. Any other statements?"

Sally nodded. "Yes. The other guests at the TLF said they had seen the Collins family out and about during the days leading up to the disappearance. All claimed the family seemed happy. The parents came across as responsible and caring."

"I remember," the chief mumbled while still chewing on the pen. "When the press realized they had left their toddler all alone in the apartment, they painted them as anything but that. I recall they were portrayed as self-centered parents whose neglect led to their child's death."

Sally let out a huff.

Chief Parlot thought back to twenty years ago. "But I was there when they were questioned, and I know they were very caring. They loved their daughter more than anything. Such a shame; their decision to go do laundry together that night ruined their lives."

"No kidding," Sally said, and sighed. "But honestly, I don't understand why they left their daughter all alone, regardless of whether she was asleep or not. Couldn't they have waited to do their laundry at a better time?"

"Well, Sally, you don't have kids yet, do you?"

She shook her head. "No, but I don't understand why that's of any importance."

"It's not, except for the fact that I had the same reaction you just did back then, twenty years ago. Since then, I've had kids myself, and now I kinda understand. When you're raising kids, those few moments you get alone with your partner are precious. And most of those moments happen only after the kids go to sleep. I bet the Collinses just wanted a few minutes to walk and talk together, as they wouldn't have had much time to do so otherwise."

Sally thought for a bit. "I see. I assume we know for sure the parents didn't have anything to do with their daughter's disappearance, aside from their absence, right?"

Chief Parlot nodded. "Correct. They looked very carefully into that back then. Didn't find anything. And I was there. I saw the unbearable pain on their faces then, and their immense joy last night when they got her back."

"And we're certain Maria Gabriella Sullivan is in fact Moana Marie Collins?"

The chief nodded again. "There's no reason to suspect Maria *isn't* Moana Marie Collins. Her parents recognized her, and she even recognized them. Their physical resemblance is uncanny, undeniable.

Still, we'll need to wait for the DNA test results to have absolute certainty."

Sally nodded.

His work cell phone rang. "Hello, Chief Parlot speaking." As he listened, he raised his eyebrows, then smiled. "Wonderful news, Aaron. Thanks for calling me. We'll be there soon." He hung up.

"Well, Sally, our star witness has come to. She should be of great help."

"You mean Maria?"

He grinned. "Yes, she woke up. I hope her memory did as well. Let's pick out some files, especially pictures, to show her. See if anything rings a bell."

"You can do that?"

"Do what?"

"Interrogate her at the hospital?"

"Sure, as long as her doctor signs off."

"And did he?"

"Um, not yet," Chief Parlot said. "I suppose we should call the doctor right away."

CHAPTER 7

"Let's call the doctor right away," Aaron said. "He can let us know when you can leave, Maria."

"Yes, Aaron's right," Brad said, standing by Maria's bed. "You can't make that decision for yourself—it's the doctor's call when to discharge you."

Elisabeth nodded and took Maria's hand, tears in her eyes. "They're right, meine Süße. I'm so happy you're feeling good, but the doctor needs to make sure you're okay."

Maria nodded and felt the warmth of the woman's hand. She wasn't sure whether to pull her hand back or not. *I feel her love for me. I know she loves me. But I don't know this woman.*

"What a treat to see you awake," Brad said, and smiled at her, then stood behind Elisabeth and put his hands on her shoulders.

Maria decided to focus on him. "COLLINS" his uniform name tag read. *My dad. Collins. Brad.* She sighed.

"We were here all night, then leave the room for like a few minutes and you decide to wake up just then? Unbelievable," Brad laughed. His laughter filled the room, so warm it even made Maria smile.

"Where did you guys go?" she asked.

"We went to take our genetic tests," Elisabeth said.

"Genetic tests?"

"Yeah, paternity and maternity tests. To make sure you're really our daughter," Brad explained. "Though I don't think anyone doubts that."

Aaron chuckled. "Definitely not. The resemblance is uncanny."

Resemblance? Maria studied the unknown couple standing beside her bed. The woman in the pixie cut with the freckles. *Same freckles, same hair color. Same straight nose as me.*

She glanced at the strong man in the camo uniform. His brown hair had a few grey streaks in it. His eyes sparkled. *Unique eyes. Hazel eyes with a mosaic of golden-and-emerald-green flecks surrounding a dark-brown center, encircled by a blue rim. My eyes. Exactly my eyes. The resemblance is uncanny. Aaron's right.*

She swallowed hard, still felt the lady with the pixie cut holding her hand. *I guess they're my parents. But we won't know for sure until the results are in.*

"So, how long until we get the test results back?" she asked, and chuckled. *Look at me, asking for evidence for once.*

The irony wasn't lost on Aaron. He grinned and winked at Maria, then said, "As far as I know, it takes at least twenty-four hours, doesn't it?"

Elisabeth and Brad shook their heads. "They said it'll take only about two hours."

"Really?" Aaron said and raised his one eyebrow. "That's super-fast."

Brad smiled. "I know. They said they'll use a rapid test to get results quickly."

"I see," Aaron said. "Makes sense to rush it."

"Yeah," Brad said. "And I sure hope they rush the interrogations as well."

"Interrogations?" Maria looked from one person to the next, not understanding.

"Yeah, they'll need to take a statement from all of us again, and you as well." Brad sighed, then stood up taller, his voice strong. "I just want to know what the heck that bastard Jonathan Sullivan has to say for himself. And Martina Sullivan."

"Mamá?" Maria sat up taller.

Elisabeth dropped Maria's hand, her face suddenly pale, her wrinkles much more visible. "Mama? You're still calling her Mama?"

Maria didn't know what to say. "Well, she did raise me and—"

"She *stole* you! She took you away. From me. She stole everything from me. All those years, lost. Look at you, you're all grown up. You're a grown woman now, and I missed all those precious years. I missed them because of her! *I hate her*, hate her so, so much."

Maria stared at the lady with the pixie cut whose face had flushed red in anger. *I don't know what to do, what to say, what to feel.* Her heart was aching, her thoughts confused. *All I know is that nobody should hate Mamá.*

"But, but... don't hate her. She's my mom."

"What? No she's not! *I am.* She's a child-stealer. A criminal. That's what she is, a disgusting criminal. She deserves to rot in hell for what she's done," Elisabeth said, her voice loud and low, her face red.

Maria felt as if she'd been sucker punched in the face. *Rot in hell? Mamá? No, she doesn't deserve that. She's a good person. I know she is. She's innocent in all this.*

She watched as Elisabeth's flushed face turned pale again, then the older woman collapsed into the uncomfortable plastic chair next to her bed and started sobbing. Maria watched silently, then felt her heart ache. *I like this woman. But she's wrong about Mamá.*

Brad tried to comfort his ex-wife. "Elisabeth, please. Think of all the good that's happened. We found our daughter. She's safe."

"But that nasty woman ruined my life! Ruined it all: my marriage, my happiness. Everything. She took everything from me when she stole my innocent little daughter and convinced her she was her mom. How sick is that? So sick. She's a disgusting criminal."

"Mrs. Collins," Aaron started, "don't forget that she might be innocent."

"*Innocent?* That video didn't prove anything. Sure, Moana said she was afraid of 'bad guys,' but it probably wasn't the Sullivan lady who did the job. Her ex did!"

"No!" Maria yelled. "No, you're wrong! You're wrong. They're innocent."

Dumbfounded, everyone stared at her.

Aaron found his words first. "What? *They're* innocent? You're referring to both Martina *and* Jonathan Sullivan? What, you're saying you suddenly remember who took you?"

Maria looked at Aaron and shook her head. With both hands, she scrunched up her bedsheet. "I don't really remember, but somehow, I have a feeling," she whispered, then her voice got stronger. "And I definitely know that you are innocent until proven guilty."

She looked at Elisabeth, who was still sobbing, then at Brad.

Brad smiled at her. "You're one smart cookie."

Maria suddenly felt small again, so small. "I know, Daddy," she whispered, then stared back at her bedsheets.

For a while, they just sat there without speaking, Elisabeth's sobs and the beeping of the hospital monitor the only sounds in the room. Maria didn't know what to do or say. What to feel. All she wanted was one thing—to get away. *I need to get out of here, away from all of this.*

But she was trapped. Trapped with her own feelings, trapped in this situation.

CHAPTER 8

*T*rapped *in this situation, in this police car. Need to get out of here.*
The handcuffs had been cutting into Martina's wrists for so
long, she didn't feel them anymore. Her arms had gone numb after
hours and hours of sitting in a car with her arms behind her back. She
could barely move, and getting comfortable was out of the question.

Despite herself, she must have dozed off a while ago because she
couldn't remember the car exiting the highway. Now the sun was rising,
the city coming into view.

¡Bello! She smiled briefly. *It's beautiful here, I have to admit.* Her
smile became a frown. *But why in the world did they bring me here? I
didn't do anything. I played by the rules.*

She sighed. *I guess I played by the wrong rules. His rules. Those rules
weren't the ones you should play by. ¡Naguará! I learned nothing from my
relationship with him. Back then, I followed his rules so carefully. Didn't
mention the pain. Hid the bruises. Finally, I broke his rules—I called the
police. Why didn't I do the same that night he dropped Maria off at my
doorstep?*

She was so wrapped up in her own thoughts that she barely
noticed when the car came to a stop in the back parking lot of a police
station. "Niceville Police Station" read the sign over a secure-looking
door.

"Mrs. Sullivan, we're here," the chatty police officer announced and looked over his shoulder at her through the metal partition. She nodded in acknowledgment, then noticed a person peeking around the side of the building at them.

Who's that lady? What's that black thing in her hand? More people appeared behind the lady. One held a big camera on his shoulders. *What's going on?*

Before she could think about it any longer, her door opened, and the police officer with the gruff voice unbuckled her, then led her out.

"Time to go inside. Come on, quickly, before the reporters swarm us."

She stared at the police officer who had taken hold of her arm and was roughly pulling her out. His chatty partner appeared by her side and took her other arm.

"Quick, before they get to us. Unless you want to talk to them and incriminate yourself?"

Martina stared at both men, then shook her head.

"Thought so. Come on, let's go inside. Quick. Here, through the back door."

Trying not to stumble over her own two feet, ignoring the pain as circulation was restored to her arms, she hurried inside, accompanied by the two police officers.

"Ready?" Chief Parlot turned to Officer Sally Johnson, who was watching Martina Sullivan through the one-sided window of the interrogation room. They'd been watching her sitting there on a metal chair behind a metal table, all by herself, facing the opaque window. She looked so small, so lost, so broken.

"I guess so," Sally said, and sighed. "I suppose I just have to jump, right, Chief?"

He smiled at her. "Right. Well, let's get to it. Watch and learn. Feel free to ask questions yourself, if you think of something."

59

She took a deep breath, nodded, and they both walked into the interrogation room.

Martina jumped in her seat when the door swung open. She stared at them as they walked in and took a seat across from her behind the table. They were carrying two folders with them.

"Good morning," the police chief greeted her.

"Good morning," the young lady in the police uniform said, and smiled at Martina.

Martina didn't say anything, she just eyed them.

"Before we get started, Mrs. Sullivan, please state your full name and date of birth."

Martina still didn't say anything.

"Please, we just need to make sure we have the right person. We need to hear it from you." The chief smiled at her. "There's no harm in that, is there, Mrs. Sullivan? Or do you prefer to be called Martina?"

She peered at him. *He seems friendly enough. But can he be trusted?* She wasn't sure. Instead, she focused on the young female police officer next to him and began speaking.

"I am Martina Sullivan. I was born Martina Marie Perez in the City of San Fernando de Atabapo, in the state of Amazonas in Venezuela on September 28, 1976."

"Thank you, Mrs. Sullivan. Or Martina?" The young police lady smiled more kindly at her.

"Martina is fine," she said, then looked down at the floor.

"Okay, thank you, Martina," the middle-aged man said. "I'm Chief Parlot, and this is Officer Sally Johnson. It's nice to meet you."

"Yes, ma'am, nice to meet you," Officer Johnson repeated, and smiled.

Martina dared to look up at them. They were smiling at her as if they were old friends she'd just accidentally met on the street. *But I'm in jail and they're interrogating me!*

She sighed, then the officer began to read her her rights. As she listened, she thought back to Maria's text. *"¡Conseguir una abogada!"*

Determined to listen to her daughter, she blurted out, "I want a lawyer!"

The chief and Officer Johnson looked at each other, surprised. "You're requesting a lawyer *now*?" Chief Parlot asked.

Martina nodded.

The chief stood up. "I assume then you've been fully aware that you raised a child that was not your own?"

Martina stared at him. *Don't nod, don't shake your head*, she reminded herself. *They will use anything and everything against me.* She withstood his stare and didn't move.

"If you're requesting a lawyer, I assume you know that this little girl"—the chief took out a picture from one of the folders and tossed it onto the table—"is in fact *not* your daughter—not Maria Gabriella Sullivan, but Moana Marie Collins."

Martina stared at the picture lying directly in front of her on the table.

What?

She saw the smiling face of a toddler, her auburn-brown hair in little pigtails, her teeth in a wide grin, her unique eyes sparkling. Martina swallowed hard and suddenly felt tears streaming down her face as she studied the picture. The hazel eyes with the blue rim encircling the iris with a mosaic of golden-and-emerald-green flecks in the dark-brown center stared back at her. She knew that straight nose covered in tiny freckles all too well.

And then she saw it, the caption below the picture: "Missing toddler Moana Marie Collins—one year and eleven months old, missing since May 2003."

¡Dios mío! She gasped, then covered her mouth with her hands, felt the hot tears streaming into them. *Maria is not Jonathan's daughter like he said? She's not the daughter he had with another woman after our divorce? She's someone else's child?*

She started sobbing now. *I've raised someone else's daughter. Someone who was looking for her. That poor, poor family must have been devastated.* She covered her whole face with her hands and started crying uncontrollably.

"Martina?" A soft voice made it to her ear, and she dared to look up. She looked right into Officer Sally Johnson's friendly face. "Do you know this child?"

Through her tears, Martina nodded.

"Is this the child you raised as Maria Gabriella Sullivan?"

She nodded again, then buried her head in her hands once more, sobbing.

"Stop crying," she heard a deep voice demand. She looked up again, this time at the chief whose face had turned to stone. "She's been missing for twenty years, and all that time you just raised her as your own. Why? Why would you do that? Why did you take her away from her parents?"

All color drained out of Martina's face. *Take her… from her parents? But I didn't!* She stared at the chief, incapable of forming words.

He slammed his fist on the table. "Don't pretend to be so shocked now. You knew she wasn't your child. Why did you kidnap her?"

Martina jumped up. "But I didn't! I didn't kidnap her. She came to me. I took her in. She needed help!"

The chief stared at her; Officer Johnson raised her eyebrows. "Look at this picture again, Martina. Look at it, take a very close look. Do it! Now!"

She winced under his roaring voice and did as she was told. She looked at the picture again.

"Go ahead and tell us what you see."

Her tears had dried up in shock. In a whisper, she started describing the picture. "This picture shows a little toddler who looks very happy. She looks well-fed. Her auburn-brown hair is shining brightly in the sun."

She stopped. *Auburn-brown hair? But that's not right!*

The little girl Jonathan dropped off at my doorstep that night didn't have auburn hair. She had dark hair. Short, dark, black hair. Not healthy hair either. *Unhealthy, uncombed black hair. Only once grown out did it get brown, reddish-brown, shiny and healthy.*

She stared at the picture.

When Maria came to me, she hadn't been well-fed. She looked sickly and neglected, completely different from this picture. The only similarity is those unique eyes. And the freckles. What happened to my little girl? What did Jonathan do to her?

Gripped by horror, she collapsed in her chair and had to hold onto the table to keep from sliding to the floor.

"Keep talking," the chief barked. "Her parents really want to know why you kidnapped their child."

Kidnapped? Martina was so confused. *Jonathan stole her from someone else. Why? When did that happen? From where?*

She now realized she had no true knowledge of the story behind the crime she was being accused of. She wished she had her phone so she could google it. She wished she could look up the case of this Moana Marie Collins. But her belongings were outside of the room, left there by the two policemen who had escorted her to Niceville. All they had given her was a cereal bar that lay untouched on the table.

She looked around the room, her horror etched on her face. *Maria was kidnapped. I raised a child that already had a loving family.* Tears threatened to spring anew.

"Martina, how did you do it? How? Together with your ex-husband, Jonathan Sullivan, right? How? Tell us!" the chief yelled at her.

Me and... Jonathan? Definitely not. He doesn't even like kids! Why would he kidnap one? There must be an explanation. And I need it, quickly. I need that explanation to help me avoid being punished by Jonathan, punished by the law for something I haven't even done.

She closed her eyes and saw an image of Maria—her adult daughter—in front of her, encouraging her to stand up for herself. She opened her eyes. "I didn't do it. I did *not* kidnap that little girl. And I will not say anything else without a lawyer!"

CHAPTER 9

"A lawyer?" Tía Mariella screamed so loudly through the cell phone's loudspeaker that Maria felt as if the whole hospital would hear her aunt.

I'm glad I sent my parents to get some breakfast and coffee. I don't want them around while I'm trying to help Mamá. She sighed. *It's so complicated. I still feel strange, knowing that these people I've always called aunt and uncle aren't actually related to me. So relieved that Aaron agreed to talk to them instead of me.*

"Why? Why does she need a lawyer?" Maria heard her tía say. "And where would we even find one?"

"Well, first of all, Mariella, your sister has been accused of having kidnapped Maria twenty years ago. We've been over that countless times," Aaron said, his voice calm. "But we can't let her go with a public defender. I feel like she might not get a fair trial."

Maria heard sobbing over the line, followed by a bunch of fast-paced Spanish in the background. She and Aaron knew Martina's extended family was gathered together in Miami.

"She's innocent, Aaron. She is! I know so, I know her. Innocent," came the shrill voice of Maria's other aunt, Tía Monica.

Aaron sighed and chose his words carefully. "Yes, I believe you. We both believe you. But we still don't know how Maria ended up with Martina, do we?"

There was complete silence on the other end of the line.

"Martina lied to you all. And we need to find out why."

Maria stared at Aaron. *He's right. We need to find out why.*

"¡Sí! We need to find out," Maria heard all her relatives agree.

"But if it involves that idiota Jonathan, she will be afraid to tell anyone," Tía Mariella said.

"Exactly," Aaron said. "And I don't know if Martina knows yet about what happened last night."

"¡No sé! Whenever she finds out, she'll be very shocked."

Everyone else in Miami agreed.

"How is our mija Maria?" Tía Monica wanted to know, deep concern in her voice.

Aaron looked at her.

He wants me to talk? But... I don't know if I want to talk to them right now.

"Aaron? How is our Maria? Our mija. We're so worried. Please, please tell us."

He pointed at her questioningly, but she shook her head. Then a communal sobbing broke out through the phone, an expression of collective fear. "Please, tell us! Is she okay?"

"Yeah, I'm fine," Maria blurted out.

"Maria? Oh, Maria. Mija. ¿Estás bien?"

There was a big commotion on the other end of the line. They were all talking over each other in a mixture of English and Spanish, a mix of laughter and cries.

Maria had to smile. "Sí, I'm fine. I'm okay. But we need to focus now. Focus on helping Mamá."

Her relatives immediately sobered up. "Sí. ¿Cómo?" Tío Eduardo wanted to know.

"Well, we need to hire a lawyer. Right away, before they assign her one. She needs someone she can trust. Someone she can afford; someone we all can afford. We need to be quick, especially since her arrival already hit the news headlines. Hope she didn't say anything yet, remembered my text."

"Espero que sí…"

"Yes, let's hope she does request a lawyer. But we should still do our part to help find a lawyer she can trust," Maria said.

"Not a man," Tía Monica blurted out immediately.

Maria nodded. "I agree."

"She's running out of time," Aaron said. "She'll be assigned a defense lawyer soon, someone willing to take on her case, unless she requests a specific lawyer."

"Specific lawyer? I don't know no lawyers," Tío Eduardo said.

"I don't know any either," Tío Mauricio said.

A discussion in English and Spanish erupted in the background. Maria and Aaron listened for a while, then looked at each other.

Aaron's face lit up. "But I do," he yelled through the phone.

"¡Muy bien! Explain please, Aaron."

"Of course, Aaron's dad is a lawyer," Maria jumped in over Aaron. "That's a great idea, Aaron!"

"Mmm, he's a man, but Martina does like him. She told us so. That would be perfect, Aaron. ¡Gracias a dios!" Tía Monica said.

Aaron grimaced. "I'm afraid Maria was mistaken. Unfortunately, my dad can't defend her."

Maria raised her eyebrows. "Why not? Isn't he a defense lawyer?"

"Yes, he is, but in the *state of Montana*. He can't legally work here in Florida. Doesn't have the license. Besides, this case is way too personal for him. It would be a conflict of interest."

That's too bad. Maria sighed and heard the others sigh as well.

"But listen," Aaron said, "my dad is part of a network of lawyers that practice across many states. He must know a good one here in Florida who could help Martina."

Maria smiled. "Awesome."

"¡Muy bien! Aaron, quickly, get Martina this good lawyer. Please, mijo," Tía Mariella said.

He grinned. "Yes, consider it done."

"Gracias."

"De nada," he said and smiled.

Maria laughed. "Aaron, I'm proud of you: you know *you're welcome* in Spanish."

"It's at least something," he protested to the sound of laughter on the other end of the line. "We better call my dad now."

"Sí, please, Aaron, please do. And, mija? Take care. ¡Nosotras queremos mucho! Always our mija," Tía Monica said.

"Gracias," Maria whispered, then hung up.

I think I love all of you too, even if we're not related. You're my family. She stared at the two empty seats on the other side of her bed. *And they're my real family.* She sighed and felt her heart ache. *My relatives in Miami love me so much. But so do the Collinses. We need to find out what happened. Just have to.*

She watched Aaron dial his dad's number. *Hope he can help. And quick. Help Mamá. How in the world did I end up at her house?*

She tried to listen in on Aaron's conversation with his dad, but her mind was racing.

CHAPTER 10

Her mind was racing as Martina stared at her reflection in the large mirror of the interrogation room. She did not look well. *This case! A kidnapping case. ¡Dios mío!*

She still couldn't believe she was caught up in this case. Accused of kidnapping a child. *Unbelievable. But at the same time, not so unbelievable. I should've seen through his fake trickery back then, twenty years ago. But he won again. Made me feel so helpless again.*

She shook her head.

Have to admit, I was grateful for the unexpected company. A little girl. A small, little girl, a human being more helpless than myself. She gave me so much strength, immense strength. Everything went so well after he left me my new daughter that night.

She sighed. She looked at herself in the huge mirror again, suspiciously. *Probably not a mirror but a one-way window. They're probably watching me right now.*

She shifted in her seat, the simple metal chair. *Why in the world does it take so long to get a lawyer?*

She was uncomfortable, hungry, upset. She so wished she could at least have access to that case file they'd waved under her nose. She knew nothing about it. Nothing except that Maria was unmistakably the child of an unfortunate couple that had lost their baby girl twenty years ago.

When exactly? I don't know.

How exactly? I don't know.

Where exactly? I assume right here around the Florida Panhandle, close by.

She got up and started pacing. It helped her think. It wasn't long before she heard a key in the door. Someone was coming in. She backed up into a corner, just in case. While she was curious to see who it was, she was also afraid it would be someone mean, like those Miami policemen. She was surprised when two women walked in: the young police officer from before and a middle-aged woman of Hispanic descent.

"Martina Sullivan, this is Valentina Garcia. She'll be your defense lawyer if you agree to it," Officer Johnson said.

"Hello, Mrs. Sullivan. It's nice to meet you," the lady with the long wavy hair said. "¡Mucho gusto!"

Martina stared at her. *She speaks Spanish?* "Hola," she whispered.

"We apologize for the long wait, but it took some time for Mrs. Garcia to get here. She came all the way over from Tallahassee after Jack Heikinnen spoke with her," Officer Johnson explained.

Martina was stunned. *Jack Heikinnen? Aaron's dad? But why? How?*

"I'll let you and Mrs. Garcia talk. Your conversation will be completely confidential. There are no cameras or audio devices recording you. This door has to remain unlocked, so someone will be on the other side standing guard. Just in case. It's protocol."

"Sure," Mrs. Garcia said. "Thank you, Officer Johnson."

"My pleasure." The young police officer left Martina with Mrs. Garcia.

Martina watched her go. *I like her. Officer Johnson seems like a good cop. Very polite to me. She might even believe I'm innocent. Innocent until proven guilty, as they say in America.*

Her face took on a determined look. *But I won't be proven guilty 'cuz I am innocent!*

"Please, Mrs. Sullivan, let's sit down and chat. Let me know if you prefer to speak in English or Spanish, and how you'd like to be addressed. But first I'll start by introducing myself. Please, dear, have a seat."

Reluctantly, Martina came over. *Just because she's a Spanish speaker and a woman doesn't mean she will understand or sympathize with me. Women are sometimes their own worst enemies. And she's a lawyer. Can a lawyer ever be trusted?*

She wasn't sure yet but nonetheless sat down across from Mrs. Garcia. She wondered what this lawyer had to tell her. And how much she would charge her for this "chat." During her divorce, Martina had almost gone bankrupt. All because of a greedy lawyer who had used her vulnerability to turn a profit. Suspiciously, Martina listened.

"I'm Valentina Garcia. I was born in Puerto Rico and came over to the States at age eight with my mom and brothers after my dad passed away. My mom was hired by the Marriott corporation and worked as a maid in one of their hotels in Helena, Montana."

Montana? The state the Heikinnens are from. Martina listened, more interested now.

"My mom was a single mom and worked very hard to get her three kids through school. I managed to get into the University of Montana in Missoula to study psychology, then went on to Harvard Law School."

Hah, Harvard Law School, of course. A super smart lady. Probably thinks nothing of me and my little business.

"After that, I practiced law on the East Coast for a while with a private firm. Over time, I came to realize so many of my own people—immigrants of modest means—were being misrepresented in court. So, I decided to practice law in Florida as a defense attorney. And here I am, ready to help you, if you'd like."

Martina was suspicious. "How much money?"

"Nothing, Mrs. Sullivan. Nada. I'm a private defense attorney, but I want to do this pro bono."

Martina raised her eyebrows. "Pro-what?"

"Oh, that's Latin. It means 'for free.' Meaning you won't have to pay me a dime. This is my calling, helping to defend people like you. Know that I don't defend just anyone, that's for sure. I have to be picky. But your case interests me. And when Jack called, I knew—"

"Jack?"

"Yes, Jack Heikinnen. I was his wife Grace's roommate in college at the University of Montana."

Martina raised her eyebrows. "University of Montana?"

"¡Sí! Grace Heikinnen studied there to become a teacher; you might recall I studied psychology there. We hit it off our first year and ended up living together all through college until we graduated."

Martina's jaw dropped. "You did?"

Valentina Garcia smiled. "Sí, we did. Grace and I are still friends to this day, still in touch. Not constantly, but I do keep up with their family."

"You do?"

Valentina nodded. "Yeah. We visit one another whenever we happen to be in the same area. Unfortunately, I haven't seen her the past couple of years. Kids keeping us too busy."

She sighed and then perked up. "We did run into each other when they dropped Aaron off at college here in Florida. Such a nice boy. A young man now, I suppose. I often joked that I would love to see my daughter hook up with him, but he obviously had other plans." She laughed and winked at Martina.

"You have a daughter?"

"Yes, a couple years younger than yours. She's Emma Heikinnen's age."

Younger than yours. Martina liked that she said that. *She seems to at least give me credit for having raised Maria. She's acting like she thinks I'm innocent. And she knows the Heikinnens.*

"Now that you know a bit about me, here's the deal, Mrs. Sullivan: it's up to you whether you'd like me to defend you. If not, you'll be assigned a public defender."

"Why did you come this far to defend me?"

"Because I got a call from Jack asking me to consider it. By the way, he passed on a message from Aaron and Maria."

"A message from Aaron… and Maria?"

Mrs. Garcia nodded. "Yes, they both know you must be scared and in need of someone to trust. They both seem to think there's someone you're afraid might hurt you. That you'll need help to tell the truth about a crime you didn't commit, without fear of retribution."

Martina stared at her. *A crime I didn't commit? Aaron and Maria actually said that?*

"Si, lo dijeron, Aaron y Maria. Ellos te creen."

Martina looked at her. Her eyes were moist. *Aaron and Maria believe me?* She smiled. "Mija believes I'm innocent?" she whispered. "Incredible. That makes me so happy. Hope she'll forgive me for everything."

Mrs. Garcia smiled. "I bet she will. I bet she can't wait to see you when she gets out of the hospital—"

Martina jumped up, her voice shrill. "¿Hospital? ¡Dios mío! ¿Por qué?"

Mrs. Garcia stared at her. "¿No lo sabes?"

Martina shook her head. The defense lawyer told her about the attack on Maria without telling her who attacked her. Martina turned ghostly white. "Who did it? Who hurt her? That person is in the hospital, too?"

"Yes, correct. But I can't yet divulge who attacked her."

"Why not? I have the right to know—"

"Unfortunately, at this moment, you *don't* have that right. Remember, you're under arrest for Maria's kidnapping, and she's not legally your daughter."

Martina's eyes narrowed as she studied Valentina Garcia's face while still standing up.

Valentina sighed. "Please understand that I believe—just like many of us here do—that you are innocent. I want to work with you to prove your innocence."

Martina's face softened. She lowered herself into her chair and kept listening.

"If you let me help you, I'll first need to hear what you have to say about how Maria came to you. That's the key to proving you are innocent. I already looked over the case file and have a feeling: if you just tell me the truth, I'll have you out of here in no time." Valentina squeezed Martina's hand. "What do you say? May I help you? Yes or no?"

Martina looked at her, this gentle but firm woman holding her hand. She looked at Valentina Garcia through tears, then took a deep breath. "¡Sí, por favor, ayúdame!"

As she started signing the paperwork to retain Valentina as her defense lawyer, shivers ran down her spine. *Someone attacked Maria. ¡Dios mío! I already have an idea who did it. Hope I'm wrong.*

But if I'm right, I hope they can protect us. My daughter and me. Both of us.

CHAPTER 11

*B*oth of us are so uncomfortable. Maria glanced over to Elisabeth, who was already very upset. *And she doesn't even know yet we got Mamá a lawyer. She'll get mad and even more upset. Even though we should be happy.*

A knock on the door drew Maria out of her thoughts. Chief Parlot entered the hospital room. "Good morning, everyone. How are you all doing? I heard our patient gets to go home today. Great news."

His smile faded quickly when he saw Elisabeth. It didn't take an expert to tell she had been crying. She was a picture of misery. The chief looked stunned.

Maria eyed him. *He doesn't seem to know what to say. He's probably not good at dealing with others' feelings—better with the facts. Typical for a police officer.*

A young female officer entered the room after the chief. "Good morning, everyone." She greeted them with a smile, but her smile disappeared once she saw Elisabeth in her chair, silently crying. "Mrs. Collins, are you okay? We still need to interview you."

"You need Elisabeth?" Brad asked.

"And you, sir," the young officer explained. "We reviewed the case file from twenty years ago. It would help us out a lot to hear your recollection of what transpired back then again, please."

Elisabeth stared at her, her teary eyes glistening in anger. "Seriously? You think something changed during the past twenty years? What happened, happened that night. We told the police everything we knew."

"I know, ma'am—"

"And who are you anyway?" Elisabeth said.

"I'm Officer Sally Johnson, Chief Parlot's partner for this case," the officer said and smiled, but her smile quickly faded when she saw Elisabeth's angry face.

"*This case?* I see. Just a case, huh?"

"Ma'am," Officer Johnson said, "we know it's not *just a case*. We understand—"

"Then you understand that I have nothing new to say," Elisabeth interrupted her, "I *told them* back then that Moana would never have walked out by herself. I *told them* she was kidnapped. And nobody believed me. Or even made a serious effort to look into it." Elisabeth's face was bright red now. She was steaming mad. "Back then, Chief Billings thought I was delusional. Making things up to take away the pain. Yeah, right! And now look at that, he was *wrong*." She pointed at Maria and continued, "They were all wrong. The FBI, base police, everyone. Everyone but me. Moana was alive and obviously had been kidnapped."

She lowered her finger and curled her hands into fists. "And now you want *us* to retell the same old story of her disappearance, instead of going after the criminals who did it? Unbelievable."

"Mrs. Collins, please," Chief Parlot started to explain, "of course we'll talk with the Sullivans, but Jonathan Sullivan still isn't awake yet and Martina Sullivan is currently with her lawyer—"

"She's *what*? With her lawyer? How dare you even give her the option of a lawyer. All she needs to do right now is talk and spill the beans. Interrogate her then lock her up!"

Maria closely watched the chief and could tell he was taken aback. *He probably didn't expect this frail-looking woman to be so confrontational.*

She sighed. *Neither did I. But maybe I take after her more than I'd like to admit?*

Officer Johnson came over and sat down beside Elisabeth. "Mrs. Collins, we understand how hard this must be for you. Having found your long-lost daughter, only to find she has affection for another woman, calls that lady 'Mom,' even though *you* are her mom." Elisabeth's face softened, though her forehead remained wrinkled in pain. "Mrs. Collins, you'll have to give it time. Take a step back and consider your daughter's needs. Right now, she doesn't really know who she is. It must be so very hard for her."

Officer Johnson glanced at Maria. *She's right, it is very hard for me. I'm so confused.* Tears started welling in Maria's eyes.

"Up until yesterday, this young lady was under the impression that Martina was her biological mom. Imagine how she must be feeling. The betrayal, the confusion, but also, all those years she led a happy life thanks to the woman who pretended to be her mom. Mrs. Collins, I don't wish to diminish your own feelings on the matter, but consider how hard this must be for your daughter. You can't blame her for feeling love for that woman. This complexity is a part of her life now and always will be. You can't make her forget her past, but you *can* remind her of the time you spent with her when she was little. Because deep down, a child remembers their first feelings of love. And that was with you! Your love!"

Maria watched the scene in fascination. Officer Johnson was talking straight to Elisabeth's heart, and Maria felt Elisabeth respond. *Wow, this officer is good. She's right.*

"You think she still loves me?" Elisabeth asked the young police officer. Her voice was so frail, so little, her tears spilling from her eyes. Everyone in the room couldn't help but feel for her.

Maria's heart was hurting. *I know this woman. I feel so bad for her, so sad.* "Yes, I love you. Hab dich lieb," she blurted out, surprising herself.

Everyone stared at Maria.

Then Officer Johnson turned back to Elisabeth, took her hand, and looked straight into her eyes. "I think you got your answer. See? She loves you. You are her mom and always will be. She never forgot you, even remembered your loving words."

Elisabeth nodded, her eyes moist.

"It seems she remembers more than we can imagine—including herself—and we'll work together to bring out those memories, to find the truth of what really happened," Officer Johnson continued. "And that means, for now, that you must stop accusing Martina Sullivan of a crime she may not have committed. Instead, I'd like you to focus on your memories of that night. Remember, all of us want the same thing: the truth."

Elisabeth sighed, then nodded.

Officer Johnson patted her hand. "Okay, then. Let's get started, shall we?"

Elisabeth nodded again.

Chief Parlot had to grin. "Well, everyone, I was going to introduce Officer Sally Johnson to you when we first walked in, but I suppose it's moot at this point. Officer Johnson will be working the case with me. It's her first major case, but I think I picked the right person for the job."

The young officer blushed. "Thank you, sir. I'm honored."

He smiled and winked at her. "Happy to be working with you. You complement me well. I'm not the best at dealing with feelings, but you clearly are."

Officer Johnson grinned. "Call it women's intuition."

"You sure described my feelings better than I could have," Maria said to the officer. "You're something else."

They all agreed.

Chief Parlot cleared his throat and said, "Well, then, I think this would be a good time to share some good news. We got the results of the maternity and paternity tests."

"Already?" Aaron said.

"Yeah. That's the nice thing about being the police chief—I have some colleagues here at the hospital who can expedite testing when I need them to." Chief Parlot winked at Aaron.

"So, what did the results say?" Elisabeth asked. Everyone in the room held their breath.

The chief clasped his hands together. "We now know with 99.99 percent certainty that this young lady is in fact your missing daughter Moana Marie Collins."

Elisabeth jumped up in excitement. "I knew it, I just knew it. It's her. My baby girl."

Brad got up, too, and hugged Elisabeth tightly. "We found her, hun, we found her," he said, his unique eyes glistening with happy tears. "I told you. Told you this trip would be worth it."

They gave each other a quick kiss, blushed with self-awareness, then stopped hugging and walked over to Maria's bed. They stopped short when it became apparent their daughter was dealing with a different set of emotions entirely.

She was staring at the empty wall. *I am... Moana? Me? Moana? Not Maria?* She sighed and looked up at the couple surrounding her. The guy with the same eyes and full lips as her, the woman with the pixie cut and the same nose and freckles. *My parents. I have a new set of parents. I think I love them.* She smiled. "Hi there... my parents."

They stood on either side of her and took her hand. Maria felt the warmth of their touch; their love streamed through her body, all the way up to her heart. She smiled.

"Well, young lady," Chief Parlot said after the moment passed, "before we start the interviews, we need to know how we should address you from now on."

"Address me?"

Aaron took Maria's other hand. "What he means is, the chief is wondering if you'd like to be called Moana or Maria. That's something I'd like to know also."

Maria looked back and forth at everyone, then focused on the Collins again. *My parents. Still so strange to think like that.* She sighed. *Moana or Maria? Don't know what name I want to use.* She was silent for a bit, as was the whole room.

The door to the room opened, breaking the tension, and a large man strode in, breathing heavily, his arms laden. "Hi, everyone, it's me, Jack. Finally made it. Got some fresh clothes here for Aaron and Maria. Excuse me for going through your stuff, Maria, but Aaron instructed me to find something."

He set down a big bag of clothes, then held out a bouquet of beautiful pink and purple flowers.

"Also got flowers for our brave girl. Maria, my future—" Jack Heikinnen stopped midsentence as he read the room and realized he'd intruded at an inopportune time. His posture sagged, and the flowers in his hand drooped a little. "Oh, I'm sorry, I didn't realize..."

"It's okay, Jack," Maria said, and let out a little chuckle. "You actually just helped me out a lot."

"Helped? Me?"

"Yeah, you. You made me realize there's a whole bunch of people out there who know me as Maria. Way more than those who know me as Moana. Not to mention I'm about to get married. Well, soon-ish, I guess." She smiled at Aaron. "So, I've decided what my name will be from now on."

"And...? The suspense is getting to be too much, my love," Aaron said, and winked at her.

"Well, if it's okay with everyone... my parents, Aaron, um, the law... I would like to be known as Maria Moana Heikinnen."

Aaron smiled. "You want to take my last name?"

"Yeah. I already thought that one through a while ago. I know I'm an independent woman, but I do like traditions. I'd like our future family to share the same last name." She smiled at him, eyes sparkling.

Aaron gave her a quick kiss on the forehead.

"And I certainly don't want Sullivan to be my last name. Not after that man attacked me!"

She turned to Brad and Elisabeth. "Is that okay with you? I love the name Moana, but I'd like it to be my middle name. It would just be hard for all my friends, for Aaron to suddenly—"

Elisabeth smiled, tears in her eyes. "You don't need to apologize, mein Engel. I adore your choice. I do. I might have a hard time getting used to calling you Maria, but I'll try."

"Thank you," Maria whispered, and waved Elisabeth over to give her a big hug. *My other mama.* She smiled and got an approving nod from Brad.

"Okay, I guess it's settled then. We'll refer to you as Maria from now on. I'll make sure my boys get started on the paperwork. Your new IDs will read 'Maria Moana Heikinnen,'" Chief Parlot said, and made a note of it in his phone. He looked up. "Sounds good?"

Everyone nodded.

"Great. Then who wants to go first for questioning? Maria? Or General and Mrs. Collins?"

Maria and the Collinses looked at each other and collectively shrugged their shoulders. Maria cleared her throat. "Would you guys be okay with going first? I'd like to catch up with Jack for a bit. And start packing so I can get out of here sometime today."

Brad and Elisabeth smiled and nodded. "Sure, that's fine by us," Brad said.

"Okay, great, thanks," Maria said, then turned to Chief Parlot. "Chief, Officer Johnson? Please go easy on my parents."

CHAPTER 12

*P*arents? *Her real parents? They ended up in Florida? Both of them? With her?* Cliff still couldn't believe it. *This was never supposed to happen. Never. They were never supposed to fucking find each other.*

He was pacing back and forth in his grand office inside the U.S. Capitol. *Wish I could fly down to Eglin right away. Be there to make sure everything goes right this time.*

He watched the news on the TV opposite his desk. The reporters were going nuts over the missing child who had reappeared after twenty years had passed. "We have just learned from Chief Parlot that DNA testing confirms the young lady—the same one who was attacked last night by Mr. Sullivan—is in fact Moana Marie Collins. The missing toddler who disappeared from Eglin Air Force Base twenty years ago."

Stupid reporter!

He switched channels, only to find they were also covering the same thing, the hot news. Every channel he turned to was obsessing over it. The disappearance, criticism of the then-authorities' conclusion that an accidental drowning had taken place.

They were all asking the same questions: was the guy who attacked Moana also her kidnapper? What about the lady who raised her? Innocent or complicit in the deed? Certain fringe newscasts were even speculating that the drowning little girl had been saved by dolphins and then carried all the way to Miami, where she was found and raised by Mrs. Sullivan.

Cliff laughed out loud. *Dolphins? That's so stupid.* He kept laughing, snorting over the idiotic conclusion those reporters speculated in. *Well, luckily, my constituents love believing in miracles and fairy tales. Most people are just plain dumb. Not capable of thinking critically. Just content in their ignorance. That fact really helped us twenty years ago.* He laughed again. *Yeah, stupid people. Easy to manipulate.*

He found his mood was improving. *The primary investigators of that case certainly had an interest in giving the people a great story rather than the truth.*

He sighed. *It was a great plan, a well-thought-out plan, an amazing plot. But it got bungled back then, and again just yesterday, by the middleman! Holy shit. How did this happen?*

He started pacing again. *Sure, I messed up back then. But I thought our guy could fix things. It was supposed to be an easy job. Just get rid of her. Hide the body well. Why did the runt have to hang on to life?*

A shudder ran down his spine, and he involuntarily shook. *I'll never forget the moment that little thing convulsed in front of us on that boat. I was certain she was dead, but no. That nasty cough, spitting up all that water and vomit. Then she opened her eyes and just looked at us.*

He stopped pacing and took a big gulp of water. *Don't know why Sully couldn't do it. He was always so angry, so aggressive. I was convinced he was the guy, perfect for getting rid of her. But he didn't. Sure didn't. He couldn't do it. In the end, he begged me not to do it. Said he had a much better plan to get rid of the child without having blood on our hands.*

Cliff sighed and drank more water. *And I went along with it. A fucking crazy, idiotic plan! Fuck, I'm an idiot. A massive idiot. Why did I agree to go along with his plan? We both swore to secrecy, and it worked— for twenty years. Thanks to that gorgeous blonde at Vital Records.*

He went to take another sip of water but realized the glass was empty. He looked up at the big TV screen, then turned down the volume. *Enough.*

He was about to call for an intern to fill his glass with water when his cell phone rang. Very few people knew his personal number. *Who's that calling me now? The police? They figured it out already? Did Sully talk?*

He started sweating. *Should I pick up? But if it's the police and I don't pick up, they might use it against me.* He wiped the sweat off his forehead and stared at his cell phone. *Maybe it's another fat-cat donor wanting to extract more concessions?*

He grabbed his phone and looked at the screen: "Unknown Caller Number." *Just breathe, just breathe.* He closed his eyes. *Wow, this mindfulness stuff really helps.* He laughed.

The phone kept ringing, vibrating in his hands. He decided to pick up. "Hello?"

"Cliff?"

"Yes. Who's this?"

"It's Bill."

He didn't recognize this voice. *Which Bill? I know hundreds of Bills.*

"Bill from the hood. The old gang."

Cliff's hands started shaking. *Of course. That Bill. The very guy I wanted to talk to. And dreaded calling.* He tried to play it cool. "Oh, hi, Bill. What's up?"

"I assume you've seen the news?"

He swallowed hard. "Of course."

"Did you know? Did you know she was still alive?"

Silence. He didn't say anything.

"What the fuck happened, Cliff? You and your middleman said you got rid of the evidence."

Silence again.

"Didn't you, Cliff?"

"Yes, yes. Things didn't go as planned."

"You don't say." Bill laughed. "You messed up. Again. Like you always do. Your father was right...."

Cliff swallowed hard, the words hitting him like a punch to the face. *Yes, I'm a loser. Always have been. From the beginning. Never good enough.*

For a while, he listened to Bill's accusations, became his human punching bag. Sat in his big leather chair behind his hand-carved mahogany desk, worth more than one year of his salary, in his big office, one of the biggest in the Capitol.

His face brightened up. *A big desk in the Capitol... I'm not a loser! I've made it big, bigger than any of the other guys. Where are they now? Retired. Spun out their mediocre careers and now they're retired. But I'm a big shot.*

With newfound confidence, he yelled, "Listen up, Bill. I didn't mess up—JB did! Big time. No wonder he killed himself. He's the loser here. And I took care of his mistake all those years ago, so well that nobody knew a thing about it for twenty years!"

The other end of the line fell silent.

"So, guess what, Bill?" Cliff didn't wait for him to answer before continuing, "*You're* going down, because they certainly know *you* were right there at the wrong place and the wrong time. You were there, working hand in hand to 'investigate' what happened—and even with all your resources, you thought you knew, but you didn't. You never did. *You're* the idiot! I don't have direct ties to this, but you do. You're going down, *Bill from the hood.*" His voice turned cold. "Now, if you want to avoid your fate, you better make sure to shut up the middleman."

And then he hung up, and laughed and laughed in his big leather chair behind the big mahogany hand-carved desk inside the U.S. Capitol in Washington, DC.

CHAPTER 13

"**W**ashington, DC?"

"Yes, sir, that's my current home," Brad Collins told Chief Parlot. "Has been for some time."

"And you still live in Germany, Mrs. Collins?"

"Yes, Chief, that is correct."

The chief pointed at an address on a piece of paper. "I can't pronounce a lick of that, but please confirm we have the correct address and phone number on file for you, Mrs. Collins."

She grinned, then looked at the piece of paper. "This is correct."

"Wonderful. Thank you, Mrs. Collins, and thank you, General Collins, for verifying your identity. We can get started now. Officer Johnson, take it away."

"Thank you, Chief," Sally said. "General Collins, Mrs. Collins, we've looked at the old case files and really need to hear it from you again. I know this will be hard on you, but please do your best. What happened the night your daughter disappeared?"

Brad and Elisabeth looked at each other. Painful memories, but they gave their statement, the same story they had given over and over twenty years ago.

They watched Brad and Elisabeth Collins walk out, hand in hand. Chief Parlot looked at his partner and saw tears in her eyes. "Sally, are you okay?"

She nodded, then reached for a tissue to blow her nose. "Yeah, sure, I guess. I just feel so bad for them. They missed all that time with their daughter, and they were right about what happened all along. Maria was kidnapped. Damn it." She blew her nose again.

"I know, Sally, I know. It's hard to deal with cases like these. They come with a lot of emotion. But you have to keep your personal feelings in check. Gotta develop a thick skin for this line of work."

She used the tissue to wipe away her tears. "I'm sorry if I've let you down, Chief," she whispered.

He laughed. "Nonsense. You haven't. You've been brilliant. Besides, it's your first real case. I'd be concerned if you weren't emotionally affected by it."

She sighed, then tucked the tissue in her pocket. She grinned. "Yeah, I was pretty good, wasn't I?"

"Sure was. So, what do you think of them?"

"Well, they repeated the same story almost verbatim. And they still couldn't think of anyone who held a grudge against them back then. They had no prior connection to either Jonathan or Martina Sullivan. Not much new information here."

"Agreed. I'd love to talk to one of the Sullivans next, but I doubt Jonathan's ready to be interrogated. And Martina is still with her lawyer. So, Maria?"

"Sounds good, Chief. Let's go."

They both got up, but before they had even made it to the door of the unassigned hospital room they'd used as an interrogation room, the chief's work phone was ringing.

Sally was excited. "Pick up, Chief. Might be the office. Maybe Martina's done talking with her lawyer and ready to be interrogated?"

The chief picked up. "Hello?"

A pause.

"Yes, this is he. I'm Chief Parlot."

Another pause.

"Oh, hello, sir. I've been meaning to call you. Guess you beat me to the punch." He gestured Sally to sit back down, then sidled over, set his phone on the table, and put it on loudspeaker.

An angry voice roared into the room, "You're damn right you should've called. Right away, if not earlier. You don't get to go it alone when the FBI was involved in the original investigation, you know that. What were you thinking, Chief?"

Chief Parlot sighed. "I wasn't sure you'd be interested in such an old case."

"Not interested? Are you nuts? Of course I'm interested. *The bureau* is interested. And we certainly need to be involved. It's a big case! And now it looks like we made a few mistakes back then, so we need to clear our name. From this point forward, you are *not* in charge of this case. Are we clear, Chief?"

He sighed again. "Yes, sir, crystal."

"Good. Because we already have an agent on the way. She'll be taking over the case. *Understood*, Chief?"

"Of course." He looked at Sally, his eyes sad, then started. "Wait.... *She?*"

"Yes, Agent Tonya Anderson is on her way."

"But shouldn't you send Agent Borman? He led the case back then. Is he at least coming, too? I feel it's important I get the chance to talk with him as well."

"I'm afraid that won't be possible."

"Why not?"

"Agent Borman passed a few years ago."

Chief Parlot stared at the phone. *I remember him being a fairly young, charming agent. He died?* "I'm sorry to hear that. I didn't know."

"That's okay. It was sudden. Anyway, Agent Anderson is on her way now with her assistant, Agent Cooper. They'll meet you at the station."

"We're at the hospital right now, not the station. Do you want us to go back? Or do you need us to pick up your people from the airport?"

"Oh no, no need for that. They're coming on a chartered flight and have access to a rental car. They'll meet you at the police station. So, get your butts back over there, and whatever you do, hold off on any further interrogations until my agents are there to supervise. Understood, Chief?"

Sally stared at the phone, then at Chief Parlot.

"Yes, sir, understood. Talk soon." He hung up the phone and let out a deep sigh.

"They can't do that," Sally protested, and got up. She started pacing. "They can't take the case away from us. From you. No way. Not fair."

"It's the Feds, Sally. It's just the way it is. They come swooping in with their own private jets and their own jumbo SUVs and do as they please."

"But that's *not fair*, Chief! Not fair. We've developed a connection with these people already. We did, not them. We should be running this case. We owe it to the Collins. And to Maria. Every time I look at those unique eyes of hers, I'm reminded of how badly the police *and the FBI* failed her twenty years ago. She was just a toddler, a small child. Those old photos show her eyes filled with such life, such curiosity. Now, her eyes are bathed in pain brought on by unspeakable trauma. It's just wrong. We have to figure out what happened to her."

Despite the unexpected turn, the chief found a big grin spreading across his face. "You're right, Sally. He said we're not allowed to interrogate anyone about the case twenty years ago—but he did *not* say we couldn't interrogate the victim of last night's attack!"

Sally stared at him, then burst out into laughter. "You're awesome, Chief."

"I know, I know, thanks, Sally." He smiled. "Let's go talk to Maria and find out why he attacked her, that bastard Jonathan Sullivan!"

CHAPTER 14

Jonathan Sullivan felt so nauseous. His head was hurting, his eyes heavy. He wasn't sure where he was. He heard a faint beeping noise in the background and moved his fingers. He found there was something on one of his fingertips. A slight pinching pressure.

What the heck? He opened his eyes, but even then it took him a while to understand. *I'm in a hospital? All these machines monitoring my oxygen, my blood pressure, my fucking everything... why?*

As he looked around and thought back to what happened, it dawned on him. He remembered. His face turned completely white; his eyes darted around the room. The beeping grew loud and furious in his ears.

"Mr. Sullivan?" He blinked, and suddenly there was someone standing by his bed.

A nurse?

"Mr. Sullivan, good to see you awake. How are you feeling?"

He looked at her. *Like shit!* But he managed a crooked smile.

"Good, good, glad to see you're feeling well. I'll let the doctor know you're awake. Be right back."

All Jonathan could do was nod, and even that was a struggle. Truth be told, he felt anything but well, pretty terrible, in fact, and could barely move his body. He began to panic.

I messed up. They won't be amused. No, not at all.
His eyes bulged.
Oh no, they'll fucking kill me! I need help!

CHAPTER 15

"**H**elp? You need *my* help?" Maria raised her eyebrows.

"Yes, like we said before—anything you can recall would be great," Chief Parlot said.

Maria sighed. "Okay. I guess I can try."

"Wonderful. Thank you, Maria," the chief said, then gave everyone else a look of gratitude. "And thank *you* for letting us talk to her in private."

Aaron, Jack, and the Collinses nodded, then left the room.

Maria watched them leave and clutched Enti tightly. *Enti still helps me. Somehow, this old dirty-looking, faded toy keeps me calm. So, let's do this, Enti.* She took in a deep breath as she watched the older police officer pull out a compact dictation device.

"Maria," Chief Parlot started in a more formal voice, "we are here today to question you about the attack last night. We will record this interview using this machine. Is that okay with you?"

Maria gripped the little toy tighter, trying to ignore how odd it must look for a grown woman to be clinging to a baby's security blanket, a duck head with three feet. She exhaled deeply, then nodded. "Okay. Sure. Yes, that's fine."

"Good. Know that this conversation is now being recorded with all parties' consent. Maria Moana Heikinnen, also known as Maria

Sullivan, please tell us what happened yesterday after you left the restaurant."

"Well, I was standing in the parking lot, holding Enti—that's this toy in my lap that my... my..." She struggled for words while holding the old toy tightly.

"...birth mom?" Officer Johnson suggested with a smile.

"Yes, that. I was holding Enti, the toy that my birth mom had given me earlier. I was just standing in the parking lot, trying to figure out what was going on. You know... My life was falling apart. I had just learned that Martina Sullivan isn't my real mamá, and met my... my... birth mom and dad."

The chief and Officer Johnson both nodded.

"And then, I remember someone coming up behind me. He put a hand on my mouth and dragged me into some bushes. I was stunned. Didn't know what to do." She stared at them in bewilderment, her hands clutching the toy so tightly that her knuckles turned white.

Officer Johnson took on a softer tone. "And what happened then? We found your shoes in the bushes by the parking lot. Did you kick them off?"

Maria shook her head. "No, one of them got caught on something and then I lost the other one somehow. Don't really remember."

"Okay, got it. Did you know who was dragging you?"

"No, not at first. I didn't recognize him until later. It was dark. We fought a bit. At one point I got away from him, but I think he caught up and hit me with something over my head. A stick maybe."

"Yes, luckily a small wound," Chief Parlot said.

"Right, but it took me out. I woke up in his lap. He was feeding me alcohol. And rambling on about something."

The chief perked up at this. "What did he say?"

"Well, I don't remember it all. But he said he would finish what he couldn't back then. That this time it would work. This time he'd make it look like an accident, like I drank too much after meeting my real parents and then drowned."

Officer Johnson looked at her. "He said 'he needed to finish what he couldn't back then'? 'This time it would work'? What did he mean by 'it'?"

Maria shrugged her shoulders. "Don't know. He mentioned something about 'plans.' Plans they had back then, and his new plan."

"'They'?" both the officer and chief asked.

"Yeah, he talked about *them* a lot. And that *they* couldn't take this new life he has built away from him now because he's actually a good guy." She laughed out loud. "Yeah right, a good guy! A good guy wouldn't attack me. This man tried to drown me, held me underwater. It's unbelievable. I *hate* being held under water."

Tears streamed down her face unchecked; her eyes had turned completely green, freakishly green. She felt small, so small. "Hate wawa. Can't swim yet. Hate wawa. So dark," she said in a little voice, and stared at the two people by her bed. *Who are they? Well, they seem nice. Interested in my story. But they're so irritating. Just keep staring at me.*

She closed her eyes, and when she opened them again, she was looking at a picture the man was showing her: a picture of a bunk bed with a few toys lying on it. She spotted her favorite.

"Enti," she yelled, her face lighting up. "That's Enti. Brand-new Enti."

She looked down at the old toy she was holding, then back at the picture again. Lying beside Enti was a pink pillow and a pacifier. "Kissen! It's Kissen! And Schnulli!"

With a big grin on her face and her eyes completely green now, she looked at the two people sitting by her bed. *I feel so strange. Who are these people?*

"Can you point to those things you just mentioned?" the man asked.

"Kissen and Schnulli?"

He nodded. "Yes, please."

He doesn't know Kissen and Schnulli? Why not? Oh, maybe he doesn't speak Mama-language words? She pointed to the pink pillow and the pacifier in the picture. "Kissen. Schnulli."

"Thank you for showing me. Do you recognize this room?"

"Yes, mine. My room."

"Yes, that's your room in the TLF at Eglin Air Force Base," the man said.

"TLF?" Maria stared at him now. The little hairs on her arms stood up. She felt a shudder run down her spine. *This place scares me.* She again studied the picture she was holding. Her hands had started sweating and were so moist, they left a wet mark on the picture.

"What do you do in this room?" she heard the man ask.

"I sleep. My bed." She pointed at the bed again. "Mama sings good-night song."

"I see. And what else happens in this room? Something bad?"

Something bad? No. Why? Maria shook her head.

She saw the man pull out another picture and handed it to her. She studied it. It showed twin rows of old-looking one-story buildings, a half-sandy-half-grassy area in between them leading directly toward a shallow shoreline.

The outside. The sandy grass that leads to the water! She clutched Enti so tight that her fingernails started to break her skin. Her breaths came fast and hard. Sweat formed on her forehead and her eyes glowed bright green. *Here. Something bad happens here. By the shore.*

With shaky hands, she pointed to the picture, to the water. "I sleep. Wake up in man's arm. Not Daddy's. Strong man. Man in uniform. Carries me."

"Where does he go? Where is he taking you?"

She was breathing so hard now and couldn't help but sob. "Wawa… Into wawa. Dark wawa swallows me." *No, no, no. Don't carry me there. Help me, please help me.*

She couldn't take it anymore and screamed an ear-splitting scream. "No wawa, no, no!" Tears were streaming down her face, but through them, she saw the middle-aged man and young woman by her bedside jump up.

"Oh my gosh, what's happening to her?" she heard the young woman ask, then saw the door to her room fly open. A bunch of strangers she didn't know came rushing in.

Who are all these grown-up people? They scare me. Moana is scared. She kept screaming, just like a toddler.

"Chief, what's going on here?" a lady in blue scrubs asked. She came over to Maria and started talking to her directly. "It's okay, sweetie, it's okay. You're safe here. I'm Nurse Hannah and I'm going to take care of you. Maria! You're safe, Maria."

Maria? Who's Maria? Safe? Here? Where am I? She stopped screaming—only now realized she'd been screaming the whole time—and looked around with bewildered green eyes.

"Close your eyes, sweetie, it's okay. Just close your eyes and take a deep breath, nice, slow, deep breath." She listened to the lady's gentle voice and did as she was told.

When she opened her eyes again, she found she was in her hospital bed, surrounded by her loved ones. The Collinses, Jack, and Aaron were all there, right by her side. In front of her, the nurse who had been speaking to her was scolding the two police officers.

"You went too far, Chief! You put her in a state of shock. Just who do you think you are, tormenting this poor girl?"

The police officers looked down at their feet. "I'm sorry," the chief mumbled, then picked up the recording device and two pictures on the end of her bed and put them inside his briefcase. "I'm sorry."

The young officer gave him a look and bit her lip. She kept quiet.

As the nurse cared for her, Maria watched the police officers slowly leave the room. They looked forlorn, penitent.

What... happened...?

At that precise moment, the blood pressure cuff on her arm, keeping to its own schedule, decided to inflate, squeezing her tight. *So tight! I don't like it. Like someone holding me, squeezing me.*

Suddenly, she remembered something. *Just like my kidnapper did—he held little me so tight, underwater, drowning me.* She shook her head to get rid of those unwanted thoughts. *But I'm alive. I didn't drown back then. And I didn't either last night. He didn't finish what he started twenty years ago. Wait, what?*

The color drained from her face. *Jonathan Sullivan said that to me last night, didn't he?*

"Maria, are you okay?" Aaron took her hand, bringing her back to the present.

She nodded.

"What is it, Maria? I can see it in your eyes. Did you remember something?"

She nodded again. "Jonathan Sullivan told me he was going to finish what he couldn't back then. That he'd come up with a better plan than the one they had twenty years ago."

Jack now stood up. "'They'?"

She stared straight at the wall, her head hurting. "Yeah, *they*. When Sullivan attacked me last night, he mentioned them a lot. I just told the police about it. I think there were other people besides Jonathan Sullivan involved in kidnapping me as a child. A whole group of guys."

"Guys?" Brad said. "You mean men? Only men, no women?"

Maria nodded again. "No women. Just guys. Yeah, bad guys kidnapped me back then. Two or three of them. Don't think I ever saw the first one again, the one who carried me... from... the TLF...."

Her breathing got faster; a splitting headache came on.

Aaron stared at Maria. "You never saw the one again—the one who carried you as a toddler? The one who kidnapped you from the TLFs? You're saying it wasn't Jonathan Sullivan who kidnapped you back then?"

Maria nodded slightly. A dull pain enveloped her forehead. "No, it wasn't him. He came later. He was working for somebody... *for them*." She found herself suddenly convinced there was more than one person behind her kidnapping twenty years ago, more than just Jonathan Sullivan.

A whole group. Bad guys took me. Oh no.

Before she could think on it any longer, her head exploded with pain. Seeking to rid herself of it, she closed her eyes and shook her head violently, back and forth, back and forth.

CHAPTER 16

Back and forth, Chief Parlot paced the length of the workroom inside the police station. He glanced at the two FBI agents standing by the door, watching him. They had just arrived.

"Chief, please believe us. We don't want to take this case from you. We're only here to help. Nothing more," FBI Agent Tonya Anderson said.

He kept eyeing her—her cornrows up in a bun, her dark-brown eyes with the long eyelashes glistening in excitement—but said nothing.

"It's an interesting case," she continued. "Looking forward to working on it with you… and this young lady here, I presume?"

The chief snapped out of it. "Correct. She's with me. This is Officer Sally Johnson."

Agent Anderson held out her hand. "Nice to meet you, Officer Sally Johnson."

"My pleasure, Agent Anderson," Sally said, and shook her hand.

"Oh no, no, girl, this all sounds so stuffy. We're supposed to be partners here, aren't we? Call me Tonya."

"Sally, then." The young officer grinned, and Tonya winked at her.

"And I'm Tom," the other agent said, and shook everyone's hand. "Also known as Agent Cooper, should the occasion arise."

Chief Parlot looked at Agent Cooper. *Young guy, probably in his early twenties. That wavy brown hair in a boy cut makes him look so young.* He held out his hand. "Nice to meet you both."

"You, too, Chief," both agents said in unison.

"Honestly, I was expecting Agent Borman," the chief said. "I didn't know that—"

"—he killed himself," Tom finished the sentence, then realized he probably shouldn't have said that aloud when he saw the chief's astonishment.

"Yes, I didn't know he'd passed," Chief Parlot said in a neutral tone. He was itching to jot down a note, wondering why a successful agent like Borman would kill himself.

Tonya jumped in to change the subject. "We looked over the old case file on our way over here. And we've been briefed on the newest developments. We were hoping you could fill us in on some details."

The chief nodded, reluctantly. The gesture did not go unnoticed by Tonya.

"Chief, I'll say it again, plain as day: We are *not* here to take your case. We're here to support you as best we can. We need to find the truth."

Chief Parlot grunted and looked at them. "That's what your predecessors said the last time."

Tonya tightened her lips. "I'm aware they took you off the case back then. But you were young, like your friend here. Only the chief was supposed to collaborate with the FBI and Agent Borman. It was protocol back then."

He looked at her, still suspicious.

"Luckily, Chief Parlot, time marches on, as do protocols and people. I can assure you, I want to work with you, not against you, nor do I want to shut you out. We all have different strengths, and I intend to use them. This is *your* precinct, *your* area. Agent Cooper and I are here to support. No matter what you've been told—that's the way

I see it and I wanna do this: You're the lead and we will all work this together."

The chief looked at her. *She's going against her boss's orders? That takes guts! I underestimated her. She seems fair. Pretty cool how she likes to keep us involved. Guess nobody needs to know how exactly we run this case.*

He grinned, then glanced at the young guy next to her. *And Agent Cooper seems like a rookie, just like Sally. Maybe Tonya and I have more in common than I thought? I do kinda like her.*

He broke out into a big smile. "Well, that's fantastic. Agree, let's all work this together! And I'm Isaac, by the way."

Tonya smiled at him and gave him a fist bump. "Alright, alright, Isaac my man. Let's go. Can you bring us up to speed?"

About an hour later, they had assembled a case wall inside one of the interrogation rooms. Hung on it were old pictures and transcripts of interrogations from twenty years ago, along with a bunch of sticky notes expressing their personal thoughts or questions or revelations.

The picture of the marina on base was a big question mark, as were the pictures of the wet, sandy spot in front of the toddler's bed, the pink pillow, and Enti. The timeline of events that fateful day remained a mystery.

They had plastered pictures of each person involved along the wall. Attached to each were statements or questions written on colorful sticky notes. Next to the Collinses' picture were the interviews from back then, along with the one taken earlier that day. Martina Sullivan's picture had a short note that read "Motive." Below was another note that read "Trace whereabouts on or around May 28, 2003" and "What do family and neighbors know?" Maria's picture was a big question mark—what would she be able to remember? Were those memories reliable? Last but not least was Jonathan Sullivan, who had earned sticky notes with "Motive" and "Who did he work with/for?" and "Connection to Collins?" in big blocky letters.

"Well, ladies and gentlemen, we did it. Good job, team," Tonya said, and gave everyone a fist bump. They all agreed their work had been thorough.

"It looks pretty cool, doesn't it?" Tom Cooper said, smiling at the case wall in admiration.

Sally nodded. "Sure does. Ahhh, I'm glad we did this here. We have so many more resources at our disposal here compared to the hospital, and it's far more secure. Good idea bringing us back, Chief."

"Thanks," he mumbled, then sighed. "I'm not very welcome at the hospital right now anyways."

Tonya patted him on the back. "Aw, it'll be okay. Maria was doing fine when we called earlier, but she might have more episodes once we start working with her. After what you've told me and that video you showed us—man, we gotta keep at it with her. Her memories could be the key to everything."

"Yeah, but first she needs to be released from the hospital. I think the best way to get at those memories is to take her places she might have been when she was abducted," Sally said.

"We'll have to be patient. We certainly can't remove her from the hospital ourselves." Tom laughed. "Then, we definitely wouldn't be welcome there anymore."

"Alright, team. It's a waiting game for now," Tonya said. "Of course, police officers and FBI agents *never* just sit around and wait. Or eat donuts."

Everyone laughed, and she winked. "That's just a stereotype, right? Anyways, let's assign jobs. Isaac, tell us what to do, man."

He looked at her and smiled. *She's funny, amazingly easy to work with. And, so far, she's kept her promise.*

"Well, Sally, you're a people person. I'm putting you in charge of coordinating with the Miami Police Department to send us a transcript of the interviews they did this morning with Martina Sullivan's family and neighbors. Do the same with the Jacksonville Police Department who questioned Jonathan Sullivan's family, friends, and colleagues."

Sally took a deep breath. "Wow, okay. Big job, but I'm on it."

"Great. Tom, you mentioned you're a wizard with technology, so I'm putting you in charge of finding out where and how Maria's fake birth certificate was created." He handed Tom the birth certificate in question.

Tom grinned. "On it." He immediately took out his laptop, along with a bunch of other forensic tools, from his bag.

"Well, Tonya, that leaves you and me. We're gonna talk to everyone who worked the former case."

She nodded. "I'd like to include Agent Borman's former assistant, Chief Billings, as well as every former Eglin base police officer. And the former base commander."

"Good idea. Though some of them might be hard to find," the chief said, and sighed.

"Nah, not for Tom. He can help look them up while we start with the people who are easy to find." Tonya looked at Tom, who just gave her a curt nod.

"Or there's another approach," she continued, eyeing Chief Parlot. "Should we start in the present?"

"The present?"

"Come on, my man. The attack. Last night. At the restaurant."

"Oh, that. You mean, see if anyone else saw something?"

"Yeah, exactly. Maybe there were some witnesses your guys missed, someone who could yield fresh evidence?"

"Hmm. It's worth checking out. How about we take a trip to the restaurant and ask around? We can leave the youngsters in charge here. What do you say?"

Tonya nodded.

"Great. Hope you're good at dodging the paparazzi."

She grinned. "Oh, yes, I'm *very* good. Better stretch before we go, though. Don't wanna pull something while we're crawling and summersaulting past them." Tonya pulled her limbs into an arm stretch, and the chief looked at her, his mouth open. She giggled. "Come on, Isaac, I'm kidding. I haven't been able to do a summersault since I was seventeen."

"Oh, good," he mumbled. "Uh, me too." His face lit up. "But I *am* good at crawling and hiding."

"Bless your heart. Well, okay then, let's go."

Just then, there was a knock at the door. Everyone stopped in their tracks. The chief went to see who it was.

Mrs. Valentina Garcia, defense lawyer pro bono, smiled at him. "Martina is ready to see you," she announced. "Is now a good time?"

The chief looked at Tonya, then at Sally and Tom. He grinned. "Actually, yes. Now's perfect. Thank you. We'll be right there."

Her missing testimony is critical to our investigation. To be more effective in the field, we need her side of the story. I have a feeling Martina Sullivan will be of great help in our pursuit of the truth.

CHAPTER 17

The truth? Nobody can ever find out the truth! You'll never tell anyone, Jonathan Sullivan. We need to keep you quiet, my dear Sully.

He looked down at the man in the hospital bed and shook his head. *It didn't have to come to this. It didn't. But now, there's no way around it. Man, this sucks. Really sucks. Too bad.*

He sighed a deep sigh and thought about how best to do it. He looked at the hospital monitor, saw that Jonathan's heart was beating well—too well—a line jumping up and down with every beat of his heart. His oxygen intake was also great.

Can I cut off his oxygen somehow? Unplug something? He just can't talk. Need to stop him from saying anything. He wasn't quite sure what to do and looked at all the cables draped around the hospital bed. *Hard to tell what's what here, just a mess of cables.* He sighed. *Whatever I do, gotta do it soon.*

He kept searching for the perfect cover-up, not really knowing what he was doing, when he saw the pulsing line on the monitor speed up. *What the fuck?*

He stared at the monitor, then back to Jonathan and had to take a step back. Jonathan's eyes were open, resting on him.

"H-hi, Jonathan," he stuttered, "h-how are you?"

But the man just stared at him, not blinking. Finally, he rasped, "Police here?" He tilted his head. "In the hospital?"

"Yes, you're in the hospital, Jonathan. And please, no need to worry about that. I'm just here to see how you're doing." He put on his hat to conceal his face, then made sure the name tag on his uniform was well hidden. "Get some rest."

He watched Jonathan nod and close his eyes again.

Phew, that was close. Shit!

Quickly, he turned around and left the room. Just as he was gently closing the door, he heard footsteps coming closer. He glanced over his shoulder and saw a young woman with long wavy reddish-brown hair waving at him from down the hall.

"Hey there, Chief. Thought you left a while ago?" she called to him in a loud voice.

Shit! Who the heck is that? I can't be seen. Need to get away from here. Wait. Did she mistake me for…?

A grin came over his face. He let go of the door handle, pulled his hat down further, and kept his back to her as he yelled back, "Yep, just leaving now." He tossed a wave at her then walked off in the opposite direction.

"See you later, Chief," he heard the young woman say.

Quick! Must get away from here. Ahhh, that girl's irritating.

Even as he walked away as fast as propriety allowed, his big grin spread wider across his face.

But she certainly was convinced I'm the chief.

CHAPTER 18

*T*he chief was acting kinda weird. Maria left the hospital kitchenette, coffee in hand, and walked back toward her own hospital room.

Guess he's still embarrassed over interrogating me and putting me into a state of shock. She sighed and took a sip of her coffee. *Oh well, I'm fine. Feeling much better without that IV and after changing into those clothes Jack brought me. And even better now—finally getting my coffee fix.*

She smiled and took another big gulp, then frowned. *Not the best coffee, but it'll do. Gotta stay sharp. I really want to help solve this case. The strange puzzle of my past.*

Deep in thought, she opened the door to her hospital room. She was surprised to find not only Aaron, Jack, and the Collinses inside but also a man in a white lab coat who turned to her immediately and said, "Ah, there you are, young lady. You were gone for some time. Had me thinking you'd flown the coop."

"Oh, hi, doc. No, just got myself a coffee. Felt like I really needed it, and the exercise. Was I really gone that long? The vending machine is just around the corner."

The doctor laughed. "Yeah, I know. Trust me, I know that vending machine well. And I might have been exaggerating a little. Your family already informed me what you were up to." He winked at her. "But next time, please ask permission before you leave your room."

Maria was stunned. "Permission? I'm twenty-one years old. Besides, I thought you were about ready to release me."

"True, you're not a child anymore, and you'll most likely go home today. But you just had a traumatic experience. I need to evaluate you first, make sure it's safe to release you."

"Okay, fine, doc," Maria said. She put her coffee on the little table then slid onto the hospital bed.

The doctor took her vitals as Aaron, Jack, and the Collinses watched on.

"Vitals look good. I'm not seeing anything that concerns me at this time," the doctor said, then looked straight at Maria. "Next time you sit down for questioning, though, I'd like you to have a trauma specialist in the room with you, young lady. No more interrogations unless the police offer you a specialist, understood?"

Maria sighed. "Yes, I understand. I need a shrink next time." She grinned and got a laugh out of the doctor. "So, may I be released today?"

"Hmm, seems like the blow to your head and mild concussion haven't dulled your wit."

"Nope, my brain works quite well," Maria assured him. "I don't have so much as a headache."

"Your vitals are fine, the swelling on your forehead is going down, and you seem eager to leave… and yet, I think it would be for the best if you stayed one more night to rest."

"But I can rest at home, doc," Maria said. "I have plenty of home care, I can assure you that. We're surrounded by people eager to care for me!" She pointed to the Collinses, Aaron, and Jack, who all nodded.

"From what I understand, you have no home here. Where will you stay?"

"We have a very nice room at the Air Force Inn on base," Aaron explained.

"Or she can stay at Eglin's Distinguished Visitor's Quarters, sir," Brad Collins offered.

"Or my hotel room in Destin," Elisabeth called out.

"Okay, okay, everyone, I get the message. Maria's got options. I just need to make sure she gets her rest—I cannot begin to express how important that is for her. Her mind is fragile. She cannot be confronted with further trauma, especially if she ends up staying on base. And you'll need to keep her away from the reporters," the doctor said.

"Reporters?" Maria asked, and looked at everyone.

"Yes, your story is all over the news. They're even camping out here in the hospital parking lot."

"Oh my…"

"I suggest she stays on base, then, doctor," Brad said. "The press isn't allowed. She should be safe there."

"If we do that, we need to make sure she stays far away from, you know… from the…" Jack trailed off, but Aaron understood what he meant.

"Of course. We won't bring her back there, Dad," Aaron said. "She can't afford to have another traumatic experience. Maybe we could go straight back to the inn?"

"Or the Distinguished Visitor's Quarters," Brad suggested. "It's a big house. Big enough for all of us to stay at. My treat."

Aaron turned to Brad. "I don't know, sir. Isn't that building also close to the water? You know, close to the…"

"Oof, you're right. Maybe the inn would be best after all? What do you think, Mo—Maria?" Brad smiled at her.

"I liked the inn. Sure."

Elisabeth looked disappointed. "That's a shame. I was hoping we could all stick together and maybe stay at Brad's place?"

"Well, folks, that's a problem for you to figure out. I'm done here," the doctor said. "Maria, I need you to come back in about a week so I can remove the stitches from your forehead. Until then, please, rest up. Honestly, a quiet place would be best."

He addressed the room. "It was nice seeing everyone.

"Maria, Nurse Hannah will be in soon with your discharge papers."

"Okay, thanks, doc," Maria said. "Thanks for everything."

"My pleasure. You're lucky the cut on your forehead was minor. But remember, you do have a mild concussion. You need your rest to fully recover."

She nodded. "Yes, sir, I hear you."

They all watched him leave.

"So, everyone, I have an idea," she said. "I think Aaron's right, I should stay at the Air Force Inn. But maybe we could all stay there? That way we can be together, but in separate rooms?"

Elisabeth's face lit up. "Mo—Maria, that's a great idea. I'd love that, mein Engel."

Brad nodded. "Guess I should ask my buddy Drew if he's down to stay at the inn."

"And my friend, Sarah," Elisabeth said.

Brad laughed. "I doubt she'll want to give up the resort in Destin for the inn at Eglin."

Elisabeth smirked. "Yeah, probably not. But will Drew want to give up the big house you were both staying at?"

Brad laughed. "I think so. He doesn't need all those extra rooms, or the kitchen. We've been doing work dinners every night while we're here."

" *We?* "

"Ah, good point. I guess he's the only one working at the moment. Technically, I should be, but…"

Aaron snorted. "Yeah, same here."

Brad walked over to him and gave him a pat on the shoulder. "Nah, no worries. You already did all your in-processing, and it's standard for them to give you vacation time to house-hunt immediately afterward. You just had to use yours to do more important things." He winked at Aaron. "You'll make for a fine second lieutenant. Just tell them you're hanging with the General now. No better way to learn the ins and outs of the Air Force."

"I guess, sir."

"So, the inn, then?" Maria said, and they all nodded. "Good. I'm pleased about that. But not about how hungry I am. Think we could get a bite to eat somewhere?"

Aaron came over. "Are you sure you'd like to go eat somewhere?" Maria nodded.

He took her hand and whispered in her ear, "You seem happy. I'm glad to see it."

She looked at him, and her smile faded. "Well, I decided I need to be. I'm happy I'm okay, I'm happy I've found my family," she whispered to Aaron. "But I'm so worried about Mamá." Her eyes filled with tears.

He gave her a kiss on the cheek. "Don't cry, my love. Focus on the good things. And don't forget, it's your *real* birthday today." Then, he turned to everyone. "Hey, we should take Maria out for her birthday. Where should we go?"

"I have an idea," Brad said, smiling. "Let's get food on base at the Officers' Club. It'll be a great place for you to see, Lieutenant, and the food there is actually really good. Great lunch buffet."

"Sounds wonderful, General," Jack said.

Brad laughed. "Please, don't call me that. I'm Brad, just Brad. Honestly, I can't wait to get out of this uniform."

"Well, Brad," Jack said, "I'm afraid I only brought new clothes for Aaron and Maria. It would've been kinda strange rummaging through your belongings."

They all laughed.

"Elisabeth and I will go ahead and get changed," Brad said. "We'll meet you on base for a late lunch?" They all nodded. "Aaron, will you let the chief know that we're relocating? He needs to be informed about Maria's discharge and where we'll be staying."

"Yes, sir," Aaron said, then flinched. "I mean, yes, Brad."

"Good, good. Let's head out then, Elisabeth."

"But I don't want to leave her...."

Brad took her hand. "We'll all be together again soon. I'll drive quick, I promise. Oh, wait... I don't have a car."

Jack laughed. "I do. I can give you both a ride."

"Perfect."

Jack and Brad waved goodbye to Maria, while Elisabeth came over and gave her a hug. "See you soon, then, right?"

"Yes, I'll see you soon," Maria reassured her, and watched them leave the hospital room. She sighed.

Focus on the good things. Get to know my parents. But what about Mamá? My dear Martina?

CHAPTER 19

Martina sat across from the police chief and an FBI agent. Her lawyer Valentina Garcia sat next to her. She was nervous.

"Let's get started then, shall we?" Chief Parlot said.

Martina's lip quivered; she felt like she was about to cry. She saw both the chief and the female FBI agent's gaze resting on her.

They've probably already made up their minds about me. Me, the weakling. Well, hopefully they'll see that I don't have the cutthroat personality it takes to be a criminal, to plan a kidnapping. Hope they see I'm emotional, that I have empathy. Something mean guys and criminals don't have.

She felt Valentina take her hand. "Estára bien," the lawyer whispered. "It'll be okay."

With a big sigh, Martina sat up a little straighter. "Yes, Chief, let's get started."

"Wonderful, Martina," the chief said. "First, a few words from my colleague here."

The FBI lady took over. "Hi, Martina, I'm Agent Tonya Anderson, FBI. I'm glad you and Chief Parlot let me be a part of this questioning."

Martina looked at her suspiciously. *I did no such thing.*

The agent laughed. "I know, I know, you didn't actually invite me. My man Isaac here did. Still, wanted you to know I'm happy to be here and would love to help you."

Martina stared at her. "Help me?"

"Yes. We all want to find out the truth, even you, I think. You took a lot of time to discuss the case with your lawyer, so I get the feeling there are a lot of unknown parts and pieces to it." She winked at Martina, a smile on her lips.

Martina smiled back at her. *Maybe she's nice after all?*

"Martina, we have to videotape this interview. I'd appreciate it if you'd sign this paperwork, please. It just grants us permission to record our interactions, and that you're aware that everything you say can and will be used against you. It also states that you have been given a lawyer to defend you. Take your time to read through it," the chief said.

Martina took the paperwork and went through it. It was written in such lawyerly jargon that she couldn't possibly understand it all, but Valentina Garcia took over and went through it again with her, helping to translate words or sentences that were too complicated and interpreting the meaning behind the words.

Martina felt a bit uneasy. *I see them watching me. Watching my every move in silence. But I need to learn and understand everything. Need to be thorough.*

Once she felt she understood it all, she signed the paperwork and pushed it across the table to Chief Parlot and Agent Anderson.

"Thank you, Martina," Agent Anderson said, and nodded to Chief Parlot, who started recording. "Please state your full name, address, and profession."

Martina nodded and answered in turn.

"And now, please tell us about your family and relatives."

She took a deep breath. "I have two younger sisters. The oldest is Mariella Lopez. She is married to Eduardo Lopez. They have two children, Stephanie and Rolando. My youngest sister is Monica Santos, married to Mauricio Santos, and she has two boys, Alejandro and Diego, both in high school. All of these relatives live in Miami."

"Great, thank you," the chief said. "Now, who is Maria Gabriella Sullivan?"

Martina looked at the chief, then at the FBI agent, and chose her words carefully. "Maria is a wonderful young lady who studies Human Factors at Embry-Riddle Aeronautical University. She just finished her junior year there and is engaged to Aaron Heikinnen, a second lieutenant in the United States Air Force."

Chief Parlot and Agent Anderson glanced at each other.

Martina saw it. *I'm sure they know I've been prepped what to say by my lawyer. Good thing she went over this with me.*

The FBI agent took over. "Martina, how do you know Maria Gabriella Sullivan?"

Martina took a deep breath. "I raised her."

"Did you give birth to her?"

"No, I did not. She came to me when she was about two years old."

Chief Parlot jumped up abruptly and slid Maria's fake birth certificate as well as a picture of her as a toddler across the table and yelled, "So, how in the world do you explain your name on this birth certificate, and the fact that the girl you raised as Maria Gabriella Sullivan is actually Moana Marie Collins, a toddler who was kidnapped twenty years ago?"

Martina's eyes went wide, her face pale. *He's so intimidating.*

Valentina Garcia took Martina's hand. "Estára bien," she whispered to her, then turned to the chief, her voice stern. "Please, you're scaring my client, Chief. There is no reason to be this aggressive all of a sudden. My client is cooperating and answering all of your questions patiently. Unless you can stay calm, my client will not say anything else, you understand?"

Chief Parlot nodded and sat back down. "I'm sorry," he whispered, "It's just been a long day." His face flushed in embarrassment. He glanced at his colleague.

Agent Anderson gave him a nod and took over. "Martina, we understand you have told your lawyer you are innocent of both the kidnapping as well as faking this legal document, but know that we intend to pursue these charges to the full extent of the law. If you are innocent, we need you to prove it. Please tell us your side of the story."

"Estára bien, go ahead," Mrs. Garcia whispered to Martina and squeezed her hand one last time, then let go of it.

Martina studied the picture of little Maria before her. Well, little Moana. *"Moana Marie Collins. Missing since May 28, 2003."* A tear rolled down her face.

She took a deep breath and said, "Here is the truth and nothing but the truth. Not a story; the truth. My recollection of how Maria came into my life. The truth!" Her voice rang out clear and strong.

She looked at the police chief and the FBI agent, then fixated on the picture of the toddler again. Tears welled in her eyes. "My ex-husband, Jonathan Sullivan, dropped this child off at my apartment. I thought it was his child, a girl he'd had with another woman. I thought the woman had left him, or that... or..."

"Or what?" Agent Anderson asked, her voice soft.

"That he had hurt the mom." Martina looked up. "Jonathan is not a nice guy. Not at all. I got a restraining order against him. He was abusive. At least he was to me. But hopefully wasn't... hopefully..." Martina started sobbing.

"Hopefully what?" Chief Parlot asked, his face now soft, his eyes no longer fiery.

"Hopefully not toward my little one," she whispered, and started crying even more. "What did he do to her? What? ¡Dios mío! You need to find out! What did he do to her those two months?"

Perplexed, Chief Parlot and the FBI agent looked at each other, then at her. "What do you mean? 'Those two months'?"

With a shaky hand, Martina pointed to the caption underneath the picture. "It says here she went missing May 2003."

"Yes, that's right," both the chief and agent said.

Tears streamed down Martina's face and her voice became hysterical. "But Jonathan dropped her off at my door in *August*. Early August! Not in May! Not in June! Not in July! In August!"

Chief Parlot and Agent Anderson stared at her. They swallowed hard.

"August? Are you sure?" the agent asked, and Martina nodded.

"Please, Martina, tell us everything," the chief urged her.

"Yes, I am, I will...." she whispered, then looked at her lawyer.

"Please continue, Martina. You are safe here. Your daughter is safe. Todas están seguras," Mrs. Garcia told her.

Martina nodded and stared at the table. "But Jonathan promised he would come back and hurt us both if I ever told anyone anything," she whispered, her voice small as a mouse.

The FBI agent reached across the table and held her hand. "I assure you, Jonathan Sullivan won't hurt you or Maria ever again."

Martina dared to look at her. Her eyes rested on Agent Anderson's. "But he's in the same hospital as Maria. What if he just walks over and—"

"We *assure* you, Martina," the chief said, "Jonathan Sullivan *will not* hurt Maria ever again. I personally posted guards at both their hospital room doors. And I have to say, he's unlikely to do any walking any time soon. Maria really did a number on him...."

Agent Anderson grinned. "Yeah, she did. That girl sure did. She was strong, Martina, and now we need you to be strong for her."

Martina took a deep breath and nodded, still holding the agent's hand. "Yes, I will be strong."

She took one last look at the picture of the missing toddler, then started telling them every detail she could recall of that fateful night in early August. The night her life had changed forever.

Even as she spoke, her mind was preoccupied.

What happened during those two months that summer? What did Jonathan do? We must learn the whole story!

CHAPTER 20

"The whole story Martina told seems sound, doesn't it?" Sally Johnson looked at her colleagues.

"Yeah, it does," Tom agreed. "It explains why she had no idea about who Maria really was. By the way, I looked through every record of her bills. She didn't own a TV or a radio for a long time. Not until 2006. That makes it less likely she'd have heard about the kidnapping, especially if she kept to herself a lot."

"Agreed. All her neighbors claim she mostly keeps to herself," Tonya said, looking over the report from the Miami Police Department that Sally had given her.

"And all of Martina's relatives described toddler Maria as being scared and having dark black hair when they met her the fall of 2003," Chief Parlot noted while skimming through the transcripts of Martina's relatives' interviews. "They were all adamant that Martina has been a great mom, practically the nicest person in the world."

"But does that prove she's innocent?" Sally looked at everyone. They all shook their heads.

"Doesn't prove anything, but certainly doesn't hurt her claim," Chief Parlot mumbled, then turned to Tom. "Any updates on that birth certificate?"

"None so far, Chief," he said. "It was definitely professionally faked. Uses the same paper, font, and printing style that Vital Records use here in Florida. I think it must have been printed by someone within Vital Records. Someone who was in on the plot."

Tonya looked up. "Are we really going with that theory? A plot? A big coup?"

They all nodded.

"Do we think Jonathan Sullivan is capable of planning something like this?"

Tom laughed. "Doubt it. I mean, look at this guy. He's not the brightest. Barely finished high school. Martina put it nicely when she said he's 'not a nice guy.' Seems he broke bad early on. He was accused of sexual assault while still in high school."

"What?" Sally stared at him, her face now pale.

"Well, I did some digging," Tom continued. "Apparently, Jonathan was the lead actor in his high school theater group. A talented actor, one critic claimed. Juilliard-bound, another wrote. But then, after opening night during his senior year fall play, the understudy played his part. That struck me as odd. I dug some more and found out the theater group had a nice fun after-party on opening night. Apparently, they all got wasted at someone's house. There, Jonathan apparently attacked a girl he liked who didn't like him back. She filed a complaint."

"He wasn't charged?"

Tom shook his head. "Nope. Apparently, nobody knew whether it was consensual or not, and the complaint just kinda went away. It was a different time. The girl was also pretty drunk, which didn't help her claim."

Sally stomped her foot. "Argh, that's so wrong. Typical. A girl can't enjoy some alcohol with a guy...." She stopped talking when she saw everyone looking at her. "Sorry. It just makes me mad."

"Yeah, no kidding. We noticed," Tonya joked. "But I like that about you. We need compassion in the police force." She smiled at Sally, who grinned back at her.

"Exactly why Sally is on this team," the chief said, grinning as well. "Anyway, back to Sullivan."

"That's not to say he didn't get punished, though," Tom continued. "He got rejected by Juilliard. Lost out on his dream. After that, seems like his life went downhill from there."

"How so?"

"Well, after graduating from high school, he just kinda disappeared. Worked odd jobs here and there. Looks like he was gambling, drinking, doing all kinds of silly things all the while. Had a fake ID that got confiscated."

"Did his parents know what was happening? What did they do?" Sally wanted to know.

"Not sure. But later on, they had a big falling-out. Apparently, he gambled away most of their belongings. They had to sell their house, their cars, all kinds of things to pay off his debt. Eventually, they stopped talking to him and disowned him."

Sally stared at Tom, then glanced at Tonya and the chief. "That's sad."

Tonya smiled. "Aw, you're too sweet, Sally. Yeah, sad, but hardly an excuse for kidnapping a child."

Sally nodded. "Definitely not. Do we know what happened then?"

"Well, looks like he got a handle on his life eventually. He got going in the plumbing business. Worked in Miami for quite a while. There, he met Martina, got married, then divorced. Seemed he started gambling again after the divorce, disappeared for a few months after a bad spending spree at some major casinos. Might have gotten sober during that time, as his life actually took a turn for the better. He worked plumbing jobs in Jacksonville and made enough money to start his own plumbing business. It's been pretty successful."

"Good digging, Tom," Chief Parlot said, and patted him on the shoulder. "Very good. Sally, what do Sullivan's colleagues say about him?"

119

"Well, Chief, the Jacksonville Police Department spoke to all his employees. They all seemed shocked when they learned what happened. Said he was hot-headed and angered easily, but they never saw him drink. Claimed he's a fair boss, pays well, teaches his guys well, and doesn't seem to be afraid of getting his own hands dirty when helping out."

"Sounds like an ideal boss, I have to admit," Tonya said. "Anything else important?"

Sally took a few moments to look through the transcripts again, then looked up. "Yes, this here, I think. Jacksonville spoke to his business's front desk lady, and she mentioned there was a nasty confrontation in the store a couple weeks back. It involved a very handsome young man—a Mr. Aaron, in the Air Force, and his fiancée, who accused Sullivan of having raped her mom, who then apparently got pregnant and had her."

Chief Parlot nodded. "Yeah, Aaron told me about that. He and Maria went to see Mr. Sullivan at his store in Jacksonville. Martina also confirmed it. She was upset Maria had gone to see him. Anything else the plumbing store employee said that stands out?"

"She said Sullivan disappeared from the store last week. Apparently, he got sick with COVID. At least, that's what he told her."

Tonya started pacing and mumbling something. They all watched her but couldn't make out what she was saying. She stopped and said, "We need to talk with Martina about this in more detail. She claimed Sullivan renewed his threats against her and Maria after he came to her store. For the first time in twenty years! Did he believe Maria was digging too deep? When exactly did he go to Miami to threaten her? Last week? How did he even end up here then?"

Tom whistled through his teeth. "Good catch."

"Agreed," Chief Parlot said. "If Mr. Sullivan renewed his threats last week, we might have the makings of a timeline. Come on, Tonya, let's ask Martina about this now." He turned to Tom. "I need you to find out if Sullivan has spent any money on his credit cards lately—when and where. Sally, draft up a search warrant. Let's have the Jacksonville Police Department search Sullivan's store."

"But, Chief, I've never—"

"Time to learn. We'll help you out after we talk to Martina. If you want to wait for us, make yourself useful by going back over the reports on the Compass Rose crime scene. The guy's vehicle was there, a green pickup truck. See what they found. Figure out where that car has been."

"His car. How will I—" Sally started, but Tom interrupted her.

"I'll help you. Easy to trace a car. Just need the license. Let's work on it together."

Sally nodded. "Great, thanks, Tom."

He grinned at her. Sally smiled, her cheeks showing her dimples, her brown eyes sparkling. Her long blonde hair framed her beautiful smile. Her beauty did not go unnoticed by Tom. He blushed.

"Okay, team, let's go," Tonya said. She fist-bumped everyone in turn, then left the room with Chief Parlot.

Tom and Sally were laughing together when the door opened and their bosses returned.

"Hey, youngsters, what's going on? I wanna laugh, too," Tonya Anderson said, and Sally and Tom stopped immediately. "What? You won't let me in on the secret?"

Sally looked up. "Tom just told me a silly joke about a goat."

Tonya raised her eyebrows. "I see. You can take the farm boy out of Kansas, but can't take Kansas out of the farm boy." She winked at Tom. "Keep your goat jokes away from me. I'm a city girl."

They all laughed until Sally asked, "So, what did Martina say?"

"Jonathan came to her store last Thursday," the chief said.

Sally jumped up. "That's when his front desk lady said he called in sick! Oh boy, I think we found something, too, right, Tom?"

121

"Sure did. Jonathan Sullivan's pickup traveled from Jacksonville to Miami really early last Thursday. Surveillance cameras show he was at a bar in Jacksonville the night before, Wednesday night, and that he left at closing time, early Thursday morning. Another camera caught his truck parked in front of Martina's Tailor Shop that same morning around nine a.m."

"Martina said he came in and threatened her right after she opened the store," Tonya said. "I assume that's around nine a.m."

Tom's hands flew across the computer's keyboard. "Yes, indeed. Nine a.m. on the dot."

"Okay, what else?" Chief Parlot wanted to know.

"He stuck around in Miami. That night, his truck was parked at some bars again. Then he's seen traveling north on the highway again, but not back to Jacksonville—he stayed in Daytona Beach until Sunday."

"Daytona Beach?"

"Yeah. Guess where the first camera picked up his truck?"

The chief and Tonya shrugged their shoulders.

"Sally, drumroll please," Tom told her, and she used her fingers to thrum out the sound on the desk. "On campus at Embry-Riddle Aeronautical University!"

"Maria's college," both the chief and Tonya said simultaneously.

"Isaac, didn't Martina say *she* was in Daytona that weekend for her future son-in-law's graduation and commissioning?"

Chief Parlot nodded, his throat dry. "He was stalking Martina all last week?"

Tom imitated the sound of a buzzer going off. "Wrong. He was stalking *Maria*."

"But how would you know—"

"Come on, Isaac my man," Tonya interrupted with a grin. "Told you that young guy over there is a wizard with technology."

Tom nodded proudly, then turned to Sally. "Keep going. Tell them what we discovered."

"We found out his truck was parked across from Aaron Heikinnen's apartment for two straight nights. His credit card statements show that he ate at a bunch of fancy restaurants around town. Including a place called the Sky Rooftop Bar. And guess what? The owner confirmed that a bunch of Embry-Riddle graduates celebrated their graduation at the bar. So, we can safely assume Maria and Aaron visited that bar after his graduation and I bet she might have been at those other places as well."

"And then the pickup drove here, to Niceville, on Sunday night," Tom told them. "We have a gas bill placing it close to the police station on Monday afternoon, then, of course, its final destination at the Compass Rose."

"Everywhere Maria went, he followed," Tonya concluded.

The two young investigators nodded. "Exactly. And guess what? Sally talked to the bartender and a waitress at the restaurant, and they both remembered him. He was out on the balcony that night, sitting right next to the Collinses' table."

"*What?*"

"Oh yes. He paid at the bar, ordered two whiskeys. Really jazzed himself up. They found a napkin he left with the cash that had his handwriting on it."

"Really?"

"Yeah, he scribbled on it that it was payment for the whiskeys and the table. The bartender says he just disappeared after that."

"Hiding in the bushes by the parking lot, I assume. Bastard." Chief Parlot's face was flushed, his forehead wrinkled. He slammed his fist on the table. "I was there! Man, I should've protected her. I should have seen what was going down much earlier, but I didn't. I failed." He stared at the desk, then at the case wall. His shoulders drooped as he covered his face with his hands.

"Come on, Isaac my man, you couldn't have known. No one did. Look at how badly the FBI and police force failed twenty years ago. But not you. You got pushed out. Now you have the chance to pick up the case again and solve it. We'll do it together." Tonya gave him an awkward pat on the back.

"Yes, Chief, we will," Sally said, smiling her big smile. "Remember, a wise person once told me you gotta develop some thick skin to make it in this business."

Chief Parlot couldn't help but smirk. *Clever, using my own words against me.*

He took in a deep breath. "Yeah, you're all right. We'll solve the case together." He sat up straight. "Great work so far, team. Let's confirm with Maria what restaurants and places they visited before driving here. And we desperately need to speak to our main suspect, Jonathan Sullivan. We somehow need to get him to talk to us, tell us everything without pleading the Fifth."

Tonya nodded. "Yes, we sure need Jonathan Sullivan to talk."

CHAPTER 21

"Talk on the street is that Maria Gabriella Sullivan, also known as Moana Marie Collins, has been declared fit for release and should be leaving the hospital at any moment. Right now, we're intently watching the hospital's front entrance, hoping to speak to her. Earlier, Brad and Elisabeth Collins were spotted leaving the hospital with another man. According to our sources, this man was Jack Heikinnen, Maria's future father-in-law. It's safe to say the missing toddler, now a grown adult, has received an outpouring of support from her family, and of course, from you, the audience. In case you missed our coverage from earlier, let me fill you in...."

Cliff turned off the TV. *Sure hope Bill's got everything under control. Man. Shit. I never should've gotten involved in this stupid plan. I'd just managed to build myself a solid reputation after those crazy early years. Was heading toward better things. Then I went and approved this absurd plan of kidnapping a child. Just because I wanted to get back at Collins.*

He shook his head. *Stupid. I've been so fucking stupid.* He started laughing, a loud coarse laugh. *I knew it would be risky, but Bullet made it sound so easy. And damn it, we did pull it off. But then that child somehow managed not to die.*

His laughter faded and he slammed his fist on the big mahogany desk. *And I was fucking stuck. I couldn't tell the others. Couldn't disappoint even more people.* He sighed. *So I came up with a new plan. A really good plan. A perfect plan. It worked out so well. Until now. Until that damn girl somehow managed to find Sullivan and then her real parents. It's crazy! I hate her!*

He grabbed the remote control again and turned the TV back on, just in time to see a mob of reporters all scrambling toward the hospital door.

The news reporter was talking fast. "Breaking news, it looks like Moana Marie Collins is just now leaving the hospital. We're all glad to see she's well enough to leave after last night's attack. Let's see if we can catch her."

Cliff drank in the flashes, the clicking, the clamor of a throng of voices talking over each other.

"There she is!"

"There, the missing girl!"

"That must be her!"

He saw there was a young guy with her, trying to shelter her from the chaos as best he could.

"Welcome home, Moana!"

"Moana, how are you feeling?"

"Are you mad at the woman who raised you under false pretenses?"

"Is she guilty?"

"What happened?"

"Were you hurt?"

Cliff watched the girl's eyes widen. The camera zoomed in on her, and he had to hold onto his big desk. *These unforgettable eyes! Just like Collins. Holy shit.*

He watched as the mob came at her, saw her duck her face under the young guy's arm. The guy tried to lead them through the crowd, his lips pressed together, his intense blue eyes focused on something in the distance.

The reporter's mic picked up the guy's loud, roaring voice. "Goodness, let us through. We need to get to our car." He started jostling reporters out of the way.

"Where are you going?"

"Are you the future husband?"

"What do you think of all this?"

"No comment," the young guy said, and kept pushing forward.

Smart to keep his mouth shut. Who is this guy? Cliff got up and stepped closer to the TV to get a good look at the handsome young man accompanying the now grown-up girl he once knew.

"Moana," he heard the reporter of the news channel cry out. As the girl drew near, the reporter grabbed her by the arm and twisted so that she turned toward the camera. Seizing the opportunity, the reporter asked, "Are you happy the authorities caught your kidnappers, Jonathan and Martina Sullivan?"

The girl stopped, shrugged off both the reporter's and the young man's grasp, and stood tall.

"Listen, lady, Martina Sullivan is a good person," she shouted into the reporter's microphone. "That's all I'll say now. No further comment. By the way, keep your hands to yourself!"

Cliff started laughing. *Sassy!* He grinned. *Yeah, that little toddler sure did grow up to be a beautiful young lady. Would love to meet her.*

He kept watching as the young couple finally made it to their car. The young man got behind the wheel while the pretty girl determinedly pushed more reporters to the side so she could climb into the passenger seat.

"That was our breaking news. Moana Marie Collins has been released and is leaving the hospital as I speak. She's in a blue Oldsmobile, presumably with her fiancé, Aaron Heikinnen. We'll keep you posted on where she's going next along with any future developments to this ongoing saga. Thanks for watching. Back to my colleagues in the studio."

Cliff switched off the TV and grinned. *At least we'll know what she's up to at all times without trying, thanks to the press. Now we just have to keep a close eye on Sully. I'm sure Bill is on it.*

He took out his stress ball and started kneading it.

Just want everything to go back to normal. Need my life to be quiet and calm.

CHAPTER 22

"Calm down? How am I supposed to calm down? That was ridiculous! Those reporters were absolutely crazy," Maria said.

Aaron sighed. "Let's at least try to, Maria. We were warned about them. I'm taking us to Eglin right away. The reporters don't have access there. It should be a safe haven for us the next couple of days." He began driving as fast as he could without risking a speeding ticket.

Maria was still staring at him, her face bright red. "A couple of days?"

"Yeah, at least. I'm afraid you've become a celebrity practically overnight," he said, then glanced at her in concern.

"But… but… it's my life! Not a soap opera or a film. I'm not playing a part. It's me. Just me. This isn't fair."

"I know it's not. I know. And I'm sorry. You certainly have enough to deal with as it is and don't need more on your plate, but it is what it is. We'll have to make the best of it."

"I don't know, Aaron…."

"Trust me, Maria. Let's make the best of it. That starts with getting a late lunch with the Collinses and my dad at the Officers' Club. It'll be okay. Might even be fun. Either way, you'll be safe on base."

Safe on base? She shuddered. "Sure," she said, but she had a feeling that wasn't true. Could never be true. She tried to ignore the uneasy feeling in her stomach and instead looked out the window. There were cameras and reporters lining the street leading into Eglin AFB.

Gosh, I hate them. Those reporters. Making news out of my life.

Her phone rang loudly, ripping her from her thoughts. She looked at the screen. "Oh, it's Keisha!"

"Good, I think you should pick up," Aaron said without taking his eyes off the road. "She's been worried about you. All our friends are. They've been texting me."

"Really?"

"Yeah, of course. Come on, pick up!"

Maria did as she was told. "Hi, Keisha."

"Hey, girl! I'm so glad to hear your voice. Oh my gosh, what the heck's been going on with you? Wait, hold up... No way! I just saw you pick up your phone. I can see you. You're on TV! Live TV. You're sitting on the passenger seat of your car, holding the phone to your ear!"

"Um, yeah... because you called?"

"Holy moly, girl!"

"Hold on, Keisha," Maria said, "we're about to go through the gate to Eglin AFB. Don't hang up."

She put down her phone and gave the guard her ID and visitor's pass. He studied it, saluted Aaron, then waved them through. Maria got back on the phone with Keisha.

"Girl, what's going on? You were attacked? By Jonathan Sullivan? Your own dad who's also *not* your dad? And now you have new parents? And you—"

Maria had to chuckle. "Come on, Keisha, you're all over the place. I can't follow a thing you're saying."

"—and you're all over TV! This is crazy!"

Maria sighed. "Yeah, it is. I guess I'm a celebrity now."

"Girl, please. What in the world's going on?"

"You seem to know more than I do. Thought you saw it all on the news?"

129

"Yeah, but I hardly understood a lick of it. What happened to you when you were little? What about your mamá? And these other people claiming to be your parents?"

"It's a long story." Maria sighed. "Honestly, I don't really understand much myself. The whole thing is like a crazy jigsaw puzzle with tons of missing pieces...."

For the first time since she got on, Keisha fell silent. Maria could almost hear her shaking her head.

"I'm sorry. This is crazy stuff you're dealing with. Unbelievable."

"Yeah," Maria said, and looked out of the window. She saw a mix of dark pine trees and tall palm trees lining the street, the sun up high in the perfectly blue sky, a bright ball blinding her. She closed her eyes and sighed.

"So, you were kidnapped?" she heard Keisha say.

"Guess so."

"I don't think your mamá did it," Keisha said, her voice strong and determined. "Do you?"

"No," Maria whispered, "I don't think so. But it's all so unclear. Well, she's with her lawyer now. Apparently being interrogated or something. I don't know."

"You haven't talked to her yet?"

"No. I wasn't allowed to."

Aaron turned around a curve, and there it was: Eglin's Officers' Club. It was a fancy place, close to the sparkling, emerald-green water, but Maria shuddered at the sight of it. She almost jumped out of her seat when she heard Keisha's voice over the phone again.

"Maria, still there?"

Aaron turned into a parking space.

"Yeah, still here. Sorry."

"It's okay. I bet you have a lot on your mind. Just wanted to check in."

"Yeah," Maria said as Aaron put the car into park and turned off the engine. "Hey, I gotta go."

"Okay, girl, sure. Good to hear from you. Know that I'm always here for you."

"Thanks."

Maria hung up and unbuckled herself.

Guess I'm ready to hang with my real parents on my birthday. Today. My new birthday. Gosh, this is so complicated. Maria sighed.

Elisabeth sighed as Jack parked the car in front of Eglin's Officers' Club. They all got out.

"Here we are," Brad said. "Thanks for driving us all over the place this afternoon, Jack."

"Sure, no problem," Jack said. "I have Aaron's car for the whole day."

They all looked at the fancy building in front of them.

"We came here, long ago," Elisabeth whispered, sadness in her face.

"Yeah, we did. Right after we moved to Eglin." Brad took her hand. "Remember that awesome Sunday morning brunch?"

"Yeah, I do. Of course I do." Elisabeth's voice broke. "It was the last brunch we had together before she disappeared."

"Yeah, I know. Remember how she was jumping around in there? Hard to keep her still."

Elisabeth nodded, tears forming in her eyes. "Yeah, she was full of energy."

Brad squeezed her hand. "And still is. Just look at her."

Brad pointed to the blue Oldsmobile that had just arrived. Maria got out. She looked beautiful in her flowery shirt and three-quarter jeggings; her long, wavy hair flowed around her, framing her elegant face. She walked determinedly in their direction.

"Hi Maria and Aaron," Jack yelled, and went to meet them.

"There's our baby girl," Elisabeth whispered. "All grown-up." She held back tears.

"I know it's hard, Elisabeth. Her presence is a reminder of lost time, isn't it?"

She nodded. "We've been robbed of her whole childhood." A tear escaped her eye and ran down her nose, right over her freckles.

"I know, hun, I know. But she's alive. Full of life. Here with us. So, let's go and celebrate her twenty-second birthday. Nobody can take another minute with her away from us."

Elisabeth looked at Brad, the handsome middle-aged man who was standing close to her, by her side again.

He's right. So much time has passed yet it feels like our connection never disappeared. Now we're picking up right where we left off. Our love is still there, still strong, mature, pure. For the first time in twenty years, we're whole again.

A family again, two parents with our grown-up daughter. She's here, and nobody will ever take her away from us again.

Little did they know that a group of bad men had other plans.

CHAPTER 23

"**P**lans?" Chief Parlot looked from Nurse Karen to the doctor.

"Yes, what are you planning, Chief? How do you plan on interrogating Mr. Sullivan without compromising his well-being?" the doctor asked. He gave the chief a wary look, then directed his attention to Agent Anderson.

She took the cue. "We assure you we'll be careful, doc. If he gets too tired, we'll stop. Everything that's said will go into the record, and you can even have Nurse Karen wait outside his door. If he calls for help, she'll hear him."

The doctor nodded, but the nurse's eyes narrowed. She was suspicious, didn't trust the chief or Agent Anderson and also threw a stern look at the young police officer and agent.

Officer Sally Johnson saw it and smiled her big smile at the nurse and the doctor. "Yes, we'll be careful," she said.

"I can only allow two of you in the room at a time," the doctor said. The nurse nodded.

"But doctor, please," the chief said, "I would like to have Officer Johnson and Agent Cooper in there with us. When we're at the station, they can watch and follow along from outside our interrogation room, but here—"

"This is a hospital, not a police station," the doctor interrupted. "Consider yourself lucky I'm even allowing you to interrogate Jonathan Sullivan at this stage. He's still very weak and really shouldn't be going through this… but we recognize the importance of your investigation."

Chief Parlot didn't know what to say.

"Thank you, doc, thank you. We appreciate your cooperation." Agent Anderson smiled and shook his hand, then turned to the chief. "Come on, Isaac my man, just the two of us then, I suppose."

Chief Parlot sighed, then nodded.

"I'll be right here, Chief, listening and making sure everything's okay," Nurse Karen said, and eyed him. He looked at her, but before he could say anything, Agent Anderson pulled him into the room with her and closed the door.

"She sure dislikes you, Isaac," the agent whispered to him. "Guess the whole hospital knows you put Maria in a state of shock."

"No kidding. Seems like Nurse Hannah talked to Nurse Karen. Can't believe it. I didn't even do anything terrible, but they seem to hate me more than our suspect here."

"Well, let's not focus on that now. Let's focus on this guy," Agent Anderson said, and walked closer to Jonathan Sullivan's bed.

The man's eyes were closed, the monitor hooked up to him beeping. The chief drew near, took out the recording device, and gave Agent Anderson the sign to proceed.

"Mr. Sullivan, the police and FBI are here to see you," a woman's voice said loudly. Jonathan slowly opened his eyes.

His eyes widened as he took in the scene. He swallowed hard. *The police again?* He looked at the police chief, then at the lady in uniform. *FBI too? Holy shit!* He closed his eyes again, hoping they would disappear.

"Mr. Sullivan, my name is Chief Parlot, and this is my colleague, Agent Anderson."

"Hi, Mr. Sullivan, I'm Agent Tonya Anderson, FBI. It's a real pleasure to meet you."

Bullshit. The only thing they love is seeing me hospitalized. Shit, what have I done? I never should've attacked her. I was so stupid, so fucking stupid.

He kept his eyes closed as his thoughts raced. *Wish I had said no. Wish I'd had the will to say no.*

But I didn't. I was tempted, just couldn't resist the temptation, then fell deep into their debt. So fucking deep that I agreed to that idiotic plan. I could have easily gone to prison back then—but this is worse, much, much worse.

I don't want to talk to them. To the FBI? Holy shit! Nope, I'll just pretend to be too weak. After all, I do feel like shit.

"Mr. Sullivan?"

"Jonathan Sullivan? Can you hear us? The doc told us you're awake."

I can do this. Just pretend. Just act. I used to be good at it. Still am. He had to hold back his smile.

"Mr. Sullivan, we need to talk to you."

Sure you do. But I won't. I'm saying "no" today. I will not *take the fall for them. I won't. Didn't even kidnap her back then. I was just the middleman, the one who was supposed to get rid of her.*

Couldn't do it. Not that I was supposed to. She was supposed to already be dead, drowned, but somehow, that little thing fought for life. I had to watch her open her eyes, those freaky, unique eyes, and have them look straight at me. He shuddered at the memory of it.

"Mr. Sullivan, come on. We know you're messing with us," he heard the FBI agent say. "We know you're a good actor. You were Juilliard-bound. Impressive stuff."

What? How do they know about that? What the fuck? So, I am going down for what happened? I'm the fall guy? But they'll need me to get to them. The smart people who used me. The rich and powerful.

135

He felt hot flashes pass through his body. He was sweating now. *I don't even have enough proof to pin on the other guys involved. Would the police even believe me if I ratted them out? Me, a plumber, a nobody? Probably not.... Fuck! What do I do?*

Sweat dripped down his forehead, but he couldn't wipe it away. Not because he was playing possum—he really was too weak to move his hand. *Fuck, I'm doomed.*

"Mr. Sullivan, we really need to talk to you. We know you attacked that young lady last night. Although we have to advise you that you have the right to remain silent..."

They're reading me my rights? I'm done, I'm so done. He stopped listening and kept his eyes shut. He doubted he could open them now, even if he tried. He felt dizzy, paralyzed, not sure what to do. He had lost his cool. All the acting he had done so well the past twenty years, gone up in smoke.

"Still don't want to talk? Well, how about we make a deal?"

A deal? He perked up.

"We know what happened last night. We know why you attacked that young lady—to finish what you couldn't back then, correct?" he heard the chief say.

"We also know you were the one who dropped off the little toddler at your ex's house, at Martina Sullivan's. That was you, wasn't it?" the female FBI agent said.

They know about that? The sweat running down his forehead seeped into his eyelids, stung his eyes, made him want to cry.

"So, Mr. Sullivan, let's talk. We know that deep down inside, you're a nice guy, aren't you?"

I am a nice guy! When I'm sober. I was a nice guy when I met Martina. I helped her fix up her store for free. But I was tempted. Tempted by the evils of the world: alcohol and girls. Not a good combination, at least not for me.

But little kids, tiny toddlers? I wouldn't hurt them, never. Sure, maybe neglect 'em... but I couldn't kill her. I tried, really tried to fulfill my debt by doing as they said, but I just couldn't do it.

Instead, I figured out where to hide that little thing. It was a great plan, leaving her with Martina. It all worked out thanks to Cliff, since he knew someone inside Vital Records.

That was the last solid Cliff ever did for me. Never saw him again after that. Never saw any of them. Do I even remember their names? Oh, fuck.

"Mr. Sullivan, open your eyes so we can make a deal with you," he heard the chief say.

"Yeah, open your eyes. Then we can talk things over. I think you'll like what we have to say," the lady agent told him. He heard her footfalls as she paced back and forth by the side of his bed. He refused to comply.

"Or, Mr. Sullivan," she said, "we can just charge you with attempted murder, kidnapping of an adult, kidnapping of a toddler—"

"—child neglect," the chief continued, "as well as sexual abuse of a child over the span of two months."

What? His mind was racing. *Sexual abuse of a child? For two months?*

"That's not true! So not true," he yelled, and opened his eyes to look at them.

"What's not true, Mr. Sullivan?" both agent and police chief asked him in unison.

"I didn't *sexually abuse* her. Are you fucking kidding me? A toddler? I like women. But a child? That's absolutely disgusting!"

The FBI agent and police chief grinned at each other.

"I see, Mr. Sullivan. So, before we charge you, you're telling me you'd rather talk with us?" The agent looked at him, a smile on her face.

"Yes, I'll talk to you. But only if we make that deal!"

"I see. Well, what sort of deal do you have in mind?"

"The one you were talking about. Whatcha got?"

"What have *we* got? I think what's more important is, what can *you* give *us*?" The lady stared at him, her smile freezing over.

"The whole story."

"The whole story…. What story? We're not playing story time here, Mr. Sullivan," the police chief said.

Seriously? How dumb is he?

"The story behind the kidnapping twenty years ago. Don't tell me you've got it figured out already." He looked back and forth between the chief and the agent.

The lady laughed. "But we do have it figured out. You kidnapped her off Eglin AFB then dropped her off at Martina's."

"That's not true."

"It's not?" She looked at him, her eyebrows raised.

"No, it's not."

"So, it's not true that you attacked the same person, now one Maria Gabriella Sullivan—who, by the way, is apparently your legal daughter—last night?"

"Well, that's true… but I only did it to protect the secret from back then."

"The secret?"

"Yes, the big coup. By the Fearless Four."

"You worked with three other people?"

"No, I didn't. I worked *for* four other people. Powerful people. Rich, powerful guys."

"Rich, powerful guys?" He saw immense interest spark on both the FBI agent's and the police chief's faces.

He grinned. *Bingo.* "Yeah, so, if you promise not to lock me up, I'll help you bring them down. How's that for a deal?"

The police chief looked at him. "You don't want to be locked up? You want to avoid jail time?"

"Correct, sir."

They both laughed now.

Irritated, he asked, "What's so funny?"

"Mr. Sullivan, you attacked a girl last night. Tried to *kill* her. We cannot let that go."

He stared at them both.

"But we can strike other charges off your list," the FBI agent said.

"Like what? How?"

"Well, we could render your sentences lighter. Less years, for example, if, say, you were *made* to act this way because someone pressured you to do so? And maybe you were *made* to help with the kidnapping back then?"

"I don't deserve to go to jail at all! She's alive because of me!"

"Is she?"

He nodded.

"Well, well. We might work out a deal after all."

He smiled. *Finally. Someone who's not playing me. Yes, I'll tell them everything.*

"So, Mr. Sullivan, you're ready to talk to us, then?"

"Yes," he said. Despite himself, he grinned. "I'll talk."

CHAPTER 24

Talk? Will he talk? Tell them everything? I hope not. That could bring us all down! Cliff is right. Sullivan needs to shut the fuck up!

Nervously, he crouched behind a spare hospital bed that had been left in the hallway. *Fuck, they're in there already. Have been for a few minutes. Did he squeal already? Does he even know enough to squeal?*

He peeked over the bed at the nurse, then also saw the young agent as well as the police officer standing outside the hospital room door. He chuckled. *How dumb to assign such inexperienced people to such a big case. Oh, Isaac, you're so dumb.*

He frowned. *Too bad I can't hear what they're saying. Maybe there's a way to find out how much they already know?*

He watched the young male agent smile at the blonde police officer. She blushed.

Oh dear. He likes her. He grinned a wide grin. *Perfect. A very welcome distraction. I'll find a way to use it to my advantage.*

As awkward as it was, he decided to keep watching them from his hiding spot behind the large, empty hospital bed standing in the corner of the hallway, right across from the men's room.

If anyone should come down this hallway, I'll slip into the men's bathroom to hide. But so far, nobody has even walked this direction.

He kept watching the door to Sullivan's room closely, trying to overhear the young police officer and agent standing in front of Sullivan's door. He clutched his hands nervously.

Better not say too much there, Sullivan.

CHAPTER 25

Sullivan was propped up in his hospital bed and looked at the police chief and FBI agent standing next to his bed. "I'm innocent. She lived a happy life up until now because of me. Because of me!"

"We hear you, Mr. Sullivan," the FBI agent said. "So, tell us about this Fearless Four group you mentioned earlier."

"I worked for them. They came up with a well-thought-through plot, and I was their middleman. Had to be their middleman. Was *forced* to be their middleman."

"Alright, thank you for that, Mr. Sullivan," the chief said. "We understand you were forced to be a part of the scheme. But how? And why?"

"Yeah, why'd you do it?" the agent lady asked. She was back to pacing around the room as she spoke. "When and where did you meet the Fearless Four?"

"In Vegas. I've always been a gambler. Just can't help it. Especially back then, after the divorce. It was hard, and gambling made me feel happy again, you know? Also gave me plenty opportunity to meet girls."

"Girls? Young girls?"

"No, no, no! Not young girls. *Women.* Though they were sometimes quite young."

"How young?"

"Fuck, I don't know. Didn't ask. But they were all definitely legal."

"You sure?"

"Yes, I'm sure!"

"Okay, back to the Fearless Four. You met them in Las Vegas… when?"

"Spring of 2003. I was there on a trip, same as them."

"A work trip?"

He laughed. "What? No. A work trip to Vegas? Hell, no, who does that? I was an employee at a plumbing store at that time. Plumbers don't go on work trips to Vegas."

"What about them? Were they on a work trip?"

"Doubt it. They were rich guys, and I doubt they were there for work. Looked like they were having a whole lot of fun."

"Did you know them before?"

"Nope. I literally stumbled into the group at a blackjack table in the MGM."

"The MGM?"

"It's a big casino in Las Vegas. Surprised you've never heard of it. We all got to playing together, had a couple of drinks, became friendly. They invited me to play poker with them."

"Invited you? To their table?"

"Nope, upstairs, to their suite."

"Just them?"

"Yeah, just that group. The guys. Wanted to play for money… *lots* of money."

"You got names for us?"

"Yeah. Cliff, Bill, and JB."

The agent and police chief looked at him. "I count three guys. What about the fourth? You're not holding out on us, are you? Are you the fourth member of the Fearless Four?" the chief said.

Sullivan laughed. "Nope, don't think so. But, you know, I was pretty wasted, and I sure became part of their group that night. So maybe they ended up including me, temporarily? But I didn't belong to their world. I was an outsider. Now that I think back, I never met the fourth guy. He was around. At one point, they called over to him, I think. Called him Bullet. He was in the back of the suite that night we played poker. At least I think there was someone. Not one hundred percent sure. Could barely see him—he was in a cloud of smoke, you know? Enjoying himself. And I was super drunk."

Chief Parlot counted on his fingers. "So we've got ourselves a Bullet, a Cliff, a Bill, and a JB."

Sullivan nodded. "I think so."

Tonya stared at him. "You think so, or you know so?"

Sullivan eyed her. "What do you mean?"

"Your story is shaky. Were there three or four guys? We gotta know," she said.

"Listen, lady, I *can't* know for sure. I was fucking wasted. I thought there was a Bullet, but I'm not sure. Never met him. I only met Cliff, Bill, and JB."

"So, you are the fourth member of the Fearless Four after all," the chief said.

"Well, maybe. Maybe they adopted me as the fourth one. Who knows? Anyway, Cliff was the leader."

"I see. You got any other names for them? Last names?" Tonya asked him.

He laughed. "What the hell? I don't got any other names for them. Those were their names! The names they gave me. Like, what the fuck? That's all I know."

"Okay, okay then," the chief said. "What happened at poker that night? Was it a lucky night for you?"

"Hell no. I lost. Lost lots of money."

"Did you have that sort of money to begin with?"

He had to laugh. "Well, see, that was the issue. I lost and couldn't pay them."

"Did they know you didn't have the money?"

"Nope, don't think they knew. Didn't stick around to find out. I left the next morning and went back to Florida."

"You left for Florida owing them money?"

"Yeah, I snuck out after they all passed out. Sure, I owed them money—that's why I drove home so quickly."

"You *drove*? In your car?"

"Yes, drove the entire way back home. Well, almost. Stopped in Shreveport."

"Shreveport, Louisiana?"

"Yes."

"Why? More gambling?"

"Yes, more gambling."

"Why?"

He laughed. "All these whys. Seriously? You stupid or what? I gambled more *because I needed the money*, of course!"

"How'd that turn out?"

He sighed. "I didn't have much luck there either."

"What then? Did you keep at it?"

"Yeah, I tried again. In New Orleans. Still on the way home from the Vegas trip."

"How did you keep coming up with the money to gamble? Weren't you in big debt by now?"

"Hell yeah, I was. How many times do I have to tell you? That's why I had to keep playing, to win money to pay my debts off."

"Pay off your debt with the Fearless Four?"

"Yeah, them, but I had other issues before that." He sighed again.

"Other issues? Like what?"

"My job. The IRS."

"How come?"

"How come? Shit, just told you. Because of money! I had no money back then, nothing. Not a dime to my name. Don't you get it?"

"Okay, Mr. Sullivan. What about your business? It seems like that's gone well for you."

"Yeah, it has. But I didn't own my plumbing business back then. I was young and stupid, just working for one. Had a stupid boss. Didn't like him. Always wanted my own business."

The agent and police chief nodded.

"You know, they actually promised me I could have my own business—could afford to open one—if I just did something for them."

"Did something? Who promised you this?"

"The Fearless Four, of course."

"I see. What did they want you to do?"

"A little favor."

"And they asked this of you in Vegas, right after you met?"

"Nope. I left, quickly, remember?"

"Help us make sense of what you're saying. When and where did they ask you for this favor?"

"They came to me."

"You mean, to your house?"

"Yes, to my house."

"How did they find you?"

He laughed. "I have no fucking idea! Cliff just showed up on my doorstep one day."

"When, exactly?"

"Not sure. Don't really remember. Sometime around May 2003."

"And Cliff showed up alone?"

Sullivan nodded.

"Is Cliff nice or scary?"

"Cliff? Oh, he's one scary dude."

"A gangster?"

Sullivan laughed out loud. "No, he's definitely no gangster. But scary. Scary mean. A real mean guy. But filthy rich."

"Rich?"

"You heard me. *Filthy* rich."

"So, what did he do then? What did Cliff want?"

"That fucking bastard bribed me! He said I owed him and his friends so much fucking money that he'd put me six feet under. Or in jail. Forever. All because I was in so much debt with him and his friends from the Vegas trip. But he told me that if I was willing to do just one little favor for them, they'd forgive me of my debt wholesale— even help me start up my own store."

"Your own store?"

"That's right. He told me he'd fund my own plumbing business."

"How did they plan to give you that money?"

"How? In cash, of course!"

"In cash?"

"Yes, cash. A shitload of cash."

"Interesting. So, what was this one little favor you had to do for them?"

"Honestly, it sounded pretty cool at first. He told me I'd have to hang out on his yacht over the summer and couldn't tell anyone. I had to hang out there until it was time for my little job. The favor that would forgive me my debt and earn me enough money to start a new life."

"Sure sounds nice. Did you find his offer attractive?"

"Yes, of course. Who wouldn't have?"

"But you didn't know what the favor was he'd ask of you, right? Why, then, did you agree?"

Jonathan laughed again. "Come on, don't be stupid. I just told you: it was an attractive offer, gave me enough money to start over. A new life. A new chance. Anyone in my situation would take it."

"Because your situation was so miserable?"

"Yeah. My life was fucking miserable at the time."

"So you wanted to start over?"

"Yes, I wanted to start over."

"Why didn't you just... do it by yourself?"

"Why? Because I *couldn't* just do it by myself. You get me? Besides, I was balls-deep in debt."

"Why'd you believe these guys would keep their word?"

"Why believe the filthy rich guys?" He laughed again. "Oh man, because they *had* the money. I knew that. He sweetened the pot by telling me I could get sober while living on his yacht. They'd even help me slowly wean off the alcohol. Thought that was good—can't start a business if you're wasted all the time, you know? Anyway, all I had to do was one thing. One little thing. One small favor. They would take care of everything else."

"Didn't that sound a bit fishy to you?"

"Did it sound fishy? Ha, of course. But not fishy enough. I signed the contract."

"A contract?"

"Yes, a very official-looking contract. Said the arrangement would remain a secret between us, and that I didn't owe them anymore, and that they'd give me money for my services, then leave me alone forever."

"I see. It was a good contract, wouldn't you say?"

"Oh yeah, a very good contract."

"Okay. Who all signed the contract? Just you?"

"Nope. Both Cliff and I signed it."

"Not the others?"

"Nope, just us. Remember, he was the leader—the only one who dealt directly with me."

"I see. You mean to say that after you signed that contract, you never saw any of the others again?"

"Nope. Well, I take that back. I saw JB once, just briefly. Otherwise, everything I did involved Cliff only."

"You're sure Cliff was the main guy."

"Yeah, I think so. He was the guy that delivered my money. Only him."

"Only him?"

"Yeah, correct. Only him."

"And he organized this *one little thing* you had to do for them?"

Jonathan shrugged his shoulders as best he could given his condition. "Don't know. He was the one in charge of me, that's for sure."

"So, that one thing you had to do for them… was that described in the contract?"

"Nope. It just said I would do this one favor for them. At one point, Cliff told me I'd have to dispose of something."

"Dispose of something?"

"Yes. Something. That's all he said."

"Didn't that sound strange to you?"

He shrugged his shoulders again. "Nope, not really. I didn't want to ask too many questions. That contract was worth a lot to me."

"I see. So, I assume you stopped going to work?"

"That's right."

"You stopped working and went to live on the yacht?"

"Yeah, I got on Cliff's yacht in Pensacola. Left my car and belongings at his private parking spot and storage area in the marina there. Boy, let me tell you, his yacht was amazing."

"Was it everything you'd hoped for?"

"Well, not everything, but it was a great life. Thought I would be in Pensacola a little longer, but it was still May when we set sail. Only a few days after Cliff had found me. We departed at night and stayed at the Destin Harbor's marina."

"Destin? As in Destin, Florida?"

"Yes, here in Florida."

"Interesting. Did you have a good time in Destin?"

He laughed. "Nope. I didn't even get to see it. Not at all. I wasn't allowed to leave the yacht."

"Why not?"

"It was in the contract. I wasn't allowed to leave until I'd done my job."

"Did you know by then what kind of job he had in store for you?"

"Nope, still didn't know, but Cliff had the money on him. I saw it. Big bag of cash."

"Cash for you and only you?"

"Yes, all for me!"

"Why didn't you just take it and run?"

"Well, shit.... You're funny. Because it was locked in a safe on the yacht. And, as I've now told you a million fucking times: I wasn't allowed to leave!"

"And you're telling us you simply obeyed his orders?"

He nodded. "Yes, I obeyed."

"Why?"

"Because they'd bribed me. More importantly, Cliff said they'd get rid of me if I didn't obey."

"Did he? And you believed him?"

"Holy shit, of course I did. Who wouldn't? They had all kinds of connections. It'd be easy for them to hunt me down and do whatever they pleased. Probably still the case."

"Stick to the narrative, please. What happened then?"

"Okay, right. Back to the story. What happened then? Well, I was told to take the yacht out to this area in the middle of the Choctawhatchee Bay at night."

"One specific night?"

"No, every night. All by myself."

"You knew how to pilot a yacht?"

"Not at first, but Cliff taught me. It's pretty easy."

"I see. So, you did that for how long?"

"Don't know. A few nights."

"That's all? Your task was to take the yacht out on a nighttime stroll in the middle of Choctawhatchee Bay a few times?"

"There's more to it. Once I got to the designated spot, I was supposed to leave the yacht behind and take a little rowboat in the direction of the shore on the other side of the bay. But not too close.

I was supposed to stay away from the little marina there, stick around just close enough. Right by this little inlet or island or whatever."

"Interesting. Did you know what was on the other side?"

"Nope, I didn't. Looked like houses. Big houses. Some town houses, maybe. A small community."

"Mmm. So, what were you supposed to do there in that rowboat after you arrived?"

"Wait. I was supposed to wait for Cliff's friend, JB, to show up."

"Like you mentioned earlier. Did you meet with JB more than once?"

"Nope. Just the once."

"And you first met him in Vegas."

"Yep, that one night in Vegas. Correct."

"Tell us more. Why were you waiting for JB?"

"Well, I was supposed to chill in the rowboat and wait for that JB guy to bring me something. What it was, I had to bring it back to the yacht and get rid of it."

"And you *still* didn't know what you were getting yourself into?"

"Nope. I wasn't sure. I didn't know what he would bring me. He'd given me a crate to put it in."

"A crate?" Tonya raised her eyebrows for the first time that interrogation.

"Yes, a crate. A wooden box with metal poles. Wood on the bottom, wood up top, metal poles all around. Looked a lot like a cage for an animal. I started to imagine I'd be handling some rare, exotic bird or animal."

"A rare... bird."

"Yes, something like that. Thought they wanted to smuggle it somewhere. 'Cuz I also had a blanket to throw over the crate. Or maybe they wanted to kill it for its meat? Who knew what they were up to. Rich people are crazy."

"Did you ever stop to think about how illegal this sounded?"

He grinned. "Illegal? Hahaha... of course."

"Why didn't you call the police?"

He laughed again. "Hahaha, very funny. Why you think? You're not very bright, are you? Of course I couldn't call the police. I had too much debt. I'd evaded taxes. I'd stolen some money."

"What?"

"You heard me."

"Who'd you steal money from?"

"My former boss. For my debts. I needed the money. So, I took it. And of course, don't forget about those death threats."

"So, you just obeyed?"

"Yes, I obeyed. I was in so deep I couldn't tell anyone at that point. Thought it for the best to just shut up."

"So, you just waited night after night for JB to come to your boat?"

"Waited there on that tiny rowboat. Took a few nights."

"Regardless of the weather?"

"Yes, in any kind of weather."

"Must've been dark. Scary, maybe?"

"Yeah, it was pretty fucking dark. And scary. Windy and wavy, sometimes. I'd be frozen by morning when I returned to the yacht."

"Did you ever see anyone else out there?"

"Nope. Not a soul either boating or on the shore. Until one rainy night, I spotted something. Cliff never mentioned how JB would get to me—that fucking bastard swam out to me!"

"He swam?"

"He swam right up to the boat. Scared the living hell out of me."

"Was it just him?"

"Not exactly. He had a toddler on him."

The chief and the agent fell silent at this revelation.

"Wasn't that shocking to you?"

"Yes, very much so. Fucking shocking."

"Keep talking."

"He told me to open the crate in the rowboat and put the child in there. Holy shit, a child! I had no idea."

"You really had no idea?"

"Nope, no fucking clue. Like I said, I thought the crate was for a bird or something. Not a child! A dead child at that."

"Dead?"

"Yes, dead. At least I *thought* so."

"Why?"

"Because she wasn't breathing. She was ice-cold."

"I see. What did you do next?"

"Man, this isn't gonna sound good.... I obeyed. I took the dead kid. JB told me to get rid of it. Row away. As fast as I could."

"Did he jump in the boat with you?"

"Nope, he swam away."

"Swam away? How did he manage to swim that far?"

"How the fuck would I know? He must've been a good swimmer."

"Was he a fit guy? Who was he, exactly?"

"Yes, very fit, very strong. I don't know who he was."

"What was he wearing?"

Sullivan thought for a while. "I don't know. Don't remember."

"A swimsuit?"

"Nope, definitely not a swimsuit. But it was dark. Couldn't really see."

"A wet suit?"

Jonathan thought about it. "Maybe so. Don't know. He was well camouflaged. As soon as I had the kid, he quickly swam away."

"Where to?"

Sullivan shrugged his shoulders. "Don't know. Not toward the marina. Different direction. Couldn't see because of that island or whatever it was."

"So, he just disappears, and you have a dead child on your hands. What did you do then?"

He closed his eyes for a bit, then took a deep breath. "I did what I'd been told. I put it in the crate, knew I needed to get rid of it. I rowed as fast as I could out to deeper water. Figured I'd dump the crate with the kid in it. It was heavy, so I figured it'd sink to the bottom of the bay."

"You think so?"

"Well, I don't fucking know, they didn't tell me anything. No fucking clue if that would've worked. How would I know? Maybe the water wasn't that deep and the crate would've been seen in the light of day. How should I know? They didn't instruct me. They didn't tell me *how* to get rid of the thing they brought me. Fuck! Those bastards didn't even hint at what they'd be roping me into."

"It was all a bit crazy, huh."

"A bit crazy? Hell yeah, more like a lot crazy! So crazy! And then the fucking rain. I was wet, so wet and cold, and I panicked. I rowed as fast as I could just trying to find a good spot to dump the crate."

"The crate with the child in it."

"Yes."

"That's very sad, Mr. Sullivan. How did you feel at the time?"

"Panicked, just panicked. So, I rowed and rowed. It was rainy and dark. Couldn't see shit. Then I heard a noise."

"What noise?"

"I thought it was a bird at first. Don't know what was up with my obsession with birds that night. There was nobody out there other than me. But it was dark, and I heard a noise. Fuck! It was terrifying."

"What kind of noise was it?"

"A... choke. I guess I heard a choking sound. Coming from my boat. Holy shit, the noise was coming from the crate! I lifted the blanket covering it, then used my flashlight to shine a light into it, and found that thing looking at me."

"That... thing?"

"Well, the child. It was looking at me. I could see it in the dark. It just opened her eyes and looked at me. Those big, exotic eyes. Like she was looking through me, into my soul. Begging. Oh my God. Fuck! I didn't know what to do. I turned off the flashlight, covered the crate with the blanket again, and rowed as fast as I could back to the yacht. Anchored the rowboat and hoisted the crate, child and all, onto the deck."

"Of the yacht?"

"Yes, the yacht."

"Where did you keep her?"

"Inside, of course. Deep inside the hull, in a room with no windows. Couldn't let anyone see her."

Agent Anderson stared at him. "Did she cry?"

"Nope, no crying. Lots of choking, whimpering, whining. It was horrible. I got a phone call from Cliff."

"There was a phone on the yacht? Cell phones weren't common two decades ago."

"Yes, there was a phone on the yacht. But he gave me a cell phone to take with me. A BlackBerry."

"Ah, a BlackBerry. I remember those."

"Yes, it was considered nice at the time."

"Where was Cliff calling from? And why?"

"Don't know where he was that night. He just called me to know what was happening. Wanted to know if I'd gotten rid of the thing. He always called the child 'thing.' Always. Told him I couldn't do that anymore, 'cuz it was still alive. He got mad. Told me to take the yacht back to the marina at Destin Harbor and wait there. But not to come out. And if I did, if I told anyone, he'd send JB to… to… kill me."

"To kill you?"

"Yes, along with 'that thing.' That's what he said."

"And you believed him?"

"Yes."

"Were you afraid?"

"Yes. Terrified. I was afraid for my fucking life. That JB guy scared me. So fit, so young. So well-trained and strong. He could've gotten rid of me easily."

"I see. So, what happened next?"

"Well, I got the yacht back to the marina at Destin Harbor and stayed below deck, just waiting for Cliff. I paced and paced until Cliff showed up wearing an expensive suit."

"Did he always wear suits?"

"No, don't think so. He was extravagant but didn't wear a suit every day when he taught me how to drive the yacht. He was usually in shorts and a polo shirt then. But that night, he wore a suit, nice blue suit, white shirt, and a fancy yellow tie. I don't know where he came from. A party or something, I think. Not sure. Anyway, he jumped when he saw the toddler was alive. Don't think he believed me when I told him over the phone."

"So, is it safe to say things didn't go according to plan?"

"They most definitely did not. Cliff took her out of the crate and put her on the floor to monitor her breathing. But she sure was alive. So he just stared at her. He seemed shocked. He mumbled something about how it wasn't supposed to be this way. How she was supposed to be dead already. And then, he told me to kill her. Kill her, then throw the body overboard. Get rid of her."

"Did you have a gun?"

"No gun. I was supposed to use my own fucking hands. But"— his voice broke—"I... I... I couldn't do it. She was whimpering."

"A lot?"

"Yes, the whole time."

"Did that annoy you?"

"Of course. It was fucking annoying. Nerve-racking. Annoyed Cliff even more. He seemed afraid someone might hear her if she got any louder."

"There were other people around?"

"Yeah, I'd docked the yacht at the marina at Destin Harbor. There were people around, especially in the bars and restaurants there. Crowds eating in nearby restaurants or having drinks at the bars. Not many walking around. I suppose the rain made them all find shelter in the buildings there that night."

"I see. Did anyone see Cliff board the yacht?"

Jonathan shrugged his shoulders. "I guess. How should I know? I was inside the ship."

"Was anyone else there other than Cliff?"

"Nope, it was just him. Always just him. Anyway, he told me to shush her. Shut her up. We found some duct tape."

"Did you... Did you really...?"

"Yeah, taped her mouth shut. But she started fighting. That little thing somehow put up a fight. We were afraid she'd run. Couldn't be sure if she could walk already, so we taped her to the crate. Taped her arms."

"So, you taped her mouth shut, then her arms?"

"Yeah. But she didn't like it. She kicked. So, we taped her legs as well."

"You taped a child to the crate."

"Yeah, I did. But I was told to. Wasn't my idea. Cliff told me to. He held her still while I did it. As I worked, he told me I couldn't leave the boat. Not for a while."

"Define 'a while.' "

"Holy shit, I don't know. Ended up feeling like forever, but it was a few weeks maybe. We took the yacht out and were on the water a few weeks."

"A few weeks?"

"Yes, it seemed that long. Not sure. Lost track of time. I stayed down below deck."

"Below deck the whole time? Why?"

"Because he fucking told me to!"

"With the child?"

"Yes, with her."

"What did you feed her?"

"We didn't."

"What? Did the boat run out of food?"

"We had food. Cliff kept me fed."

"But you didn't feed the child?"

He looked down. "Cliff told me not to feed her. Fuck! He said to let her starve. But then, then... she kept watching me. Looked at me every time I ate. Begging. Begging with her exotic eyes, those long eyelashes. I felt bad. She looked so hungry. She lost so much weight."

"Was it that obvious?"

"Well, her clothes got looser. Her eyes seemed to get bigger and bigger. It got to be too much for me. Eventually, I just couldn't do it. I couldn't. Not with those eyes begging me. So, I gave her some water, some bites to eat. Now and then, whenever I knew Cliff wouldn't see."

"So, her mouth wasn't taped shut anymore?"

"It was. But I'd briefly remove the tape to feed her."

"Did Cliff ever find out?"

"Yeah, he did, when she stopped wasting away entirely. Fuck, he was so mad, steaming mad. So mad, he slapped me. But he's not a big guy, so I defended myself. He started yelling. Told me he would hand me over to the police along with the child. That the police would arrest me for kidnapping her, not to mention running from my debts. I got fucking scared. He told me we needed to get rid of her. He was growing impatient, told me he'd have me killed. Me and her, if I didn't obey. If I didn't get rid of her. But I couldn't. And she fought, fought against us, fought for her life, hanging on to her life. Barely had anything to eat or drink, but hung on to her life."

"I see. Did you change her diaper?"

"What? No. We just let her go in the crate."

"Didn't it stink?"

"Yes, it stank, but we hosed it down a few times."

"Tell me you took her out of the crate while hosing it down."

"Nope, we just left her in it."

"Unbelievable."

"Look, I took care of it."

"Took care of what?"

"Everything. At some point, I realized I either had to do the deed, or else take care of her. And, fuck, I just couldn't kill her. Couldn't do it. Those eyes of hers. I don't like children, but those eyes…. Yes, she was annoying, but you don't kill people just because they annoy you."

"I see. Did you keep from drinking this whole time?"

"You mean like, alcohol?"

Both police chief and agent nodded.

"Nope, I didn't have any drinks. Just water. Nothing fun to drink on that ship, no alcohol."

"I see. So, eventually you decided to bring her to Martina's."

"Yeah. Cliff gave me an ultimatum: I either had to get rid of her within the next few days or he'd hand me over. Or call his buddy to kill us. And this time, he meant it. I was so scared. So fucking scared. I needed to do something. And then the idea came to me, a brilliant idea: I'd give her away to a woman who'd raise the child as their own. Right away, I thought of Martina, my ex. She'd always been caring. Always wanted a baby. Naïve, though. Told Cliff how fucking naïve she was, and easily intimidated. Told him my plan would work—I just needed to give her a real good scare. Then she'd never talk."

"And Cliff went along with it?"

"Not at first. But he sat on it for a while. I kept telling him this would solve our problem. He kept thinking, and thinking, and then told me he'd come up with a plan. Said we needed paperwork to make the plan airtight. The perfect story for Martina. He told me to tell her the child was mine, that I'd had her with a girlfriend who'd disappeared and that I couldn't care for the child. He said he'd arrange everything else, the paperwork and stuff. All I had to do was drop her off. And scare the bejesus out of Martina."

The agent and chief looked at each other. "You agreed to this?"

"Yes."

"Explain what you mean by 'paperwork.'"

"Well, a birth certificate. And a social security card. Cliff knew someone. Told me he'd put my name and Martina's name on the kid's birth certificate."

"You agreed to have your name on a falsified legal document?"

"Of course. By that point, I just wanted to get out of there."

"How'd the paperwork come to you?"

"Cliff somehow arranged it. Don't know how. We parked the yacht and he left for the day. Came back early the next morning with the paperwork and some other stuff."

"What stuff?"

"Scissors and hair dye. He made me cut the kid's hair super short. Put black dye in it."

"Did she cooperate?"

"Nope, not one bit. But she was pretty weak by then. Once that was done, we took her out of the crate for good. Cliff said it was time to be rid of her and that the plan had better work. He went over what to tell my ex. It was a good story. He said if it worked out, I was a free man."

"How did you find Martina?"

"Cliff knew someone. I'm telling you, he knows all kinds of people. He found out. He also arranged to bring my car to Miami."

"The car you'd left in Pensacola?"

"Yeah, exactly."

"He had it brought to Miami?"

"Yes, because that's where Martina lived. Still lives in Miami."

"How'd you end up in Miami?"

"By boat, of course. Cliff docked his yacht there and I got off."

"Cliff seems pretty well-connected."

"Oh yeah, he is. Very powerful guy."

"Who helped him? The others you met in Vegas?"

"I'm not sure. Don't know who else was in on it."

"You say his name is Cliff. Do you have any other information you can share on him?"

"No, I only know his first name."

"Can you spell it?"

"*C, L, I,* double *F*. Cliff. First name. Only knew first names for all of them."

"And you said the others are… Bill and JB? And maybe Bullet?"

"Yes. Correct."

"Bullet is a first name? Or a last name?"

He laughed now. "No clue. Never saw the guy, much less collected his résumé. Vegas was a blur. I was fucking wasted."

"You told us that before."

"Exactly. Again, I only met Cliff, Bill, and JB."

"Did you ever see Bill again?"

Jonathan shook his head. "Nope. He was my emergency contact on the yacht, but I never had a reason to call him. Had his number programmed into the BlackBerry."

"So you never contacted him again?"

"Nope, not really."

"Not really? That's a yes-or-no question, Mr. Sullivan."

He sighed. "Well, I contacted him recently—after the girl showed up at my store. Told him we needed to come up with a plan to deal with her."

"And did you?"

Sullivan laughed. "Nope. He told me *I* was the one who had a fucking problem and that he wouldn't help. He had no idea she was still alive."

"I see. Only you and Cliff knew?"

"I guess so. Never saw the others again. It was always Cliff. Just Cliff. Only ever Cliff."

"Okay, we hear you. So, the night you took the child to Martina…"

"Oh, okay, sure. Back to that night. Well, I got off the yacht. Got into my car that Cliff somehow brought to Miami. I got the kid in the backseat and drove to the address Cliff had given me."

"Did Cliff come along for the ride?"

"No, it was just me and the girl."

"Did you have a car seat?"

He chuckled. "Hell no. I just laid her down in the backseat."

"You had no car seat?" He shook his head. "Did you buckle her?" He shook his head again. "So, you just laid her down in the backseat of your car?"

He wiggled nervously in his bed. "Yes, for the hundredth time. Why's that so important?"

"Just wondering," the chief said. "Did she cry?"

"Nope, she was quiet. Pretty weak by then. I knew we'd been on the water a while, but had no way of knowing how much time had passed."

"I see. May I point out that at this point you found yourself in your own car, no longer supervised. Why didn't you just drive away, escape?"

"Haha… Funny. You cops are funny. Because I had that little girl with me and needed to get rid of her. And Cliff was following me."

"He was?"

"In his car."

"What type of car?"

"Not sure. Black BMW. Fancy European car. He followed. He told me I'd get my money once I'd dropped her off."

"And you trusted him?"

"Yeah. Really had no fucking choice, now did I? Anyway, I trusted him. Because I had to. So, I drove to Martina's apartment. It was late. Nighttime. I parked across the street and had a quick drink."

"A quick… drink?"

"Yeah, Cliff finally got his hands on some whiskey for me. Liquid courage, he said. Man, I felt it after being sober for so long…. Anyway, walked over to her apartment with the girl."

"Rest your voice. Let me read Martina's statement to you, Mr. Sullivan," the chief said, and took out a piece of paper.

Sullivan listened for a while.

The chief snapped his report folder shut. "Is that accounting correct, Mr. Sullivan?"

"Yeah, yeah, more or less. Told you she's naïve. Very easily intimidated. And it worked. For twenty fucking years!"

"It sure did, Mr. Sullivan. What did you do after the drop-off?"

"Well, I started a new life. With the money."

"Cliff actually pulled through?"

"Yes, he actually did. Well, sort of." He laughed a coarse laugh. "He only gave me twenty thousand bucks. Got me out of debt, but definitely not enough money to start a business."

"Were you mad at him?"

"Yes, of course I was mad. But he left before I could think about doing anything about it. Just drove off. And honestly, I was happy it was over and done. It was rough. Rough few months."

"You knew by then it had been a few months?"

"Yes, noticed that night it was probably August already. You know how the heat here takes on a life of its own in August, even at night.... Yep, long time. But it was done and over. I got to start a new life after that."

"Did you ever hear back from them?"

"Nope, never saw or heard from the Fearless Four again. But, like I said, I called Bill when the girl showed up at my store a few weeks ago."

"Yes, you did say that. You must have called Bill on your old BlackBerry."

"Correct."

"Why him? Why not Cliff?"

"'Cuz I was told to contact Bill if anything ever went wrong."

"I see. Remind me, what did he say again?"

"He told me that *they* didn't have a problem, only *I* did!"

"How did that make you feel?"

"Fucking scared. I'd built a good life for myself. But the girl's alive because of me. And these powerful, powerful people were pissed to learn of it!"

"They are? Who are they again?"

"Aren't you paying any fucking attention? Bill, Cliff, JB.... They're rich and powerful. They know people. And they will fucking kill me if I don't handle this right."

"Handle what right?"

"The... Who else could it be? The girl!"

"Aha. You mean Moana, also known as Maria?"

"Of course. I just wanted to make the problem go away...."

"By... what, trying to drown her? Again?"

"Yeah, exactly...." He sighed. "Look, we had a deal, right? I won't be charged for kidnapping the kid?"

Agent Tonya Anderson and Chief Parlot were looking at him, staring straight at him, smiling.

Jonathan found this unnerving. "But we had a deal! I tell you the whole story, give you names, I don't get arrested. Besides, I didn't kidnap the girl when she was little, and I sure didn't fake any legal document. Cliff did. And his friends."

"Yes, you said that. Several times," Agent Anderson agreed.

"Exactly! You can't charge me with that now."

"We'll see. We still have to verify all of this," Chief Parlot said.

Jonathan Sullivan looked at him, his heart sinking. "What does that mean?"

"So far, you've been telling us your side of the story. We need to verify everything you've told us."

"What? How? It's been twenty years!"

"Exactly, Mr. Sullivan," Agent Anderson said. "And that's why we're sure you'll understand... this might take a while."

"What?"

"In the meantime, you can stay here in this lovely hospital and get healthy, then come to our station and check into one of our nice prison-cell suites while we verify your account," Chief Parlot said, and grinned.

Jonathan turned pale. "No, no, you can't do this to me! You cannot! I told you everything you wanted to know! It's true! I didn't do anything that deserves being locked up!"

"You didn't?" both Agent Anderson and Chief Parlot asked in unison.

"I didn't kidnap her. I didn't fake those documents. You can't pin that on me! I'm innocent. You have to drop the charges against me." He looked at both of them, his body shuddering. "You can't lock me up for kidnapping the toddler. I didn't actually kidnap her."

"We know. You said so. So you're right, we can't arrest you for that," Chief Parlot said.

Jonathan Sullivan sighed and looked relieved.

Agent Anderson spoke. "But we can and will arrest you for being an accessory to kidnapping Moana Marie Collins, as well as severely neglecting a child, threatening your ex-wife, using illegal money for your own benefit, kidnapping an adult, and attempted murder. I think those charges should be enough for us to hold you for a long, long time!"

Jonathan's face turned even more pale, until he was ghostly white.

"Don't be too sad, Mr. Sullivan. The hospital here is very good. They'll nurse you back to health, and then you'll be fit to enjoy our cells here in Niceville. They're not bad either. Pretty *nice*, actually. Get it? 'Nice,' as in *Nice*ville…"

Chief Parlot smiled, and Tonya smirked. Satisfied, they both rose to their feet.

"Thank you, Mr. Sullivan, for your cooperation."

"But, but… No! No! No!" he screamed. "You can't do this. It's just words. Just my words."

"Correct, Mr. Sullivan, just your words. We would love to hear more from you, but for now, what you said today is enough. Remember? 'Anything you do or say can and will be used against you.' You will be punished to the full extent of the law."

"This isn't fair," Jonathan yelled, flailing in his bed. "This isn't fair! I helped her, I fed her, I kept her alive! It's not fair! Cliff and Bill and JB did it! They need to pay for this! They do, not me! I'm not the bad guy here!" He started bawling.

"That's for the jury to decide," Agent Anderson said. They waved goodbye.

"No, please! No! Help me, please! I'm not a bad guy, I'm not. I quit drinking, I stopped gambling, I turned my life around. Please! Help me! Ahhhhhhh!"

"Does that lawyer sound good right about now, Mr. Sullivan?" Chief Parlot yelled over Jonathan's screams.

Jonathan Sullivan stopped and nodded, tears in his eyes, his expression dead.

"Okay, then. We'll bring you the paperwork. Let's hope one of them can help you."

CHAPTER 26

Help you? No one can save you now.

From behind the empty bed in the hospital hallway, Bill watched the chief and his crew walk down the opposite end of the hallway until they turned out of sight. The nurse entered Jonathan's hospital room immediately. He decided to watch and wait until she came back out.

A police officer came down the hallway and plopped down in the chair in front of the door. He recognized him. *Same guy guarding the room as last time. Officer Miller. Good guy. I'll deal with him. Bet he still remembers me.* He grinned.

It'll all be okay. And this is perfect timing. They'll think the interrogation was too much. Went quite long anyway. And whatever Sullivan told them, he doesn't know shit. Doesn't even know our real names.

He smiled, but then his smile turned to a frown. *Is the risk worth it? So far, I've only obstructed the twenty-year-old case. Any other involvement back then will be hard to prove. But if anyone ever finds out I was involved, my reputation is ruined.*

He stood up, relishing the renewed blood flow to his legs, and strolled over to a nearby vending machine. He knew it was quiet up here and nobody would bother to take a close look at him. He easily blended in. He inserted a one-dollar bill into the vending machine and bought a coffee. He took mental notes on how long it took the machine to brew the coffee, how long it took him to complete the transaction. He took a few sips as he casually strolled back toward Sullivan's door.

Cliff's right, though. I need to shut him up. If Jonathan keeps talking, they might figure out who Cliff is, and that could lead them to the rest of us. It would ruin everything—my reputation, my legacy, my family name.

I can't have that.

I know enough to make it look like an accident. Yeah, sure do. Comes with the job. I know how to make things look just right, what'll be searched.

He took another sip of his warm coffee. The hot liquid washed away all his doubts, and he took a few casual steps toward the door. He saw the nurse come out, the officer reading in his chair.

A few more minutes, then it'll be perfect.

"Hello, Officer Miller!"

The middle-aged police officer looked up from his phone. "Oh, hi there again, sir. Still interested in the case, huh?"

"Yeah, naturally. And guess what? I just ran into Parlot and he updated me on a few things. Man, who knew. It was Sullivan the whole time, huh? Well, glad they finally got him."

"Yes, sir, that is good. To think he almost got away with it. Seems to have no real connection to her, does he? Guess he went a bit crazy, attacking her again after all these years. They never would've found him otherwise."

He wanted to frown, but laughed instead. "Yeah, no kidding. Dumb mistake. Well, in the end, they all make mistakes. All get caught one way or another." He bit his lip. *Hopefully not* all *of them.*

"So true, sir, so true. Well, better get back to it."

"Oh sure. You've been here a while, huh?"

"Yeah. It's a twelve-hour shift. Started early this morning."

"Yeah, I remember us talking earlier." He sighed and sipped his coffee. "You know what? It's probably coffee-time for you, too. There's a nice vending machine just around the corner. Makes great coffee. I just got some myself."

He showed the officer his cup and took another sip. "Should've gotten one for you. Sorry about that."

"It's alright, sir. Yeah, I could go for a coffee, but I can't leave here. It'll be fine."

"You work so hard, though. It's a tough job, sitting there all day long for twelve freaking hours. Wow."

"Yeah, it's a lot," Officer Miller agreed, and yawned. "That coffee sure smells good though."

He smiled at the officer and took another sip. "Tell you what, Officer... I can take over for a bit while you get coffee. Nothing's gonna happen around here."

The officer looked at him. "I can't just leave my post."

"But you wouldn't really be leaving it unguarded. You'll have me. And you know you can trust me. Obviously. Just look at me." He winked.

"Yeah, I know, sir. The blue blood runs thick, huh?"

"Aye, that it does. And Parlot wouldn't mind. I would know. I know that guy, remember?"

Officer Miller yawned again, then nodded. "Are you sure it'll be okay?"

He winked at the officer again and took another sip of his coffee. "Of course. Nobody will know. Not like you're planning on a trip to Starbucks, are you? The vending machine is just around the corner. Won't take you longer than five minutes."

Officer Miller nodded. "Yeah. Okay. Nothing important can happen in five minutes, right?"

"Nope, nothing can. So go, run along. I'll keep your seat warm."

"Okay. Thanks again, sir."

Officer Miller was about to leave when he checked his pockets.

He knew exactly what the officer was up to. "Ah, right, here's a few bucks. On the house."

"Awesome, thanks, sir. I'll be right back."

"Sounds good. I got you."

He sat down and watched the officer closely. As soon as he rounded the corner, he set his coffee cup under the chair and slipped into Sullivan's room.

Sullivan was sleeping soundly. The nurse had clearly given him something for his agitation. He had rolled onto his side in his sleep, as much as the cables allowed him.

He grinned. *Perfect. He's making it easy for me.*

Quickly, he put on hospital gloves. With his gloved hands, he tilted Sullivan's head back, toward the end of the big, fluffy pillow it rested on.

He looked at his watch, had it all timed out.

Now. I have to do it now.

He folded the free side of the pillow over Sullivan's mouth and nose, used his other hand to push Sullivan's head further into the pillow. Soon enough, he saw the lines on the monitor begin to jump and squiggle. He pushed harder and harder. He felt Sullivan's body convulse, and pushed harder and harder until he heard a long, drawn-out beep. The line on the monitor went flat.

Done.

He slipped off his gloves, shoved them inside his pocket, then slipped out the door and sat back down in the chair. He gingerly sipped at his coffee. *Hmm. A touch hot. Needs more sugar.* He had just managed to take another sip when Officer Miller turned the corner, walking fast toward him.

"I'm back, sir. Did anything happen?"

He grinned. "No, nothing at all. All quiet here. Very quiet!"

CHAPTER 27

"Quiet? Yeah, guess I'm being kinda quiet. I just don't know what to say. It's just... awkward," Maria whispered to Aaron.

He smiled and put an arm around her. "Well, at least your future in-laws get along well."

Maria looked at him. "In-laws?"

"Yeah, your parents, my dad—soon-to-be in-laws."

"Oh yeah."

"You forgot about our engagement?"

She smirked. "Of course not. More like I forgot I had new parents for a bit." She sighed. "I don't know. I don't hate her."

"Who?"

"Mamá. I don't think she did anything. You were right.... Why would she kidnap a child with her ex she was so afraid of?"

"We'll find out what happened soon enough, Maria. We will. Don't worry."

She sighed and took a sip of her ice water. They were sitting at the table at the Officers' Club overlooking the beautiful Emerald Coast. Putting on the appearance of a real family. Elisabeth and Brad were chatting with Jack. Maria was seated next to Elisabeth, Aaron in between his dad and Maria.

She sipped her water again and stared out at the beautiful, calm, emerald-green water. *We may look like a real family, but we sure don't feel like one.* She sighed. *It's so hard. The tension is awful. Neither my birth parents nor I really know what to say. And when we do chat, they get nostalgic and overly emotional.*

Aaron looked at her. "I'm gonna get more food from the buffet. Want to tag along? I think they're serving the main course now."

Maria shook her head and started nibbling at her salad again. Aaron got up and wandered off. When he returned, the Collinses were still fixated on their conversation with Jack. Maria was still staring out the window while picking at her salad.

Aaron sat back down. He gave her a friendly nudge. "I think that salad is done for, Maria."

She looked at her plate and now noticed only a few leafy greens remained. "Oh, yeah, guess so." She put down her fork.

"But look at this, Maria," he said with a grin, "they're serving wonderfully burnt green beans and super-soggy sweet potatoes."

"Burnt green beans and soggy sweet potatoes?" Maria inspected Aaron's plate and smiled. "Yummy!"

Jack, Brad, and Elisabeth overheard them and studied Aaron's plate as well.

"Burnt green beans? Yummy, indeed," Elisabeth said. "Safe to say this place exceeds its reputation, Brad."

Brad blushed.

Maria turned to her. "Ah, you like burnt green beans also?"

Elisabeth nodded. "I do. And soggy, buttery sweet potatoes. I haven't eaten that in so long. Germany doesn't have many sweet potatoes. Not popular. But I love them."

"Me, too." Maria smiled.

"In that case, how about both of you indulge in some? You can go together," Aaron encouraged them.

The ladies nodded and went to the buffet together. Elisabeth handed Maria a plate. "What else do you love to eat?"

The mood shifted, and suddenly their conversation started flowing much more naturally. They even laughed together. They soon realized how much they had in common, all the things they liked. They were still talking when they returned to the table.

"Thank you, Aaron," Brad whispered as Elisabeth and Maria sat down. "Those nasty green beans and sweet potatoes saved this lunch, I think."

Jack started laughing. Aaron and Brad joined him as the ladies continued to talk about food.

"And, of course, I love tamales. Venezuelan pastries, too," Maria said, still smiling innocently. "Especially the ones my mamá and her sisters make."

Elisabeth's fork clattered onto her plate. "Your... *mom?*"

Maria's smile faded when she realized her faux pas. "Oh, I mean... yes, I—"

"But you're *my* daughter," Elisabeth screamed. "Mine! Just mine. Meine Tochter!"

"Mama, ja," Maria burst out in a childlike, singsong voice. "Ja, Mama."

Brad almost choked on his food. Jack and Aaron went quiet. Maria's eyes had turned green again, as emerald-green as the water outside the window.

The moment passed, leaving Maria deep in thought. *What do they want from me? Years, so many years living a life apart from them made me into who I am. A stranger to them—and they are strangers to me.*

I was so little when we knew each other. Too little to even remember them fully. I feel there's a connection, but not one defined by memory like they have. I was shaped by the way I grew up, a life they know nothing about. She sighed and hung her head low. *I look like them but we're strangers to one another.*

She could see that Elisabeth was shaking. Brad was keeping quiet, his eyes also a deep emerald green.

"She didn't mean any harm," Aaron said.

"I know," Brad whispered, and looked at his two women. Both had the same food on their plates, both had been eating with perfect manners prior to the altercation. He grinned. "Look at you both, eating your food with a knife in your right hand, fork in your left instead of stuffing the food into your mouth with the fork only—like all of us do."

The other men at the table glanced at their own utensils. They had all been gripping just a fork in their right hand.

"Psh. You need both knife and fork. That's the way it should be," Elisabeth said, and Maria nodded in agreement.

"Yet another thing you both share in common," Aaron commented.

"He's right," Brad said. "You have to focus on what you have in common, not your differences. I bet there's a lot."

Everyone else nodded.

Brad turned to Elisabeth. "Hun, we can't treat our long-lost daughter like the toddler we knew. We can't expect her to hug us, call for us, need our help. She's her own person now, and she's phenomenal, that much is clear."

Maria blushed a little, then smiled. "Aw, thank you."

That put Brad in a good mood. "I tell you what, ladies: I think we need to start all over again. Start from scratch, from zero. Focus on the here and now, not the then. I would love to hear, for example, more about what you're doing now, Maria. More about your friends. And how exactly you met this guy over there." Brad pointed at Aaron with a wink.

"Yes, how did you two meet?" Elisabeth said, her eyes sparkling, a smile wiping away her fear. "I know it was in college, but how exactly? Would love to hear the whole story."

Conversation flowed anew, but differently this time; it was as if a burden had been lifted, like they were friends that were getting to know each other. *Like meeting a new person but knowing already you'll like each other*, Maria thought. Soon, they were laughing and joking until, all of a sudden, Jack's face drained of color.

"Dad? Are you okay? You aren't choking on something, are you?"

But Jack couldn't say anything. Aaron rose and rushed over in a panic, preparing to administer the Heimlich maneuver, but Jack shook his head and pointed at the small TV broadcasting in the corner of the restaurant.

Then they saw it.

Maria's fork left her hand and clattered to the floor.

On the screen was a reporter standing outside of the hospital they'd all come from earlier that day. At the bottom was a banner that sucked the air out of the room.

BREAKING NEWS: JONATHAN SULLIVAN FOUND DEAD IN HOSPITAL.

CHAPTER 28

Jonathan Sullivan found dead in the hospital? Cliff sat up in his big, comfy chair as he watched the news. *Can't believe it. How did that happen, Bill?* He whistled through his teeth. *Man, he really gets shit done. No more middleman to worry about now.*

He was in between meetings and didn't have much time to dawdle, but found he had a strong urge to call one of his old buddies.

Can't do it now and probably shouldn't anyway. Now that Sullivan is dead, he won't be talking to anyone. He leaned back in his chair and thought for a bit. *Everything should be good now. I took care of everything.*

He smiled, but then the smile froze in a grimace. *Or did the police already talk to him? Did he say something before he died?*

He hopped up and started pacing. *I'll have to watch the news conference covering this later. Just have to.*

Any other loose ends? He thought back and stopped pacing. *No, nothing more. The secret died with him.*

He sighed. *Guess you can never be assured of anyone keeping a secret. Especially a big secret. People talk, especially when they're pressured into it. Unless, of course, they're dead. Convenient that he's dead now. Can't talk anymore.*

He grinned again, then it faded just as quickly. *The hot blonde at Vital Records. Will she freak out and talk? She's super influenceable. I know that better than anyone. And I know the police are good at getting to those types of people.*

His face flushed. *Unless she, too, disappeared. Otherwise, I can't be one hundred percent sure she won't talk.*

He started sweating, sweating so much he had to loosen the tie around his neck. *I have to take care of her somehow, take care of the hot blonde at Vital Records. Somehow. However I do it, I need her not to say anything. Have to make sure!*

CHAPTER 29

"Sure? You're one hundred percent sure, Nurse Karen?" Chief Parlot said.

His mind was racing. *He can't be dead. He just can't. Maybe he went into a coma and they'll be able to wake him again?* The phone was on loudspeaker—the whole team was staring at it, gathered together in their workroom inside the police station.

"We *are* sure, Chief," came Nurse Karen's quavering voice over the line. "We tried everything. *I* tried everything. Sullivan could not be resuscitated."

"But… we were just there an hour ago. He was doing fine. What happened?" Officer Johnson asked.

"Well, his heart just stopped. All of a sudden. We're not sure why yet. The coroner will have to test to find out. Trust me, you'll be the first to know of his findings."

"Okay, thank you," Chief Parlot said. "And you have no idea what happened?"

"Well, not really, but I have a feeling. Maybe it was… just too much stress?"

Tonya prickled at that. "What do you mean, 'just too much stress'?"

"Seems like the interrogation was too much for him. We asked you to be gentle, but it seems you took matters into your own hands. And this is the outcome!"

They all looked at each other.

The chief cleared his throat. "Nurse Karen, please, we were—"

"First you put your star witness into a state of shock, then your key suspect passes minutes after interrogation. So, it is what it is. Have a great day, Chief."

The line went dead.

She just hung up? Seriously? And she accused us of making Sullivan's heart stop?

They all stared at the phone, not saying a word, listening to the unnerving dial tone.

Tonya hung up and smirked. "Oh dear, Isaac my man. Sounds like you and I somehow made ourselves a big enemy in the medical world. Better hope Nurse Karen doesn't ever have to care for any of us."

He grunted. "No kidding. We weren't... We didn't push too hard, did we?"

"Goodness, no, Isaac. We did not. We were gentle as lambs. Besides, he did most of the talking, basically told us what happened with minimal prompting."

"Yeah, I know... but what about how we slammed him at the end?"

She shook her head. "No. If he had two brain cells to rub together, he'd've known he wouldn't walk after attacking Maria."

Tom shook his head. "Well, he wasn't the brightest."

Sally stared at the wall. "Oh my gosh, he's dead. That's not good, not good at all. We needed him to identify his coconspirators."

The chief nodded. *No kidding. We needed him. Really would've needed him. Something here's not right!* "Sally's right," he said. "We gotta find out if the names Sullivan gave us hold water. Were these people just made up or did they actually exist?"

"You mean we gotta find one Bill out of a million?" Sally asked.

G. P. SCHUMACHER

He nodded. "Yeah, and the others. That's our task."

Tom sighed. "It'll be hard. Such common names."

The chief slammed his fist on the table. "Damn it. This sucks, just really sucks. Sullivan would've talked more, I know it. And how in the world did the press learn of his death so quickly?"

Tonya came over and gave him a pat on the back. "You know the press. The moment one of them catches wind of something, they blurt it out to everyone."

The chief shook his head and sighed.

Tonya kept patting his back. "I know, Isaac, I know. But we can't give up, *won't* give up. Gotta keep moving. So, what's next?"

"Well," Sally said, "isn't it clear Martina told us the truth?"

They all looked at each other and nodded.

"Yes, Jonathan Sullivan corroborated her testimony. We have every reason to believe she wasn't involved in the girl's kidnapping or in faking her birth certificate," Tonya said.

"So, she's free to go?" Sally said, trying not to sound too excited.

"Yeah, no reason to hold her any longer," the chief said. "She did right by the kid. At least that's some good news."

"But she should stay in town," Tom said. "In case we have more questions."

"Yeah, good call. She'll need to be kept away from the reporters. Maybe we can sneak her out while Tonya and I hold the press conference?"

"Great idea, Isaac my man. But where should she stay?"

"Maybe on base with the others?" Sally suggested.

"Might get a bit heated if we put them all together, don't you think?" Tom said.

Tonya grinned. "He has a point. But maybe that's exactly what we want?"

"Wait, what?" Tom was confused.

"Yeah, the messier, the better," Tonya continued. "Might learn more about the lot of them. We can have one of our people listen in."

Sally's eyes were big. "Wow, good thinking. We could send someone to act as Martina's escort. Just need to make sure they know Spanish." They all looked at her with curiosity. "You know, for when Martina talks to Maria in Spanish. Wouldn't it be good to have someone there who could, let's say, *accidentally overhear?*"

Tonya whistled through her teeth. "Haha, what a smart young lady! Love it."

The chief nodded. "Sally, since this is your baby, why don't you arrange for all of that? Talk to base police to see if they'll allow her on base. And recruit an escort who speaks Spanish."

Sally nodded.

"What should I do, boss?" Tom asked.

"We learned toddler Maria was held on a boat. A yacht. If that story's true, then we need to find that yacht. A white yacht, Sullivan mentioned, parked at the local marina back then. See what you can find."

"But we're in Florida, there's like a million yachts.… Ack, I'm on it," Tom said.

Sally's cheeks were flushed in eagerness. "Don't we still need to check out the area on base where she was taken from? That might lead us to more clues. And I think we need to talk to Maria again soon. She might remember more when we share what we've learned."

Chief Parlot looked at his watch. "I agree, but first, I have a press conference to run. And you, FBI Agent Anderson, will go out there with me to face down the mob of reporters. Let's try not to turn this into a PR debacle."

"Alright, alright, alright, my man, for sure. Let's step out to go over our speech and leave the youngsters to their research, shall we?"

"Yes, let's." The chief sighed. "I hate reporters and their questions."

Tonya patted him on the back. "It'll be fine, my man. We have a lot of red meat to feed the hungry sharks with. A key suspect passed away, and another is going to be released—quite the story!"

Isaac nodded. *Yeah, quite the story. But I don't like where all this is going.*

181

CHAPTER 30

I don't like where all this is going! A shudder ran down Maria's spine as she watched the press conference covering her case. Jack, Aaron, and the Collinses had already surrounded the restaurant TV to better watch and listen.

This is so surreal. They're talking about me, my attacker—and Mamá? Immediately, Maria was glued to the screen with the rest. She listened carefully. Then came the magic words, and she jumped up, whooping. "Yeah, that's awesome! Mamá's getting released. She's innocent!"

She fell into Aaron's arms and hugged him. She glanced at the Collinses over his shoulder and noticed both of them were clenching their jaws. *I know they're not happy, but this is good news. I just knew Mamá didn't kidnap me, I just knew.*

She trained her attention on the TV again, where the police chief was speaking. "Before Mr. Sullivan passed away, he verified with us that his ex-wife, Martina Sullivan, had no idea who the child was. He was the one who dropped the child off at Mrs. Sullivan's apartment, and supplied documents that made her believe the child was his."

"Nonsense," Elisabeth screamed. "She should've known we were looking for her. It was all over TV!"

Maria bit her lip and watched the Collinses hug each other in grief. Her mind wandered off before tuning back in just in time to hear the chief make a plea to the press. "We need your help in finding the people who enabled this kidnapping that Mr. Sullivan told us about."

"The Fearless Four?" a reporter interrupted.

"Yes, exactly. It's unclear if Mr. Sullivan himself was the fourth member of this group, or if there's another man going by the name Bullet involved. For now, we're looking to locate a Bill, a JB, and a Cliff."

Maria stared at the TV. *Bill? JB? Cliff?* She thought long and hard about these names. *I don't know a Bill. Or a JB. But Cliff? That sounds familiar.*

"Oh dear, the poor chief," Maria heard Jack say, and focused on the TV again.

"I can assure you, my department had nothing to do with Sullivan's death. Yes, we interrogated him, but not harshly. It was a very civilized interrogation."

"So you weren't playing 'bad cop'? You didn't induce a heart attack by being too mean?" a reporter asked.

"Certainly not, ladies and gentlemen," FBI Agent Anderson said, and looked directly into the camera, her brown eyes fiery. "Chief Parlot is a professional and knows what he's doing. I was there and can assure you—we did not violate protocol. Neither one of us. We have a recording of the interrogation that clearly shows we had a civilized conversation. So Chief Parlot certainly isn't a so-called 'bad cop.' Got it? Any other questions?"

Maria stared at the screen. *A bad... cop?* A shudder ran down her spine as she remembered. *I saw him. The chief. This morning. At Sullivan's door.*

"We have to go," Maria muttered. "Right away. I need to see Chief Parlot. I need to ask him something."

They all stared at her.

"What?"

"Why?"

"Now?"

But Maria was already out of the door and walking to her car. Aaron quickly ran after her, waving goodbye to the others. Stunned, Jack, Brad, and Elisabeth watched them speed away.

Maria was sitting in one of the interrogation rooms at the Niceville Police Department, waiting for the chief and his team to come in. Aaron sat next to her. Her arms were crossed in front of her chest, her slightly green eyes shining in anger.

"I hate those reporters. We can't drive or go anywhere without them hounding us."

"I know, Maria. We just have to bear it for now—they'll get bored and go away eventually. Besides, you did great handling them when we came here. Just ignored them and said you had no comment. That's exactly the way they should be dealt with."

Maria was tapping her fingers on the desk, her lips pressed together.

"But you're also treating *me* like those reporters," Aaron said, and put his hand on hers so that she couldn't tap her fingers on the desk anymore. "I can't say I'm a fan of that."

She turned to him. "What do you mean, Aaron?"

"On the way over here. You didn't give me anything either, 'no comment' on what was so urgent we had to rush over here. You just sat there, silent. What's going on? What's wrong?"

"I don't know yet… can't tell you yet." She made a fist with her hand despite it being held by Aaron.

"Maria, you need to relax. I know it's a setback that Sullivan died, but the team has everything under control, and the chief—"

She snorted. *Yeah, the chief. What did he do? I know what I saw. I'm very interested in hearing his explanation.*

Aaron's eyes rested on her. "Please just tell me what's going on."

Her angry green eyes looked back at him, but before she could say anything, the door opened and in came the whole team: Chief Parlot, Officer Johnson, and their respective assistants.

"Hello, Maria, great to see you again," Chief Parlot said, and sat down across from her. The others shook Maria's and Aaron's hands as well and found a seat at the table.

"So, what brings you in so urgently?" Agent Anderson asked Maria, a friendly smile on her face.

"This guy," Maria said, and pointed at Chief Parlot.

"Me?"

"Yeah, you. You've got a lot of explaining to do."

"Huh, me? Why? What did I do?"

"Excellent question, Chief Parlot," she said, then stood up and started pacing the room, her eyes locked on him, shutting out everyone else. The others couldn't help but watch her pace back and forth, back and forth.

"I saw you. This morning. While I was getting my coffee."

Perplexed, the chief withstood her stare. "I have no idea what you're talking about, Maria. Yes, we saw you this morning in your room. But you didn't have coffee on you there."

"That's right, I didn't. I got it later on. Left my room to find a vending machine inside the hospital."

"Okay. Good. I'm still not following."

"Well, Chief, isn't it interesting that I saw you this morning *right after you were in my room?*"

He shrugged his shoulders. "Well, I was in and out of the hospital all day on business, so yes, you might have seen me. That doesn't strike me as particularly interesting."

"You didn't see me?"

He shook his head. "Nope. Just in your room that morning when we talked to you."

Maria abruptly stopped pacing and leveled her finger at the chief again. "Liar! That's a lie! You waved to me, recognized me. You don't remember? We spoke. I told you I thought you'd left already and you replied, 'Yep, just leaving now.'"

The room fell silent. Maria looked from one person to the next. *They all look stunned, dumbfounded. Yeah, didn't see that coming, did they? The chief is a liar. Maybe a murderer?*

Chief Parlot just looked at her, then shook his head. "That's not right, Maria."

"What? Of course it is. I know what I saw. You're a liar! You were right outside of Sullivan's room, had the door handle in your hand. I saw you! What were you doing in there? Already prepping his heart attack?"

"Maria..." Aaron jumped up, pushing down her arm that had been stretched out pointing at the chief. "You can't just go around accusing people of murder. Not without evidence."

She turned to Aaron. "But I *have* evidence this time: my own two eyes!" She ripped free of his grasp and crossed her arms in front of her. *I know what I saw. Aaron has to believe me.*

"But... Chief Parlot was with me the whole time," Agent Anderson said. "All morning."

"We were there, too," Officer Johnson said, and Agent Cooper nodded.

"So you're all in this together? Silencing your key suspect? What do you have to gain from that?"

"Maria," Aaron tried again, "you've got to calm down. Stop the accusations. What's gotten into you?"

She ignored him, focused on the chief, until a tug on her arm, gentle at first, then demanding, pulled her back down into her chair. She turned to Aaron, her green eyes piercing through him.

"Just relax, Maria. Breathe, just breathe. Come on, let's be civil about this."

She stared at him. *Civil? I'm fed up with people messing up my life. Hiding things. Keeping secrets. I'm done with them. With everyone.*

"Maria, I assure you my team and I gained nothing from Sullivan's death. Regardless of his character and obvious guilt, we're very upset he passed away. He was being very talkative, gave us insight we've yet to discuss with you. More pieces to the puzzle."

Maria was taken aback. "That wasn't you at his door? But I saw you! Don't tell me I didn't see what I saw!"

"I assure you, whoever you saw, it wasn't me."

Maria pressed her lips together and was about to stand up and speak her mind, but the chief continued, "I believe you, to the extent that you saw *someone* when you got your coffee. It just wasn't me. But this might be of utter importance. Please, describe this person."

Maria cocked her head and eyed him. *Is he trustworthy? Before this I kinda liked him, thought he was a good person— but is he?*

"Please describe who you saw. I believe you when you say someone was there, especially since I highly doubt Mr. Sullivan died of natural causes."

Everyone stared at the chief.

What? He thinks someone did him in after all? But he's claiming innocence? Maria wasn't sure what to think.

"Describe the encounter to us, please," Agent Anderson said. "And we'd like to record this, if that's okay?"

Maria nodded, then took a deep breath and thought back to that morning. "It was definitely a policeman. About your height, your build, Chief. White guy. Was convinced it was you."

"I see. What kind of uniform was he wearing?"

Maria thought for a bit. "A blue police uniform—"

"Maybe it was your guy guarding Sullivan's door?" Officer Johnson interrupted, but got shushed by Chief Parlot.

Maria shook her head. "No, it wasn't a regular police uniform. A chief's uniform, complete with a matching hat."

"Chief's uniform?" the chief said.

Maria nodded. "Yeah. Just like what you have on now. That's why I assumed it was you."

"But… didn't you leave your hat in the car? You never brought it into the hospital," Agent Anderson said.

The chief nodded. He looked disturbed.

"So, that wasn't you?" Maria asked in a small voice.

He shook his head. "Please continue. What was the person doing? You said you saw him standing just outside Sullivan's room? And he talked to you?"

"Well, he had his back to me, but answered when I said 'I thought you'd left a while ago.' He waved over his shoulder at me and walked off. Looked like he'd just come out of Sullivan's room." She thought for a minute. "I guess I'm not sure whether that was his room. I assumed so because it was under guard."

"Wait, the guard was there then?" Agent Anderson asked.

Maria shook her head. "No, just the chair, identical to the setup outside my room. It was empty."

The FBI agent and police chief looked at each other. "Officer Miller wasn't at his post? We need to confirm this, Tonya."

Aaron said, "But who's this guy that supposedly looks like you? Or was pretending to be you? Is there another police chief who's like… your twin brother?"

Officer Johnson burst out laughing. "No, we're a very small department here in Niceville. There's only one chief, and you're looking at him."

The young officer's laughter trailed off and the room lapsed into silence.

"You're the only chief here?" Maria asked again, trying to wrap her head around this new twist.

They all nodded.

"I mean, there's the former chief. But he retired…. Hey, Chief, didn't he work Maria's case way back when?" Officer Johnson asked.

Maria looked at the young police officer, her long blonde hair in a low bun. *The former chief worked my case? He sure didn't do his job well. Certainly didn't find me. Must not have worked hard on it.*

Then she remembered what Elisabeth had said.

"My birth mom said the team lead twenty years ago was condescending. They didn't believe her kidnapping theory. Just dismissed it."

"That's right, Maria," Agent Anderson said.

"Don't you think that's strange? She was right all along and they just dismissed her concerns. Why?"

"Well, it's a long story." Chief Parlot sighed. "They had good reason to believe you wandered away and drowned. Of course, they were wrong."

"Why didn't they even consider a kidnapping?"

"Like I said, it's a long story, Maria," the chief said.

"Yeah, but we got it all mapped out on our case wall," Officer Johnson blurted out, earning her a look from both agent and chief.

Maria was curious. *They've got a case wall? With pictures and everything?*

"Could I see that case wall, please?"

"I don't know, Maria. It might trigger memories and I can't guarantee that—"

"It's fine, Chief, I'll be fine. It's just pictures, nothing too crazy, right?"

"Lots of writing, paper notes… a mess, really, but a nicely organized mess," Agent Cooper said with a smirk on his face.

"Okay, now I have to see this. I want to know why the former chief thought I just walked out." Maria was already up on her feet and walking toward the door.

Quickly, the chief and Agent Anderson rose to join her outside the hallway.

"It's right across the way," the FBI agent explained, and opened the workroom's door. She and the chief stepped inside ahead of Maria.

She stopped in the doorframe and glanced about in awe. Covering the entirety of the far wall were pictures of people she knew: the Collinses, her mamá, Jonathan Sullivan. She saw herself as a grown woman, and as a toddler. There were pictures of the TLF, and tons of sticky notes in different colors with handwritten words scrawled across them. Some held only a solitary question mark.

Oh my gosh, it's my life on that wall. Maria closed her eyes for a second. *But I have to see this. Need to make sense of this confusing case.* Determined, she entered the room, her eyes fixed on the case wall.

She stepped closer and noticed a picture in the corner of the wall. It featured two men, posing for the camera. Carefully, she studied them. "Agent Borman and Chief Billings—2003 Team Leads," read the caption. Maria stared at the picture of the FBI agent and the former police chief.

Do I know you? Do I know you guys from somewhere? She had to hold onto the table to not fall over; her heart was pounding.

CHAPTER 31

Her heart was pounding as she left the station.

"Careful there. Right in front of you, Martina, there's a big step. Three of them. You see it now?" Valentina Garcia said.

Martina nodded, barely able to see from beneath the giant sun hat they had given her. It was to hide her from the throng of reporters surrounding the police station, they'd said. "Gracias," she told her lawyer.

A young police officer, a security guard from Eglin AFB who introduced himself as Lieutenant Pablo Martinez, opened the car door for her so she could get into the backseat.

"¡Me alegré de que vayas de aqui!" Valentina Garcia told her, and smiled.

No kidding. I'm glad too. Still can't believe I'm free to go. She smiled back at Mrs. Garcia. "¡Sí, gracias a tí!"

"De nada," her lawyer told her, and turned to Lieutenant Martinez. "Take good care of my client."

"¡Sí! Por supesto, señora," Lieutenant Martinez replied, and started the car. Martina was waving to Mrs. Garcia when she saw a snoopy reporter with a microphone peek around the corner and point at her car.

"¡Vamos! ¡Los periodistas están por ahí!" she told the lieutenant, and he quickly took off. Tires squealing, he turned the corner and left the police station and its reporters behind.

Phew! We made it. And I'm out of jail. They believed me. She smiled and sat tall. A big burden fell off her. Years of secrecy. *I hated lying to Maria. Hated lying to everyone. But now, I don't have to anymore.*

And I guess Jonathan is dead? She sighed. *Never was a nice guy, but still, he didn't deserve to die. He had his good moments.*

The color left her face. *Did he die because Maria fought him off during the attack? She injured him? ¡Dios mío! Well, guess he deserved it then.* She stared outside the window.

"Mrs. Sullivan, we'll arrive at Eglin Air Force Base soon. Until then, just relax. ¿Lo entiendes?"

Martina nodded and smiled. "Gracias."

Lieutenant Martinez held the door for her as she got out of the car. "This is the Air Force Inn, Mrs. Sullivan. They have a room ready for you."

Martina nodded and looked around. She saw a car arrive and recognized it. Aaron's car. She smiled, tears welling in her eyes. *Is that Aaron? And maybe also Maria? ¡Mija! I've missed her so, so much. Can't believe she was in so much danger. And now, I can finally tell her about how she came to be my daughter.*

She saw Jack get out of Aaron's car and started waving. Then two other people got out as well, but neither of them were Aaron or Maria. Her arm sank down midwave as she stared at the couple. A tall, slender woman with auburn-brown hair in a pixie cut. She looked frail, but at the same time, intimidating. Especially to Martina. The Florida sun reflected in the women's hair, and Martina knew at that instant who she was.

¡Dios mío! The exact same hair color. The same slender figure. The same long neck. The same elegant nose. The same freckles. She stared at the woman. *That's my daughter's mother! The resemblance is uncanny, undeniable.*

Martina swallowed hard. She was about to face a woman who had missed out on twenty years of her daughter's life because Martina had raised her child instead. A tear escaped Martina's big brown eyes, and she now looked at the man standing next to the woman. Even though she was standing a few feet away, she saw it.

Those eyes. The same eyes she had looked into with love for years were staring back at her from an unfamiliar face. *¡Dios mío! He has Maria's eyes! Her unusual, exotic, beautiful eyes!*

She took a step back and almost tripped over Lieutenant Martinez's shoe. *Jonathan lied to me and I was stupid enough to believe him. I should've known that scared little toddler wasn't his. Should've known he was only using me. Again. And this time not for his entertainment or pleasure, but to cover up his crime. A crime he committed. A child kidnapped, taken away from that couple.*

Martina started sobbing. She couldn't take it anymore. She felt the couple's pain; she could imagine how desperate they must have been trying to find their little girl.

Their little girl, taken from them and hidden away, raised differently by a stupid woman. By such a stupid woman. By me. I'm so, so sorry. But I didn't know. Tears were streaming down her face when she heard it.

Jack was calling to her. "Martina! I'm so glad they released you!" He walked over and gave her a big hug. She sobbed loudly as she hugged him back.

"We knew you were innocent," Jack whispered to her, and the warmth of his hug, the kindness of his words made her smile through her tears.

"You? You! It was you!" came an angry female voice.

Martina looked up and found the lady with the pixie cut pointing at her. The man was holding her other hand, one arm around her

193

shoulder, but Martina could tell he wasn't going to be able to hold onto this woman, hold her back much longer. And soon enough, that lady struggled out of his grasp and approached Martina.

"How dare you! How dare you steal my child!" The woman's voice was low, so low and dangerous that both Jack and Martina backed away in fear. The woman's blue eyes were shining with disgust, sparkling in anger.

"I missed it all, missed all that time with my daughter. Missed watching her grow up, get older, become a school child, a teenager, an adult. Missed sending her off to college. I missed it all. Because of you!" She was still pointing at Martina. Her words sliced the hot, humid air and swirled around in Martina's head.

Me. Because of me. It's all my fault. I was stupid. Perdón, perdóname. Martina stared at the lady who looked like an older version of her daughter. Tears were welling in her eyes. Her lips trembled. "I'm so, so sorry. I'm sorry."

"What did you say? You said you're sorry? Yeah, you should be sorry, *will* be sorry—you will pay for this, I promise!"

All color drained from Martina's face. *But I'm innocent. I saved her.*

The lady turned to Lieutenant Martinez. "Officer, sir, Lieutenant, whoever you are, why is this lady even out here? Why isn't she in jail?"

Lieutenant Martinez stared at her. His eyes widened, darted back and forth as if looking around to find a friendly face. "Ma'am, Martina Sullivan was released from jail an hour ago."

"What? Why? But she's—"

"Elisabeth, please," the man with Maria's eyes interrupted. He came over and stood next to her. "I'm sure the chief's rationale was sound. Didn't you hear what he said at the press conference?"

"Brad is right," Jack said, standing beside Martina. "This woman is innocent. The chief told the public as much and dropped all charges against her. It's clear Maria was dropped off at Martina's doorstep by Jonathan Sullivan."

Brad nodded, but Elisabeth raised her eyebrows and turned back to Brad. "You actually believe that?"

"I do," he whispered.

"Me, too," Jack said. "It makes sense, doesn't it? Like Aaron said, why would a divorced couple that can't stand each other bother to kidnap a child together? Sounds like the police agree. Martina's name's been cleared."

"Sí," Martina said with sudden confidence, and stood a bit taller. "It's the truth. I told the chief the truth, and he released me. He said my ex, Jonathan Sullivan, confirmed it."

"That's excellent," Jack said. "Sounds like they got quite a lot of info out of him before he died."

Brad nodded along. Elisabeth just stared at Martina.

Martina shifted from one leg to the other under Elisabeth's uncomfortable stare. "Yes, I'm innocent. And have a great lawyer who will prove it to anyone who doubts me." She took in a deep breath, then turned to Elisabeth. "I took care of her when my ex brought her to me. I thought she was a child he'd had with another woman."

Elisabeth didn't move. "What? How stupid are you?"

Martina's lip started quivering. *I'm* not *stupid. Why is she insulting me?* She closed her eyes for a split second and could hear Maria's words in her head as if she were standing next to her. *"Mamá, you're not stupid! Look at all the things you've accomplished in life. You should be proud of yourself!"* That memory made Martina smile. *Mija. I love you. Love you as my own.*

With newfound courage, she spoke. "I gave her unconditional love all these years, even though I knew she wasn't my own child."

"Exactly," Elisabeth screamed, "you *knew* that little girl wasn't your child. You knew! Just like you must have known that everyone was still looking for her, searching for her, for the missing toddler. It was all over the news! Why didn't you call the police?"

"Because he threatened me. Threatened me and the child. Made me agree to never tell anyone. Said if I did, he'd come back and kill us both."

Everyone stared at Martina.

"Oh, Martina…" Jack said quietly. "I'm so sorry."

"But… but… didn't you see all our pleas on the news? Didn't you think of how it felt for us?" Elisabeth started sobbing. "We lost our only daughter."

"I didn't know," Martina whispered. "I didn't know. I had no TV, didn't listen to the radio. Even if I had, not sure if I would've recognized her face. When she came to me, she didn't look like the girl in the pictures the police showed me today. She was a very small, malnourished, scared little girl."

"Malnourished? Scared?" Elisabeth asked, her voice quiet.

"Yes, she was in bad shape when she came to me that August. And her hair was short and pitch-black."

Elisabeth and Brad now stared at her. "Black hair? Wait, August? Did you say August?"

"Yes, it was August. I know for sure she came to me in August."

Silence. Nobody said anything. All eyes rested on Martina. Elisabeth threw her hands over her mouth.

The color drained from Jack's face. "Late May to early August… that's two whole months from when she was kidnapped to when she entered your custody."

"Two missing months? We need to find out what happened during those two months," Brad said, his voice a bark, the voice of a general. "Two months with a bad guy. Oh my gosh, my baby girl."

Elisabeth lost it then. She started sobbing hysterically. Even Brad was so affected that a wave of nausea enveloped him, and he had to swallow hard to avoid vomiting.

Jack took over. "We need to find out what happened during those two months unaccounted for. Or do you already know, Martina?"

Martina shook her head. "No, the chief is still working on it. I think he got more out of Jonathan, but they didn't tell me. They just said I'm free to go, but need to stay in the area for future questioning."

Elisabeth wiped her tears away, her breath shaking. "Why did that man take her? We never knew him. Had never heard of him before."

Jack turned to the Collinses. "There were other names mentioned on TV. Did any of them ring a bell? Someone connected to Jonathan Sullivan? Could you have made an enemy of any of these other guys?"

Elisabeth and Brad shook their heads, then Brad turned to Martina.

¡Dios mío, those eyes. Exactly like Maria's.

"Was your ex ever in the military?" Brad asked her. She shook her head. "Maybe not even a service member, but in training? Like at the Academy?"

Martina looked at him. "Academy?"

"Yeah, like the Air Force Academy in Colorado Springs?"

Martina thought for a moment, then shook her head. "No. Jonathan had a rough time after high school. Didn't go to college or anything, went straight into the plumbing business. Learned on the job."

"I see."

"Why are you asking, Brad?" Jack wanted to know. "What are you thinking? That he might have attended the Academy at some point? Did you know a Jonathan there? Any bad blood with other trainees?"

Brad shrugged his shoulders. "Can't say I had any enemies. Yeah, there was this one guy who didn't like me. I think his first name was actually Jonathan, but he had a different last name. And then there was this one guy who got a bit mad at me."

"Who was mad at you?" Elisabeth asked.

"Well, you know… Mike…"

"Oh," she said, and nodded.

"That's silly, though," Brad said. "Mike couldn't have known Jonathan Sullivan. He'd be way too stuck up to even talk to a person who never went to college."

Elisabeth nodded and wiped away the sweat forming on her forehead. "It's so hot out here."

"Let's head inside then," Jack said. "I assume you're staying here, too, Martina?"

Martina nodded. She sighed. *Such a strange situation. She's so mad at me. But I understand. I wasn't stupid, but I was a fool.* Tears formed in her eyes as she glanced at Elisabeth, who appeared to be preoccupied with her own thoughts.

"Yeah, Mike would never hang out with a plumber," Elisabeth said. "They wouldn't have cause to know each other. He'd never talk to someone like Jonathan Sullivan. Never."

Martina followed them as they all walked inside. She was quiet, but not only because of the strangeness of this whole situation. No, at that moment, there was a certain saying haunting her ruminations.

Never say never.

CHAPTER 32

"**N**ever met them before?" Maria was still staring at the photo of Agent Borman and Chief Billings.

Aaron shook his head. "No, you couldn't have. Just think about it. We only know the people on the team in this room: Chief Parlot, Officer Johnson, Agent Anderson, and Agent Cooper. No one else."

Maria nodded but looked back at the photo. *Somehow, they still look familiar.* She brushed off the thought and sat down at the table, focusing instead on the pictures the team was pulling out of the old case file.

"This one here is the reason the police arrived at the conclusion an accidental drowning took place. See that? That pink pacifier in the sand? It was yours. Your pacifier washed ashore," Agent Anderson explained.

Everyone studied the picture. The pink pacifier had been discovered on the beach right where the grassy and sandy area in between the TLFs ended. Not far from Maria's old apartment. There was no fence.

Maria swallowed hard. *Stay with it. Stay sane.* She did some of her breathing exercises. Aaron noticed and took her hand, then squeezed it. That made her feel better, stronger. She briefly closed her eyes, allowing her mind to sharpen again. *Stay calm and think, just think. Logically. Like these investigators do.*

"Did they find my footprints in the sand?" Maria asked.

"Great question," Officer Johnson said, and riffled through the files. "Ah, here it is." She read aloud: "'No footprints found due to rainy conditions the night of the kidnapping. Heavy surf and waves washing ashore. No articles of clothing found.'"

No footprints. Rain. Maria swallowed hard. *So much rain. Water.*

Officer Johnson continued. "A footprint was found in a clump of wet sand on the carpet in front of the toddler's bed inside of her bedroom. Forensic evaluation ascertained it was locally sourced, most likely tracked in by a big boot, perhaps a military boot. The police concluded the footprint left in the wet sand must have come from the dad's military footwear."

"I see," was all that Maria could say. She tried hard to focus on the conversation and not let her feelings take over.

Officer Johnson continued. "Here's another note: 'Elisabeth Collins insists she always made her husband take off his boots before coming into the house. She claims the wet sand spread in the outline of a footprint couldn't have been from one of his boots.'"

Maria closed her eyes and suddenly, her brain formed a long-lost sentence. She heard it clear as day, as if someone were whispering it in her ear—her real mom, her German mom. *"Nein, meine Süße, zieh deine Schuhe aus im Haus,"* she heard her say. Maria's brain automatically translated the sentence. *"No, sweetie, take off your shoes in the house."*

She opened her eyes, the green flecks in the dark-brown center now prominent, almost shiny. "That's right," she said. "My mom always made us take off shoes. Always."

The chief started chewing on his pencil. "What did her dad say to that?"

Officer Johnson rummaged through the files. "He wasn't sure. All he remembered was that he had worn tennis shoes to the laundry facility that night but said it was possible he'd left that mess in front of the kid's bed earlier that day. He did claim he had the habit of taking off his boots at the entrance but wasn't one hundred percent sure he'd done so that night."

"Let me see that picture again," Chief Parlot said, and Officer Johnson handed it to him. He looked it over, then grabbed a magnifying glass to inspect for details. "Yeah, even though it's grainy, I can make out a print, a faint footprint outlined in the wet sand spread across the carpet. Sure looks to me like the print of a boot. Any military boot. Possibly Brad Collins's boot."

"But that's not right," Maria said. "Somehow I know that's not right. Let me see!"

Before anyone could say anything, she had ripped the picture out of Chief Parlot's hand.

Irritated, they all watched her.

"Something about this bothers me," she said.

Her eyes bore through the picture. *Sure looks like a footprint outlined in the clump of wet sand. Like something you'd bring in on your shoes after walking on the beach on a rainy day. Wait. Rainy day?*

She looked up from the picture, her eyes bright green now. "Was it a rainy day?"

"Rainy day?" Agent Anderson repeated Maria's question. "What do you mean?"

"Think about it," Maria said, "if my dad usually took off his boots but forgot to that day, he could've walked in with his boots on after work. And he said he wore tennis shoes when they... you know... when they—"

"—left for the laundry facility," Aaron completed her sentence. "Yes, you're right! The only way this wet bootprint could be from Brad Collins is if it was raining earlier the day of the kidnapping—he only wore his boots earlier in the day, not that night."

Chief Parlot began to thumb through the files like a maniac. "We gotta find a description of the weather that day. Where is it?"

Officer Johnson and Agent Anderson helped him search.

"I found it. Here," Officer Johnson said. "Sounds like it was a regular May Florida day. Sunny, humid, ninety-two degree high. At night, damp, slight rain, then heavier rain. The rain didn't start until about nine thirty p.m."

"Damn," the chief exclaimed. "The rain started right around the time of the disappearance?"

Officer Johnson nodded.

"So the kids are right," Agent Anderson said. "That clump of sand definitely didn't come from the tennis shoes Brad Collins wore that night. Forensics was sure it came from a boot. But when Brad Collins returned home from work that day, even if he didn't take off his boots at the front door like his wife wanted him to, he *couldn't* have made that stain. That stain was wet. *Wet.* It could only be wet if it had rained. So someone tracked in a clump of wet sand. And it wasn't the parents!"

Officer Johnson jumped up. "You're saying the kidnapper wore boots? Military boots?"

The chief grunted, still pacing.

Agent Cooper raised his eyebrows. "So we're looking for someone in the military? Damn."

"This fits with what Maria said when we were at the TLF," Aaron said. "When I recorded her while she was... you know... in that special state. She said she was afraid of bad guys in uniform!"

"Jonathan Sullivan told us the truth. He didn't kidnap her. Someone else did. Someone in the military," Officer Johnson concluded.

"JB," Chief Parlot said. "Sullivan said a guy named JB brought her to him."

Agent Anderson sighed. "It'll be hard to find a JB in the military. That's a common abbreviation. We don't even know what it stands for."

They were all talking over each other, discussing connections, throwing out theories. They went through more files, old pictures scattered across the table. Nobody paid attention to Maria, who was looking at a certain picture, a close-up of a man that had landed right in front of her on the table. She stared at it and without warning, her thoughts were thrown back to a long-ago time. A memory formed in her mind, so clear it was as if she was watching a movie of herself, of little Moana.

She was being carried, swaying from side to side, secured by big, strong arms. She smiled contentedly and sucked on her pacifier.

Daddy. He's taking me somewhere.

But suddenly, she grew uneasy.

Tight. So tight. Arms holding me so tight.

She tried to open her eyes, but it was dark all around her. The air smelled salty and little rain drops fell on her head. She heard the woosh of large waves crashing ashore.

Where am I?

She wiggled but only got tucked in tighter, so tight within those big arms that no longer felt safe. She listened to the footsteps.

Squish, squeak, squish.

Fast, fast, walking fast.

She shuddered.

It's not Daddy. He doesn't walk that fast.

Panic rose in her, but all she heard were the fast footsteps and the squishy squeakiness they made on the ground. *I hate that sound!*

Who is this? Who's carrying me?

She looked up again, tried to see. Her eyes adjusted to the darkness, and in the faint light shining from the porch of the TLF, she made out a uniform. A green, camouflaged uniform.

Like Daddy's. But not Daddy!

She lay sideways in those big, strong, dangerous arms, her face squished against a strong tummy.

Big muscles. Like Daddy.

She looked up to see the man's face. Saw a big chin, a big jaw, almost boxy-looking.

Not like Daddy's.

She realized this guy wasn't wearing a hat.

Daddy says he must wear a hat when outside. A green camo hat.

No hat. Not Daddy.

She saw a strand of hair hanging down, wet from the rain that had grown heavier. This hair was dark as the night, jet-black.

Not like Daddy's.

She was sure now the guy who was carrying her wasn't her Daddy. She had never met him before.

Man in uniform.

Fast, fast, walking fast. Squish, squeak.

He's mad. I know he's mad. Walking fast.

She knew she had to get away from this stranger. She wiggled, then spat out her pacifier and tried to scream, but she was tucked in so tight and deep against him that her screams were muffled. Then suddenly, she was surrounded by wetness.

Rain?

No.... Water! Cold water! Muddy water!

Squish, squeak, squish.

Swish.

Oh no! Cold, muddy, murky water.

Man in uniform with black hair and big jaw. Dragging me deeper into the water.

Swish, swash.

Help! Help me!

She felt her hot tears mix with the cold water around her. She was crying now, and then she swallowed water, a whole mouthful of water.

Mucky, murky water.

No, no, no!

Please help! Help me!

But no one heard her pleas, and everything went black around her. Pitch-black, just like the man's hair.

"Maria?" a voice softly called to her. "Are you okay?"

She opened her eyes and realized she was lying with her head between her arms, elbows on the table, her hands grasping her skull through her hair.

"Are you okay, Maria?" There was that voice again, coming from her right. She lifted her head sideways and saw it was Aaron. Irritated, she just stared at him.

He raised one eyebrow. "Do you have a headache? What's going on?"

"Not sure," she whispered. She lifted her head and laid both arms on the table. Only then did she realize she was grasping something. A picture.

"You looked at that photograph and suddenly started holding your head," Aaron explained, pointing at the picture in her hands.

Maria now studied it. It was a headshot of a man in an FBI windbreaker, smiling into the camera. He had jet-black hair, a big, boxy jaw, and pearly-white teeth.

The picture fell from her hands and, with a scream, she jumped up. Astonished, the whole team watched the picture flutter down onto the table, swirling about until it came to a stop. They looked up at Maria. She was shaking, her arm hairs standing on end. Sweat beaded her forehead.

Aaron was by her side in an instant. "Maria, what is it? What's scaring you?"

With a shaky hand, she pointed at the picture on the table. "Who is that guy? The one in the picture?"

Agent Anderson came over and picked up the photograph. "This guy? That's Agent Borman, the FBI guy who worked your case."

Chief Parlot's eyes narrowed. "Why do you ask?"

"I know him," Maria whispered. "I *know* him. He took me!"

Everyone stared at her. Aaron held her tight, worried she'd collapse any minute.

"Agent Borman?" Agent Cooper said. "Say what?"

Agent Anderson shushed her colleague. "Maria, why do you think that?"

"His jaw. I recognize it."

"His... jaw?"

Maria nodded, breathing hard. "And his hair. Jet-black. Dark like the night. Same as the guy who took me."

Officer Johnson closed her gaping mouth and found words. "But we thought it must be a military man...."

"He wore a camo uniform," Maria said. "I'm sure of it."

Aaron struggled to believe. "You really recognize this guy?"

Maria nodded. "I think so."

Agent Cooper shook his head. "But Sullivan said a guy named JB brought Maria to—"

"Wait a minute! JB?" Agent Anderson interrupted her young colleague again. "What's Agent Borman's first name?"

Officer Johnson looked it up. "James. Agent James Borman."

"James Borman. James Borman! Holy cow," Chief Parlot said. "They're initials. Sullivan gave us initials. Not for a first and middle name, but a first and last name!"

Aaron's eyes widened. "You're saying an *FBI agent* kidnapped Maria from Eglin? The same agent that then worked her case to find her?"

"Damn," was all Agent Cooper could say.

"But are we sure?" Agent Anderson said. "Maria, can you really identify him?"

Maria just stared ahead, breathing heavily.

206

Officer Johnson eyed Maria. "She's going into shock. Now *that's* a classic PTSD flashback. I assume that's a good-enough response to run with this lead?"

The others nodded.

"You gotta fly that guy in," Aaron said. "In cuffs, if necessary. Then we can really identify him. Stuff him in a uniform, see if Maria recognizes him."

"Well, we can't." Chief Parlot sighed. "Unfortunately, he passed away."

"Oh."

"But we *can* put him in a uniform," Agent Anderson said, and smiled, her brown eyes sparkling. She started laughing. "Don't look so confounded, my peeps. Tom here is our resident tech wizard. He can get a picture of Borman and photoshop him wearing a camo uniform that matches Maria's description."

"Wow," Aaron said, still holding on to Maria, who was doing her breathing exercises. Aaron encouraged her, whispering into her ear that she was safe here. Maria started relaxing, her eyes turned hazel again.

Agent Cooper's hands flew across the keyboard, hammering into it. The sound of the hammering keys made Maria snap out of her shock and—just like the others—she watched the young agent work his magic on the computer. Within a few minutes, he was done.

"Ta-da!" Agent Cooper showed off his masterpiece with a goofy grin on his face. It showed FBI Agent James Borman in a camo uniform, his cold blue eyes staring out at them from the screen, his jet-black hair hanging into his face, his big, boxy jaw a wide smile.

"Is that him, Maria?" Chief Parlot asked.

She nodded. "I think so. But I was little. He was holding me. I saw him from below. Looked right up at his chin. I think I was sideways in his arm."

"Oh, no problem," Agent Cooper said. He clicked a few more buttons and made the image spin in 3D. He was able to adjust the view so that it was if someone was lying in the agent's arm.

Maria's eyes widened. "That's. Definitely. Him," she said under quick staccato breaths. "That guy. Carried me. Into the. Water. I'm sure."

Chief Parlot slammed his fist on the table. "Damn it! Agent James Borman is JB? What the heck?"

They all stared at the screen in horror.

"I can't believe it," Chief Parlot said, his face flushed. "A big coup from on high? Why? How? I wonder who else was involved."

CHAPTER 33

"**W**ho else was involved in the tragic kidnapping of Moana Marie Collins? The police are sure Martina Sullivan is innocent, but not so for her ex-husband Jonathan Sullivan. Unfortunately, as our viewers well know, he passed away and can no longer help identify the people whose names the police shared earlier," the news reporter said.

Martina and Jack were watching the news together in the Air Force Inn's lobby, waiting for Maria and Aaron to return. Lieutenant Martinez stood nearby, while Elisabeth and Brad had gone upstairs to their room to be alone.

Who kidnapped her? Jonathan? Really? Why? He doesn't—well, didn't—even like children.

Martina wiped away a tear and focused on the TV screen. All news channels were going nuts over the case of Moana Marie Collins. The kidnapping case. The little toddler who supposedly drowned yet lived.

Martina was deep in thought. *Jonathan didn't like kids. Only money. Always the money. Did he do this for money?*

It didn't take much to convince her. She jumped up and said, "Money! He did it for the money!"

"What?" Jack turned to her. "What are you talking about, Martina?"

"Jonathan would do anything if it meant getting paid well."

"You think he got paid to kidnap Maria?"

Martina nodded. "It's the only explanation."

"You think he was part of this plot involving those other people they mentioned?"

"Sí, possible."

"But where would he befriend people like that?"

Martina shrugged her shoulders. "Don't know. But Jonathan loved to drink. And gamble. Even before he met me, he was always gambling."

"Gambling? Interesting." Jack thought for a while.

Martina focused back on the TV.

"It's still not clear how the little toddler was smuggled off base. There were no witnesses to the crime," the reporter said, then drew closer to the camera. "But after looking deeper into it, really looking at all angles, our news team is convinced the kidnappers must have fled by water. Eglin Air Force Base is surrounded by water after all."

¡Dios mío! Water? Surrounded by water? The base?

Martina jumped up again. "That's why she was always so afraid of water. I bet they tried to drown her!"

"What?" Jack looked at her.

"Maria! When she came to me, she was afraid of water. Especially bathtime. Tried to get her started with swimming lessons, but she freaked out. But then, an exchange student from Germany helped her get over her fear of water. That sweet German girl calmed her down."

Jack stared at Martina.

"And now I know why. She reminded Maria of her mom, Elisabeth! I just figured that out. ¡Dios mío! I raised someone else's child, still can't believe it." Big tears fell from her eyes.

Jack stood up and rubbed her back in comfort. "You didn't know, Martina. You didn't."

She shook her head, then buried it in both hands. "Mija, she's gone through a lot. That poor baby girl. Almost drowned, then spent two months with bad guys."

"I know, Martina, I know. It's a lot. We'll just have to find out who did this. And why. Such a shame.... The Collinses had just moved here."

Martina sobbed. *Wait? What? Just moved here?* She turned to Jack. "They had just moved to Eglin? So they barely knew anyone here?"

Jack nodded. "Yeah, I suppose. Why?"

"¡Dios mío! Someone must not have liked them. Hated them. Everyone keeps saying this was a well-planned kidnapping. But Jonathan, he's not a planner. And not clever enough. Someone else must have planned this for months."

Jack stared at her. "You think someone planned this in advance? If so, they must have known the Collinses would be at this place at this exact time."

Martina's mouth was all dry now. "¡Sí! It was a well-planned kidnapping, no? Well-planned, months in advance. Someone must have known they'd be at the TLF at that time."

"Down to the exact unit they occupied," Jack mumbled. "Oh my gosh. Someone was waiting for this opportunity to hurt the Collinses. Who? Who could hate them that much?"

"¡No sé! But someone important. A big enemy!"

CHAPTER 34

"**A** big enemy—yeah, at least one person in the FBI qualifies as that. But why? Did he act alone, or did he have help within the agency? What do they have to do with the Collinses?" Chief Parlot kept pacing back and forth. "Does Borman have any connection to the Collinses?"

The investigative team collectively shrugged their shoulders.

"I have no idea," Agent Tonya Anderson said, "but I'll call the boss immediately to report this. Corruption within the FBI? Oh man, oh man, oh man. This is crazy and calls for launching an investigation!"

The chief stared at the agent. "Sure, report this. But I'm telling you—*we* will look into this and figure this out! They can do their own investigation into the corrupt Agent Borman, but we will not give up this case!"

Agent Anderson grinned at him. "Relax, my man Isaac. Trust me—it'll take days with this kinda stuff to get all the paperwork done for investigating one of their own. By the time the FBI gets going, we will hopefully have solved this case. I'll just have to report it—but you better believe Tom and I are on your side. Got it?"

The chief nodded and the team went to work. While Agent Anderson stepped out to call the FBI boss, the others kept looking through files, meticulous and alert, and took notes as they went, completely ignoring their guests, Aaron and Maria.

The two of them sat on the couch in the little resting area inside the room, next to the snack table and coffee machine. Aaron stayed with Maria, an arm around her shoulder. She rested her head on his chest and closed her eyes, but her mind kept racing. *I'm exhausted. Mentally exhausted. I just want to go home. This is hard. Don't want to hear talk about enemies.*

But she didn't have the strength to say anything, just sat there on the couch in the police workroom. Agent Anderson stepped back in and got to work as well. It was quiet in the room as everyone worked, aside from the constant hammering of Agent Tom Cooper's fingers on his keyboard.

Maria covered her ears. *His fast typing is giving me a headache.*

Agent Cooper suddenly stopped attacking his keyboard. "Did Chief Billings know Agent Borman?"

"Not before they worked the case together," the chief said. "Why?"

"That makes this interesting then," Agent Cooper said, and waved the team over. Aaron and Maria listened from the couch. "Might not be important, but at least I find it interesting. Billings liked to vacation in Salt Lake City, while Borman enjoyed trips to Destin."

"I don't get it," Officer Johnson said. "Who cares whether someone vacations one place or another?"

"Sally has a point. Any national park fanatic is super interested in Utah. It's quite the place," Agent Anderson said.

"Agreed. Tom, why do you find these trips interesting? What does that have to do with Billings or Borman?" Chief Parlot said.

"Agent Borman was stationed in Utah. At the Salt Lake City FBI field office. Quite a while before he moved on to DC headquarters."

They all thought for a while.

"So, if we put the puzzle pieces together… this means Billings worked here in Niceville around the time Agent Borman visited Destin, Florida, on a frequent basis. But then the chief liked to visit Salt Lake City, where Agent Borman was stationed," Officer Johnson said, and Agent Cooper nodded. "That *is* interesting."

Agent Cooper grinned. "The dates line up. Even more interesting, Chief Billings never returned to Salt Lake City after Borman left there."

"Very interesting," Chief Parlot mumbled. "What about the other way around?"

Agent Cooper attacked his computer keyboard again.

Maria sighed. *Argh, that sound again. What's he doing? I guess finding information. Wonder what sites he's using?* She stood up and walked over to join the group huddled around Agent Cooper's chair. Aaron followed.

"Found it. Borman's last visit to Destin was in May 2003."

"May 2003?" Aaron yelped, and everyone turned to face him except for Agent Cooper.

The young agent went on, "Yes, he took leave from DC until mid-June, but returned early, only a few days into his trip. He checked in to the Sandestin Golf and Beach Resort from May twenty-fifth through May twenty-ninth."

"He left May 29, 2003? Isn't that the day after Maria was kidnapped?" Aaron said.

"Yes, indeed," the chief said.

Officer Johnson was confused. "But wasn't Agent Borman here to work the case?"

"Yep, he sure was," Tom said. "He was called back here only a day later, on May 30, 2003, to work the missing toddler case. With Chief Billings."

"Interesting, very interesting," Agent Anderson said. "We gotta talk to Chief Billings. See if any of this holds up."

"Dang," Aaron said. "If they knew each other before the case, and James Borman is JB—the JB who kidnapped Maria—then it's no wonder they acted the way they did."

Chief Parlot looked at him. "What do you mean, Aaron?"

"Well, I think that Billings–Borman team came to their conclusion about an accidental drowning taking place way too quickly. They dismissed Elisabeth Collins's kidnapping theory, and didn't even take into consideration there is a nearby marina."

"A marina?" Agent Cooper asked.

"Yeah, you know, the base is surrounded by water. It represents a huge security risk. Anyone can just swim onto base to get around the ID checkpoints."

They all stared at Aaron, then Agent Cooper broke into laughter. "Damn, the young guy's good. Ever consider working for the FBI instead of the Air Force?"

Everyone chuckled, except for Maria. She was breathing heavily again, her thoughts racing. *Water. Surrounded by water. Gotta swim, but don't know how.*

She closed her eyes and started talking, slowly. "I was there. In the water. He took me in. He carried me through the rain into the water. Lots of wetness, suddenly, all around. All around."

Aaron put a hand on her shoulder. "It's okay, Maria, it's okay. You're safe here."

But it was too late. Maria had crossed over, was talking with the voice of a grown woman but with toddlerlike mannerisms. "It's wet, so wet. So dark, it's so dark. It's water, water all around me. Some boats, but we're passing them. Not going onto those boats. No, we go into the water. Deeper into the water. Oh no, no, no. I can't breathe. Please, please help me. Water all around, so black. Murky, muddy water. Swallowing it while crying, I swallow so much. It's yucky, so yucky. Can't breathe. I can't see anything. So black. It's so black. It hurts to breathe."

She held her breath for a bit, then kept talking. "But then it doesn't hurt anymore, I'm not cold anymore. I feel warm in the cold, dark, mucky water, so warm as I sink into the blackness. Mama? Daddy? Are you there?"

She collapsed into Aaron's arms as everything went black around her.

When she opened her eyes, there was a hustle and bustle about her, people talking all over each other.

"Jeez, I'll get in trouble again. They told me to get a child trauma specialist involved," she heard an unfamiliar voice say.

"It's okay, Isaac, it's okay," another voice said.

Where am I? Maria looked around and realized she was back on the couch in the police workroom.

"She's awake," she heard Aaron yell. He was sitting at the end of the couch, her head in his lap. He looked down at her. "Hi there, are you okay?"

"Yeah, I'm fine. Why?" She sat up.

"Well, you fainted, my love," Aaron said, and sighed.

"Oh no, I did?"

"Yep, you sure did, girl. Just crashed down. But your fiancé reacted quickly," Agent Anderson said, and smiled at her.

Maria frowned. "Yeah, guess Aaron is used to me fainting by now, unfortunately."

"Yeah, this was probably too much, young lady. Why don't you head home?" the chief said. "Enjoy the rest of your day. You've already helped us a lot. We understand how you got off base—by being carried through the water. Confirms Sullivan's report. And thanks to you, we now know Agent James Borman was most likely JB. That's a big breakthrough."

"Still gotta find Bill and Cliff and a possible fourth guy—Bullet man." Officer Johnson sighed. "Unless Sullivan really was the fourth in that group. Too bad he wasn't sure himself."

They all nodded, then the young officer went on, "It'll be tough to find them. Such common names. Bill, a name so common, everyone knows one. And Cliff. Also common. Not super common, but common enough. Yikes."

"It's okay, Sally, there's still work to do. Let's have Maria and Aaron head home. You kids did enough today." Chief Parlot winked at them. "Me and my team will focus on getting Chief Billings over here."

"Please do. You gotta find out if he was in on it with Borman," Aaron said. He stood up, ready to go.

"Chief... Billings? Another chief?" Maria asked.

Aaron raised his one eyebrow. "Are you sure you're okay? Don't you remember? He's the guy who worked on your case twenty years ago."

Maria turned to Chief Parlot. "Does he still live here?"

"Yep, he retired here. It's his community, his home. He loves it here. So yes, Chief Billings is still in town," Chief Parlot said.

"So maybe I saw him?" Maria blurted out.

"What?" Nobody followed her train of thought.

"Remember, we came in today because I saw a guy in a police uniform at the hospital, a uniform like yours, Chief Parlot. It must've been him—the guy I saw in the hospital."

Agent Anderson reacted quickly. She ran over to the case wall, took Chief Billings's picture off the wall, and returned to Maria. "Is this the guy you saw?"

Maria studied the photo. "I can't say for sure. I only saw his backside. But maybe?"

"But why in the world would Chief Billings show up at the hospital now?" Agent Cooper said. "Shouldn't he be busy fishing or something?"

"To shut Jonathan Sullivan up," Aaron concluded. "You would've needed him to identify all those people he mentioned. The Fearless Four. We know JB was one of them, and maybe Billings is, too? If he was in on it with JB? Either way, it's very convenient that Sullivan can't talk anymore. And somehow, I have a feeling he didn't just drop dead because you interrogated him too harshly."

"That's right, we sure didn't," Agent Anderson said. "But, phew, my man Aaron, you just accused the former chief of not only taking part in Maria's kidnapping, but murdering Sullivan?"

Aaron turned red and looked at his shoes. "I guess. I just have a feeling..."

Maria laughed sharply. "Look at that, Aaron. *You've got a feeling?* I thought you went by evidence and proof only?" She took his hand and squeezed it. He glanced at her and grinned back.

"Speaking of proof," Agent Anderson said, "Maria, you're *sure* you saw someone in a chief's uniform outside Sullivan's hospital door?"

"Yes, I'm sure."

"But she can't be a witness," Officer Johnson blurted out. "They'll question her state of mind."

Maria raised her eyebrows and gave the young police officer a look. *My state of mind? Who the heck does she think she is?*

Before Maria could say anything, the young officer went on. "I'm sorry, no offense, Maria. I know I'm getting ahead of myself, that the investigation just started. But I *know* the courts will jump on your mental fitness given what's been happening to you lately."

Guess she's right? Maria just nodded.

"Sally's correct in that we need to find out more. Make sure Billings really was at the hospital," Chief Parlot said. "Tom, we need you to check the hospital surveillance cameras they have mounted by the entrance around the time of Sullivan's death. See if you can find Billings at the scene."

"Yep, we need to dig deeper into this," Agent Anderson said. "Man, this is getting intense. Can't believe it. We're talking about the former police chief. Chief Billings, man, Billings!"

Billings? Chief Billings? Maria's brain repeated his name in a loop, and suddenly it hit her. "Bill..." she said. "Didn't you say that was one of the names Sullivan gave you?"

The team nodded.

"If James Borman is JB... Billings is Bill."

They all stared at her.

"You just said they all knew each other. And you mentioned earlier these names Sullivan gave you might not be first names. Bill is part of Chief Billings's last name.... Why not go by Bill if you want to cover something up?"

Silence ruled the room. Officer Johnson's mouth was wide open. Maria grinned. *Guess the police officer isn't questioning my state of mind anymore, now is she?*

"If you're right, and an FBI agent and police chief conspired to cover up the kidnapping… this is huge. A big deal!" Chief Parlot swallowed hard. "Tom, I need you to work your magic. Find out whether you can locate Billings's car around the hospital the past few days. Then, look back to 2003 and see if he or Borman were into gambling. Sullivan said he met them in Vegas. Find credit card statements, anything that fits the timeline."

The young agent sat down in his chair and turned toward his laptop. "I can certainly do that. I'm on it."

"Okay, great, thanks. Sally, I need you and your people skills. Make contact with Billings. Have him come in. Make him think it's just to question him about his work on the former case. Don't let him know he's a suspect. I need him to come in unperturbed."

"Got it, Chief."

"Tonya, you and I will talk to the coroner at the hospital. We need to be sure Sullivan didn't die of random heart failure, that we do actually have a murder on our hands here."

She nodded and opened the door. "Let's go, my man."

"And I need you, Aaron and Maria… to go home and enjoy the rest of your day. Get some dinner, do something fun. You've helped a lot—but now it's time for the police and FBI to take over. We'll keep you posted. Come with me. I'll arrange an escort to get you back to base and shield you from reporters."

"Sounds good," Aaron said. He waved at Officer Johnson and Agent Cooper, then walked out of the door Agent Anderson held open.

Maria followed, deep in thought. *Chief Billings. One of the bad guys? But I don't remember him at all. What did he have to do with my kidnapping? Either way, we need to find out what he did. They will, I trust them. Time to go now, it's getting late. Time to leave the police station.*

CHAPTER 35

The police station was quiet when the former chief, Chief Jim Billings, finally arrived. Chief Parlot greeted his former boss and was deep in thought when he walked down the hallway with him into one of the interrogation rooms.

He'll pay for this. For whatever shady dealings he's done. Never liked him. Chief Parlot watched his former boss plop down in one of the chairs, a grin on his face. *Cocky guy. Always was.*

"So, you wanted to talk to me about the old case?" Jim Billings looked first at Chief Parlot, then eyed the rest of the team.

"Yes, Chief Billings, we do," Sally said.

Billings turned to her. "This young chicken is helping out with your investigation?"

Tom's mouth fell open. Sally was stunned. "Excuse me?"

Chief Parlot's face reddened in anger. "Yes, sir, she's a part of our team leading the investigation. Emphasis on *team*. You know, *teamwork*… always better than flying solo. And that doesn't even take into account how very bright Officer Johnson is, an excellent judge of character."

"You don't say, Isaac." Jim Billings laughed.

"Well, she sure *is* an excellent judge of character. So, with all due respect, I'd be careful if I were you. Just saying."

Tonya grinned as Jim Billings stared at his former employee.

"So, can we get started?" Chief Parlot said.

"Sure. Whatever."

"Well, let's start with your rights. You know that everything you say—"

"Jeez, Isaac, I know my rights. Everything I say can and will be used against me in the court of law, blah, blah, blah…. Don't forget, *I* was the chief of this police station for decades!"

"How can anyone forget?" Chief Parlot mumbled.

"Chief Billings, can you please tell us everything you remember about working the case back then," Tonya said.

"It's all in the files."

"Yes, we know. We've read them. So I need to ask you again, what do you recall? Come on, work with me here."

"Fine, I'll tell you what I remember." Jim Billings reiterated everything the new team had read in the files, gave the same explanations, the same conclusions.

"Why didn't you look into the marina more?" Tonya asked.

"What marina? You're talking about a suspect fleeing by boat? There was no boat missing, no sign of a boat even being tied to the dock. The other residents by the water said it was a quiet, rainy night. No boats passed by."

Sally looked at him. "Other residents? You mean in the TLFs?"

"Yes, and the people who live along the shore of the bay. All along the route a boat intruding in Eglin AFB waters would need to go. No one heard a peep."

"Who didn't, exactly?" Tonya asked again.

"Jeez, woman, I just told you! The local residents."

"Her name is Agent Anderson, not *woman*," Chief Parlot said, his face red, his lips pressed together, his hands in a fist. He slammed one onto the table. "Show some respect."

"Right, Isaac, respect. Well, I expect the same from all of you. I'm the former chief, and I worked hard on this case."

"Obviously not hard enough," Officer Johnson mumbled loud enough for the room to hear.

"What was that?" Jim Billings looked at her, his eyebrows raised.

"Oh, Chief Billings, I'm just saying you seem to have overlooked something," she said with a smile. "Obviously. The girl lived."

Jim Billings's face turned red with anger. "Nobody knew that back then. All signs pointed to a drowning. If you doubt me, just ask your lady Fed friend here. The Feds were the ones who took over the case. Blame them. Like that loser guy Borman. Heard he killed himself. And it's no wonder..."

The investigative team stared at the former chief in shock.

Tom swallowed hard and said, "Agent Borman was not a loser. He may have made some questionable choices, but he was a good agent."

Jim Billings laughed. "Yeah right. A good agent. Obsessed with porn, I heard. No wonder he got suspended. Didn't see a way out in the end."

Agent Borman was suspended? Over possession of porn? Chief Parlot had to try hard to keep his mouth closed. He glanced at Tonya and Tom. Both agents showed no emotion.

"I wouldn't be surprised if he fawned over that little girl," Jim Billings said, and tapped his finger on the desk, pointing to the picture of the missing toddler.

Sally stared at him, then turned to Chief Parlot. She looked pale, a bit greenish. He knew what she was thinking. *A cute little toddler.* He saw the nausea take her quickly.

"Excuse me," she said, and left the room hastily.

Poor Sally. But I don't think that's right. Not according to Sullivan. Not even sure why Billings brought it up. Misdirection? He focused on his former boss again.

"He was a little too confident back then," Jim Billings went on. "Quickly came to the conclusion the little one had just wandered out of the TLF. In his defense, I do have to say, everything did point in that direction."

"Mr. Billings," Tonya said. "These accusations against Agent Borman are new. You didn't say a word back then."

"No. It just came to me this very minute as I thought back on it."

"I see," Tonya said. "How do you even know he got suspended over graphic material? When did you learn about this? You kept up with him after the case?"

Jim Billings shook his head quickly.

The chief raised his eyebrows. *Maybe a little too quickly.*

"Nope, didn't know the guy. First time I ever saw him was the day he came to town and took over the case. I'm just throwing out ideas here; as you said yourselves, we might have overlooked something back then. Obviously, the girl is alive."

"I see," Tonya said. "I'm just wondering why you say the Feds took over the case."

"They did. Just ask our friend Isaac here. Right, Isaac?"

"Well, yeah, sure, I remember the day Agent Borman came in. It was a bit shocking," Parlot said.

Billings grinned. "See?"

Chief Parlot rose to his feet. "Well, I clearly remember *you*, Chief Billings, introducing me as the officer who was working with you on that case 'for now.' Yeah, you emphasized *for now*, and Borman laughed, then repeated, 'For now.' I remember he then told me he was Agent Borman and would be working the case exclusively *with you*, Billings, from that point forward. Note that my colleagues' puzzled expressions are because Borman never said he was there to 'take over'—that would go outside his mandate. Then, both of you just left me standing there, didn't invite me to join you."

Billings made a pouty face. "Aw, poor little Isaac, no one wanted to play with you. But I assure you, it was all Borman's idea."

"Was it?" Isaac raised his eyebrows. "And you're sure you'd never seen him before that case?"

"Yes, absolutely sure. Already told you everything I know about the case back then. I think you need to look into Agent Borman more.

He was the driving force behind wrapping up the case. He's the guy who determined it was an accidental drowning. I knew him from working the case together and that's it."

"I see, I see," Tonya said, then slid a printout covered with dates over to him. "Well, somehow you and Borman ended up in the same place together quite often back in the day. You went to Utah; he visited Destin a lot."

Billings sat up taller in his chair and stared at the printout, then shrugged his shoulders. "So what? I love Utah. Love hiking and visiting the national parks. And Destin is quite the tourist town. You'd begrudge a man for vacationing in Florida of all places? This proves nothing. I'm telling you, I didn't know Borman before the case!"

"And you didn't know... JB?"

"No, I didn't," Billings said and shifted in his seat, then shook his head quickly.

Chief Parlot grinned. *Got you now, Billings. You didn't even ask us who JB is.* He looked over and saw Tonya grinning as well.

"Well, we have credit card statements that show the two of you were at the same venues at the same time."

Billings leaned back in his chair, his eyes darting back and forth between Tonya and Chief Parlot. He cleared his throat. "What? That's ridiculous. That was years ago. What does this even have to do with the case?"

"Well, you tell us, Bill," Tonya said.

Isaac grinned and watched his former boss turn pale now. *Yeah, we got you sweating now, Billings, don't we?*

He continued, "Sullivan told us he met a group of guys while gambling in Vegas back in 2003. One of them went by JB. Another called himself Bill. Sullivan lost badly that night, wound up owing them money, couldn't pay his debt. So, they made him a deal: one small favor, and everything would be forgiven. That small favor involved getting rid of something. Turned out to be a small child. Any of this ringing any bells?"

Jim Billings shook his head.

"It doesn't?"

He shook his head again.

"But you and your friend JB *were* pretty involved, weren't you, Bill?"

"I'm not Bill. My name is Jim," Billings said.

Tonya grinned and pulled out another picture, a copy of a grainy high school yearbook. "Oh yeah, Billings. Your name *is* Jim. Indeed."

Billings nodded. "Exactly. I'm Jim."

Tonya continued, "But you thought there were too many Jims in your high school, didn't you? So, you started going by Bill. Says so right here in your old yearbook. We even talked to a former classmate who confirmed this."

Billings now stared at her.

Chief Parlot took over. "Well, Jim Billings, a.k.a. Bill, looks like you and your friend James Borman, a.k.a. JB, were thick as thieves in all of this, weren't you? No wonder both of you came to the conclusions you did. Very convenient way to cover up your crime, wasn't it?"

Chief Billings swallowed. His wide eyes wandered back and forth between his former colleague and the FBI agent.

There we go. The cracks are starting to show. Just wait until we show you what else we have up our sleeves. Chief Parlot grinned, then nodded at Tonya.

That was her cue. "Jim Billings, we need to talk to you about Sullivan's death."

He raised his eyebrows. "Sullivan's death? You mean… Jonathan Sullivan? Your primary suspect thanks to recent events?"

"Yeah, that guy," Chief Parlot said. "Do you know him from somewhere?"

"Me? No, definitely not."

Chief Parlot tossed other printouts his way. "How do you explain, then, that you and Sullivan were at the same casino in Las Vegas in 2003?"

Billings laughed. "Same casino? You're saying I met that clown in a casino in Vegas? Do you know how big the casinos there are? Tens of thousands of people visit every day. You're saying I was there the same time as Sullivan? That doesn't prove anything. Sure, I visit Vegas time to time. But I don't know a Jonathan Sullivan."

"I see, you're saying you don't know him."

Billings nodded. "You're damn right I don't know him! Not from a casino or anywhere!"

"I understand. But why were you interested in visiting him, then?"

"What are you on about, Isaac?"

Tonya stood up and started pacing back and forth, her eyes always on Chief Billings. "Well, my man Isaac here is talking about the visits you paid our main suspect in the hospital."

"What?"

"Yeah, on the day he died. Isn't that ironic?"

"I have no idea what you're talking about. I didn't visit him. Don't even know the guy."

"You don't?" Tonya stopped pacing and nodded at Chief Parlot.

"Well, then, Jim Billings," he said, "if you don't know him, why were you at the hospital?" He slid over a grainy printout. A zoomed-in photo of a car parked in a large parking lot. "Your car. It was at the hospital. This morning."

Now Tonya slid over another picture. "Surveillance camera caught you leaving the hospital right after Jonathan Sullivan died."

Billings looked at them both, then at the pictures. He shifted in his seat, then laughed. "Well, I was just there out of curiosity. You know, it used to be my case."

"It sure was, wasn't it?" Tonya pointed at his form in the still image taken from the surveillance camera. "And you wore your old police chief uniform just because... you were curious? Perhaps feeling a little nostalgic?"

"Well, you know... I like putting it on and... wanted to get some information on how the investigation was going. Out of curiosity."

"I see. And that's why you talked to the guard at Sullivan's door? Officer Miller?"

Chief Billings nodded. "Yeah. You know, he used to work for me and—"

"He did, we know. We already talked to him," Chief Parlot said, and smiled. "Sounds like you were being really supportive of him. Helped him out by encouraging him to get a coffee."

Billings cleared his throat. "He was working a long shift... I figured he needed it."

Tonya eyed him. "How *kind* of you."

Billings grinned through thin lips. "Yeah, that's me. Always like to lend a hand."

"So, *Jimmy*," Chief Parlot said with a grin. *He always hated it when folks used that nickname around the station.* "If you wanted to help out, why didn't you just bring Officer Miller a cup of coffee instead of inviting him to leave his post and get it himself?"

Billings stared at Parlot. "Well, he'd been sitting a long time. Wanted to stretch his legs a little."

"Did he?" Tonya looked at him. "According to him, *you* were the one that encouraged him to go."

Billings laughed. "What a load of crock!"

"Well, either way, it puts you at Sullivan's door exactly when he suffocated on his own pillow."

Billings stared at his former colleague.

"So, Chief, that makes *you* our main suspect in the murder of Jonathan Sullivan."

They saw him swallow. His face turned ashen. "You s-said... murder?"

Tonya and Isaac nodded. "Yes, *murder*. How else would he suffocate on a pillow while lying on his back?"

Billings shrugged his shoulders; his face regained its color. "I know this game. Sounds to me like you're fishing here, boy. You don't got proof, *real* proof, that Sullivan was murdered, do you, Isaac?"

God, I hate him. He's such a smug person. But guess what, Jimmy, you're going down.

"The coroner confirmed an hour ago that Jonathan Sullivan died by asphyxiation. He suffocated. On his own pillow. They found fibers from his hospital pillow in his lungs and mouth."

"That doesn't prove someone killed him," Chief Billings croaked.

Chief Parlot would have laughed if the subject weren't so grim. "Of course it does. To suffocate a person, it takes a few minutes of pressing a pillow against their face to block their breathing. As you damn well know, Chief, you can't kill yourself that way; anyone who tried would pass out and start breathing again long before they experienced any real danger. No, Sullivan was murdered."

"But—"

"We have two witnesses pegging you at Sullivan's door. Not a good look, Chief Billings, not a good look," Tonya said, and made a sad face.

Jim Billings stared at her, sweat beading his forehead. "*Two* witnesses?"

Everyone nodded.

Parlot saw Billings swallow hard. He grinned. "Jim Billings, you are under arrest for the kidnapping of Moana Marie Collins and the murder of Jonathan Sullivan. You have the right to remain silent—"

Billings was as pale as a ghost. "I want a lawyer."

"Yeah, good idea, Bill, good idea," Tonya said. "We can't wait to hear how you'll get out of this one."

Billings flinched.

Chief Parlot saw it. "You'll be punished, Billings. I'll personally make sure of that. And your friends as well. You're all going down!"

CHAPTER 36

"**Y**ou're down with it? Really, you sure, Maria?" Aaron nodded toward the noisy entrance to Eglin's bowling alley. "Are you sure it won't be too much to handle? You do have a slight concussion."

"Yeah, I'm sure. It's because of that concussion we can't watch TV or go to the movies. I wanna do something fun, since... you know... since... it's my actual birthday today. And I really need something to take my mind off everything."

Aaron nodded and let go of her hand, then held the door open for Martina, who was clutching her purse.

"Vamos, Martina," he said playfully, encouraging her onward.

"¡Gracias, mijo! Thanks, Aaron."

He laughed. "I understood what you said, Martina. You don't need to translate the easy stuff for me."

She gave him a brief smile. "Okay, mijo, okay. Thanks."

Aaron let go of the door after Lieutenant Martinez, who was escorting Martina, passed through. She stopped walking and hugged her purse tightly. Aaron walked over to her and linked arms with her. "It's okay, don't be nervous. There's nothing to fear. We all believe you're innocent."

"All of you?" She glanced up at Aaron, sadness blanketing her big, brown eyes.

"Well, most of us. I don't know about Elisabeth Collins, but—"

"She hates me. Will hate me forever. And I can't even blame her for it." A tear rolled down Martina's nose.

"It's a complicated situation, I know. But Maria insisted on inviting everyone here for her birthday. Just stick with me and Dad. And who knows, maybe Mr. Markas is a good guy to chat with tonight? He already grabbed a lane over there." Aaron pointed at a guy in a suit.

"Who is he again?" Martina asked.

"Drew Markas. He's Brad Collins's best friend and colleague. He's here on a business trip with Brad, was at the restaurant when Maria found her... you know, her—"

"—parents." Martina finished Aaron's sentence, and sighed. They saw Maria shake Drew Markas's hand. He looked uncomfortable.

"See, we're not the only ones who feel awkward around here," Aaron said, and grinned at Martina. "And look over there."

Aaron pointed to a tall middle-aged woman with light-brown hair who was shaking Maria's hand now. She looked unsure of what to do and her already sunburnt face turned even more red. "Looks like Elisabeth's friend Sarah seems equally uncomfortable."

Martina stopped walking. "Sarah? A friend of Elisabeth? She's here too? Where did she come from?"

"She's from Germany also and here in Florida with Elisabeth on vacation. Sarah was at the restaurant, too, when they all met. She's staying at a resort in Destin, but I guess Elisabeth invited her to come tonight to celebrate Maria's birthday," Aaron explained.

"I see," Martina said, her lip quivering. "Her friend. Elisabeth's friend. ¡Dios mío! She probably hates me, too." She sighed, tears welling in her eyes.

"Oh, Martina. I know this will be hard. But come on, it'll be fine. We'll make the best of it. For Maria."

Martina took a deep breath in, then nodded. "You're right, Aaron. Fine. ¡Vamos! Let's do this together. No matter how strange. Let's do this for Maria, our mija."

Aaron smiled at her and they walked over to join the group idling near one of the bowling lanes.

"This was a great idea, Aaron," Brad told him, and put a hand on his shoulder. "Just look at the girls. Who knew they would all get along so well?"

Aaron and Brad were watching Maria, Elisabeth, Martina, and Sarah cutting up with one another. It was Martina's turn, and she awkwardly tried to throw the bowling ball down the lane, but it dropped out of her hand early, hit the floor with a loud *bang*, then rolled in a zig-zag motion right into the gutter.

"¡Naguará! Another zero!"

Sarah, Elisabeth, and Maria laughed hard together, holding their bellies.

"She's worse than both of you," Maria told Elisabeth and Sarah and kept laughing. Then, she called over to Martina, "You've gotta hold onto the ball longer, Mamá. Otherwise, you'll dent the poor floors."

"Nonsense. Who cares about the floors? It hurt my hand! These balls, so heavy," Martina yelled back. She took her second turn. The ball slipped out of her hand again, but this time while she was swinging her arm backward, and landed right on the floor behind her.

The women burst into even more laughter.

"That's worse than a zero! It didn't even make it into the lane," Elisabeth laughed, then turned to Martina. "Here, let me show you the German way."

"Oh ja, the German way. Good idea, Elisabeth," Sarah said and clapped her hands. "That will be easier. We call it *kegeln*."

"Exactly," Elisabeth said and picked up a bowling ball with both hands. "Forget those stupid finger holes. Just grab the ball like this."

With both hands firmly around the ball, Elisabeth walked down the bowling lane and positioned herself at the end of it. She stood with both legs apart, the ball between them and used her hands to roll it down the lane.

Even Lieutenant Martinez, who still seemed uncomfortable as he stood at attention behind the seats Aaron and Brad occupied, broke into a chuckle at the unorthodox technique. The men watched as Elisabeth's bowling ball slowly rolled down the lane before tipping into the gutter.

"You still got a zero," Martina said and grinned at Elisabeth.

"I know, I can't believe it. Another zero!"

"Gutter, it's called a *gutter*, ladies," Brad called over to them. "You're throwing gutter balls."

"Who cares what it's called? We just can't hit any of the pins." Maria laughed.

"We're pitiful," Martina agreed. "But let's try Elisabeth's way. The German way."

"Yes, try it on your next turn, Martina," Elisabeth said with a smile.

"I wanna try it, too," Maria said.

"Yes, we all should play the German way," Sarah agreed. They all nodded.

Maria stood next to Elisabeth. She smiled at her. "This is fun. Thanks for coming and hanging out with everyone."

"Of course, mein Engel," Elisabeth said and put an arm around her. They both stood there in a half-embrace. Maria squeezed her, then walked over to pick up her bowling ball and started bowling the German way.

She jumped into the air on the second try. "I hit one! I knocked it over! Wow!"

They all high-fived each other, then it was Sarah's turn.

"Yeah, this really was a great idea," Aaron said to Brad. "It's amazing to see them all talking and laughing with one another. Been an emotional day, hasn't it?"

Brad nodded.

"Well, sir, I wish I could take credit for this idea, but it was all Maria's. She wanted to celebrate her birthday with both of you and Martina, and thought a game like this would help everyone get their minds off recent events. She was right. It's nice to let loose and chat without silently staring at each other over the dinner table."

Brad laughed. "I would have fancied dinner, but greasy pizza and Tater Tots will have to do. I'd rather have those than good food and awkward conversation. Maria was right. Much better to sweat a little."

Aaron nodded. "Looks like my dad and your friend are very much into their game. They're really going at it."

Brad smirked. "No kidding. Didn't even wait for us before they got started. But I guess Drew is too competitive. Can't believe your dad beat him that first round. Nobody ever does."

Aaron grinned. "Well, my dad loves bowling. No one ever beats him."

They watched the guys for a while. They were silently playing with no downtime, each hitting spares and strikes. They were in the zone.

"Well, guess we get to eat more junk food and just watch, huh?"

"Yeah, let's chill and enjoy," Brad agreed. He turned to Lieutenant Martinez. "Please, Lieutenant, come join us. There's more than enough pizza here, and you need to eat something, too. Come on, sit down."

Pablo Martinez cleared his throat. "Okay, sir, thank you. Appreciate it, General."

"Sure, come on, sit!" Brad pointed to the seat next to him and the lieutenant finally sat down.

"I'm so thirsty," Maria said as she came over to the table where Aaron, Brad, and Lieutenant Martinez were sitting. She grabbed her glass of water and gulped it down in big sips. "This game is hard. Really works up a sweat."

Aaron laughed. "Oh, yeah? From what? Throwing gutters?"

Brad smirked.

"Haha, very funny, guys, very funny. And yes, it *is* hard nailing zeros every time."

"*Gutters*," Brad and Aaron corrected her at the same time.

Maria rolled her eyes. "Whatever!" She took another sip of water. "Why aren't you guys playing?"

They pointed at Jack and Drew, who were still focused on their game, silently throwing one fast ball after another.

"Those guys are way too competitive," Brad said.

"Too competitive? Aw, is the poor wittle general scared?"

Lieutenant Martinez almost choked on his pizza and Aaron's mouth fell open at Maria's childish remark. But Brad just smirked, amused, his eyes shining brightly.

"You're just like your mother. Always teasing me. More effective now than you were as a two-year-old." He grinned, and Maria smiled back at him.

I could get used to this. Having a dad around. She turned around and saw Sarah, Elisabeth, and Martina laughing together over another gutter ball. *Even having two moms.*

An idea came to her. Maria beckoned for Martina and Elisabeth. They looked at each other, then came over, Sarah in tow.

"What is it, mija?" Martina wanted to know.

"I think I made up my mind."

"About what?" Elisabeth asked.

"About what to call both of you." She pointed at the two moms. Both their smiles slowly faded. Sarah quickly moved to the side and sat down next to Aaron and Brad.

They all listened to Maria. "Well, 'Mamá' and 'Mama' aren't going to work. The Spanish and German words are just too close. But I don't want to ignore the fact that you're both my mom. One by birth, the other because she raised me."

Both Martina and Elisabeth got quiet and stared at the floor.

"I know this is hard, but I want to honor you. Both of you. Because you both mean so much to me. So, I would like to stick to Mamá for Martina, and I would like to call you"—she pointed at Elisabeth—"Mom!"

Martina glanced at Elisabeth, who was staring at Maria.

Maria continued, "I think 'Mom' makes the most sense because I've forgotten a lot of my German—well, most of my German, I suppose—and mostly speak in English with you. And I think 'Mom' is good because I'd like to call this guy over here"—she now pointed at Brad—"Dad. So, you'd be 'Mom and Dad.' Is that okay?"

Shyly, Maria glanced at Elisabeth, then at Brad. He was smiling a wide smile; Elisabeth looked stunned. "Are you okay with that, Mom?"

Suddenly, Elisabeth rushed over and gave Maria a big hug. "Of course, mein Engel, of course. 'Mom' is fantastic." She started crying. "My baby girl, my grown-up girl, my daughter. I love you. Hab dich lieb."

Maria smiled at her. "Hab dich auch lieb, Mom!"

Suddenly, Martina started sobbing. "I… I… am so, *so* sorry. Look at you both. ¡Dios mío! You're mother and daughter. Just the two of you. I don't deserve to be called Mamá, I really don't. Elisabeth, she's your daughter, just yours. I stole all those years from you! I did! I'm a bad person! I raised your daughter instead of you. You must have been so lost, so broken after losing her… I'm so, so sorry. I was stupid. I should've called the police."

Elisabeth turned to Martina, the small, little round woman with the big brown eyes. Tears streamed down her friendly face. Despite what she had said, she herself was the picture of a woman lost and broken.

The sight of her almost broke Maria's heart. She was just about to say something when Elisabeth said, "But you didn't know."

"I should have known. I'm so, so sorry. You must hate me, will hate me forever. Like you said earlier. And I will understand why. I raised your child. The child you should've raised." Martina sobbed.

A single tear rolled down Elisabeth's face. "You're right, Martina. At first, I couldn't stand to look at the woman who kept my daughter these past twenty years. Twenty long, agonizing years. That whole time I wasn't able to think, do, even feel anything. I was numb, had forgotten how to live. I'd lost both my daughter and my husband, lost my life, and the whole time you were loving, cuddling, laughing with *my* daughter. With the daughter I missed so terribly."

Martina buried her face in her hands. Her head hung low as tears streamed through her fingers. "I'm so very, very sorry. I really am. I'm sorry. It's horrible. It must have been so hard."

Elisabeth nodded. "Yes, it was. I cried for her every day. For twenty years."

"Yes, she cried every day," Sarah said, tears in her eyes as well.

"Yeah, I did," Elisabeth continued. "And in the end, I convinced myself that she was dead, that I had lost her forever. But look at her."

She gently touched Martina's arm and pointed at Maria. Martina looked up, her face covered in tears, her mascara smeared.

"Just *look* at her. She's alive. And she's well. She's smart, she's witty, well-socialized, well-educated. All because of *you*."

Martina stared up at Elisabeth, her tears suddenly dried up. "¿Qué?"

"She became the phenomenal young woman she is *because of you*, Martina. Because you took her in and loved her. Not knowing the truth about where she came from, whom she belonged to. You never meant any harm raising her. You did so out of love. You were convinced she was Jonathan's daughter yet loved her all the same. You did the right thing. You took her in and raised her to become this wonderful young lady. You kept her safe and—"

"But she's *your* daughter," Martina interrupted her. "Yours!"

Elisabeth shook her head. "Not so. She loves you. I know that."

"But it must be so horrible for you. It must be so hard. Knowing this pains me.... I understand what I need to do. If you want me to get out of her life—"

"No, Mamá!" Maria cried out, tears streaming down her face as well.

"Maria, mija, you found your real mom now. I can't stand in her way. I can't take more time away from the two of you. I just can't. Tonight was fun, but I must go now. She hates me, and I understand." Martina started sobbing again.

Maria turned to Elisabeth, who was crying now, too.

Elisabeth took a deep breath in, then reached out and held Martina tight. "I know you're sorry. But you didn't know. You couldn't have. It wasn't your fault."

Martina's forehead was wrinkled in sorrow. "¿Qué?"

"I don't hate you, Martina," Elisabeth whispered. "I forgive you."

Through her tears, Martina stared up at Elisabeth. "¡Dios mío! You forgive me?"

Elisabeth cried harder, but nodded. "I do. Thank you for keeping her safe!"

Martina broke out into violent sobs. "Thank you, thank you, thank you for forgiving me. It means the world to me!"

The women looked at each other through their tears then hugged each other fiercely, bawled together right there in the bowling alley.

Maria threw her hands over her mouth. *I can't believe it. My two moms. They made peace with each other! This is just amazing. I won't have to choose who to be with, who to love. I can love them both.*

She threw her arms around both of them and they all cried together. "I love you both, Mom and Mamá!"

"Cheers to a new start and a new life together," Brad announced, and the whole group toasted with their beer in plastic cups.

"Hear, hear," Drew said, and winked, then took a big sip of his beer.

"Salud," Martina said, and made sure to cling the plastic glasses with everyone.

"Prost," Sarah yelled, and they all clanged cups again.

"Yes, prost, cheers, salud," Elisabeth said and raised her cup. "To all of us!"

Brad had the biggest smile of them all. "To my two girls!"

"To my new crazy family-in-law," Aaron grinned. "And hope I won't have to learn Spanish *and* German now."

Jack laughed. "To all of us, especially our beautiful, healthy Maria, who fought off her attacker and managed to find not only her family, but identify her kidnapper. Soon, we'll bring everyone involved to justice!"

"Hear, hear," Drew said again, and took another big gulp of his beer, then clanged his cup so hard against Maria's that her water spilled.

"Oh no," she said, as she watched the water drench the beautiful, shiny light-tan floor of the bowling alley.

"Don't worry, Maria, it's just water. I mean, that *is* water, isn't it? You didn't sneak some beer, did you? Remember, you're only supposed to have water because of your concussion."

"Of course I remembered, Aaron. Duh!" She rolled her eyes. "But that spill still needs to get cleaned up or someone might slip on it."

She grabbed a napkin then bent down to wipe up the mess. She let the napkin lie there, soaking up all the water, then gently wiped the fancy wooden floor.

The very shiny wooden floor.

The freshly polished wooden floor.

She stared at it.

Is it moving? Is the floor moving? Oh yeah, it's moving. Definitely moving. Swaying back and forth.

Her head was hurting. She tried to shake the feeling off as she stared at the shiny wooden floor. A bright light appeared in front of her eyes and suddenly, she felt herself being transported back to a long-forgotten time. A time when she was staring at a fancy light-tan wooden floor.

CHAPTER 37

A fancy light-tan wooden floor was all she could see. Through the small hole. A corner left uncovered. A prick of light. Everything else around her was dark, so very dark.

Always dark.

She was having a hard time breathing. She couldn't open her mouth.

I hate this. I want to open my mouth, open it and say something. Or eat something. Drink something. Open my mouth to suck my thumb. Since I don't have Schnulli.

Schnulli. I still remember you. It's been so long. So long.

Mama and Daddy.

Are you still there? Do you have Schnulli?

She stared through the hole and saw it again.

Light coming through, a few rays. Dampened light, slight light.

That's right. There's light. All around me. But can't see it. I'm under a fuzzy, black blanket.

The light still shone through.

Wish I could move the blanket away. Can't reach it.

Can't move my arms. Or legs. Or mouth. Can't move anything. I feel stuck. Stuck on some metal poles. Stuck with something sticky. I'm all stuck, stuck in this dark place.

She looked around again. The blanket wasn't over her; it was over a cage.

My cage. Smells bad in here.

Oh yeah, that's my fault. My diaper is too full.

She had never liked diaper changes, but now she longed for one. For when Mama would lift her up onto that beautiful table with the mobile of colorful fish. Then Mama would gently wipe her bottom. Put a new diaper on. "All fresh, all nice," she'd say.

But it hasn't happened in so long. Can barely remember the last time. So here I am, in the dark, with a stinky diaper on. Under a blanket in this strange box. Hello?

She looked around again and saw the big metal poles. Her feet and hands were tied to them. With that sticky something. Something sticky but strong. So strong she couldn't move. Her sides felt sore, blistery almost.

And her diaper was leaking.

No, focus on the light. The light in the darkness.

Then there were the voices. She heard them sometimes. *Two bad guys.*

There's the one who sometimes talks to me, gently. But other times he's mean. It hurts when he rips off the thing covering my mouth. Hurts oh so bad.

But then he's nice again and gives me water.

She longed for water. And food. She longed to eat.

He gives me food, sometimes. Bread or something. Just a small piece. It's good. It was bad at first, not very tasty, but now it's good. I like it. I want it. Want more.

The guys were yelling now.

Oh no! I don't like the other guy. The curly-haired blonde one. Hair like sand on the beach. He's worse than the grey-eyed blonde one.

She thought about it. *I'm scared of the curly-haired blonde one even though he never really does anything. Except yell at the other guy. The guy who gives me food.*

"What's that smell? Yikes, it stinks in here," she heard.

"It's her."

"That thing? What the fuck? Why? What'd she do?"

The curly-haired blonde one sounded very upset. She listened closely, tried to see through the blanket but couldn't. All she could do was listen. She had learned to listen silently.

Any squeak from me freaks them out. Makes them readjust the thing over my mouth, the sticky thing. That hurts! Better not make a peep.

Just want them to leave me alone. Alone in the darkness.

"Guess she had to use the bathroom," she heard the grey-eyed blonde one say.

"The bathroom? What the fuck you talking about?"

"You know. She pooped, I guess. Isn't that what toddlers do?"

"What the heck? That thing is stinking up my whole boat. It's yucky! Clean it!"

"Me?"

"Yes, of course you."

"How? Do you have a new diaper for her?"

There was laughter. Evil laughter. It made her shiver. "Diapers? What the heck? Why would there be diapers on this ship?"

"But, but…"

"You clean up that poop or whatever mess this thing makes, or *you get rid of her.* Got it?"

Silence for a bit.

"Yes, you got it? Good, very good! So, clean it up. Now. Do it however you want. I don't care. Hose her down if you have to."

Hose… down? What does that mean?

She remembered "hose." It was a weird word. *Mama has one for gardening. It sprays water on the pretty flowers. Sometimes, Mama lets me use it. With her help, usually.*

She thought back to the happy times. Happy times with food. With new diapers. With love. Tears ran down her face. She didn't know why.

241

Am I sad? Yeah, maybe I'm sad.

She made sure to be very quiet, though. She had to be quiet to be left alone.

If I'm not quiet, they'll slap me. Or do the thing to my mouth.

Once, one of them had made her stop whining by wrapping his hands around her neck and squeezing it tight.

It didn't feel good. It was hard to breathe. Don't want to feel like that ever again. Felt really, really bad. Really, really scary!

Without warning, the blanket above her disappeared. She squinted against the sudden light.

And there was the guy, holding something.

What's that long thing with the opening? Looks like an open mouth. Oh, wait, that's a hose, isn't it? But why? No flowers here to spray with water.

And before she knew it, she was the flower.

Freezing cold water, hard water. It was so hard, she squeaked when it hit her. Her eyes widened in fear as her body got soaked.

With the hose still running, her little cage opened up and rough hands reached in to rip off her diaper. The water ran over her naked bottom and she whimpered.

Doesn't feel good. Too much water. Too hard.

Then she saw a broom.

A broom? For cleaning? Cleaning what?

And before she knew it, she got scrubbed with it. The bristles hurt her. She started crying. She looked at him, eyes wide open.

"Oh, don't do that! Don't look at me!"

But she did, looked straight at him. Whimpering.

He stopped brushing with the broom, and she stopped crying.

"Oh, did that hurt?"

Her little head nodded.

"Oh, sorry," the man mumbled. He dropped the broom, then fumbled with the hose, and the water turned off.

Good, so much better!

She tried to smile at him, but couldn't, really. The sticky thing wouldn't let her.

But somehow he saw it. And smiled back. "Well, all clean," he said, and walked away.

She was completely soaked. She started shivering. Shivered more and more.

When he returned, he saw it. "Cold, huh?"

He left again. Came back with a towel.

Wiped the floor first, then the cage, then her, briefly. Then he left again and returned with another towel, a new towel. He wrapped it around her little bottom and mumbled, "Don't know what I'm doing, but this should work. Just don't poop again."

She looked at him, her eyes showing thanks.

He briefly smiled, then looked away quickly, mumbling something, as if scolding someone.

Who? Me?

Himself? He's scolding himself?

Maybe.

He does deserve timeout for the broom thing. Not fun!

"What's going on down there?" she heard the other guy yell.

Oh no, not him! Don't like him. She looked around but couldn't see the light-blonde guy.

"Nothing," the grey-eyed guy yelled back. "All clean now."

"Finally you do something right."

She looked at the guy crouching over her.

"Shhh…" he said, and threw the black blanket back over the cage.

Her new house. Her tiny play area. Her everything. An empty cage. Dark.

But wait… not so dark anymore. Right by her eyes, a whole corner left uncovered. *More light now than ever before. I like that.*

And for the next few hours, days, weeks, however long it may have been, she peered through that uncovered corner at the shiny light-tan wooden floor of the yacht.

A very shiny, freshly polished wooden floor.

"Maria? I think the water is all wiped up now," she heard a voice say, then a hand touched her shoulder. She flinched, then looked up.

Aaron was taken aback. Maria's exotic eyes were completely green, freakishly green. He kneeled beside her. "You okay?"

"This floor. It's the same," she whispered, and stared back down at it.

"What?"

A tear ran down her nose, then she started sobbing. Her hands touched the shiny tan wooden floor, feeling it, over and over again.

"The boat had this type of floor," she whispered. "The same floor."

"The boat?" Aaron looked at her. Quickly, he set down his beer on the table and pulled out his phone.

"What's going on, Aaron?" Brad and Elisabeth glanced at him then Maria with looks of concern.

Maria was rocking back and forth, her hands scrabbling at the wooden floor.

"She's having a flashback, I'm sure. Her eyes are doing the thing. She's crossing over." He started recording her on his phone.

The room fell silent. Everyone watched Aaron and Maria.

He gently touched her shoulder. "Where are you right now?"

"On the boat, the big boat," she said, her voice small like a toddler's. She rocked back and forth now even more. "Rocking. Rocking me. The waves. The boat's out, far away. In deep wawa."

"Are you on the floor?"

"No," she whispered. "In my tiny play area. My cage. But I see it. The floor. This floor. Shiny tan wooden floor."

"What else do you see?"

She covered her eyes. "Bad guys. Holding me. Moana. On the boat."

They all gasped and looked at each other. Martina and Elisabeth held each other as they helplessly watched their daughter.

"Moana is held on a boat?"

She nodded. "Long, long, long time. With two bad guys."

"What do the bad guys look like?"

She closed her eyes. "Don't know."

"You have to try to see them. Just see them. What do they look like?"

She sat down on the floor, her head in her hands, rocking back and forth. "One smaller, grey-eyed, blonde hair. Not too mean. The other, light blonde. Hair like sand on the beach. Curly. Mean. Mean to other guy."

"Oh my gosh, my baby girl," Brad yelled. He came over and started rubbing her back.

She looked up at him, her green eyes piercing through him. "Don't *touch* me! Don't tie me up!" She pushed him away and got up. Her face was pale, her eyes wide, as though she were seeing through all the people standing around her.

Jack snapped his fingers loudly.

Surprised, everyone looked at him, including Maria. Her eyes returned to exotic hazel-brown again, the green confined to emerald-green flecks as big as the golden flecks in the dark-brown center encircled by a blue ring. She touched her head.

Aaron stopped recording and put away his phone.

"I have a bad headache," she mumbled, and Aaron ran to catch her. He sat her down on the bench behind the table with all their beer cups on it. "I think I need to lie down."

"Sure, Maria, we can leave. I'll take you back to the hotel," Aaron said.

She nodded and rubbed her temples.

"What was *that*?" Drew asked, his mouth agape.

"Flashback," Jack replied.

Drew grabbed another beer and downed it. "Freaky," he said between gulps.

"Very scary. My goodness," Sarah said and downed her drink as well.

Elisabeth and Martina were crying, holding each other.

"¡Pobrecita!"

"Mein armes Engelchen."

"Our poor girl," they both said, tears running down their cheeks. They watched as Aaron helped Maria unlace her bowling shoes.

"We should call the chief," Jack said, and looked at Brad, who was just getting up off the floor, then turned to Elisabeth and Martina. "Maria gave us new information here."

They all nodded.

He continued, "We have to tell the chief we're looking for two guys who held her on a boat. A fancy yacht, I assume, if it had floors like what she described."

"Jonathan had blonde hair and blueish-grey eyes," Martina whispered. "But he didn't have a boat or yacht. No money."

"He fits the description? And then a rich guy with light-blonde curly hair and a fancy yacht who held my daughter... Why?" Elisabeth's voice was shrill as she looked at Martina. "Why would they do this?"

Elisabeth turned to Brad. "Do you know a rich, handsome blonde guy? Someone who would have wanted to punish us?"

Brad shrugged his shoulders. "No, I don't. I mean, a lot of guys fit that description... But who would want to punish us? And for what?"

Sarah, Drew, and Lieutenant Martinez all stared at the floor, uncomfortably shifting from one leg to the next.

Aaron took Maria by the hand. "I'll take her back to the inn to lie down."

They all nodded and watched them leave the bowling alley. Maria was still rubbing her temples, walking slowly next to Aaron, who took care to make sure she didn't trip or fall.

PUZZLE OF THE PAST

"A curly-haired blonde guy who didn't like you? Who *didn't* like General Collins?" Maria heard Elisabeth say before stepping outside.

Her headache was unbearable. Thoughts were racing through her head. Pictures and sentences flashed in front of her from a long-ago time. She briefly closed her eyes.

Through the uncovered corner of her cage, she watched the light-blonde curly-haired guy pacing back and forth atop the shiny tan wooden floor.

"I hate Collins. Fucking *hate* him. Want him to suffer. Gotta get back at him for what he did to me. Just wanna get back at him!"

247

CHAPTER 38

I just wanted to get back at him all those years ago, but now we're all going down. All because mistakes were made. He had to loosen his tie to wipe the sweat off the back of his neck so his light beach-blonde curly hair wouldn't stick to it.

He could hardly believe what they had said on the news just now.

"The former police chief who worked the infamous case of missing toddler Moana Marie Collins was interrogated this evening and subsequently arrested. Sources tell us he's assumed to have been in on it. Part of a group calling themselves the Fearless Four. Chief Billings was also interrogated about Jonathan Sullivan's death—he might be somehow involved. He's now being held at the Niceville Police Station. A shocking turn of events," the reporter said, and went on to engage in dubious speculation.

Cliff kept dabbing his forehead with a tissue while watching the news. *Holy shit, Sullivan* did *talk. I knew it. Gave them our code names. And they already figured out Billings is Bill? Fuck! How much did Sully share with them? How much did he even know? Probably not enough.*

He swallowed hard. *Probably? That's not very calming. In fact, that's fucking uncalming! You can never ever assume what people do or don't know, what they do or don't understand.*

He started pacing back and forth in his big office, glancing up at the TV from time to time, listening closely even while his thoughts were racing. *What does Bill know? Not much either. He played his part well. Didn't even know the brat was alive until that stupid pig Sully called him. How much does he know?*

He kept wiping his glistening forehead. *I need to figure out how much they know. Need to make sure nobody mentions me. Or Bullet.*

"The former Niceville PD chief, Chief Billings, requested a lawyer immediately after being charged. We have no information yet on who will defend him," the reporter said. "But it's not looking good for Chief Billings. He better choose a very good lawyer."

Lawyer?

Cliff stopped pacing. *That's it! Bill needs a good lawyer.* He grinned. *And so he shall get one. I'll make sure he gets the best fucking lawyer of the panhandle.*

He ran to his desk, snatched up his address book, and riffled through it. Finding what he was looking for, he picked up the phone and dialed the number. It rang a few times, then someone picked up.

"Shuster and Harris Law Firm. How may I help you?"

"Hello," Cliff said, "I'd like to speak to lawyer Hank Harris, please."

"You're in need of a criminal defense attorney?"

Cliff grinned. "Yes, correct. I need Mr. Harris."

"I'm afraid he already went home for the night."

He frowned. "It's very important I speak with him straightaway. I'm a good friend of Hank and need him to consider taking on a case. A high-profile case."

"I see. I'll give you his work cell phone number. Would that be okay with you?"

"Oh yes, that would be great. Thank you. I assume he's good about picking up?"

"Yes, Mr. Harris picks up every call he gets on his work cell, including holidays," the lady said. "Even late at night."

CHAPTER 39

Night. Nighttime is here. I can tell it's getting dark out. I see it through the curtain. And on the TV. Maria was lying in bed inside their hotel room. Her head was still hurting, pounding, her thoughts spinning.

Aaron turned off the news channel and sat next to her. He gently stroked her shoulder. "You're awake? Thought you were sleeping."

She shook her head.

"It'll be good to rest and sleep after the long, eventful day you had. The doctor said you need to rest. Make sure you rest to heal the concussion." Aaron sighed, then hit the bed with his fist. "Damn. We shouldn't have gone bowling. I knew we shouldn't have gone bowling. It was way too much for you. Way too much."

She frowned. "Come on, Aaron. It wasn't too much. And remember, I only have a mild concussion—it's not that bad." She sighed. "What's too much is this whole situation. The memories coming back and everything. This whole crazy situation. And look, I'm still all over the news." She pointed to the TV and closed her eyes again, then touched her temples. A dull, aching pain behind them.

"It'll be alright, Maria. We'll all make sure you're alright. You know we love you."

They love me? I sure hope so. She sighed. *I still feel like I'm letting my new mom down. I feel an unmistakable connection to her, but she*

250

really can't expect me to just forget the past twenty years, the way I grew up without her. She can't expect me to love her unconditionally. She looks a lot like me, but she still feels like a stranger.

"I know you're deep in thought, Maria, but talk to me. What's going on?"

She looked at Aaron. His blue eyes showed concern, sadness. *My Aaron. My sweet, handsome Aaron.*

"Well, you know," she said. "I just can't help but wonder what my life would've been like if I hadn't been kidnapped."

Aaron shrugged. "Very different, I suppose. For starters, you wouldn't have met a lot of people you know so well now."

Maria froze. *He's right. I would never have met Mamá. I'd only have known Elisabeth, my real mom.*

She shook off these strange thoughts. "I guess. Well, now I have two moms. That's just the way it is. And maybe… it's a good thing to have two?"

Aaron nodded. "Yes, it's good, I suppose."

"But what happened to me? Why did someone kidnap me? Who did it? Why me? Why?"

"Please, calm yourself. We don't have all the answers yet. But don't worry. We'll find them. We have more suspects to chase now. Jonathan Sullivan was certainly involved, and apparently the former police chief as well."

Maria nodded and kept thinking.

Aaron turned off the lights and got under the covers. He scooted close to her and hugged her from behind. She felt his warm body against hers and it gave her strength, made her headache disappear.

"You know, Aaron, it's just so strange. I don't really remember Chief Billings. I don't think I've met him before—like twenty years ago. First time I saw him was at that hospital."

Aaron nodded. "I know. You said so."

"Yeah, so I don't get how he was involved. Maybe he helped plan?"

"Plan what?"

"You know, the kidnapping. Maybe he was part of the planning but wasn't directly involved in the act."

"Maybe."

She sat up. "I'm sure of it, Aaron. And I think two blonde guys held me on a boat. But Billings has dark hair."

She lay back down and Aaron held her again. She felt him shrug his shoulders. "Well, guess Billings could've dyed his hair?"

Maria shook her head. "Don't think so. He doesn't scare me the way the others do. Don't think I know him."

"Well, when we met Jonathan Sullivan at his plumbing store in Jacksonville, he didn't scare you that much either. Yet he was deeply involved, right?"

She sighed. "Yeah, I suppose so. Don't know why I didn't recognize him back then. Guess I was too focused on finding my real dad. And maybe his appearance changed?"

Aaron chuckled. "Yeah, people do look different when they get older. And you might not remember everything clearly."

"I guess so," she mumbled. "But I did feel a bit intimidated by Sullivan at the store. I don't get that feeling at all with Chief Billings. So, how was he involved?"

Aaron held her tighter. "Don't know. But the police are working on it. We have a great team helping us. They'll let us know what they find, I'm sure. They were busy when I called them earlier."

"You called them?"

"Yeah, I did. Told them about your flashback. But they already knew you'd been held on a boat."

"They knew?"

"Well, suspected it, I suppose. But yeah, apparently Sullivan told them about it. Told them he was there."

Maria abruptly sat up again. "Sullivan was there? He was one of the guys holding me captive?" Her headache came back suddenly, violently. "One of the two blonde guys... was... Sullivan?"

Aaron sat up as well. "Yeah, something like that. But please, Maria, let's try to get some sleep, okay? I know it's not super late yet, but I can tell your head is hurting you again. You need some rest. And honestly, I'm exhausted."

Maria let out a deep breath, then turned to give him a kiss before lying back down. Aaron joined her and wrapped his arms around her.

"Good night, my love," he said. "I'm glad you're okay. Finally out of the hospital. Right here with me. You're safe here in our little hotel room."

She nodded, but her arm hairs stood up in alert. *Our little room?* She shook off the thought and listened to Aaron's calm, slow breathing. She smiled. *Of course. He's asleep already. That's his superpower.*

Maria closed her eyes and tried to fall asleep as well. She started counting sheep, imagining the fluffy white animals all lined up in a barn. And soon enough, sleep took her.

She was in a very small area.

Where am I? A barn? Or is it a room?

She tried to see, but her eyesight didn't seem to work right. It was all very blurry.

Why can't I see?

"No, we'll stay put right here. For however long it takes. It's safe on the boat," she heard a male voice say.

Is that Daddy? Doesn't sound like Daddy.

She tried to see the man behind the voice, but he was too fuzzy.

And suddenly, she knew. The bad guys. It's the bad guys! Oh no! The bad guys! They never let me go anywhere. They keep me in the box. In this small place.

She looked around. Her vision was still blurry, so fuzzy. She couldn't make out the speaker's face. She sighed, then her eyes grew wide.

I can't see right anymore. Hard to think. Always so hungry and so filthy. So dirty. Wet, pee, everything all over me.

She started sobbing.

I fought, but got weak. So hungry. Drift in and out of sleep. No more fighting. Lost my will. And Enti. And my parents. Everyone. I just have the box. And splinters.

"No, we'll stay put!" *she heard again.*

She sighed, sobbed.

Yes, of course. Stay here. Always here. In the box. They don't want to talk to me. They hush me. Sometimes hurt me. Slap me, yell at me to keep my mouth shut. Hold it shut. Stick it shut with the sticky thing.

The sticky thing—tape as they call it—holds my mouth shut. Holds me. I'm stuck, stuck in this box, this small crate. Stuck to it with the sticky thing. Always.

Despite her tiredness, a shiver ran down her spine. Her hairs stood up.

It scares me. I hate it. Just hate it so, so much! Hate the box. The wooden box full of splinters, full of dirt. The cold metal poles all around it. I hate it. I need to get out of here.

She threw herself from side to side over and over again, her hair flying wildly about her face, slapping her as she shook her head.

A hand reached in through the poles.

No, not again. Don't hold me down!

She started screaming.

"Maria, wake up! You're dreaming! Wake up, open your eyes!"

She opened her eyes and saw darkness all around her, except for a little ray of light coming from her right-hand side. *The hole in the box?*

No. Light coming through the curtains. *Moonlight? A street lamp?*

Her eyes adjusted to the darkness, and she saw Aaron sitting in bed next to her, his hand on her shoulder. "Aaron?"

"Maria, oh my gosh, you were dreaming. Nightmares again?"

She nodded, her mouth all dry. "I think I was in a box. A wooden box. Wood on the bottom and the top, metal poles all around it. Like a cage."

"Excuse me?"

"The two bad guys on the boat... they kept me in a cage-like box!"

CHAPTER 40

"**B**ox? What box? You mean this box of chocolates? You want me to FedEx it overnight?" Olivia asked him.

Cliff nodded. "Yes, please. The box of chocolates and this envelope with a note in it. And here's the address it's going to."

"Okay, I'll take care of it," she said with a big smile, her long brown hair framing her face nicely.

He smiled back at the young intern and looked her up and down. *Such a pretty smile. A beautiful young lady. Hot.*

"Thanks, I owe you one. So glad you stuck around after everyone else already went home for the day. Way to make it obvious who's the best intern out the bunch." He winked at her.

She blushed.

Cute! Real cute. A cute hottie. He grinned.

"Well, why don't you scoot off and mail that box of chocolates, then come back and let me know how it went?"

"Okay, I can do that." At the door, she turned around quickly and said, "See you soon, then, boss?"

He nodded and sat back down behind his big mahogany desk. "Yes, see you in a little bit. Thanks, Olivia."

He watched her leave his office and grinned. *It's a great plan. The chocolates. The note. And I have a feeling tonight will be great as well.*

He checked his watch and sighed. *Well, guess I won't make it to my martial arts class tonight. Shoot. I love karate. But I'm already amazing at it—got a black belt to prove it. Guess this here tonight is more important. Gotta wait for Olivia to come back. And maybe, just maybe, she'll make up for me missing my karate class.*

He grinned and busied himself with work while waiting for the girl to return.

It was growing very late. A knock on the door.

"Who's there? I'm about to leave," Cliff yelled through the closed office door. He rose, grabbed his bag, and switched off the lights, then opened the door and came face-to-face with his young intern.

"Oh, there you are." He smiled a big smile, his white teeth almost shiny in the darkened room. "Was beginning to wonder whether you were coming back."

Olivia shook her head. "I wouldn't do that to you. You told me to come back, so of course I'd come back."

He broke out into a big smile. "Great. I love workers *who carefully listen to instructions and comply.*"

She blushed again.

"So, did it go well?"

She nodded. "It's taken care of. Took a while to find a location open this late that could do overnight. I'm sorry, I didn't mean to keep you waiting here. I know the hour's late."

"Think nothing of it, Olivia. It was a lot to ask of you, and you did splendidly. And I was the one who told you to come back afterward, wasn't I? So, no worries please. Thank you for doing me this favor."

"You're very welcome."

He smiled. "So, what are your plans for tonight?" He took a step closer to her and leaned one arm into the doorframe. The intern was about the height of his armpit. He smiled. *A hot shortie.*

"Well, you know… not much going on," she said.

"No? Well, maybe I could interest you in doing something together?"

"You and me? You sure?"

"Absolutely," he grinned, his nose almost touching her hair. He could smell the fruity shampoo she must use. *Sweet, innocent smell!*

"Well, maybe yeah. I guess I'd like to learn more," she whispered, her warm breath on his muscular chest.

"About what, Olivia?"

"Well, you know… How things work around here." She glanced up at him and took a step closer, her chest brushing his.

He grinned. *Oh, I can certainly show you how things work around here.* "Why don't you come into my office then?"

She nodded. "Oh, okay." She ducked under his arm to walk into the office, her body brushing against his as she passed.

He grinned and turned around. *Oh yes, tonight's turning out to be a good night for sure.*

He pulled the door shut behind him. As soon as it closed, he dropped the bag he was holding and grabbed her, started kissing her. The intern seemed surprised by his boldness, then started kissing him back. He lifted her up onto his desk; she never let her lips leave his. Moaning, she reached up with one hand to grasp his thick curly blonde hair in the dark.

CHAPTER 41

In the dark they lay, arm in arm, cradling in bed inside their hotel room. Elisabeth had her head on Brad's bare chest. He felt her short hair on his skin, tickling it.

He had to smile. *Can't believe she's here. She's back. My wife. The love of my life.* He gave her a kiss on the head. *Wonder what she's thinking about?*

"Are you happy, Elisabeth?"

He felt her nod. Her hair tickled his chest again.

"Yeah, just thrilled we found our daughter. I'm happy she's alive. I think Martina and I might get along okay, too."

He grinned. "I think so. The two of you sure hit it off tonight."

"Yeah, it was good. I'm thankful she took good care of our daughter all those years... still wish it went differently."

He sighed. "I know, hun, I know. But she's here now. And we're gonna find out who did this."

"I hope so."

"We will. Don't give up hope, Elisabeth."

"I won't. I just can't believe how much trauma our daughter's gone through. Dragged through the bay to a boat? Unthinkable. And now they're saying the former police chief is involved?"

"And the FBI guy who worked the case. Remember Aaron told us Maria identified him?"

"Of course I remember," Elisabeth said, her voice shrill. "How could I forget? I can't believe they had something to do with it—the men we were supposed to trust to find her. Despicable!"

"Unbelievable, I know. What did we ever do to them? Why did they take our girl? We didn't even know them."

Elisabeth lifted her head off his chest and looked directly at him. He felt her stare in the dark. "I know," she said, "we *don't* know them. Never did. That's all I've been able to think about. So I've come to a conclusion."

"What's that?"

"It's the fourth one who knew us."

"The fourth one?" Brad raised his eyebrows, trying to understand.

"Yes, the fourth member of the Fearless Four. Remember, the police talked about that silly, evil group? Four people were involved."

He nodded. *She's right. We already identified three of four. Who's the last one? Who hated us so much that they would kidnap our only child?*

"It doesn't make any sense, does it, Brad?" Elisabeth said. "Why would a police chief, an FBI agent, and a plumber take any interest in kidnapping an Air Force captain's daughter? You were a captain then, a lower-ranking officer at the time. We had just moved to Eglin. You couldn't have pissed off that many people in the span of a few days, right?"

Brad thought about it. *She's right. It doesn't make sense. We're missing a piece to the puzzle.*

"So it must have been someone we pissed off when we were young, long before the kidnapping," Elisabeth said.

"You're right. It was a well-thought-out plot, planned months in advance. Someone knew we were coming. Someone knew we'd end up in a TLF right by the water. Someone knew."

"But who knew we'd end up there?"

"Practically everyone in Utah. We told everyone we were moving there, remember?"

Elisabeth nodded. "But we didn't make any enemies in Utah. The only enemy you ever had was Mike."

Brad raised his eyebrows. "You're bringing him up again? My old buddy Mike? He didn't know we were moving to Eglin."

Elisabeth sighed. "I guess not. But he seems to be the only person who's ever held a grudge against you. He might have had something to do with the kidnapping."

"What? Don't be ridiculous. We had nothing to do with each other back when our little one disappeared. I haven't seen him in forever. The last time was the spring of my senior year at the Academy. A long time ago."

Elisabeth squinted her eyes. "Are you sure about that? I recall you said you just saw him recently."

"Oh, well… yeah, I guess so. But how is that relevant? He works in DC, as do I. It's not unusual for him to show up at the Pentagon from time to time. It was about the F-35 program."

She nodded. "Exactly. Didn't you say he was still upset with you?"

Brad shook his head. "No, not with *me*. With the program I oversee."

"Same difference."

"Not really. We just happened to cross paths again. Besides, he has no excuse to be mad at me. Not graduating from the Academy worked out well for him, didn't it? Look at him now—he's a big shot. Florida's senator. Wildly popular. Keeps getting re-elected. Why would he still be upset with me?"

Elisabeth sighed. "I don't know. I just have a feeling there's more to it. Look, I googled him. Not much to find out other than what he wants everyone to know. A few scandals with young women, but the voters don't seem to care."

Brad sighed. "Yeah, no kidding. He's well-liked. A real Florida sunshine boy. The older ladies all love him. I guess the fact that he attended the Academy—even if only for a short time—lends him a lot of credibility and trust with men. That his dad was a general helps as well, I assume."

Elisabeth nodded. "Put that way, he sounds pretty nice, doesn't he?"

Brad laughed out loud. "Yeah, *on paper*. But boy, he has a temper. Still does. And so stubborn. Does things his own way, and whoever gets in the way gets pushed aside. Too bad. He really is a likable guy but carries so many flaws. Guess he didn't have a stable family life growing up, from what I recall."

Elisabeth frowned. "If he has a bad temper, is stubborn, and pushes opponents out of his way… wouldn't that fit with being a criminal?"

Brad laughed. *That's silly. Mike's a pain in the butt, not a criminal.* "Guess those are some criminal character traits, but—"

"*And* he's smart," Elisabeth interrupted. "He's a very smart guy. And powerful. Just think about it!"

Despite the dark room, Brad saw her blue eyes piercing through him, her freckles glowing on her flushed face. A big knot formed in his throat.

Is she serious? She came up with good arguments—as always—but this is too far-fetched. Mike? Why would he kidnap our daughter years after the Academy incident?

Brad cleared his throat. "I don't know, Elisabeth. Mike wasn't powerful back then, twenty years ago. I doubt he made friends with police chiefs and FBI agents in his spare time. Seems more likely he'd know a plumber than anything, even though he'd been too stuck up to talk to someone like him."

"You can always meet people, anyone, even high-class ones, anywhere. Take Sullivan, for instance. How did he meet that group of powerful men? He was a nobody."

Brad thought for a bit. *Guess she's right. You can always run into anyone on the street. But it's so unlikely…. Doesn't make sense.*

"Well," he said, clearing his throat, "even if Mike befriended them, none of them could've known our family was going to move to Eglin. And Mike didn't even have access to the base. Frankly, I think your theory's a bit far-fetched—"

"Far-fetched?" Elisabeth sprang out of the bed and started pacing. "That's *exactly* what you told me when I said I knew our daughter had been kidnapped. And look at that—I was right all along, wasn't I?"

He watched her cross her arms in defiance. *Oh, Elisabeth, I hate seeing you this angry with me. But it's true, I didn't believe you back then. And I've regretted it ever since. Does this mean I should believe you no matter what? I'm not sure.*

"You're right," he whispered. "I was wrong to doubt you back then. But Mike? You really think he had something to do with it? How? How could he pull off a stunt like that?"

"It wasn't a stunt—it was *our daughter*." Elisabeth glared at him, then uncrossed her arms and sat back down on the bed beside him. She hung her head low. "I don't know. Nothing makes sense. I guess I just don't know."

Brad scooted over and gave her a hug. "It's okay, Elisabeth, it's okay. We'll keep searching for answers. For now, let's get some sleep, shall we? We can talk to the police again tomorrow."

She put her head on his strong shoulder and he felt her nod. Her short hair tickled his chin. He smiled and gave her a kiss on the forehead. "Come on, let's lie down. I just want to hold you. I missed you."

Elisabeth did as she was told and cuddled up with him. "Me too. I missed you, too. We were so stupid to go our separate ways, weren't we?"

Brad had to smile. "We were. Young and stupid. I love you so much, Elisabeth. Now we have our daughter back. A phenomenal young lady. Life is good."

"You're right," she said. "Good night, hun."

"Good night." He gave her one last kiss and held her close. Contentedly, he just held her tight, then felt her even breathing, a warm breath of air on his bare chest. She had fallen asleep.

He smiled, but then his smile faded. *She's right. The only person who's ever said, "I hate you," to my face was Mike. My old buddy Mike. But how could he hold a grudge that long, years after the fact, to the point that he'd orchestrate a kidnapping? My daughter's kidnapping? I just don't know.*

CHAPTER 42

"I just don't know yet," Hank Harris told the reporter who was immediately by his side the moment he arrived at the Niceville Police Station the next morning. "I've yet to commit to representing Chief Billings."

Despite the sun just rising, the place was already swarming with reporters. Hank closed his car door and clutched his briefcase. More and more reporters crowded around him as he made his way toward the police station.

"You're a long way from home. Why are you interested in this case?"

"Do you believe Chief Billings is guilty?"

"How will you prove his innocence?"

The lawyer waved from atop the steps of the police station entrance and smiled. "No further comment."

The door swung open and a young female police officer waved him in.

"Good morning," she greeted him. "I'm Officer Sally Johnson. I assume you're Mr. Harris, here for an initial consultation with Jim Billings?"

"Correct," he said. "Where's my client?"

"In his cell."

"A cell?" He raised his eyebrows. "You held Mr. Billings overnight in a cell?"

"Of course, sir. He *is* under arrest, after all. It's only reasonable any suspect charged with murder and kidnapping would be held in a cell. What do you think he deserves? A hotel?"

Hank Harris stared blandly at her. Her smile was wide and pretty, with just a hint of malice.

"You couldn't make an exception for the former chief of this fine establishment?"

"Definitely not, Mr. Harris. We treat everyone equally here at the Niceville Police Station. No matter their pedigree." With a grin on her face, Officer Johnson turned around and started walking down the hallway of the station.

"Jim Billings, you have a visitor," he heard, and opened his eyes.

He stared at the blank wall and felt his body aching. *Where am I?*

He looked around and quickly realized he wasn't dreaming. *They're actually holding me in a cell inside my own police station. The audacity...* He sat up and felt every bone in his body groan.

"Sleep well, Jim?"

He looked up and saw Chief Parlot standing outside the cell in his police chief uniform, grinning at him. *What an asshole! He's enjoying this!*

Billings stretched out his sore arms and heard his shoulders pop. *It's fucking uncomfortable on this concrete bed.* "Go away. I gotta take a piss."

"Better do it quick. Your lawyer is here."

His sluggish mind struggled to catch up. "Oh, good. Time to finally get out of this ridiculous situation."

"We'll see," Chief Parlot said, and smiled as a guard opened the cell door. The big metal key clanked as it rattled inside the lock. "Ready to go, then?"

Billings stood up and heard his back pop. He rubbed it. *Man, last night was so incredibly uncomfortable. Feels like I pulled something in my back.*

The guard entered the cell with handcuffs in hand.

Billings's eyes widened. "Don't you dare," he growled.

The guard immediately stopped in his tracks and turned to Isaac. "Chief?"

Billings saw Chief Parlot sigh and wave the guard out. "Fine then, I'll do it myself." The chief took the handcuffs out of the guard's hand and sauntered over to Billings.

"Don't you dare, Isaac!" Billings yelled.

"I'm afraid I'm only following protocol," Chief Parlot said, already by his side. "Sorry, Jim—or should I say 'Bill'?"

The chief grasped Billings's arm and was about to turn him to handcuff him, when Billings wiggled out.

"What's this? Are you resisting, Billings?"

"Come on, Isaac man, please...."

"That's *Chief Parlot* to you," the chief roared at him, then grabbed his arm forcefully.

"No, please, I need to pee first," Billings said. "Can't do that handcuffed."

Chief Parlot sighed. "Fine. Go ahead then."

Billings gave his former colleague an irritated look. "What do you mean?"

Chief Parlot pointed at the metal toilet in the corner of the cell.

Is he fucking serious? His face bright red in anger, Billings stared at the younger man who used to work for him. "I will certainly not use that toilet, not with you lording over me. The door's already open. I'll use the one down the hall."

The chief broke out into laughter, then shook his head. "You're funny, you're so funny, Jim!"

Billings watched him laugh. *What the fuck?*

"Those restrooms are for police officers only. The others for visitors. And at this point in time, Jim, you're neither."

What? Is he fucking crazy?

"The moment you committed a crime—oh, wait, *two* crimes—you unfortunately lost your privileges, Jim. I'm sorry."

Billings stared at his successor. "Isaac—err—Chief Parlot, I mean… Please. Just make an exception this one time. Please?"

Chief Parlot shook his head. "Nope, no exceptions in my police station. Everyone is treated with equal regard, the way they deserve to be treated. You have your rights as a suspect. And there's your right. In the corner." He pointed at the metal toilet again. "You can have your privacy. We'll leave. Just holler when you've done your business."

What the fuck?

Before he could say anything else, Chief Parlot turned around and walked away. He heard the clink of the big metal key as the guard locked the metal door to his cell.

Holy shit! What have I gotten myself into? Billings shuddered, his face pale. It rapidly regained its color, flushed red. *What did* Cliff *get me into? I should have never listened to him. The fucker. I'll make sure to rat him out!*

Despite the circumstances, he caught himself grinning. He shuffled over the toilet to pee. *Yeah, I sure will. I'll hire this lawyer and tell him what really happened. I've been used. I'm innocent in all this. Every one of them used me and threatened me, Cliff most of all.*

He kept smiling. *Good plan, yeah? Great plan, actually!*

CHAPTER 43

"**A**ctually, we were just about to go see the police as well," Brad said between mouthfuls.

Elisabeth, Drew, Aaron, Maria, Jack, and Martina were all eating breakfast together in the dining room of the Air Force Inn.

"You were? Why?" Maria asked.

"Well," Brad said, taking another bite of his waffle, "we made a troubling connection last night. It's a bit far-fetched…"

"…but worth mentioning, right?" Elisabeth said.

"Anything will help," Jack said. "But Maria and Aaron, why were you planning to go?"

"Well," Aaron said, "Maria had a dream—another memory, we're assuming. We were going to tell the chief about it."

"Another memory?" Elisabeth raised her eyebrows.

All eyes rested on Maria now. She sighed and laid her fork next to her waffles. "Yeah. But I really don't want to talk about it right now."

Martina sighed. "Aw, poor mija."

"We understand, sweetie," Brad said. "Are you sure you can handle it? Handle being back at the police station? Seeing those old pictures must be very, um, triggering."

Everyone agreed.

"Well, it sounds like they'll have a childhood trauma specialist there today. Someone who'll work with me and ensure I'm safe. Dr. Davies is his name, I think."

"Yes, Dr. Elijah Davies," Aaron said. "I googled him this morning after we spoke with the chief. He seems very professional."

"It'll be good to have a specialist working with you," Elisabeth said.

Maria frowned. *Yeah, my personal shrink. Great.*

"Yeah, real good," Brad said, then stuffed another piece of waffle into his mouth.

The rest of the group returned to their breakfast and prior conversation again. Maria picked up her fork to join them but hesitated. *Can I do this? Can I handle going down the rabbit hole once more to help with the case?* She sighed.

Aaron noticed, swallowed his bite of pancake, then turned to her. "You okay?"

Maria nodded. "Yeah. Just nervous, I guess." Sadness and doubt washed over her face.

Aaron put down his fork and took her free hand. "You are strong, Maria. And whatever you remember *will* help. It'll help you find closure. Find the truth. Remember that. Besides, there's no wrong way of going about this."

"I hope so," she whispered. She looked into his ocean-blue eyes and wished she could lose herself in them, just swim away in that gentle ocean, away from all the pain and confusion.

Away from the reporters outside of the base. Away from the police questioning. Away from suddenly having two moms. Away from it all.

"You got this, Maria," Aaron encouraged her.

She squeezed his hand and held it tight while forcing down her waffle.

They were standing in the foyer of the police station.

Chief Parlot introduced his colleague. "Maria, this is Dr. Elijah Davies, psychiatrist, a specialist in PTSD and childhood trauma. He and I go way back. He's a trusted colleague of mine—even though I always hate calling him in. Tough cases, any time he's involved."

Maria noticed a wave of sadness wash over the chief's face. *I like the chief. He cares deeply.*

"Anyway, Dr. Davies here is fantastic. Not only does he work well with children, he often lends an ear for my own worries, disappointments, and disgusts any time we work a case together."

Maria smiled. *Good. I trust the chief's judgment. Looks like he has friends from all walks of life. Just like me.* She sighed. *I miss my friends. Keisha. Brandy. Even Nick and Jim.*

"Hello, Maria, pleasure to meet you," Dr. Davies said, and shook her hand, ripping her from her thoughts.

"Yes, nice to meet you, too, doctor," she said, returning the handshake while studying him. *Older guy, probably in his fifties. Short haircut, tight black curls, a hint of grey in his curly hair.*

Dr. Davies let go of her hand and now rested his brown eyes on Aaron. "You must be the fiancé, Aaron Heikinnen?"

"Yes, sir," Aaron said, and shook his hand as well.

Dr. Davies turned to Brad and Elisabeth. "And you're Maria's parents?"

They nodded and shook his hand also.

"And all of you must remember Agent Tonya Anderson, I'm sure," Chief Parlot asked.

They all nodded and greeted her. Maria noticed two other people in uniform walking down the hallway. A young man and woman.

Officer Sally Johnson and Agent Tom Cooper are here also. Where are they going? To question the former police chief? Did he already confess to murdering Sullivan?

"Maria," Dr. Davies said, drawing her back to the present again, "I think it's best you and I get to know each other a bit before we talk about your case. Shall we?"

He pointed to a room on the left.

"Can Aaron come?" she asked.

"Sure," Dr. Davies said, and both Maria and Aaron followed him into the small room.

"We'll be over here if you need us," Maria heard Chief Parlot say, and she turned to wave to her parents before they disappeared into another interrogation room.

She sighed. *Busy here this morning. Hope they can find the other guy from the boat. The curly blonde-haired guy. Maybe the former police chief knows him? He must.*

And the former chief better talk and tell them everything. I sure hope he'll talk, that Chief Billings!

CHAPTER 44

Chief Billings eyed the lawyer. "Why should I hire you? More importantly, why are you offering to represent me for free, Mr. Harris?"

"Because, Chief, you're a respected man in your community. When I heard about what happened, I harbored serious doubts you were involved in this kidnapping and decided I wanted to help you. I assume you simply failed to figure out the truth back then, and now someone is getting back at you for having made a genuine mistake. And killing a prime suspect? Hah. Why would you, a retired police chief, kill a suspect? Too many wild claims. Too much bad-mouthing out there," Hank said.

Billings eyed him. *Makes sense. I need someone who is on my side. This guy just might be it.*

"And I'm not alone in my thinking, Chief. My cohorts all agree: we think you're a victim of revenge by a former colleague who never really liked you. The one you took off the case back then. And now he's getting back at you, tarnishing your name."

Exactly. He's thinking exactly what I need everyone else to think. Gotta go with this guy.

"So, Mr. Harris, what are your credentials? Where did you go to school?"

"Princeton for my undergrad, then Yale Law School, then—"

"Yale?" Chief Billings interrupted.

Hank nodded.

"Say no more. You're hired. Where's the paperwork?"

Hank grinned. "In my briefcase."

"Get it out then, Mr. Harris, what's the delay? I'd love for you to represent me."

"Wonderful, wonderful," Hank said, and grinned widely. "Great choice. It'll be an honor to defend you. And a bunch of my good friends will be very happy to hear you chose me as your defense attorney."

"Great! Good for me, then." Jim Billings smiled contentedly.

Hank pulled out the paperwork and a pen and placed them in front of Billings. He snatched the pen and signed the contract right away, sight unseen.

Hank Harris grinned. "Yeah, good for you, good for *you*. Let's hand this over to the cops, then we can get started, shall we?"

Chief Billings nodded and smiled. *Yes, we shall.*

"I want to start with the story of how I met *them*. The Fearless Four. We all met while gambling. Poker, blackjack—"

"Whoa, hold up now... blackjack? You're telling me you loved to gamble and you made some buddies along the way? What does this have to do with the charges brought against you? The girl's kidnapping, Sullivan's death?"

"Well, if you'll let me get to it... It's the story of how I met *them*— the ones that forced me to do all this. I intend to give up all their names. Because I didn't do it, *they made me do it.* Just like you said, I'm innocent. *They* made me do it."

Hank's face flushed. He loosened the tie around his neck.

274

"If I give the police their names, I bet we can cut a deal with them, don't you think?"

Hank swallowed hard and kept loosening his tie. "Sure, I suppose."

"Okay, then. Great. Let's start with those names." Jim grinned and leaned back in his chair. *Yeah, rat 'em out. All of them.*

"Chief, before we do that, why don't you start by telling me what you mean by, 'They made me do it'?"

Jim shrugged his shoulders. "If you want." He eyed Hank Harris. *Why isn't he getting it? Is he slow? Thought he went to Yale. It's obvious I was forced into doing this.*

"Chief Billings, can you describe what it is they made you do?"

"Well, for starters, they told me to look the other way. Told me to tell the world the girl had died from an accidental drowning, and to tell it quick. JB rode me hard."

"JB?"

"Yeah, James Borman. Agent James Borman."

"An agent... as in the FBI?"

"Yeah. Now *there's* a guy who was deeply involved in the kidnapping. He came over here to help me 'solve the case'—you can probably guess what I mean by that—basically had me lead the whole team to the wrong conclusion."

Hank raised his eyebrows. "An FBI agent..."

Jim grinned. *Ha, he didn't see that one coming, did he? Just wait till I tell them who else is involved. All of Florida will be shocked.* "Yeah, he was one of the main guys. But not the only one."

"I see," Hank croaked. He swallowed hard, then wiped sweat from his forehead.

Jim stared at him. *Why is he acting so nervous all of a sudden?*

"What about Sullivan?"

Jim laughed. "Sullivan? A small fish in the big pond. He was their middleman, some random guy they hired to do their dirty work. He was supposed to get rid of the girl."

"So he kidnapped her?"

Jim shook his head. "No, he was supposed to hide the body. Don't know the details, but he was to dispose of it after JB kidnapped her."

"The FBI agent?" Hank raised both eyebrows again, sweat pooling in every crease on his forehead.

"Yes, Agent James Borman. He was the only one skilled enough to abduct that little girl right out of her bed. Again, don't know the details, don't know how he pulled it off. Super-secret mission. All I had to do was look the other way, you know?"

Jim saw the lawyer nod. *He looks pale. Nervous. Why? He can't believe it? An agent gone bad?* Jim grinned. "As I said, I didn't have anything to do with that mess. I was just told to make sure the investigation concluded with an 'accidental drowning.'"

Hank Harris jumped up. "Her death? But she's alive."

Jim sighed. "Yeah, they forgot to mention that part...."

"So, they meant to kill the little girl?"

Jim nodded. "That was the plan. And I thought it happened."

Hank exhaled, then wiped his forehead again. He sat back down. "So, you aided in covering up a murder, Chief? Without a guilty conscience?"

Jim Billings laughed. "Who says I didn't feel bad about it?"

"I see."

"You gotta understand, Agent Borman was my buddy. They had some sort of dirt on him—you know, the gambling, girls—and he begged me to help him. Told me I had to help a friend, do him a small favor. Told me to just look the other way in this case. So I did as I was told. He bribed me to go along with his investigation. And—you know—it did make sense that the little one just walked out. It did and could've been. 'Cuz after all, he was a good agent."

"A good agent that... kidnaps *children?*"

"Well, up until then, I mean," Jim said. "He was my friend. He just had a few issues."

"So you helped with the cover-up." Hank raised his eyebrows again and stared at the former police chief.

Why is he focusing on me so much? He should be asking me more about them. *The other Fearless Four.* "Let's focus on the big picture here," Jim said. "I have more names."

"Good, that's good," Hank said, and smiled.

Huh. That looks awfully like a fake smile! What's going on here?

At that very moment, Hank Harris got up. "Excuse me for a second, Chief Billings. I'll be right back."

"Okay," Jim said, and watched him leave the room. *What's he up to?*

After a few minutes, Hank came back into the interrogation room.

Jim Billings eyed him. *He's acting strangely.* "Everything okay?"

"Yeah," Hank said. "Just dandy. I have a sick kid at home and needed to check on him real quick."

Jim Billings raised his eyebrows. *Really?* "Okay, then… but don't forget your top priority—*me.*" He grinned as the lawyer sat down again.

"I won't. So, let's pick up where we left off. Tell me more about JB and Sullivan and their involvement in the old case."

Billings raised an eyebrow. *Again? I already told him about that. Something smells funny here. What's going on?*

CHAPTER 45

"What's going on, General Collins? You said you needed to talk to us?" Chief Parlot said. "About a possible lead?"

Brad nodded. "Yeah. Elisabeth and I thought you might find this important. We think I may have made an enemy back during my training days. I still have no idea why he'd kidnap our daughter or how he planned it, don't know how he'd know the others or figured out where our family was living at the time—"

"Hold on, General, you're going ninety to nothing," Agent Tonya Anderson interrupted. "Slow down and take it from the beginning. Go ahead and tell us what you know. But pace yourself."

Brad sighed. He felt Elisabeth take his hand and squeeze it. He knew what that meant: *"You can do this, hun."*

He sighed again. *But what if I'm wrong? What if I wind up accusing an innocent guy of a crime he had nothing to do with?*

He felt another squeeze, and his doubts fell away. He found his courage. "So listen, the guy I was thinking of was enrolled in the Air Force Academy same time as me. He actually threatened me."

"Why didn't you think of him earlier, General?" Chief Parlot asked. "During our questioning?"

"Because I considered the idea he had anything to do with it a bit far-fetched. And goodness, back when our little one disappeared, not once did this guy cross my mind. Even then, our run-in was old history."

"Okay, we understand, General, we understand," Agent Anderson said. "May we record this conversation?"

Brad shrugged his shoulders. "Sure, I guess."

"Okay. You said this guy threatened you. Can you tell us about what happened?"

Brad let out another deep sigh and stared at the wall. The white wall illuminated by a big, ugly fluorescent light fixture.

Terrible choice of lighting. Just as bad as the light in Sijan Hall at the Air Force Academy. Had to stare up at that fluorescent light so many times that first year. But at least I had the upper bunk. Drew got the lower one. Mike the single bed on the wall.

Mike. Our buddy. Part of our BDM Team—Brad, Drew, Mike. How could he be involved?

"General, are you ready?" Chief Parlot's question drew Brad out of his memories.

"Yeah, I guess." Brad sighed. "I can't shake the feeling this is irrelevant. I'm really not sure what that guy was even mad about. But I do know he didn't belong in the Air Force. Wasn't a good fit for him. Countless hours of training—hard, physical, punishing—not to mention all that studying, those harsh rules. Not much fun. But Mike loved fun. Loved to drink and party."

"Mike?" the agent asked.

"Yeah, Mike. He was our buddy at the Air Force Academy."

"*Our* buddy?"

"Yeah, my best friend Drew Markas and mine. We lived together the whole time we were all there at the Academy. It was a tough time."

"Yeah, so I've heard," Chief Parlot said.

"We were barely allowed to leave campus. Then we finally reached our senior year and could leave. We sure loved going out to Colorado Springs, but were constantly reminded to be on our best behavior, a shining example to the public. Polite cadets of the Academy, you know? While other college kids spent their time in college partying and drinking, us cadets were supposed to stay sober, keep a clean slate, not do anything stupid."

"That does sound hard," Agent Anderson said. "Especially since college is a time for young people to make mistakes, isn't it?"

Brad nodded and sighed. "Yeah, it should be. But not for us cadets. It was hard on all of us, but especially Mike. I remember that all too well. Mike got reprimanded quite often, while both Drew and I stayed out of trouble as best we could. We both had steady girlfriends, never really liked drinking, and were awkward dancers anyway. More than anything, we really, *really* just wanted to fly those jets."

"I see," the chief said.

"Yeah, we were goal-oriented, Drew and I. But not Mike. Wonder if he did it on purpose. To rebel against his dad, a general in the Air Force at the time. I remember how often he told Drew and me he didn't want to turn out like his pops. Still feel bad for him, even now. I don't like the idea of being pushed into becoming someone you don't wanna be."

"Yes, General, that's pretty sad, but please, get to the point," the chief said. "I assume the enemy you're thinking of is this Mike guy?"

"Yeah, Mike. You know, he's not a bad guy. But he brought about his own downfall. It certainly didn't help that Mike really loved the women. He was such a player. Still is, I guess."

Agent Anderson raised her eyebrows. "What does any of this have to do with the kidnapping of your daughter, General?"

But Brad was on a roll, caught up in memories of long-gone times. "Mike not only loved women, he loved gambling. Mostly within the walls of the Academy, betting pennies on poker. He was good at it. But we didn't really have the time to gamble, and definitely weren't supposed to."

"Gambling…" Chief Parlot took note of this.

"Yeah, not much gambling to be had out there. But there were women. Barely any within the walls of the Academy, but plenty in Colorado Springs. And they all loved the cadets, especially the pilots."

Brad almost laughed out loud. "Mike was the splitting image of a *Top Gun* pilot, a Tom Cruise type, and the girls loved it. His sports car, bought and paid for by his rich daddy, sure sold that image. The guy was a literal chick magnet."

Thinking back on that red Corvette made Brad smile. *Beautiful car. But I wasn't in it much. Mike often drove it alone, without me or Drew. It only had two seats, and Mike needed the extra seat for the hotties he'd pick up at night.*

"General? We need to get back to our work soon. Please get to the point," the chief said.

Brad nodded and pushed the memories away. He focused on the chief and agent before him. He felt Elisabeth squeeze his hand.

"So far, General, it sounds like you guys were best buds," Agent Anderson said. "One more into partying than the others, but that doesn't make for enemies, now does it?"

Brad shook his head.

The chief said, "When exactly did Mike become your so-called enemy, then, General? You said he threatened you?"

Brad sighed, then nodded. "Yeah. There was an incident. At the Triple Nickel Tavern, when we were out enjoying ourselves the spring of our senior year. That was the night our falling-out happened—the night our friendship ended."

Sadness washed over Brad's face. He didn't want to think of it, but knew he had to tell them. As he kept talking, his mind went back to that night, so clear it might as well have been yesterday, as the scene played out before him.

"Look at Mike," Drew said, struggling to speak clearly while pointing.

Brad giggled, knowing his friend had had way too much to drink. *Good thing I'm driving tonight. I don't mind sipping coke and being the*

DD. Brad followed his friend's finger and saw Mike making out with girl number four that evening.

"Such a player," Drew said, and took another sip of his drink. "The ladies go gaga over him."

Brad laughed. "They sure do. So cheers to *our* girls."

Mike and Brad clanged glasses.

"Yeah, cheers to Sylvia and Elisabeth," Drew said, and his eyes almost crossed as he carefully watched his drink transit to his mouth, taking care not to spill any of the precious liquid.

Brad looked on with an amused smirk on his lips.

"Too bad they live so far away," Drew said, then took another sip of his drink. "I miss Sylvia."

Brad patted his friend on the shoulder. "I know, man, I know. I miss Elisabeth, too. But don't worry. They'll be here soon. For graduation!"

Another one of the cadets turned to them. "Did I hear someone say 'graduation'?" And soon enough, they were standing in a big group, toasting one another's imminent success.

Mike sauntered over to the group, a girl on his hand. "Hey, guys, we're gonna head out," he said. He winked. "We'll party *our* way, right, sweetheart?"

The blonde girl in the miniskirt giggled and pressed herself against him. He waved goodbye, turned around, tried to take a few steps, and stumbled, barely able to walk straight. The crowd burst into laughter.

"Holy cow, Mike's totally wasted," one of the cadets said. "Good luck finding your zipper by the time you get your date home!"

The cadets laughed even harder as they watched Mike stumble away while fumbling in his pocket for his car keys.

Brad had a bad feeling. *They're right. He's totally wasted. Can't let him go like that.* And before he knew it, he was yelling after Mike, "Come on, man, you've had a few too many. It's not safe to drive."

Mike turned around. "What? Come on, Brad, don't tell me what to do. I'm a big boy! I can handle myself. I'm a good driver."

"We know that, man, but Brad is right," Drew said. "It's not safe to drive like that. Better call a cab or ride with us."

Mike laughed, standing arm in arm with the blonde chick he'd just picked up. "Ride with *you*? Really? You got room for this hottie, too?"

Drew and Brad looked at each other and shook their heads.

"See? No room, no can do. Won't work. Becca and I have this *exclusive* thing going on here tonight."

"Exclusive? Really?" Brad laughed out loud. "How exclusive can it be if she's girl number four? Were the other ones just as exclusive, Mike?"

Mike stared at Brad, his expression full of loathing.

The blonde girl in his arms looked at him. "What other girls?"

"Don't worry, darling," Mike said, and gave her a kiss. "Give us a moment. Just need to chat with my friend real quick."

She nodded as Mike staggered closer to Brad. He smiled coolly, then his face became downright ugly. "Shut the *fuck up*! You're just jealous!"

Brad was taken aback. "Sure, Mike, sure, just jealous.... But please, man, don't drive tonight. Think of the young lady here." He pointed at her. "Becca, was it?"

She nodded and smiled a beautiful smile.

Mike stared from her to him. "What about her? She's mine, Collins!"

"Whoa, take it easy, man. I'm just saying, *think of her*. You've had way too much to drink. Come on.... You can barely walk in a straight line."

"Not true! Shut the fuck up! Go be someone else's daddy!"

More cadets crowded around them, voicing agreement with Brad. Without warning, Mike sucker punched one of them, right in the face.

Yells and screams filled the tavern. Brad and Drew rushed in to break up the fight before it could get further out of hand. Brad wrapped his arms around Mike and held him back. *Such an asshole when he drinks. But I gotta help him.*

"Mike, please, don't throw away your career," Brad said. "You've had too much. Calm down and make good decisions. Apologize to that guy you hit. And don't drive. Not tonight. Get a taxi. Or stay here and leave with us." He could see Mike was relaxing more and more. "We're worried about you, man. You're our buddy; we need you to stay safe!"

"Fine, fine then," Mike said. "Let go of me, man."

Once he was free, he turned to the cadet he had just punched. Everyone knew this cadet; he was a good guy. "Sorry, man." The cadet just nodded. Luckily, the punch hadn't been too hard. "Fine, everyone, I'll stay."

The guys all cheered and had another drink to toast Mike coming to his senses. Becca, the girl who'd been hanging onto him, moved off to the side.

She looks a bit scared. The commotion was probably too much for her. Brad could see it in her eyes, but before he could say anything, Mike grabbed her hand and dragged her along to the far side of the tavern.

Brad shrugged. The evening wore on as they danced to the music, laughing and cheering.

"Hey, Drew, I'll be right back. That coke's run through," Brad said, and got up to use the restroom.

As he pushed up against the men's room door, he heard it: "No, no! Please no!"

Confused, he went in and saw nothing. He paused, wondering if he should go ahead and use the urinal when he heard it again, a desperate plea. "No, please no! I don't want to!"

He looked around. *Where's that coming from? One of the stalls?*

A loud banging noise came from behind the only closed stall door, then more pleas, then a shrill scream. "Stop it! No, you're hurting me! Stop, please stop!"

"Come on, Becca, don't be silly!"

Becca? Oh no… Don't tell me…

Before he could think about it any further, Brad walked over to the stall, determined to help. He had heard enough. He knocked loudly. "Open up!" he shouted. His voice came out in a roar so deep, he barely recognized himself.

"Go away, we're busy in here!"

A knot formed in Brad's throat. *That's Mike's voice. What the heck is he doing? What's he thinking? My friend Mike? Unbelievable!* He swallowed hard. *I have to save that girl... Save her from whatever my friend is doing to her!*

"Mike, open up! Now!" he roared. He shook the door to the stall. "Or I'm coming in!"

"Go away! Leave us alone!"

The girl cried harder.

"Open up!" Brad roared.

"No, she's mine!"

Then he heard movement in the stall, a rustling of clothes then a tearing sound, more crying and pleading.

"No, stop!" Becca screamed.

"Open up or I'll tear down the door!"

"What the fuck? What kind of idiot am I talking to?"

"Mike, it's me, Brad."

"Collins? Oh *shit*! Are you fucking crazy?"

"No, *you* are, Mike! What are you doing? Leave her alone. She doesn't want you."

Mike laughed. "Sure, she does. Get your own girl, Collins, and leave us the fuck alone!"

"I can't do that. I can't let you do this, Mike! You're hurting her. She doesn't want to. Just listen to her."

"Go away!"

"Mike, you *can't* do this. You don't even *need* to do this. You're a good-looking guy, you have girls lining up to be with you."

"You're right. But this one tried to skip out of line, and I won't let her. It's her turn now."

Becca sobbed.

"Mike, don't do this. This will *ruin* her life. This will ruin *your* life. Please, Mike, just let her go."

"No! She wants this, I know she does. She didn't mind fooling around earlier, so I know she wants it."

"No, I don't! I don't want this," Becca screamed.

Finally.

"What the fuck did you say," Mike said in a low voice from the other side of the door. "You were all flirty and kissy just a minute ago out there. Now this? That's not right... You *wanted* this!"

"No," she whispered.

"Bitch!" Mike yelled.

Brad heard a loud slap, then crying. *Oh my God, he slapped her. I can't believe it!* "Mike, stop this nonsense! Come on out, or I'll break down this door!"

Brad's thundering was met with silence. Then he heard Becca's short, sharp sobs. Just as he stepped back to run at the stall full force, the door opened, and Mike stepped out.

His hair was wild, his cheeks flushed, his bottom lip quivering. "You're a fucking terrible friend, Brad. An ass, actually."

Brad stared at Mike, then glanced past into the stall to see if the girl was okay. She was crouching by the wall next to the toilet. The strap of her shirt hung down, torn. Her skirt lay near her feet. Her panties were all crooked.

My goodness. I came at just the right time.

"Fucking asshole," Mike said again, standing there in front of him.

"No, that would be you, actually. Mike, what have you done? This is serious. You know I'll have to report this!"

Mike glared at him. "What?"

"I'll have to report you, Mike. This is assault. It violates the code and—"

Before Brad could finish, his world spun, followed by an explosion of pain across his face. Mike had punched him! Punched hard. He had to take a few steps back to not lose his balance, then saw his friend coming at him again.

This time, he was prepared and fought back. Before long, the two guys were rolling around the dirty bathroom floor, punching and wrestling with each other. Mike wound up on top of him, his fist raised. Brad glanced over to the bathroom stall and saw the girl just standing there.

Why hasn't she moved? Now's her chance to get away!

"Get out of here, Becca," he yelled at her while trying to block Mike's blows. Wide-eyed, she pulled up her skirt and ran for the exit.

Mike let go of Brad for a second, trying to grab the girl's leg as she passed them. But Brad reacted fast and pulled him back down. He tackled him, and before long, gained the upper hand. He pinned Mike to the dirty bathroom floor. "Mike, you made a *big* mistake. I'll have to report you. I'm sorry."

Mike's blue eyes gleamed with hatred. "Some friend you are. So, what's your plan, you gonna hold me down here forever?"

Slowly, Brad eased his grip. "No, I'll let you go… but know that I'm reporting you."

"You fucking know this will ruin me! My career!" Mike said, tears in his eyes. "Fuck, Collins! This will ruin me. Don't do it. You're my friend!"

"Yeah, I am. That's exactly why I have to do this. Help you learn to be a better man. The man I know you can be."

"Fucking nonsense, Collins. Fuck you. You report me, you'll be making a big mistake."

"No, *you're* the one who made a big mistake, doing what you did here tonight. What the heck, man?" Mike just stared at him. Brad rose to his feet then offered Mike a hand. "Come on. Let me at least give you a lift home."

Mike stared at Brad's hand, then spat at it. The wad of spit missed by two feet. Undeterred, Mike got up and dusted off his pants, his eyes still resting on Brad, his face bright red. "No, I don't want you to *drive me home*. I don't want to be in the same fucking car as you ever again! The same fucking room. And if you *do* report me, our friendship is over, you hear me?"

"Mike..." Brad swallowed hard. "I have to...."

Mike didn't say anything for a moment, just opened and closed his mouth several times. Finally, he said, "I can't believe it. You'll regret this. You will."

"Come on, Mike, we can—" But before Brad could finish his sentence, Mike was out of the door. Stunned, Brad sagged, needed a few seconds to process what had just happened.

Then he ran as fast as he could, out the bathroom door, through the tavern, past the table where his friends were all sitting, disregarding their shouts; he ran out the tavern entrance, but he was too late. Mike was already in his car.

"Mike, stop! Please! You shouldn't drive. You could hurt someone, or yourself!"

"Too late for that, Collins, you already fucked me! And I swear to you right here and now, you'll pay for this. I swear to God. You messed with the wrong guy. *You'll fucking pay for this!*"

With a face the color of his Corvette, Mike tore out of the parking lot and sped away.

Agent Anderson whistled through her teeth. "So you told your superiors about this, which led to Mike getting kicked out of the Air Force Academy. About a month before graduation?"

"Yeah," Brad said. "He was furious with me."

Chief Parlot stared at him. "So he threatened you back then. Twenty-five years ago."

Brad nodded. "Yeah. Told me I'd pay for what I did. I thought it was all talk."

He felt Elisabeth's hand in his and noticed she was still holding on to him, holding on tightly, despite his own palm being so sweaty. The squeeze of her hand calmed him, helped him to relax after reliving the painful memory of that night.

"Based off your recounting, that person *definitely* qualifies as an enemy, General. It doesn't matter if it happened well before your daughter's kidnapping. People hold grudges for a long, *long* time," Agent Anderson said.

"Agreed," the chief said. "General, who is this 'Mike,' exactly? Do you have a last name?"

"Yeah. Clifford. It's Mike Clifford."

Chief Parlot raised his eyebrows. "Clifford? *The* Michael Clifford? As in the Florida senator?"

Brad nodded. "Yeah, that's him. Senator Mike Clifford."

"Wow, that's a big enemy to have," Agent Anderson said. "Thank you for sharing, General. Good stuff. We'll be looking into Mike Clifford more."

CHAPTER 46

"**M**ore? There's more you'd like to share?" Hank Harris said.

Billings nodded and watched his lawyer bend down to open his briefcase. He pulled out a box of praline chocolates. "Before we continue, might I ask: are you hungry? I got some chocolates here."

Billings eyed him, then the box of chocolates. *Yeah, I'm freaking hungry. Been hours since I've last eaten. But chocolate? I'd rather have a nice steak or fish.* He licked his lips. "I'm starving. Sure. Give it here."

"Okay, great." Hank fumbled with the plastic wrap protecting the box of fancy-looking confections. He was finally able to unwrap it, then popped the lid and offered the box to Jim.

He chose one topped with a chocolate-covered coffee bean and stuffed it inside his mouth. "Oh, these *are* delicious," Jim said. "Very fancy. Nice and smooth."

Hank studied the box. "Yeah, European, I guess. They make good chocolates."

"No kidding," Jim said, and grabbed another piece. *Yum. This isn't steak, but at least it'll keep me going.* He licked his fingers, then snatched a third piece.

Hank watched him for a bit, then went back to studying his notes.

"You really should try one, Hank," Jim said, as he stuffed a fourth praline into his mouth. "They're amazing."

"I'm sure they are, but can't say I'm a chocolate fan. I don't really like chocolate."

"Really? You're missing out, Hank."

Hank laughed. "That's what my wife always tells me, but I'd rather eat gummies. You know, Sour Patch Kids—that's my kind of candy."

Jim nodded, then took another praline. "A shame. These are to die for!"

Hank laughed again. "Well, glad you like them. They were a special gift."

As he chewed, Jim looked at his lawyer. "Oh yeah? Special gift?" Suddenly, he started coughing.

"Woah, you okay there, Chief?" Hank asked, watching him with raised eyebrows.

Jim was having a hard time controlling his coughing spree. He caught his breath and nodded, his face red. "Yeah, guess it went down the wrong pipe or something. I might need some water."

"Sure, right over there," Hank said, pointing to an unopened plastic bottle on the table.

Jim Billings grabbed it and unscrewed the lid, his hands shaky. Hank watched as Jim lifted the bottle to his mouth, his whole arm quivering; he spilled half the water before it even made it to his mouth. He started coughing again.

Hank sat up tall in his chair. "My goodness, Chief Billings, are you okay?"

Jim stopped coughing and nodded. He set the water bottle back down on the table. "I think so," he croaked, his voice hoarse, his forehead sweaty. "What's in those chocolates?"

Hank shrugged his shoulders. "I don't know. The usual stuff, I assume." He put the lid back on, flipped over the box, and studied the ingredients label. "Are you allergic to nuts?"

Jim started coughing again and shook his head. "No," he said in between coughs, "no allergies. But throat tight." His coughing became a harsh wheeze.

Hank jumped up. "What? Oh my gosh, this does seem like an allergic reaction. Maybe you're allergic to something you didn't know about?"

Jim looked at his lawyer and wheezed again and again, hard, loud, barely able to catch his breath in between the violent coughs. "Where... did... you... get... chocolates?"

"They were sent to me. Just arrived today. With a note for you."

Jim's face had turned red, he was sweating, he couldn't talk anymore. *Sent? With a note? For me?*

"It said to gift them to you. Signed by a benefactor who sincerely wishes you'll be proven innocent soon."

Jim stared at his lawyer in between all his coughing and wheezing. His face was turning slightly blue now. *What the fuck? A benefactor? For me?* "Who?" he managed to whisper.

"One of your old friends in DC sent them."

Jim stared at Hank. *Oh fuck, an old friend from DC? Cliff! Shit, they're trying to shut me up. I should've known!* He coughed so violently he threw up right there on the floor of the interrogation room.

"Chief Billings!" Hank dashed into the hallway. "Help! Someone, help!"

Jim felt his throat tightening more and more. *Fuck! I'm doomed. They got to me before I could even rat them out.* He took quick breaths as he stared at the chocolates, his eyes bulging. *And Hank Harris was stalling me. Stalled my statement on purpose. Should've known. He's one of Cliff's puppets.*

He held his throat and an awful wheezing sound escaped his lungs before he collapsed sideways out of his chair onto the cold, hard floor.

CHAPTER 47

"**F**loor? You remember the boat's floor?" Officer Sally Johnson said.

Maria nodded. "Yes, it was the same as the floor of the bowling alley on base. The one we were at last night."

"Can we see the video again, please, Lieutenant Heikinnen?" Agent Tom Cooper said.

"Of course," Aaron said. He pulled out his phone and accessed the recording he'd taken of Maria last night.

The officer, the agent, and Dr. Davies watched the recording. Maria kept her eyes down, watching her arm hairs stand up, until she finally closed them. She did some breathing exercises. *I don't want to see that video. I really don't.*

When she opened her eyes again, she almost jumped upon seeing Dr. Davies staring directly at her.

"Classic childhood PTSD," Dr. Davies said. "How do you feel, Maria?"

She shrugged her shoulders. "Don't know, hard to say. How do I... feel? Silly? Strange? Weird? Yeah, definitely weird. And definitely strange. All of this is just so strange. So unbelievable."

"That's understandable, Maria. In fact, it's perfectly fine. Just know it'll all be okay. For this next part, I'd like to bring you back to that time on the boat, okay? Just focus on me, please," Dr. Davies said, his voice calm, a friendly smile on his lips.

"I'll try," Maria whispered.

"That's good. Thanks, Maria. Now, please close your eyes and listen to my voice, just my voice."

Maria did as she was told, leaned back in her chair and listened. She heard Agent Cooper walking around in the room, then heard his footsteps stop and heard a rustling sound instead, as if he was searching for something in his bag. Maria heard Sally sit down in a chair to her left, felt Aaron's hand on her thigh. She took in a deep breath and tried to focus on Dr. Davies' calming voice, when suddenly, she heard a scream—a loud scream, a plea for help, doors banging open and closed.

She opened her eyes and looked at Dr. Davies in fear.

"Maria, please, I'd like you to—"

"Shhh... Do you hear that?"

Everyone froze and listened. They heard feet running down the hallway in the one direction, lots of yelling, then more feet running the opposite direction. Chief Parlot's voice rattled the walls of the building. "Call 911 immediately!"

"What's going on out there?" Officer Johnson wondered, and got up. She walked to the door and opened it, just to see Agent Anderson sprinting past. "Tonya!" the officer called after her, "what's going on?"

By now, Agent Cooper, Dr. Davies, Maria, and Aaron were all crowding around the doorframe behind Officer Johnson, trying to catch a glimpse of the commotion.

Agent Anderson came running back the other way to them. "It's Billings," she said. "He collapsed. Sally, Tom, I need you. Now!"

The three of them took off. Maria watched them disappear inside a room at the end of the hallway. *Billings? The former chief?*

"Maria, Aaron," she heard from the other end of the hall. She turned and saw both Brad and Elisabeth peeking outside their designated room.

Aaron waved. "Any idea what's going on?"

Brad shrugged. "Not sure. Something happened to the former chief while he was with his lawyer. He collapsed or something."

"What?" Aaron and Dr. Davies said at the same time, and exchanged glances.

"That's odd," Aaron mumbled. He took Maria's hand and they walked over to join her parents.

"Let's clear the hallway. We can all go in here," Dr. Davies said, ushering them inside Brad and Elisabeth's room. Once everyone was inside, he shut the door. "Hang tight. Let's just wait to see what's happening, okay?"

They all nodded and took seats around the table. No one was in the mood to talk. They listened to the hustle and bustle outside; at one point, the paramedics arrived, and they all stared at the floor when they overheard the loud clicking sound of the defibrillator's shocks.

"Doesn't sound good," Brad said.

Aaron agreed. "Certainly not. If they're trying to revive him, then that means…"

"Gosh, if he dies, we're back to knowing nothing." Elisabeth's face was flushed, her freckles shiny. "Or did the police talk to him already?"

"Doubt it," Aaron said. "If he was still one-on-one with his lawyer when he collapsed, that means they didn't get the chance to interrogate him yet. He would've talked only after reviewing his legal situation with his lawyer."

"Hope they save him," Dr. Davies said.

They all nodded.

Brad sighed. "Man, another perp we really needed to help us put the puzzle pieces together. This is crazy."

Maria perked up. *He has a point. A good point. This sure* is *crazy. Convenient, if someone wanted to keep all this a big secret, isn't it?*

They sat there, cramped inside the small interrogation room, in silence. They heard the paramedics leave through the hallway, a muted shuffle. They listened for the sound of emergency sirens outside, but they never came.

Maria felt forlorn. *Either the walls are too thick or there's no need to rush him to the hospital. If there's no need to rush, that means he's dead.*

Everyone in the room exchanged glances, sad looks on their faces. Aaron voiced what was on everyone's mind. "Don't think he made it...."

The door banged open and Chief Parlot strode in.

Brad stood up. "Chief! What's happened?"

Door handle still in his hand, the chief sighed, then shook his head. "We lost him. Couldn't revive him. Jim Billings has passed away."

A gasp rose up through the whole room.

Maria stared at the chief. *I knew it. We lost him. He can't talk anymore.*

"How could this happen?" Dr. Davies wanted to know.

"He just collapsed, his lawyer said. Not sure why," Chief Parlot said.

"Heart attack?" Elisabeth asked.

Chief Parlot shrugged his shoulders. "Not sure. Regardless, we have to focus on his death right now. Find out what exactly happened, talk to his lawyer, inform the press, and... and..."

Dr. Davies stood up, walked over to the chief, and gave him a pat on the shoulder. "We get it, Isaac. You're busy. We can talk later."

"Thanks, Elijah," Chief Parlot said. He gave his friend a grim smile. "Please make sure these fine folks get home safely. Out of the back door—away from the press."

"Yes, I'll make sure. Go ahead and do your thing, Isaac." Dr. Davies gave him another encouraging pat on the shoulder. The chief nodded, turned around, and closed the door behind him.

Maria stared at the door. *This is crazy! He's actually dead? Just dropped dead? He seemed so healthy. Something's not right.*

"Let's head back to base then," Brad said, and got up.

Elisabeth sighed, picked up her purse, and rose from her chair. "Yeah, I guess so. Nothing more we can do here."

"Wait a minute," Maria said. "Am I the only person who thinks this is strange? People are dropping dead left and right. First Jonathan Sullivan, now Chief Billings. And that FBI agent who died a while back. This is *weird*, isn't it? Everyone who knows something about this case—my case—dies."

"I don't know, sweetie, it could all be one big coincidence," Brad said. "Jonathan Sullivan was weak from fighting with you, might have had a heart attack after the interrogation and…"

"No, he was definitely killed," Maria said, her arms crossed. "Killed by the former chief, Chief Billings."

"Maybe," Brad said. "But we don't know for sure yet, do we? Anyway, now the former chief died. But we don't know why. He might have had a simple heart attack; it happens to people his age. And the former FBI agent… who knows? It could just be coincidence."

Aaron raised his one eyebrow. "Two people, supposedly part of the same evil group and possessing sensitive information on Maria's kidnapping, suddenly die within days of each other? That's more than just coincidence, don't you think?"

Elisabeth stopped moving and crossed her arms in front of her chest. "Aaron and Maria are right. It's very unusual to have two suspects drop dead like that."

"Exactly. Two people who could've given us more clues to the past," Aaron said. "It's too convenient."

"But convenient for who?" Brad asked, looking at each of them in turn.

"That's the question," Maria said. "Who benefits from them not being around to talk anymore?"

"Seems obvious to me: the one guy remaining," Aaron said, his voice sharp. "The police told us there were four guys involved. We already know of three, right? Sullivan, Billings, Borman. Who was the fourth?"

"I don't know, but someone in this building might," Maria said. "Come on, everyone, let's hop over to the investigators' workroom next door and see what we can find."

The group was already on their way out the door when Dr. Davies threw up his hands. "Please, hold on, everyone. You can't just butt into an ongoing investigation. Especially if it means handling evidence without police supervision! No way!"

"Come on, doc," Maria said, and gave him an elbow bump. "*You're* supervising us. And you're my shrink—who better to help us take a closer look into my past?"

Dr. Davies shook his head. "No, absolutely not. It's against the rules. And goes against my orders. I'm responsible for your well-being, supposed to take you home. So, that's what's going to happen."

Maria saw the determination on his face and knew it was of no use pressing him any further. *Besides, he's probably right. Can't just waltz in there without the chief's consent.*

She sighed and followed Dr. Davies down the hallway.

Maria watched the palm trees fly by. She was sitting next to Elisabeth, with Aaron up front and Brad driving. Their vehicle was surrounded by a police escort.

She felt a hand on her shoulder. Elisabeth's. "Don't worry, mein Engel, we'll find out more soon. Did you get to talk to Dr. Davies about that boat you were held on?"

Maria turned to her mom and shook her head. "No, we barely got to talk about anything. Sucks. Thought I'd get the chance to remember more. Remember *them*. You know… the ones who took me."

"Well, you already identified the corrupt FBI agent. That was huge. Give it time. The memories might come back. Once you're confronted with the trauma, I suppose. Sounds exhausting and painful, though."

Maria sighed. "Yeah, maybe. But I need closure. Need to see the ones responsible behind bars. I mean, who kidnaps a kid off a military base? What kind of person does that?"

Elisabeth sighed. "Trust me, I've asked myself the same questions, day and night these past twenty years." She squeezed Maria's shoulder.

"I still wonder where you guys could have made such an enemy. Maybe back at the duty station you were at, before Eglin?"

"You mean Utah?" Elisabeth said. "I don't think so. We had a great time there."

Aaron turned around. "What did you guys do in Utah?"

"Nothing out of the ordinary," Brad now said. "I worked at the 86th Fighter Weapons Squadron while Elisabeth was first caring for baby Moana—I mean, Maria…."

"Yeah, I was home with her at the time. And I was part of the Spouses' Club."

"What's that?" Maria asked.

"A support system for military spouses. You should join one, too," Elisabeth told her daughter. "They're pretty fun, you know. They're welcoming, give you lots of information about the new area, offer monthly meetings, and smaller clubs for hobbies you might be interested in. Board games. Book clubs. Mommy groups. Things like that. It's a good way to get to know people and make friends in a new community."

"I see," Maria said. "So, make any enemies in mommy group?"

Elisabeth snorted.

Brad laughed out loud. "No, no enemies there. They all *loved* Elisabeth. Absolutely loved her. Elisabeth got famous there in Utah. She was even featured in the *Air Force Times*."

Stunned, Maria turned to her mom. "Famous? *Air Force Times*?"

Elisabeth blushed. "Well, I wouldn't say *famous*. But that newspaper did an article on one of the clubs I founded as part of the Spouses' Club."

"What kind of club?" Aaron asked her.

"The H.O.P.E. Club," Elisabeth said.

"Hope Club?"

"Yeah. It stands for 'Hear Our Personal Experience,'" Elisabeth explained. "When you take the first letter of each of those words and put them together—*H*, *O*, *P*, *E*—it spells 'hope.' And hope is what those women needed."

"What women? The spouses?" Maria asked.

Elisabeth shook her head. "No, not just the spouses. This club was for every woman: married or unmarried, active duty or reserve, officer or enlisted. For any woman who got harassed, put down, abused."

Maria gasped. "*Abused?*"

Elisabeth nodded. "Yeah, there was more domestic or work-related abuse going on than anyone ever imagined."

Aaron raised his eyebrow. "Work-related abuse?"

"Unfortunately, yeah. Especially back then, twenty years ago. Not many women were even in the Air Force, but those who were—often young enlisted or officers—were often put down and not taken seriously," Brad said. He sighed. "Or worse: Harassed. Abused. This often involved older men in power."

"Yuck," Maria exclaimed. "That's disgusting! And horrible! And so unfair! All these guys thinking they're better and stronger, believing they can do whatever they want, especially in a male-dominated workplace. But they can't! They need to learn that we women can't be put down."

Through the rearview mirror, Brad saw Maria's face flush with passion as she continued her passionate speech. "Women are so much more than what some guy sees in us. We're not some kinda object. We're smart, powerful, and beautiful. We all just need to speak up and stand together."

Elisabeth agreed. "Exactly, we *do* need to stand up for each other. Women's rights have come far, but not far enough. We need to move them further along."

Brad smirked. "Like mother, like daughter, I suppose."

Maria and Elisabeth winked at each other.

Elisabeth squeezed her daughter's shoulder again. "Du bist fantastisch. Just a phenomenal young lady."

Maria smiled and blinked back tears. *I guess we're a lot alike, my mom and me.*

Elisabeth's smile faded. "You know what? I really believe I *have* forgiven her—your mamá. Because she raised you so very well. She instilled in you such wholesome values, I probably couldn't have done it better myself. She's done a fantastic job raising a vulnerable, confused, traumatized young toddler. Traumatized after being kidnapped, almost drowning, held captive by bad guys on a boat for months." A big tear formed in her eye. "We must find out who did this to you."

"Agreed," Aaron said. "Wait, you *did* already come up with a probable family enemy, didn't you? You told the police about them this morning. Who? Someone from Utah?"

Brad shook his head. "No, certainly no enemies in Utah. Definitely not. I never pissed off anyone there the way I did in the Academy."

Maria perked up. "The Academy?"

"Yeah, the Air Force Academy. I had a friend there once. He got kicked out."

Aaron raised an eyebrow. "Kicked out? Because of you?"

Brad pressed his lips together. "No, can't really say it was because of me. He did it to himself. Bad behavior. Blatant. But yeah, I was the one who told on Mike to our superiors."

"Did this Mike guy know James Borman or Chief Billings?" Aaron asked.

"See, that's exactly why I still can't see how he had anything to do with this. Sure, he hates my guts. But I doubt he knew those guys. Mike was a nobody back then, and tried real hard to stay away from the police—especially after that first drinking-and-driving incident."

"Is that why he got kicked out?"

"Well, that and the girls," Brad mumbled. "Sad, really sad. He tried hard, but just couldn't keep away from temptation. Alcohol and girls brought him down."

Maria got angry and her face flushed again. "*Girls* brought him down? Sounds like he wasn't the victim in this—the girls were! Or am I wrong?"

Brad sighed.

"Ha, knew it. Your friend was just an asshole who couldn't control himself, wasn't he?"

"I guess so. You're right, Maria. But enough about that. I already told the police the whole story. For now, I think we should focus on finding someone who was connected to both the FBI agent and former chief, someone high up back then. Mike was a small little nobody, so it couldn't be him. No, we're dealing with someone high up, and I can only imagine they've amassed even more power by now. Someone who knows how to manipulate people."

They all nodded. The car went silent for the remainder of the drive. Eventually, they made their way through Eglin's security checkpoint and the two police cars escorting them turned back. They all flashed their IDs then continued on toward the inn.

Maria's question ended the silence. "What's the Academy guy's name again?"

"Mike," Brad said. "Mike Clifford."

"I see," she said, and looked outside the window.

She got lost in thought. *Mike Clifford. Mike… Clifford? Clifford? Something seems familiar about that name. Or does it?*

For some reason, her brain kept repeating his name in a loop. *Mike. Mike Clifford. Clifford. Have I heard about you before? Like on the news?*

CHAPTER 48

The news channel anchor talked quickly into her microphone. "We just learned that Jim Billings, the retired chief of the Niceville Police Department, gasped his last breath on the cold, hard ground of an interrogation room inside his own former police station. Irony abounds! The question is: how did this happen?"

Cliff slapped his thigh in laughter. *So dramatic! And fucking hilarious. Yeah, good luck figuring out how that happened.* He grinned. *Good job, Hank. Not that you were in on it. But you certainly nailed the job, stalling good old Bill to make sure he didn't say anything.*

Cliff turned off the TV in his big office and sat back in his leather chair. He started playing with his pen. *Yeah, I took care of everything. Thank God people are so easily manipulated. Hank didn't want to lose his lawyer's license, didn't want anyone to find out he cheated on the bar exam. He won't rat me out.*

He laughed again and nodded. *Yeah, Hank's in my pocket. Bet he's super-surprised, but he won't say a word—else, he can kiss his career goodbye. Even if he does squeal, he doesn't know it's me—at least can't be sure it's actually me. 'Cuz all I did was set him up with this job of defending Billings. And I didn't even send the chocolates. Olivia did. From a supporter in DC who happened to know about Hank's bar exam.*

Cliff grinned, returned the pen to his desk, and got up. *Yeah, thought of everything. My secret is safe. I'm safe now. Bullet should be safe.*

He sighed. *It didn't have to come to this. All this collateral damage. Too bad. Poor Sully. Poor Bill. Oh well. I blame* her. *Fucking Moana Collins.*

He nodded and sighed. *The Collins girl just* had *to go searching for her past. Too bad. It was such a good plan me and Sully came up with on that boat. With all my connections, I had no issue getting her a fake social security number and birth certificate. All thanks to that hot blonde at Vital Records.*

Ah, now there was a beaut. Cliff grinned. *It didn't take much to convince her to fake that birth certificate. Gave her a couple diamond necklaces—and a few months in an amazing relationship. Mostly amazing for doing one thing.*

Cliff laughed out loud and contentedly smiled, thinking back. *Yeah, it was enough to shut her up.* His grin faded. *But would it be now? Fuck! Not sure. It's been so long.*

He started sweating and paced back and forth in his grand office. *I can't forget about her—she's a possible threat to the secret.... I'll need to call her and make sure she won't talk. Maybe pony up a few more diamond necklaces? More time with me?*

He thought about it. *She loved status, that girl. Maybe a very personalized tour of DC. The White House and U.S. Capitol Building? Yes and yes. That should be enough to renew her loyalty.* He stopped pacing. *Yes, that's a brilliant plan. Just need to call her. Not using my office phone, of course.*

He pulled out his cell phone and an old address book from his desk drawer. He paged through it. *Oh dear. What's her name again? Do I even have her number in my address book? It's been twenty years!*

He flipped through faster and faster, past pages and pages of numbers and names. Normally, he took pride in looking through those entries, all the women he'd slept with over the years. His conquests. *It's fun to scroll through and think about how successful I am. Successful in finding girls. And they all love me. Every single one of them says so, and I always tell them I love them, too.*

He laughed, then his smile turned to a frown. *I do believe it. I believe I love them in those moments. But do I really know what love is?* He sighed. *Certainly didn't get much love from my parents. Mom was gone a lot and I was basically raised by nannies—but they were rotated in and out of service so quickly, I never got the time to grow close to any of them. My dad's doing. He was always gone a lot also.*

Cliff closed his eyes and blinked back tears. *Dad. Man, I've tried. I've tried hard. Tried to follow in his footsteps like he expected of me. But I failed before I even began.*

He opened his eyes and stared straight ahead at the wall in front of him. *Failed out, thanks to Collins. Asshole Collins. Tattletale Collins.*

His face red, Cliff was about to start pacing the office again, but managed to stop himself.

Breathe, just breathe. Think back to that gorgeous blonde. Jenna? Jillian? Joy?

Nope, that wasn't it. More like Jenna. Jenny?

Nope.

Janice! Yes, that's her name, I remember it now. Janice.

He looked through the address book and found it. Her name. And there was her number.

Hopefully still her number? Hmm, if not, I have my ways of finding people. Yes, indeed. I'll find her. I sure will.

And I'll make sure Janice won't put two and two together to realize whose birth certificate she actually faked back then. Can't let her make the connection to the current case. Yeah, I'll tell her another lie she'll believe, another good story.

CHAPTER 49

"**A** story? It's not just some convenient *story*! You have to believe me! Chief Billings just suddenly collapsed after experiencing a severe allergic reaction," Hank Harris said, his voice cracking in between sobs.

"Chief, you have to believe me! My nephew is allergic to nuts, I saw it once at a family reunion. He started sweating and complaining about his throat, then started vomiting and almost fell unconscious, but luckily, there was an EpiPen on hand and that helped. He still had to go to the hospital."

Agent Anderson and the chief exchanged glances. "Mr. Harris, why are you telling us this story?" she asked.

"Because Chief Billings went through the exact same thing as my nephew. I thought Billings might have an unknown nut allergy or something. He stopped breathing. I called for help. Didn't you hear me?"

"We did. That's why we came running."

"But you didn't administer an EpiPen. Gosh, he just died, right over there," Hank said, his voice quiet, tears streaming down his face.

"It is tragic, Mr. Harris. We know," the chief said. "But an EpiPen wouldn't have saved him."

"How do you even know that?"

"We don't know if Chief Billings was allergic to nuts or any other foods," Agent Anderson said, and slid a piece of paper across the table toward Hank Harris. "But we *do* know that he was poisoned."

Hank stared at the agent, then at the chief. All color left his face, leaving it a ghostly white. "Poisoned?" He quickly glanced down at the autopsy report Agent Anderson had slid across the table. "What… they found poison? But why? How?"

"We have the exact same questions, Mr. Harris," Chief Parlot said, and started pacing the small interrogation room. "You came here to defend him, and now your client is dead! Does that benefit you in some manner? What do you have to hide, Mr. Harris?"

"Me? Nothing!"

Agent Anderson took a step closer to Hank Harris and looked deeply into his eyes. They were filled with tears. A tear escaped and ran down his pale face.

Chief Parlot watched him closely. *He looks like a deer caught in the headlights. Scared. Really scared. Why? Because he killed him? Or because he's afraid of someone?*

"Mr. Harris," Agent Anderson said, "you're telling us you had nothing to do with this?"

"No, I didn't," he screamed. "Why would I poison my client?"

"You tell us, Mr. Harris," the chief barked. "Why would you?"

The lawyer sobbed in his chair. "I… I… *didn't*. How would I even have done that? I don't have any poison on me. You know that."

"Not *on* you, that's right, Mr. Harris," Agent Anderson said, her voice very calm. "But you did bring in these chocolate pralines, didn't you?" She slid a picture of the box of chocolates across the table. It landed right in front of Hank. He studied it, then looked up again.

The chief watched his body language, watched every move. *He looks dumbfounded. Shocked. Innocent?*

"Yeah, I… I did. Was bringing in food prohibited?"

"Oh, it's no problem bringing in some chocolates," the agent said. "But next time, I'd make the murder weapon less obvious."

Chief Parlot stared at Hank. *He's either a really good actor, or actually doesn't have a clue.*

The lawyer's face was blank. "What? I don't understand."

"Well, Mr. Harris," Agent Anderson said in that calm voice of hers, taunting him, "why did you feed him chocolates without enjoying even a single piece yourself?"

"'Cuz I don't like chocolate at all. I only eat gummy candy."

"Convenient, Mr. Harris," the chief said. "Very convenient. And not very convincing."

"Convincing?"

Chief Parlot raised his eyebrows. *Jeez. He's a lawyer! How does he not get this?*

"Mr. Harris, our lab determined those chocolate pralines were filled with strychnine," Agent Anderson said, and slid another lab report across the table toward Hank.

He glanced down and started reading. As he read, his eyes widened, his mouth dropped open. He jumped up. "It wasn't me! It wasn't. This is the first time I've ever heard of strychnine. I don't even know what it is or where to get that kind of stuff." He burst into tears anew.

"Hey, sit down and look at the report," Agent Anderson said, and Hank complied. "Everything's spelled out right there. See?"

She walked over and started reading over his shoulder out loud. "'Strychnine is a white, odorless, bitter crystalline powder and a very strong poison. Absorbing only a tiny amount produces severe biological effects. It impedes the proper operation of the chemical that controls nerve signals to the muscles. This chemical is necessary as an off-switch for the body's muscles. If this process is prevented from working properly—as happens when strychnine is inhaled or ingested—muscles throughout the human body experience severe, painful spasms and eventually tire. At that point, asphyxiation is all but guaranteed.'"

Hank was a picture of misery as he sat in his chair and sobbed uncontrollably. He had to take in a deep breath before he spoke.

"But… but… I didn't put any poison in the chocolates. Where would I even find such a powerful poison?"

"Perhaps you own a plant from southern Asia or Australia called *Strychnos nux-vomica*?" Chief Parlot asked. "The *kuchla* plant?"

Hank shook his head violently.

"Or maybe you have rat poison at home?" Agent Anderson said.

"No, I don't. I don't… really… I… I… don't, I—" Hank sank deep into his chair and cried like a baby. "No, no, no!"

The chief walked over and sat down in the chair opposite Hank. "Well, Mr. Harris, how then do you explain that poison's presence inside those chocolates you brought in? How? Tell us!"

Hank jumped up again. "I didn't even buy them! They were unopened when I got them and I brought them in! I had no idea!"

The chief stared at him. *He might be innocent. Forensics did find plastic wrap belonging to the chocolate box inside the room's trash can. But I can't back down now.*

"Where did you get the chocolates then, Mr. Harris?" he roared, his voice deep.

Hank practically fell into his chair. "It was a gift for Chief Billings I was supposed to deliver."

What the heck? A gift?

Agent Anderson had similar thoughts. "A gift? A gift from whom?"

Hank Harris sobbed again and shook his head. "I… I… I can't tell you. I really can't tell you…"

"You *can't* tell us?" the chief said. He stood up to loom over the lawyer.

"No, I can't. Don't know who they're from. They were FedEx'd to me. With a note," Hank whispered.

Tonya raised her eyebrows. "A note? What kind of note? What did it say?"

"It told me to bring the chocolates in here and offer them to Billings. Told me to stall his statement and make sure he ate those chocolates."

"Good lord, why would you comply with such a strange request?" Chief Parlot roared. "Explain, Mr. Harris!"

"Because *they know*. They know about my bar exam," Hank whispered.

The chief raised his eyebrows. *The bar exam? What bar exam?*

"Explain, Mr. Harris," Agent Anderson said.

"Well, I might have... you know... might have... ahh, I can't tell you. If anyone finds out, it'll end my career," Hank said, his head low.

The chief nodded. *I get it. He probably cheated on his bar exam. Or bought his way in. And someone knows and blackmailed him, said they'd tell everyone what he did if he didn't deliver the chocolates to Billings.*

He laughed out loud. "You're very funny, Mr. Harris, very funny. Can't tell anyone about cheating on the bar exam? Afraid that might end your career? I'll tell you what: you may have gotten away with it so far, but killing a former police chief—*your own client*—during an attorney-client session is a criminal act that'll definitely *end your career!*"

"But... but... I... I didn't kill him! Those weren't even my chocolates. I was just the mule."

Agent Anderson had caught on to the chief's plan. "Exactly, Mr. Harris," she said, her voice as calm as ever, "you were just playing postman today. So, who did you deliver this gift of expensive chocolate pralines for? Tell us, and we might be able to save your career. You're a lawyer. You know a poor middleman, used to deliver poisonous chocolates because he feared for his own career, maybe his very life, might walk if he never intended to cause harm, right?"

Hank lifted his head again and looked back and forth between the FBI agent and the police chief. He nodded slightly.

"Okay, then, Mr. Harris. Tell us. How did you come by those chocolates?" Agent Anderson said, smiling.

"They were sent to me by mail. I already told you. Arrived right at my doorstep via FedEx with that note inside the shipping wrap."

"What town did it come from? Somewhere local?" Tonya asked.

"Washington, DC," Hank whispered.

DC? What the heck? The chief was confused. "Who sent the chocolates from DC?" he roared. "Who, Mr. Harris?"

"I don't know! It just said it was from an old friend and supporter of Chief Billings."

Friend? Supporter? Yeah right! What a great way to support someone. The chief shook his head. *We gotta find this so-called friend. A killer in Washington, DC.*

CHAPTER 50

Washington, DC? Mike Clifford, my dad's former buddy, is based in Washington, DC? What's he do there? Maria kept googling him on her phone. Ever since they got back from the police station, she found herself obsessing over him.

She was sprawled across a couch in the lobby of the Air Force Inn, researching the senator on her phone, while everyone crowded around the TV watching the news. She heard them talking over one another, discussing the newest information about Billings's death.

Apparently, Billings was poisoned. But why? Maria sighed and focused on her Google search again. *"Senator Mike Clifford, raised in Florida's Panhandle, proudly represents the state of Florida in the U.S. Senate in Washington, DC,"* she read.

So he's a senator in DC? But he represents Florida? The panhandle? This place? She kept skimming articles about him. *"Well-liked." "Hometown boy." "Made his mark in DC." "Represents the common man."*

"What are you reading about, Maria?" Aaron said, and she was so surprised that she almost dropped her phone. Aaron laughed. "I get the impression you're researching something illegal."

Maria shook her head. "No, not at all. I just keep thinking this Mike guy is important. I've been doing some research on him."

"Oh, the Academy dude?"

Maria nodded. "Yeah. He's a senator now. In Washington, DC."

Aaron whistled through his teeth. "Wow. He went far despite getting kicked out of the Academy. Made it big. Real high up there."

Maria nodded, and Aaron shifted his focus back on the news.

She turned abruptly pale. Something her dad had said earlier in the car came back to her. *"No, we're dealing with someone high up, and I can only imagine they've amassed even more power by now. Someone who knows how to manipulate people."*

She swallowed hard, her tongue all dry. *A senator is pretty high up there. He wields power. He manipulates people! Could it be this guy has something to do with it? Senator Mike Clifford?*

The phone slipped out of her hand. *That name! Clifford! Oh my gosh!*

Aaron saw her phone fall and picked it up for her. He handed it back while studying her face. "Maria, are you okay?"

She couldn't answer. Her skin was pale, so pale that it contrasted sharply with her freckles. She stared right ahead into nowhere. She felt a headache coming on. *Clifford. That name. Something's rotten with that name!*

"¿Mija, estás bien?" she heard her mamá ask.

"What's going on? Are you okay, Engel?" Her mom's voice made it to her ear.

"Maria, sweetie, are you alright? Are you still with us?" her dad said.

Aaron took her hand, her sweaty hand. "Maria, please, what's going on?"

The touch of his hand made her snap out of it. She nodded, then looked at each and every one of them. Jack, the Collinses, her mamá, Aaron.

"What were the names of the guys the police were looking for?" she asked them.

Aaron raised his one eyebrow. "You mean the names of the Fearless Four they mentioned in the press conference?"

Maria nodded.

"Well, there was Bill, JB, and Cliff, as far as I recall," Jack said.

Aaron nodded. "Yeah, exactly. Those three. Plus, we all know Jonathan Sullivan was involved."

Martina sighed. "Sí, we do know that. So he's the fourth one, no?"

Elisabeth's face turned red. "That means one of those criminals is still on the loose! We know Chief Billings was Bill and Agent James Borman was JB. So we're just missing that Cliff guy! We better find him!"

"I think I already have," Maria mumbled.

"Say what?" Elisabeth said and they all stared at Maria.

"Cliff! I think I know who he is. Couldn't Mike Clifford be Cliff?" Maria said. "Just think about it: Chief Billings was Bill, Agent James Borman was JB, and I bet they had a nickname for Sullivan also. See what they all have in common? They're not first names. The Fearless Four didn't use first names. We're looking for *nicknames*—often a play on their last name."

"Clifford is... Cliff?" Aaron mumbled, then suddenly jumped up. "Oh my gosh, Clifford is Cliff. We even have a motive for the kidnapping: revenge." Everyone stared at him in silence.

"B-but, but..." Brad stammered.

"If that's true, we need to figure out what connects Clifford with the others. How did he come to know them? Where could they have met?" Jack said.

"I think I found something in this one article," Maria said. "Chief Billings endorsed Senator Clifford the very first time he ran for Florida senator. He came along on a few of his campaign stops touring the panhandle. Wait, I have the article right here. Um... the former chief says he's endorsing him 'because he's a boy from the hood and grew up here in Niceville,' then goes on to mention 'they're old friends.'"

"Old friends?" Aaron said.

Maria shrugged her shoulders. "Don't know. That's all it says."

"We have to inform Chief Parlot. Here we were, standing slack-jawed around the TV, and you were over here plugging away doing awesome research. Proud of you, Maria," Brad said. He took out his phone. "Let's share our findings with him before it gets too late. Almost dinnertime. Who knows how long he'll be up working tonight?"

"Well, you'd think they'd be at it nonstop," Jack said. "They sure have their hands full. Two deaths, one kidnapping. Sounds like an all-nighter to me."

"Go ahead then, Brad, call the chief," Elisabeth said. "I have a feeling we're onto something here with Mike Clifford. If it's really him, he's *so* going down!" She punched her palm.

Brad sighed, then nodded and started dialing. Nobody noticed Maria, who was staring at her phone again. She had pulled up a picture of Senator Clifford. She looked straight at the handsome middle-aged man with curly beach-blonde hair, a wonderful Florida tan, and stunning blue eyes.

Do I know you, Senator Clifford?

CHAPTER 51

"**S**enator Clifford is Cliff?" Sally raised her eyebrows.

Chief Parlot nodded. "Yep, that's what General Collins thinks. He just told me about it. He made a compelling argument. I suppose it could be true? That Senator Clifford is Cliff. It all comes down to potential motive: taking revenge on tattletale Collins."

"Alright, alright, alright, we might be onto something here. But we'll need to be careful tiptoeing around such a public figure," Tonya said, and turned to Tom. "Well, Tom, it's up to you to work your magic again. First of all, we need proof that Clifford is actually Cliff. Find a connection between him and the others."

"Yes, ma'am," he said, his fingers already flying across the keyboard.

Tonya, Sally, and the chief walked back over to the worktable covered in pictures and reports. Chief Parlot studied the report detailing what Hank Harris had told them about his time with Jim Billings.

He read it over and over. *They "made him do it"? What exactly did Billings mean by that? Is he talking about killing Sullivan? Or ramming through the false conclusion of an accidental drowning twenty years ago?* The chief sighed. *Wish I knew.*

He kept reading on. *Here it says he had names. Billings expressed a willingness to name names, but never did. Collapsed before he could?* He sighed again. *That sucks, really sucks. But awfully convenient for whoever didn't want to be named. His "friend from DC"? Wait, what?*

He turned pale. "Holy cow. Could Senator Clifford be 'the friend from DC'?"

"You mean the thoughtful friend who mailed poisonous chocolates to lawyer Hank Harris and bribed him to feed them to Billings?" Sally said, and smirked.

"Well, I'm sure the senator has a DC address," Tonya said. "Tom, you gotta find out which FedEx location those chocolates originated from and who dropped them off."

Tom smirked. "Will do. But kinda busy right now with the first task. Give me a few more seconds."

Sally chuckled. "*Seconds*? Don't you mean minutes?"

Tom shook his head. His fingers banged out a few more lines of code, then he loudly clicked a button and waved them over.

"Got it," was all he said.

The others rushed to his side and stared at the screen. It was covered in a mess of receipts. Confused, they all looked at Tom.

He grinned. "Ladies and gentlemen you're looking at old credit card receipts I found on the dark web. Cards belonging to one Michael Clifford. And take a look at where they were used."

Tonya, Sally, and the chief leaned in closer.

"Can't read that, it's too small," Chief Parlot muttered, and fumbled in his pants pocket. "I'll need my reading glasses. Where did I leave them?"

"Don't worry, Chief, I can blow it up for ya," Tom said.

The chief raised his eyebrows in consternation. "Blow it up?"

The others burst into laughter.

"He means he can make the font bigger and easier to read. No explosions necessary." Sally laughed.

Of course. Silly me, Chief Parlot silently scolded himself.

"But to summarize," Tom said, "his credit cards were, at various times, used in Utah, Florida, and Las Vegas."

The chief's mouth fell open. *What? Utah, Florida, and Vegas? Wait a minute! Seriously?* "Don't tell me they were used at the same times and places as Agent James Borman's and Chief Billings's cards?"

Tom grinned. "Yep, that's exactly right. Mike Clifford met with those guys."

Holy cow. That's unbelievable. The chief had to swallow hard. A knot had formed in his throat.

"Notably, all three visited a certain Las Vegas casino the same night Jonathan Sullivan did. In the spring of 2003, not long before Moana Collins's disappearance," Tom said, still grinning.

"Yay, we got them, we made the connection. Great job, Tom, great job," Sally said, and patted him on the back.

"Don't celebrate prematurely. We still need to place Clifford in the area around Eglin Air Force Base in May 2003. If Sullivan's story is right, Cliff was the mastermind who planned the whole thing out," Tonya said, and started chewing on her pen. "We know that Cliff was on that boat dealing with Sullivan and the child. The child who was unfortunately still alive."

Boat? A boat. A yacht! Chief Parlot's face turned pale. *A fancy boat with shiny floors, according to Maria's memories.*

"Tom, find out if Clifford owned a yacht in 2003. A fancy white boat with shiny wooden floors. If so, we have solid proof he was involved in the kidnapping. If he was willing to murder a child, he wouldn't hesitate to off an adult. He'd have good reason to kill Billings if it meant avoiding his buddy ratting him out. A clear motive," the chief said. "We gotta find that boat."

"Yes, I'll find out, Chief. On it," Tom said.

"This is crazy," Sally said as they returned to the worktable and sat down. "Lots of powerful people involved, if we're right."

"Yeah. This week has been sloppy, smacks of desperation, but the original kidnapping was a well-planned coup," Tonya said, and sighed. "A big master plan."

CHAPTER 52

*A*big master plan! I managed those loose ends so well. They'll never be able to trace anything back to me. Or will they?

Cliff tugged at his tie as doubt crept into his mind. *No. I took care of everything. Sullivan and Billings were silenced. The chocolates were delivered in a seemingly unopened package—if that ever somehow comes back to me, I can claim I reused a gift I got from a secret admirer. I get gifts all the time, and senators are often victims of attempted harm.*

He grinned. *Oh yeah, that's good. I can use that excuse and it's my word against the cop's. There's no hard proof linking those poisonous chocolates to me. Except that stupid lawyer. But Hank won't talk. Too scared to lose his license, his career.* He grinned and looked around his office. *Plus, I was smart enough to have my intern mail them. My hands are clean.*

He started packing up his things. *And Janice? She should've received her new diamonds tonight, plus an invitation to a special tour of DC. She's been bought off.*

He closed his briefcase and looked around again. *I'm good. Got it all figured out. And just look at this beautiful office. And my awesome penthouse apartment. I sure made it big. Made it to the top. I won't let anyone stand in my way. But they won't. Everyone's already been taken care of.*

Feeling content, he turned off the lights, locked up, and was about to walk down the hall when he suddenly stopped in his tracks.

But what about her? *What about that little girl, Moana? A grown woman now. Maria. Will she be a threat to my safety?*

Sweat beaded his forehead. *She'll need to be kept in line. How? Don't know yet. I'll figure something out when I get home. Think about it over a glass of cognac out on the balcony of my penthouse apartment overlooking the Potomac.*

I'll come up with a solution to make sure the pretty girl doesn't stand in my way, won't dig where she has no business digging. Hmm. Might have to convince her myself.

Yeah, might have to run into you again, Maria.

CHAPTER 53

M aria was lying wide awake in her bed at the Air Force Inn. She couldn't sleep. *Can't believe everyone involved in my case keeps dropping dead. Could that senator really be behind it all?*

She felt her arm hairs stand up, a shudder run down her spine. But Aaron's warm breath on her shoulder comforted her. He was sound asleep next to her.

She smirked. *At least Aaron will get some sleep tonight. My sweet Aaron. Always there for me. And he's right. Chief Parlot and his team will take care of things. They'll uncover proof that ties the senator to all this. Then it'll just be a matter of bringing him to justice.*

She sighed. *I need to let go of the case for now. Get some sleep. Let the police do their work. There's always tomorrow.*

Maria turned onto her side and felt her ring catch on the bedsheets. Instinctively, she brought her right hand up to feel the ring on her left. *I'm engaged. To this sweet guy here. Aaron. My fiancé. Can't wait to marry him. And now, I even have a dad to walk me down the aisle.*

She broke out into a smile. *Yeah, my dad. A real dad. And I have two moms. I want them all at my wedding. Better start planning it. That'll be a welcome distraction. For everyone.*

She leaned over to give Aaron a kiss on the forehead, then tossed and turned until she found a comfortable position. She sank her head into the pillow and yawned. *It's been crazy this week. So tiring. I'm exhausted.*

Maria forced herself to think of her wedding plans only. *A spring wedding. Yeah, Aaron agreed to that. It'll be fun. So many festive colors for the flowers. What color should the bridesmaid dresses be? Blue?*

She thought about it. *Blue is my favorite color and it'll look good on everyone: my friends Keisha and Brandy, Aaron's little sis Emma. Yep, blue works with blonde and dark hair. But it's such a cold color. Maybe I should choose a warmer color? Red, maybe? Pink? Purple?*

She squished her head deeper into the pillow. *Yeah, all of those would work with Keisha's dark hair and Brandy's and Emma's blonde hair. Mmm. Blonde hair?*

She felt her arm hairs raise slightly and wasn't sure why. *I'm just being silly.*

Maria kept thinking of all the different color options for the bridesmaids' dresses and how they'd match her friends' hair color, until she fell asleep.

She opened her eyes and found herself staring straight into a mass of curly blonde hair.

Curls? Who is this? Emma and Brandy have straight blonde hair. And why's this head of hair so close to me?

She realized she was lying down on something hard. The hair was so close to her she could taste it. It brushed against her face, tickled her. She involuntarily moved her mouth.

She almost had to laugh but couldn't. Breathing felt hard. She realized she was shivering.

It's cold. So cold, so uncomfortable. Hard to breathe.

She took another deep breath in and felt a big hand on her chest. She squirmed.

Whose hand is that? Why is it lying on my chest? Why is it so big?

She realized she was small again, very small. Just a toddler. Her eyes widened in discomfort and fear.

Mama? Daddy? Where are you?

She took in another deep breath. So hard to breathe!

She started coughing, coughing hard, uncontrollably. Her little body shook from those awful coughs. She felt the need to throw up.

Mama? Daddy? I need you!

Tears formed in her eyes as her little body convulsed, and suddenly, she spat up a big mouthful of liquid, disgusting-tasting water. It flew right into the blonde curls that were still so close to her.

"Fuck, that's disgusting! The little brat threw up on me," *she heard a man yell, then felt the hand retreat from her chest. The head of vomit-coated curly blonde hair disappeared.*

"Told you she's alive. No need to monitor her breathing," *another man said.*

Who else is there? Who are these guys?

She spat up more water, then started crying.

It hurts so much, it hurts. Mama, help me! Please!

"What the fuck?" *the curly blonde-haired guy said, and rose to his full height, towering over her.*

She realized she was lying on the floor. The two men stood on either side, staring down to her.

Her eyes widened. Who are these guys? I don't know them. Mama? Help!

But her mom didn't come to help her, and she just lay there, on the cold, hard floor. For some reason her clothes were soaking wet, her diaper full. All she could do was listen.

"What the fuck? What did you do, Sully?"

"Me?" *she heard the other one say.* "Nothing. I did nothing. Did exactly as you told me to. Got a little something from JB and was about to get rid of that little something when… she opened her eyes."

This man, also blonde but with straight hair, started walking back and forth next to her on the opposite side of the curly-haired blonde man, mumbling, "A little something, a little something.... Are you fucking kidding me? A little girl? *I was supposed to get rid of a little girl? Why? What the fuck?"*

"Well, she was supposed to be dead. Drowned."

"But she isn't. Told you she's alive. Look at her. She's alive!"

"I fucking see that! Now, I need you to shut the fuck up so that I can think of what to do with her."

"What to do with her? What do you mean? Just take her back."

"What? Are you insane? Do you fucking hear yourself? She can never *go back, never ever! You don't kidnap a child to just bring it back. She'll never see home again."*

Never see home again? Why not? But I want to go home. Want to see Mama and Daddy. I don't like these guys. No, no, no. They scare me. I want my mama!

She started crying louder, whimpering.

"You made her cry," the straight-haired one said, "the poor thing."

"I fucking made her cry? No, you did, because you didn't finish the assignment," the curly-haired one said.

They stood over her arguing, accusing each other of having done something wrong.

I don't understand. I just want to go home. Get warm, get a big hug from Mama and Daddy. Go back to my bed. With Enti. With Schnulli. I need them. I need them.

Tears were streaming down her face as she sobbed on the floor, shivering in her wet clothes.

I wanna go home.

Her tears felt hot on her cold little face.

And then she remembered. "Use your words. Tell us what you want." Yes, that's what Mama and Daddy always tell me. I need to use my words.

She stopped sobbing, then whispered, "Home. Go home. Need Mama."

Both men stopped arguing.

"*Did she just say something?*" the straight-haired one said, and knelt down next to her.

As he bent down, she could see him better. Straight blonde hair, blueish-grey eyes, big jaw, broad shoulders.

Who is this? I've never seen him before. He looks big, scary.

She studied his face.

But not too mad. No, he doesn't look too mad. I need to use my words to tell him what I want.

"*Home,*" she said again, louder this time. "*Go home! Now! Need Mama! Need Daddy!*"

He raised his eyebrows. "*I think she says she wants to go home.*"

She nodded. *Use the magic word,* she remembered. "*Please,*" she said.

A quick smile flashed across the straight-haired man's face and showed his crooked yellow teeth.

"*Aw, she said 'please.' Kinda cute,*" he said. He looked up at the other man.

"*Cute? You think she's cute? What the fuck. We need to get rid of her. She can't say anything. I need her to shut the fuck up!*"

She started sobbing again.

He's not nice. He's mean. I don't like him.

She looked over at the other one again.

"*You're scaring her, Cliff. Don't yell at her.*"

"*What the fuck, Sully? Don't yell at her? I have every right to be mad, and I am—at both of you! You fucking messed up.*"

The nicer one stood up again. "*I did* not *mess up, JB fucking did! And all of you! What the fuck were you thinking, taking a kid? That's not 'something,' it's a little girl! Someone's child! Just bring her back.*"

"*Yeah, right, and then we all get arrested. Fine. Both you and I will go down together. You're just as guilty of kidnapping her as me. Fine, go to jail then, for all I care.*"

The two men glared at each other.

"*I thought you wanted your reward? Thought you wanted to start over with the money? Remember? You even signed the contract, Sully.*"

"I did," the straight-haired one yelled, "but I had no fucking idea you wanted me to get rid of a little girl. I thought it was… something. A thing. An animal. But a little girl? What the fuck?"

"Well, it's not much different than an animal, is it?"

I don't like them screaming. I don't like it. I want to go home. Use my words, just use my words. Tell them what I want. Maybe they didn't understand me? "Home!" she yelled with all her strength. "Mama!"

The straight-haired one pointed at her. "See, that's way different than an animal. She talks. She can think. Holy shit. A girl!"

"She needs to shut the fuck up. Go on, shut her up."

"What? I will definitely not shut her up. What does that even mean?"

"Kill her, Sully. Kill her and finish your assignment."

A big argument erupted between the two men. She watched them, her beautiful, unique eyes wide, freakishly green, just watched the scene play out above her. She curled up, shivering, crying.

I want to go home. Mama, Daddy, please, help me. I'm so scared, so scared.

She sobbed. Then she screamed, so loud, so shrill, an ear-splitting scream that seemed to cut through the air.

For a second, the two men stopped arguing and stared at her as she continued to scream. Then the curly-haired one knelt down next to her. When she focused on him, she stopped screaming.

With wide eyes, she studied his face. An angry face, tan from the sun. Bright-blue eyes. Beautiful curly blonde hair. She eyed his body now, the broad shoulders, the big hands.

I know he's not nice, but he looks nice. Is he playing dress-up? Has a fancy yellow thing around his neck—what does Daddy call it?—oh yeah, a tie. He has a fancy yellow tie, a white shirt, a pretty blue suit. Looks like a prince from a Disney movie. The prince from Belle.

Except that prince isn't blonde, he has brown hair. Wavy, not curly. Wavy like the fur of the beast he used to be.

Is this man as mean as the beast in the movie? But the beast turned nice in the end. Maybe he'll turn nice, too? Just have to ask again, use my words.

"Home, please," she said, her little voice determined, her lip quivering.

"Shut the fuck up," he grunted. "You'll never go home again!"

Never again? No, Mama, Daddy!

Tears were streaming down her face, her little mind racing. She missed her parents so much, couldn't bear the thought of not seeing them here or ever again. She needed them, now!

She started screaming again, yelling for her parents. Before she knew it, the curly-haired man's big hand was covering not only her mouth but also her nose.

She wiggled as she struggled to breathe.

Please, I can't breathe. Please, stop it, take your hand off me! Please stop! Mama, help me!

But he just pressed his hand harder against her mouth and nose.

She kept struggling, but couldn't get away.

He's strong. So strong. It's so hard to breathe. This prince is hurting me. Can't breathe.

Her head started hurting as she tried to take in quick breaths through his fingers. Her eyes went wide, tearing up, staring at him.

No, he's not nice. He's mean, so mean.

Mama says to fight when someone is really mean.

This is really mean, isn't it?

Need to fight!

With all her might, she managed to open her mouth just a little bit and bit his fingers.

"Argh… She fucking bit me!" He darted his hand back and shook it to soothe the pain.

She coughed as air filled her empty lungs once more, then she started screaming again.

"That nasty little fucker has to stop screaming! Shut her up, Sully. Now! Do it now! I'm not touching her anymore."

She screamed as loud and as long as she could, always watching the two men. She saw the straight-haired guy, the one the other called Sully, searching for something.

"Ha, found it. Duct tape," he said, and lifted a thing up in his hand.

Duck tape? What's that? Whatever, don't care. Need Mama and Daddy. Help!

"Mama," she screamed, and watched the Sully guy kneel next to her, that strange, big roll in his hand. He unrolled a part of it, ripped a piece off, and before she knew it, it was stuck to her mouth.

Her eyes widened. She couldn't work her mouth anymore—couldn't scream, speak, or breathe through it anymore.

She heard the curly blonde-haired one laugh. "Good job, Sully! First good idea you've had today."

It's like glue. Sticky.

She tried to push her tongue through her lips that were pressed together by the sticky thing over her mouth. She succeeded and tasted it.

Tastes like glue. Disgusting.

She took a long breath in through her nose.

At least I can breathe. But I don't like this sticky thing. Needs to come off! Now!

She lifted her hands and tugged at it.

"Hey, she's trying to rip it off," the curly-haired one yelled. "Quick, put a stop to it."

"I don't know how," Sully said. "What do you want me to do?"

"Fucking hold her hands, idiot," the other one yelled, and Sully did what he was told. He held her little arms still so that she couldn't move them anymore.

"I have an idea," the curly-haired one said. "We'll tape her to the crate. Press her against it and wind the tape around her. If it can shut her mouth, it can keep her from moving as well."

"Okay," Sully said, and suddenly hoisted her off the ground.

She squirmed and wiggled, tried to fight as much as she could, but it was useless. She got put in a wooden box with metal poles. He bound her hands to one of them, her feet to another one.

I hate this sticky stuff. I hate it. I just want Mama. Please.

Tears ran down her little face, over her freckles, and pooled around the tape covering her mouth.

She heard that mean laugh again, the cruel, mean laugh of the good-looking, curly-blonde-haired guy in the blue suit.

He's a beast for sure, not a prince. A mean, mean beast. A monster!

She shivered and sobbed, breathing through her little nose only, and threw her head back and forth, back and forth.

Back and forth, she threw her head, until she felt a warm touch on her shoulder.

Who's that? The beast? The monster?

She abruptly sat up and was surprised to find she could move freely. She moved her arms, her legs. *Free, I'm free! Oh my gosh, I'm free!*

A low male voice sounded in her ears. "Maria?"

Maria? For a second, she had to think about who Maria was. *Me. That's me.*

"Maria, wake up! Please, you're having a strange dream again," said the soft voice next to her.

She closed her eyes, and when she opened them again, she was in her soft bed, next to Aaron, her fiancé.

"Maria? Are you okay?"

Her eyes adjusted to the dark and she could make out Aaron's body next to hers. She felt the warmth of his touch, the warmth of his breath. *I'm safe. I had a dream.*

"Maria, please say something." She felt his touch; he was rubbing her shoulder now.

"I'm okay," she whispered, "I'm okay."

"Good. Was it a bad dream? Or a memory?"

Her mind was still paralyzed, blank. "I guess so. All I know is that it was scary."

Aaron snorted. "Yeah, I'll say. You kept screaming. Tossing and turning and swaying back and forth."

"What? Swaying?"

"I guess," Aaron said. "As if you were trying to move but couldn't."

For a second, Maria closed her eyes, and it all came back to her. She gripped Aaron's arm tight, so tight that he winced. "Oh my gosh, Aaron. I remember. I was on the boat. I was tied to the inside of a crate, this box they held me in."

"A memory, then," Aaron mumbled. "But you already told us about that. How you were tied up. Or was there more you remembered?"

She nodded slightly, then whispered, "I saw them. The bad guys. I overheard them."

Aaron sat up at that. Maria felt him wiggling the arm she was holding, then realized she was holding on too tight, her nails digging into his skin. She let go. "Sorry," she mumbled.

"It's okay, Maria, it's okay. I'm gonna record what you say, okay? Hold onto your dream, your memory. What do you remember?"

Maria took in a deep breath and closed her eyes. "A guy named Sully was there. He wasn't that bad. He tried to convince the other guy to give me back to my parents."

"Sully?"

She nodded. "Yeah, I understand now he was Sullivan, Jonathan Sullivan."

Aaron gasped.

"The other guy was Cliff. He had curly blonde hair, blue eyes, white teeth. A handsome young man. Dressed in a blue suit and a yellow tie. He is mean, real mean. He wants to... wants to..." She started sobbing. Her heart was pounding, her head hurting. She touched her temples.

"Stop, Maria, that's enough," Aaron said. "Listen, you're grown up now. You're not on a boat, you're safe here. Safe with me. Okay, Maria? You know that, right? You're sitting on a bed in a hotel room inside the Air Force Inn with me, Aaron. Feel those soft sheets against your fingers?"

She nodded. The pain in her temples lessened. "Yes."

Aaron looked at his phone, its little light illuminating the dark hotel room. "Let's hold off on this for now, Maria. This is something we need to do with Dr. Davies. Try to get some rest. It's still nighttime. Three thirty-four."

She watched him set his phone down on the nightstand, then turn to her and give her a kiss. "You're safe here. Safe here with me. I won't let anything bad happen to you again."

Maria nodded. "I know. Just hold me tight, Aaron."

He gave her a kiss on the forehead then cuddled up with her, his arm around her, holding her tight. Soon enough, she felt his warm, even breath on her neck, indicating he'd gone back to sleep.

Yet Maria was wide awake, her heart beating fast. Despite Aaron's warmth, her body was shivering. *It's okay. I'm safe here. I love it when he holds me. No reason to be afraid anymore. I'll be safe here.*

CHAPTER 54

"**H**ere, look at him. So handsome with his curly beach-blonde hair, Florida tan, and stunning blue eyes." Sally was holding a picture of the senator from a few years ago. "Senator Clifford sure is a good-looking guy. Can't deny it."

"Agreed," Tonya said, and took another sip of her coffee. "His dad looks very similar to him, doesn't he?" She showed Sally a picture of an Air Force general, Richard Clifford.

Sally nodded. "Yeah, no kidding. Too bad they don't get along anymore."

"Not since his precious son Michael Clifford got kicked out of the Air Force Academy," the chief said, and gulped down his coffee. "That certainly put a wedge between them."

"Yeah, too bad," Tonya said. "Happens a lot when parents have a certain path in mind for their offspring. They get pissed when their children choose a different path."

"But becoming a Florida senator seems like a pretty damn good path," Sally said, shaking her head. "Very weird. I don't get why they're estranged like all these articles claim. A real shame."

"Yep, for sure. But that isn't a sane excuse to go rogue and kidnap a child," the chief said. He wiped his mouth, then stared at his empty cup. "More coffee, anyone?"

"I'm good," Sally said. "Had my energy drink. Prefer that over coffee. I'm wide awake now."

Tonya shook her head also. Tom didn't say anything either, so the chief got up to pour himself more coffee.

"We still need to place the senator in the Destin area around May 2003," Tonya said. "That would prove once and for all he's actually Cliff."

Sally nodded, then turned to Tom, who was sitting in a swivel chair in front of his computer screen.

"Tom," she called over, "find anything yet on whether Mike Clifford was at Eglin back then?"

The young FBI agent didn't reply.

Tonya looked up at him. "Tom?"

Still no answer.

Chief Parlot walked back over to the two ladies, another steaming cup of coffee in hand. He yawned, then noticed Tonya and Sally trying to prompt a response from Tom, who continued to sit in front of his computer. Unlike the chief, they couldn't see the computer screen was black. He took in the scene then burst into laughter.

"What's so funny, Chief?" Sally wanted to know.

"Tom's fast asleep in his chair," Chief Parlot said, and slapped his thigh while snorting. "The poor guy fell asleep just sitting there, right in front of his computer. Hilarious."

Sally and Tonya started giggling as well. Sally got up and walked over to Tom's chair, then turned it around. Tom's head flopped sideways, a string of drool dripping down one corner of his mouth onto his shirt.

"Yep. Fast asleep," she giggled.

"I can see that," Tonya said laughing. "But in his defense, it's almost four in the morning."

The chief frowned. *Oh dear, did I keep everyone that late? Guess we all need a break.*

Sally poked Tom's shoulder. The touch made him jerk up in his sleep, and he abruptly opened his eyes. "The party!" he yelled, sitting up straight, staring directly at his colleagues.

They laughed and laughed.

"No party, my man." Tonya giggled. "Wish we were at one. But nope, you fell asleep at the helm, Tom."

It took him a few seconds to understand what was going on. He shook himself and yawned. "Man, I'm tired," he said.

Sally and Tonya yawned in reply. Chief Parlot watched them all. *Such a tired team. I need to send them home.* "Well, everyone, you're right, it's way too late. Let's call it a night and convene here later on this morning, shall we?"

Tonya and Sally nodded, but Tom shook his head. "No, no, wait, I found something right before I fell asleep. I was going to show you, but then, well, I guess I just kinda dozed off and—"

"It's fine, Tom. Save it for tomorrow. Let's call it a night," the chief said.

"No, please, it's important," Tom insisted.

Chief Parlot took a sip of his coffee. *Color me intrigued.* He looked over to Sally and Tonya.

"Ah, shucks.... Tom, show us," Tonya said, and got up to join him.

They gathered behind Tom, staring at the computer screen.

"Ta-da!" Tom said with a smug grin on his face. "There was a party on base just a few houses down from the TLFs the very night Moana Marie Collins disappeared. Look, here's the invite. And the guest list to the party."

"So? Why is that important?" Sally didn't quite follow what Tom saw in this.

"Let me read...." Tonya said. "A promotion party for a general. A guy named General Jones. Why is that important?"

"Come on, guys, look at the guest list." Tom pointed to the second window on his computer screen.

Tonya, Sally, and the chief started reading off the listed names in alphabetical order. Sally's eyes widened and she threw her hands over her mouth, while Chief Parlot had to grip his coffee mug tight to keep from dropping it. *Holy cow. Unbelievable.*

Tonya grinned. "Well now… there it is. Black on white. Gotta love the fact that military protocol furnished the final clue: the general had to put a guest list together so the base could allow visitors access to his base housing."

The chief swallowed hard. "No kidding. They're all here. Jim Billings. James Borman. Mike Clifford. All guests at the promotion party. Wow."

"Yep," Tom said. "It places them there the night of little Moana's disappearance."

Tonya whistled through her teeth, then looked at Tom, who had a smug grin on his face. "And how in the world did you manage to fall asleep on this revelation, my man Tom?"

"Yeah, no kidding," Sally said and shook her head in disbelief. "How did you manage?"

Tom's face turned red in embarrassment. "Guess I was just super tired," he mumbled. "And—in my defense—I didn't get my energy drink. Someone else had it." He pointed at Sally.

"Oh dear, I guess we need to stock the breakroom with energy drinks now to keep the non-coffee drinking new generation awake, huh?" Tonya said and gave Chief Parlot an elbow bump.

The chief almost spilled his coffee, but held on to it tight. He wasn't listening and was deep in thought. *Is this guest list proof enough, though?*

"Well, it doesn't strictly prove they were involved, though, does it?" Sally said, voicing the chief's very question.

Tonya shook her head, her cornrow bun flopping from left to right. "Nope, not yet." Then she started pacing. "It places them at the scene, but at the same time gives them an alibi."

"But Sullivan clearly stated that JB—Agent James Borman—kidnapped Moana and brought her to his boat. He swam there," Sally said. "And then he said the little one woke up in the crate while he was on the rowboat. He went back to the yacht, got a call from Cliff, and told him she was still alive. Then, Cliff came to the yacht at the marina at Destin Harbor to see for himself. He found that Sullivan was right: the little girl was still alive, so he had to figure out what to do with her."

Tonya was still pacing. "You're right, Sally. That's the story. Guess they could've snuck away from the party? Especially JB. The general's house was only a few rows down from Moana's TLF, facing the same part of the bay. He could've easily slipped out, carried out the mission, and come back."

The chief took another sip of his coffee and found his arm hairs suddenly standing up. *Something's not right. I feel like we're still missing something here. Just can't say what.*

"Wouldn't JB be all wet, though? Wouldn't the party guests have noticed him soaked head to toe?" Sally crinkled her forehead, deep in thought.

"Not unless he changed in and out of that military uniform Maria said he wore," Tom said. "Maybe he changed at the party?"

Tonya stopped pacing. "Plausible, Tom. Maria identified JB as the guy carrying her into the cold water, and claimed he wore a military uniform. Explains the bootprint in her TLF. Being on base for that party, he would've had potential access to military uniforms."

Chief Parlot slurped his coffee, deep in thought. "Why would the general lend JB a uniform? Or did JB steal it from the general's residence? And why were all these guys even at that promotion party?"

Everyone shrugged their shoulders.

"I assume at least one of them knew the general," Tonya suggested. "He was the commanding general at Eglin at the time, right?"

Tom nodded. "Correct. After the promotion, he left. Not too many jobs for a two-star, I suppose."

PUZZLE OF THE PAST

"He may have worked with the local police while he was stationed here and knew Chief Billings that way," Sally said.

"It's possible," Tonya and Tom both said.

Chief Parlot was very quiet and sipped his steaming coffee. *Something's bothering me. But what? I can't say. Just a feeling.*

"Either way," Tonya said, "we now have proof that not only did Mike Clifford know James Borman and Jim Billings, he was at the same party as them the night of the kidnapping. That can't possibly be a coincidence."

Sally shook her head. "Nope, definitely not. There are no coincidences like that."

"Agreed," Tom said. "But we still need hard proof Senator Mike Clifford is the 'Cliff' Sullivan mentioned."

Everyone but the chief nodded.

"Isaac my man, you still with us?" Tonya nudged him with her elbow. The interruption almost made him spill his coffee again, but helped him snap out of his thoughts and focus back on the conversation.

"Yeah, yeah," he mumbled, then turned to Tom. "We *do* need proof that Clifford is Cliff. Desperately. Until then, everything remains circumstantial. Tom, keep looking for that boat, that yacht. Remember? We still need to figure out if Clifford owned a yacht that anchored at Destin around the time of the kidnapping. We get that, we'll have damn good proof Mike Clifford is Cliff. Sullivan said it was Cliff's yacht, that Cliff boarded it that night. Gotta check the records of the marina at Destin Harbor."

Everyone nodded.

"Sullivan said Cliff had all these connections. Shouldn't we also look into whether he knew someone at Vital Records? According to Sullivan, Cliff was the one who furnished the fake documents, right?" Sally said.

The chief nearly choked on his last sip of coffee. *That's it! The birth certificate and social security card. Between that and the boat, we should drum up enough evidence to justify bringing Senator Clifford in. Perfect.*

He was about to give orders to do exactly that when he saw both Tonya and Sally yawn. Tom rubbed his eyes. Chief Parlot looked at the clock. *Four thirty in the morning. We've been up for hours, worked nonstop for days. Gotta let everyone rest so we can be at our best.*

"Sally, write down a note for me, please: 'yacht and Vital Records.' Then let's all go home. Nobody's in danger right now. If Senator Clifford *is* involved, I don't see how he could possibly know we're onto him, meaning there's no rush to grab him just now. We have strong leads. You've all done an amazing job so far. I'm proud of you. Let's get some well-deserved rest, shall we?"

"Sounds great, my man," Tonya mumbled while yawning. Sally and Tom agreed.

They agreed to meet later that morning and started packing up. Chief Parlot watched his team depart. Against his better judgment, he decided to remain at the station. *Something is still bothering me. The party? The general? The connections?*

He couldn't pinpoint it. *I'll find it. Everything has begun to revolve around Mike Clifford. Need to learn more about him. Smug Senator Mike Clifford.*

CHAPTER 55

Senator Mike Clifford was in a good mood early that morning. *And it's no wonder—I have a great plan in place now. It'll be excellent.*

He watched the sun crest the horizon, a beautiful bright ball lighting up the flight line at Andrews Air Force Base. With a smile on his face, he waved to the pilot of his private plane, gripped his bag tighter, and climbed aboard.

Great to get a private plane all to myself. And it's free. Well, on taxpayers' dime. Thank you, loyal taxpayers. He grinned and sat down in his comfortable leather seat. He looked outside the window and saw the big plane with a blue stripe on it parked across from his small one. *A Boeing 747 fit for a king. Or more accurately, a president.* He couldn't stop grinning. *I love being important. Being admired, being loved. They all love me. My interns, my colleagues, my constituents.*

A frown came over his face as he buckled up. *See, Dad, I knew I could do it. I didn't need you or Mom telling me what to do. I'm the hotshot now.*

The door closed. Mike felt the vibration of the engines under his seat. The small plane's frame shook under the power of its engines' thrust. He glanced at the big plane across from him again. *Air Force One. Beautiful machine. Much bigger than this one. Ah well. Maybe, just maybe, it'll be me flying in that plane one day.*

But first, I need to take care of business. Need to know exactly what's going on in my old hood. Need to find out what the police know, how much Sully and Bill shared before they passed away.

He sighed as the plane started rolling down the tarmac. *Well, Billings family, here I come for moral support. Support for your family in your time of need—the family of a good old friend of mine. A loyal friend and supporter. Too bad he had to die, but he knew too much. He was weak. He would've faltered under interrogation.*

Seemed strong on the outside, but never was. I know that. Big tough guy on the outside, a small little nobody on the inside. Well, he died a hero. A hometown hero. Their former police chief—definitely a hero.

He scratched his chin. *I'll make sure his heroic image remains intact. I owe him that much, that's for sure. "He had nothing to do with it," is all I need to say. He just looked the other way—as he was told.*

Mike watched the sun light up the sky, the bright blue sky he'd take off into any minute now. *Nothing but clear horizons in front of me. I can paint my own world.*

His smile returned. *Yeah, I can, and I will. My own world, one that I run. No one can stop me. Not the police. Not the girl. Nobody.*

"Senator Clifford," he heard the pilot say over loudspeaker, "we are cleared for takeoff. Please sit back and enjoy your three-hour flight to Eglin Air Force Base."

CHAPTER 56

*E*glin Air Force Base. My new home. Aaron sighed and watched the sunrise through the small opening between the curtains. The bright rays lit up the teal wall of the Air Force Inn. *It's been a mess since I got here. Not much fun here at Eglin.*

He almost had to chuckle. *Fun? No, definitely not. My fiancée got attacked and two key witnesses to her kidnapping twenty years ago are now dead. Unbelievable.*

He turned over to look at Maria. She was still in a deep sleep next to him, her breathing even. Gently, he pulled a strand of hair from her face, but it got stuck on the sticky bandage on her forehead.

Aaron frowned. *Her stitches. Luckily just a small head wound. Still can't believe it. Jonathan Sullivan just attacked her. And he was in on the big conspiracy.*

His hand rested on her cheek. Her eyelids fluttered. Aaron felt the warm breath from her nose on his hand. He smiled. *She's so beautiful. My Maria, my fiancée, my soon-to-be wife. At least you know your real family now. Your mom and dad. And you still have Martina. Everything is good.*

For a while, he just watched her sleep. Eventually, he rolled onto his back and stared at the ceiling. *But something's not right. Something is strange. It's quite the sociopath who takes revenge on a former friend. Kidnapping his child. Years after the fact.*

Aaron sighed, then suddenly sat up straight in bed. *Wait a minute. Maria had another nightmare last night. She remembered Sullivan and a blonde curly-haired guy holding her hostage on that boat. Why did she remember that now? What triggered that? There must have been a trigger.*

He thought back to the day. *I know a lot happened. No wonder her mind grew turbulent, brought back her trauma. But surely there must have been one specific event that triggered remembering her captors on that boat. What was it?*

Aaron thought harder. *We watched the news. Then we went to bed. I suppose Maria researched that senator and realized who he was... Wait. That must be it! She's remembering Mike Clifford as her captor, as Cliff. So clearly that she might be able to identify him? Maybe that'll be enough to bring him in?*

He was so deep in thought as he sat in bed, staring at the closed curtains and the little ray of sunshine peeking through the crack, that he almost jumped when he felt a light touch on his arm.

"Aaron? You okay?"

He turned and saw Maria next to him, now propped up on her elbow, smiling at him. "Hey, you're up. Good morning, my love."

"Good morning," she whispered, then sat up tall to give him a long, sensual kiss on the lips.

"Oh, hey there," he said, and lay back down while still kissing her.

He rolled flat onto his back and tried to bring Maria along for the ride, but she paused, stared at him, then pulled away from him. Her unique hazel eyes studied his every move, her one hand still on his chest. "My love, what are you thinking about so intensely just now?"

"Well," he said, and sat up again, his nose touching hers, "I suppose it can wait. I can tell you later."

"No, no, no, you've got to tell me now, Aaron. I know that look. The I-need-to-find-out-more look."

He sighed. *She knows me so well.*

"What were you thinking about?"

He lay back down and started playing with her wavy auburn hair. "Well, I was just thinking that it's strange you had a nightmare again. Now. Tonight. After you researched Mike Clifford." He felt the strand of hair in his hands wrap around his fingers as Maria sat up straighter.

"Yeah. You know… I really do think Mike Clifford is Cliff. It makes sense. Fits the pattern using his last name."

Aaron nodded. "It does make sense. And the senator sure has blonde hair, like you recalled. If you saw him in person, do you think you could identify him?"

Maria was deep in thought. Aaron watched her think. "I don't know, Aaron. Why?"

"Well, I just thought if you identified him as your captor on that boat, a jury would have—"

"—lots of reasons to tear it apart. C'mon. A memory from twenty years ago? When I was a toddler? That wouldn't help at all. Just think about it. A high-up person like him? You'd need real proof to bring such a powerful man down."

Aaron sighed. "You're right. I just hope the police found something. Something to prove that Senator Mike Clifford is in fact Cliff—your captor."

"We'll get him. Don't get too worked up about it." She turned to him again, lay back down, and snuggled up in his arms. He wrapped his arms around her and gave her a kiss on the forehead, right next to the bandage covering the stitches.

"I know, you're right," he said. "We'll just have to wait and see what the police can find. At least you're here with me, your family, your mamá. We'll keep you safe."

"I know, Aaron."

She leaned her head on his shoulder and they just lay there like that for a while, happy to be together, happy to know they had each other, happy to know Maria was safe. Aaron got goosebumps. *Is she safe, though, is she really safe? I still have a feeling something isn't right.*

What if Clifford finds out we're onto him? What if he plans to complete his revenge on Maria now?

A shiver ran down his spine, but he decided to ignore it. *I'm just being silly. Starting to be like Maria—having strong feelings, but no real proof. No proof at all. And Clifford lives nowhere near here. He's a far-off threat, not close.*

CHAPTER 57

Close enough to touch his prone form, Tonya stood behind the chief. She turned around and put a finger to her mouth. "Shhhh," she whispered, then bent over to take an even closer look at Chief Parlot. "I think he's sleeping."

Both Sally and Tom giggled as they carefully closed the door to the investigative workroom. Chief Parlot's head was on the table, his arms splayed out, his right hand still holding a pen.

"Funny, after ordering us home to bed," Sally whispered. "He just fell asleep right here in the workroom."

"Yeah, I'll say. Face-planted right into the middle of a bunch of files, pictures, and reports," Tom said. "Should we wake him now that we're all refreshed and ready to work?"

Tonya shook her head. "Nah, let him sleep a while longer. My poor man Isaac. He works too hard. Let's brew some coffee and see if he wakes up to the delicious smell."

Tom and Sally nodded and were about to walk over to the room's coffee machine when the room's phone rang, shrill and loud. The ringing cut through the air.

The chief's head shot up. "What the heck?" For a minute, he looked like a deer in headlights, but quickly assessed the situation and was wide awake. He picked up the ringing phone. "Chief Parlot speaking."

"Hi, good morning," a female voice whispered on the other end.

"Good morning, ma'am. How can I help you?"

"Well, I-I think... I... I might have... you know... information about that little girl's kidnapping twenty years ago."

The chief quickly put the phone on loudspeaker and gestured for his team to come over and listen.

"You do, ma'am? Well, I'm here to listen. Please go on. For the record, may I please ask for your first and last name?"

His question was met with silence.

"Ma'am?"

"Yes, still here," she whispered. "I'd rather not say."

Chief Parlot raised his eyebrows. "Come again?"

"I'd rather not say who I am. I'd like to stay, you know... anonymous," said the lady on the other end of the line.

"I see, ma'am. That's okay. We'll appreciate any information we can get," the chief said, and winked at Tom, who understood right away.

Tom quickly sat down and started working his magic. Chief Parlot smiled. *Good thing he's such a wizard with technology. He'll have this phone call traced in no time.*

"Ma'am, please tell us what you know," Chief Parlot said, his voice calm.

"Okay," she said, and they heard her take a deep breath as if to encourage herself. "I can tell you the little one's birth certificate and social security card were faked."

Tonya, Sally, and the chief all looked at each other. Chief Parlot rolled his eyes. *Thought this call would be promising, but I'm getting the impression we're dealing with someone who just wants some attention.*

"Ma'am, we already know the documents are fake. That's nothing new. In fact, it's all over the news."

Another deep breath on the other end. "Yeah, but I can tell you where it was made and who ordered it made."

Chief Parlot started grinning again. *Now we're talking.*

Sally gave everyone a thumbs-up and they listened, interested in hearing what the lady had to say.

"Twenty years ago, I worked my first job—at the Miami Vital Records office. I was a clerk there."

"I see. So, you knew someone there who made the fake documents?"

"Yes and yes," she whispered. "I know... ahem... that *someone*. That's right. But that someone was young and naïve and had no idea she was helping to cover up a kidnapping. If she had known, she would've never done her boyfriend a favor by making that birth certificate for him as well as a social security card. A forgery for a little girl named Maria Gabriella Sullivan."

The officers and agents all looked at each other. Chief Parlot smirked. *Sure, someone. She knows someone. A friend, I bet.* He had to make sure he didn't chuckle.

"So, when were the documents made? Let's start with the birth certificate. Can you tell me who else was on it?"

"Both documents were printed in early August 2003. The parents were Jonathan Eric Sullivan and Martina Marie Perez."

Chief Parlot smiled. *Well, she's legit. She knows everything that's on the certificate. Only a person who has seen the certificate would know all that, and we've kept the forgery closely guarded.* "Correct, ma'am. So, who approached you... err, your friend to make these documents? You said it was a favor for her boyfriend?"

"Yeah, kinda," she whispered.

The chief raised his eyebrows. *What does that mean?* He glanced at Tonya and Sally, who just shrugged their shoulders.

"Kinda her boyfriend? Explain please, ma'am," Chief Parlot said.

"Well, her ex-boyfriend at the time. You see, she was still in love with him. *Really* in love. But he... you know... he had just left her."

"The boyfriend?"

"Yes. Until one night..."

"The night he showed up at the Vital Records office?"

"What? No, at her doorstep. With jewelry. Expensive stuff."

The chief was confused. *What's she talking about?* "Jewelry, ma'am?"

"Yeah. My friend's—I mean, I told my friend—you know, the one that faked the documents—that this guy wasn't boyfriend material, but she was just really into him. A good-looking guy, so dreamy, so charming, such a good kisser, and so—"

"—rich, I assume?"

She sighed. "Yeah, rich. Back then, but even more so now."

"I see. So, this rich ex-boyfriend shows up at your... friend's... doorstep and brings her jewelry?"

"Yeah. Crazy, right?"

The chief looked at his colleagues. They gestured him to continue talking. "Crazy," was all he could think of saying.

"I know, right? So he shows up out of the blue one night and has flowers on him, a beautiful necklace. He takes her out to dinner."

"And what happened then?"

"He told her he still loved her. That really charmed her, you know. But she wondered if he would stay with her this time since, you know, he left her before. She just wasn't sure what to think."

"Mm-hmm," Chief Parlot said, and looked over to Tom, who was still working on tracing the call.

"He told her he'd love her forever from now on, wanted to shower her with gifts of jewelry."

The chief rolled his eyes. *She needs to get to the point.*

"Told her that he'd love her forever... if she'd do him this one favor."

"Favor?" Chief Parlot perked up. *Now we're talking.* "What kind of favor?"

"He said all she needed to do was create a social security card and a birth certificate at her everyday job. He had it all written out. Said it was for a friend of his, a poor illegal immigrant who just wanted his little daughter to have U.S. citizenship, a good life in the United States."

"I see. And you belie—I mean, your friend believed this story?"

"Oh, yes, yes, it was a very convincing story. And my friend, you know, was a very romantic girl at that time. She always wanted to help out however she could, and just wanted to be loved. Especially by him."

"I see. So, what happened then?"

"Well, I... She took him to the office that night after dinner. You know, forging a birth certificate is very easy, actually. And so is printing a social security card. All you need is the right office with the right machines, of course. All she wanted was to help that poor illegal immigrant girl belonging to her boyfriend's friend."

"Oh, I bet," Chief Parlot said, and glanced over at Tom. He gave him a smile and a big thumbs-up.

The chief returned the gesture. *Good. He's got her.*

As he watched Tom scribble something on a sticky note, Chief Parlot concentrated on the call again. "I understand that this friend of yours had no idea she was covering up a kidnapping and—"

"—that's right. No idea," the caller said. "She didn't follow the news back then and hadn't heard about the case of the missing toddler. She didn't put it all together! She's innocent in all of this, you know, and feels really, really bad about how things turned out. And she's scared, you know, to even contact the police."

The lady on the other end of the line stopped speaking and held her breath.

"Well, ma'am, you can assure your friend she won't be punished for what she did. What she *should* do is contact us immediately. Especially if she remembers the name of her ex-boyfriend. Sharing that will work wonders for her situation."

"Really?"

Tom came over and handed the sticky note to Chief Parlot. He read the name on it and gave the hacker a pat on the shoulder.

"Yes, really, Janice," the chief said, and heard the woman gasp.

"How… how do you… know…"

"Well, Janice, we *are* the police. And we do appreciate your call. We understand you have information for us that nobody else does. We've already investigated where the fake documents were made, but the results were inconclusive. If you can provide proof, we'll happily reward you."

"Reward me?"

"Yes, Janice, we will. You… or is it your friend?"

She went silent for a bit. "Well, I… you know, don't *really* don't want to go to jail—I-I mean, gosh, don't want her to go to jail, a-and…" Her voice broke down into sobs.

Chief Parlot's voice turned soft. "It's okay, Janice. It's okay. There is no real friend, is there?"

"No," she said between sobs.

"It's okay, Janice. Really. I'm very glad you called. You did the right thing."

"I did? Well, I was told it wouldn't be the right thing to do."

The chief raised his eyebrows. "But it was. I can assure you it was."

"Good."

"Janice, who advised you against this? Did someone threaten you?"

"Not really," she whispered. "But I got more jewelry, you know, very expensive jewelry, to remind me of our deal from back then to never say anything to anyone."

"I see."

"And an invitation."

"An invitation?" Chief Parlot was confused.

"Yeah, I was invited to go see the Capitol. And get a private tour of the White House. You know, I've always wanted to see it."

"A private tour of the U.S. Capitol and the White House?" The chief, Tonya, Tom, and Sally all huddled around the phone, hardly able to believe their ears.

"Yeah, he promised. But in turn, I could never talk about that night I made the fake documents."

"You did the right thing, Janice, by calling us. We're proud of you."

"You are?"

"Yes, we really are. And we can assure you, you won't be going to jail. All we need to know is, who made you do it? Who's the ex-boyfriend, the man who invited you on a personal tour in DC? Tell us, Janice."

All they heard was the woman's heavy breathing.

"Don't be afraid, Janice. As a key witness, we can protect you if this guy threatens you."

"You can protect me?"

"Yes, for sure."

"And my family? You know, I have two little kids and I…" She started crying again, big sobs through the phone. "I'm scared. You know, he… he's a very powerful man now."

"Janice, we'll protect you and your family. We can send someone over to your house right now. But we need a name to know who to protect you from, who to arrest."

"Okay," she whispered. "It's Mike. Michael Clifford. He was my boyfriend back then. He asked me to make that fake birth certificate and the social security card for Maria Gabriella Sullivan. It was him. Senator Mike Clifford."

Chief Parlot grinned. *Bingo. We've got him. There's our hard proof. Clifford is Cliff. Just like Sullivan said. Cliff got that birth certificate made to cover up the kidnapping.*

He frowned. *Damn it! Senator Mike Clifford? I voted for that guy. Can't believe he masterminded the whole thing. Kidnapping. Attempted murder. Actual murder. Just to take revenge?*

Guess so. Well, it's the end of the line for him. Time to take Cliff down.

CHAPTER 58

*D*own we go, he grinned as he felt the plane's descent into Eglin Air Force Base. *Well, VPS airport. I'm back. Back home. Taking care of business.* Mike Clifford looked out of the window as his private plane touched down on the tarmac.

"Welcome to Valparaiso and Fort Walton Beach," the pilot announced. "Welcome home, Senator."

"Thank you," Mike yelled out, and grinned. He saw the palm trees in the distance as the plane taxied to a stop. He watched the ground crew push the mobile stairs up to the plane, then unbuckled himself and waited. Within minutes, he was climbing down the ramp.

"Hello, Senator." The driver of a black SUV greeted him right there on the tarmac. "Are you ready to go?"

Mike switched his briefcase from the right hand to the left, then shook hands with the driver. "Yes, sir, ready to go."

"Wonderful," the driver said. "Please get into the car."

Mike walked past the driver, who was holding the door to the fancy car's backseat open for him, and climbed into it.

The driver gently pushed his door shut and got into the front seat. He turned around to Mike. "It's very nice of you to make time in your busy schedule to fly out here and support your community in turmoil. Having that kidnapped girl reappear after twenty years is one thing, but losing the former chief really hit the community hard. I'm glad you're here now, Senator."

Mike smiled at him. "Yeah, me, too. As I've always said, I am who I am thanks to this community's trust. I represent them and take pride in doing so. It's my duty to support them. So, naturally, I needed to come back to support the Billings family in their time of need."

"Yes, Senator. I'll take you to them straightaway. They're waiting for you, their good friend."

"I know," Mike said. "Let's get going then."

The driver nodded, turned the key, and started the car. "Yes, sir, let's go."

CHAPTER 59

"**L**et's *go*," Maria insisted, and looked at everyone.

"Well, Brad and I are technically still on the clock. We have a bunch of meetings to go to today," Drew said, and glanced at his friend.

Brad pushed a piece of pancake into his mouth. He was in a good mood. He was focused on the future now, the here and now, with the two favorite girls in his whole life. He finished chewing, then turned to Elisabeth, who was cutting her own pancake with a knife and fork. He smirked.

"Aw, Elisabeth, you're so foreign. Nobody cuts a pancake with a knife. Just use your fork."

Elisabeth shook her head. "No, that's way too hard. And so awkward. I mean, just look at them." She pointed at Drew, Aaron, and Jack, who were all hacking away at their pancakes. "You all need to learn some manners. Only the ladies around here seem to have any."

Maria and Martina agreed and laughed. Lieutenant Martinez, who was still there to keep an eye on Martina, smirked from his corner.

Brad shook his head in disbelief, then turned to Maria. "Well, Maria, I would love to accompany you on Aaron's apartment search, but I should probably go along with Drew here and do my job for once. He covered my meetings the past few days, so maybe it's time I show up to a few of them."

He turned to Elisabeth. "Unless your mother would rather I—"

"No, no, go with Drew," Elisabeth said. "I think we will be fine. But I'm not sure if going off base is such a good idea, Mo—Maria?"

Maria shrugged her shoulders. "I bet we can sneak out and avoid the paparazzi, right?"

"I think so. Chief Parlot said he can always send a police car to escort us," Aaron said.

"Ah, though he did tell me to not leave the base," Martina said, and looked down to the table.

"Aw, Mamá, that's too bad," Maria said. She turned to Lieutenant Martinez in the corner. "Or can she go off base if you're there?"

Lieutenant Martinez shook his head. "No, she must stay here for now. Those are the orders. She can move around on base, but not off base."

Everyone looked disappointed, especially Martina.

"Well, I'm not in the mood for paparazzi at all. I'd love to see apartments and visit my friend Sarah, but she texted the reporters are all over at the resort, too," Elisabeth said and sighed. "So maybe I will stay here with Martina."

"¿Aquí conmigo?" Martina looked at Elisabeth. "You really want to stay here with me?"

Elisabeth nodded. "Yes, I'd love to hear more stories of my little girl's childhood. Maybe you have pictures, too?"

"¡Ah, sí!" Martina smiled at her, then looked at Lieutenant Martinez. "Is that allowed?"

"Sí," he said, and smiled. "I just need to be there."

"Fine," both Elisabeth and Martina said at the same time, and sighed, then laughed together.

Aaron looked around. "So, that leaves my dad, Maria, and me to go look at apartments." He turned to Maria. "Is that okay with you, my love?"

She nodded. "Sure."

Everyone finished their breakfast then went their separate ways. Maria waved to Brad and Drew as they drove off to attend their meetings.

Wish my dad would have gone with me. She turned around, then gave both Elisabeth and Martina a hug. *Same goes for my two moms. But oh well, guess it's me and the Heikinnens today.*

She followed Aaron and his dad to the car and waved at Elisabeth and Martina, who remained behind in the lobby. As the hotel's sliding door closed behind her, Maria suddenly had a bad feeling. Shivers ran down her spine. She shook a little to rid herself of the strange feeling. *I'm just being silly. It's perfectly fine to go off base. I'll be fine. It's safe.*

Why do I feel afraid, then? Because of the paparazzi? Yeah, maybe. I hate them. She sighed and got into the backseat of Aaron's car. As they left the parking lot, she watched her arm hairs stand up. *Pff, it's nothing. I'm just being silly.*

But somehow, deep down inside, Maria knew that something terrible was about to happen. Something much more terrible than paparazzi was menacing the area.

CHAPTER 60

"The area around Eglin AFB the day of the disappearance remains our core focus right now," Chief Parlot said, looking around at his team.

"Agreed. We need to construct a timeline of where Clifford was at all times that day and night," Tonya said, rummaging through a bunch of papers in front of her. "Here it is. According to the guest list, General Jones's promotion party started on base at six p.m. and ended at eleven p.m."

Sally nodded, her cheeks flush with excitement. "Correct. The kidnapping occurred during that time span, around nine p.m. We know Clifford was at that party with his buddies. Between this and everything else, don't we have enough to go arrest him right now?"

The chief shook his head. "No. To catch a big fish like him, we need to be airtight, have the whole story down pat. We need to know the exact time he left base, need to know his every move. Tom?"

"Patience, guys, patience," Tom urged. "I'm working on it, but this was, like, twenty years ago. You know that. Takes some time when the digital record is so ancient."

Sally sighed. "Yeah, we know."

"Look, I can't do this alone." Tom briefly glanced up from his screen at his colleagues sitting around the table. "Call the witnesses."

Sally was confused. "What witnesses?"

"He means the people who attended the general's party. He's right. Call them up, see if they recall anything notable about our criminal friends," Tonya said.

Sally nodded. "Oh, I see. Like whether they noticed Agent Borman was gone for a while. Same with Clifford?"

"Exactly," Chief Parlot said. "So chop-chop, let's start calling while Tom pores over archived receipts or still existent security footage to trace Clifford's movements that night."

"Awesome!" Sally's cheeks flushed even more. "Who should we call first from that guest list? Maybe General Jones himself?"

"No, let's start with the guests," Tonya suggested. "They're usually more observant of their surroundings than the host, right, Isaac my man?"

The chief just nodded and divvied up the guest list in thirds. "Sally, you take the top third of the list, but leave out Billings, Borman, and Clifford, for obvious reasons. You'll have to track down current phone numbers, then call and ask about that night. About the senator in particular. Make sure not to stir up suspicion; we don't want folks tipping him off."

"Got it," Sally said, and grinned. "I have my ways to getting information without being too obvious about what I'm up to."

Tonya laughed. "Of course, you do, girl. That's why you're a police officer."

"Yep," Sally said, and chuckled, then got to work. Her smile faded fast. "Do you think people will remember that night?"

Chief Parlot shrugged his shoulders. "Only one way to find out."

"Guys, I've got him!" Tom jumped up, both arms raised in a triumphant pose. Irritated, the others just looked at him. "Clifford pulled a parking ticket at Destin Harbor at ten thirty p.m. that night."

Tonya raised her eyebrows. "Parking ticket at Destin Harbor? Elaborate."

"Clifford parked his car at the Destin Harbor at ten thirty that May night in 2003. The night of the disappearance. He left the party and went to the harbor, just like we thought he did."

Sally looked up from her list. "I can confirm. I have a party guest who remembers Clifford leaving early after a phone call. The guest couldn't remember when, exactly, but it was right after the dancing took off, so he figured around ten that night."

"The phone call with Sullivan," the chief said.

Tonya whistled through her teeth. "Man, Sullivan was telling the truth all along, wasn't he? Maybe not such a bad guy after all."

"Probably not the worst. For all his faults, seems like he's the reason Maria is still alive today," Chief Parlot said, and sighed. "He didn't deserve to die. Why did Billings kill him?"

Tom sat back down in his seat. "Seems obvious to me: he was saving his own ass. Err, I mean... saving face." He blushed a little. The team laughed.

Chief Parlot walked over to stand next to Tom's chair and pat him on the back. "Anyway, back to Clifford. Tom, it sounds like you have hard proof he was there at the harbor to meet Sullivan?"

"Well, no."

"What?" The chief glanced at Tonya and Sally and saw they were just as disappointed as he was.

Tom grinned. "But I do have proof he paid that night for having parked a boat at the Destin Harbor's marina."

"What?" they all said in unison, and gathered around Tom's laptop.

"Yeah, got a copy of the credit card statement right here. He paid for a white yacht. And this particular yacht then set sail that night. Left its mooring slip around eleven thirty, according to the marina's records."

The chief stared at Tom. "The boat... the yacht where they held little Moana captive."

Tom nodded. "I assume so. Because this particular yacht was owned by Michael Clifford, had arrived at Destin a few days prior. Manifest shows it came from Pensacola."

"Pensacola?" Tonya grinned now. "Just like Sullivan said. That's where he boarded that boat, right?"

Everyone nodded.

"While at Destin, it only left at night for a little bit, same time every day. Otherwise, was always parked there in that specific boat slip all day long," Tom said.

Sally's eyes widened. "Wow, Clifford's boat! And that's where Maria ended up that whole time. So now we've got proof, right? Hard enough to arrest him?" She hopped from one foot to the other. "Oh boy, oh boy, that is a huge case. My first huge case, nearly in the bag."

"Hold on, youngster," Tonya said, putting a hand on Sally's shoulder, "hold your horses. Let's go through the motions. We need to know if Clifford and his boat wound up in Miami next."

"And we still need to link him to those chocolates that killed Billings," Chief Parlot said. "Safe to assume he was the one who sent them from DC."

"Good call, Isaac my man. Let's keep going until we nail the bastard. Let him think he's safe for now," Tonya said. "No rush. He can't know for sure he's a suspect, thinks he's safe right there in Washington, DC. He doesn't know we talked to Janice, found his yacht. He doesn't know we're onto him. No need to poke the bear."

"Agreed," the chief said. "Even if he does suspect something, let him sweat it out in his big gilded office in the Capitol. Luckily, he's far away."

CHAPTER 61

"Far away?" Aaron said, and shook his head. "No, not at all. Just a quick sixteen-minute drive from base."

Maria and Jack nodded, then looked around again. *Nice apartment. Close to Eglin, close to the bay. I can even see the water from the balcony window.*

The water. The bay. Maria sighed. *Still a strange place to me. But it sure is beautiful.*

Determined not to let her fears bother her, she stepped outside. "Wow, the view is breathtaking. 'Waterfront living in Fort Walton Beach'? They weren't kidding. Come see it for yourselves."

Jack and Aaron followed her out onto the balcony.

"Oh yeah, I see the bay from here. That must be Cinco Bayou," Jack said.

Aaron laughed. "Of course it's Cinco Bayou, Dad. That's why this complex is called the 'The Cove Apartments on Cinco Bayou.' Without the bayou, they'd have to change the name." He turned to Maria. "You're okay with the view?"

"Okay with it? Are you kidding? This is awesome, absolutely fantastic."

"Really?"

Maria laughed. "Of course. You know I love watching sunrises. Or sunsets. I'll take either. And this balcony is perfect for that, I bet."

"Agreed," Jack said and turned to Maria. "You'll get your sunrise here. The balcony is facing east—hence this building is called 'Sunrise Tower,' I assume."

"Awesome." Maria grinned and gave Aaron a hug, "Let's take it."

Aaron stiffened up in Maria's hug. *What's wrong with him? He doesn't seem excited, he seems worried.*

"You're sure you're okay with this?"

Maria let go of him. "Aaron, *of course.* This apartment is more than okay—it's awesome. The kitchen is super nice and updated, even though I prefer white cabinets over pinewood ones. But I love the flooring, the neutral wall color, the nice bedroom. And this view! Can't beat that. And then there's—"

"So, you're not afraid?" Aaron interrupted her.

Surprised, she took a step back. "Afraid?"

"Yeah, you know... every day you'll be able to see the water that's part of the same bay you... you know... where you almost... you know..."

Maria's face softened. She took a step closer and held his hands. "Aaron, you don't have to worry about me. I'm not afraid. Not anymore. Sometimes, I feel a bit uneasy, but I understand what happened now, I've processed it, and I'm not afraid anymore. I know that I'm safe now. And I can swim now."

Aaron nodded, and Maria gave him a kiss. "I really do love the view. I think this is the right place for you." Then she turned to Jack. "Don't you agree?"

"Yes," Jack said. "Love the amenities, too. It's more expensive than some of the other options we saw, but you can't beat the location."

Aaron nodded again, a smile on his face now. Maria was glad to see it. *He doesn't need to worry. I'm safe now. What could happen?* A shudder ran down her spine. *Am I really safe here?* Quickly, she shook off her negative thoughts and feelings and smiled at Aaron.

"Alright, then. Let's sign," Aaron said, and grinned.

"Yay!" Maria fell around his neck and Aaron kissed her deeply.

"Good choice," Jack said, and walked inside, leaving the couple alone for a bit.

"I love it, Aaron," Maria whispered.

"And I love *you*," he said. They kissed again, right there on the balcony, the breeze in their hair, the far-off noise of breaking waves in their ears.

Click!

Their eyes flew open. They stared at one another, lips touching.

Suddenly, they heard all kinds of clicking noises, then soft voices. They looked down and saw reporters flooding the parking lot, cameras pointing their way.

"Oh no, the paparazzi found us." Aaron frowned and quickly pulled Maria into the apartment. He found Jack in the dining room. "Let's go, Dad. Come on, quickly."

Perplexed, Jack watched Aaron and Maria rush past him toward the front door.

"The paparazzi found us," Aaron yelled back over his shoulder. "Let's hurry to the front office before they realize we're gone."

Jack quickly followed them, made sure Aaron had the key, then shut the door behind him. They rushed down the flights of steps and ran across the parking lot toward the apartment complex's front office.

"Faster," Jack yelled; the reporters had spotted them and were now in close pursuit. But before they could catch up, they had reached the front office and closed the door behind them. They paused in the middle of the entryway to catch their breath.

"Well, that flight of stairs won't be fun to run up and down while we're moving in," Maria said, breathing fast from running.

"So true," Jack said, and wheezed a deep breath in. "Sad to see I'm so out of shape."

G. P. SCHUMACHER

Aaron laughed. He was the only one not affected by their little sprint. "Guess you both gotta get more into running, huh? At least when we move in, you'll certainly get your steps in."

That's when they noticed the property manager looking up at them from her desk, irritated by their loud conversation. "Everything alright? Did you already see the place?"

"Yeah, yeah, we just didn't want to have our pictures taken," Aaron said, and grinned.

"Pictures?" The property manager had a blank look on her face.

"Paparazzi," Jack said, and pointed outside. By now, a bunch of reporters were gathered outside the front door, trying to point their camera lenses inside.

Maria was furious. *Idiots. It's my life. Leave me alone!*

The manager stood up, her eyes wide. "Oh my, y'all. What do they want?"

"More pictures of me. To make even more of a drama out of my life. Gosh, I hate them. They tracked us down again and now they won't leave us alone. I just want to live my life in peace," Maria said, pacing back and forth, her face red.

The manager was still irritated as she watched Maria pace. "Remind me, you are...?"

"That's Maria," Aaron said, pointing at his fiancée. "Also known as Moana Marie Collins."

The manager's mouth dropped open. "The missing toddler?"

"Not really much of a toddler anymore," Jack said, and winked at her, but the property manager just kept staring at Maria, her mouth still hanging open.

She suddenly closed her mouth and exclaimed, "I see it now, oh my goodness, I do, I do. It's the missing girl!" She turned to Aaron and Jack. "That means you two must be her fiancé and future father-in-law."

They nodded.

"And I'd like to be a future resident," Aaron said. He held up the key to the apartment they'd just been previewing. "We love the apartment."

"Oh, yes, fantastic. In that case, I'll get the paperwork ready for you right away, Lieutenant Heikinnen," she said, and winked at Aaron. "I remember your name from hearing it on TV."

Aaron raised an eyebrow.

"Oh, and from earlier, when you checked in," the manager continued. "Guess I didn't put two and two together at the time." She glanced at Maria, who was still pacing, mumbling something, throwing mad glances outside. "Can I do anything to help her?"

Aaron shook his head. "No, don't think so. I guess we'll have to ask the police for an escort back to base once all the paperwork is done."

The manager nodded and disappeared in the back to get the leasing documents. She returned and said, "Here you go, Lieutenant Heikinnen, please take all of this and go see Marcy in the room to the right. She's our leasing agent and will take care of everything. I'm afraid it's a lot of paperwork, so it might take a while. Your dad and fiancée are welcome to go with you or stay in our waiting room. It does have a TV—and luckily, your fiancée's story is not on." The manager smiled at Jack and Aaron.

"Thank you, appreciate it. Yeah, my dad and Maria can go wait in there."

She gave an approving nod and showed Aaron where to go first, then returned and gestured to both Jack and Maria to follow her. Maria stopped pacing and followed the manager and Jack. They walked into a nicely decorated waiting room with a beachy feel to it. Pictures of sea animals and shells on teal walls, a table with seashells, and a lamp in the form of a conch. The couch was sand-colored and had a pattern of little blue waves on it.

Maria looked around. *Cute theme. I could do something like that for Aaron's apartment.*

Jack plopped down onto the cute couch. A TV hung on the wall across from it.

The clerk came back into the room. "Here are two waters for you." She handed each of them a bottle. "Anything else I can bring you while you wait?"

"No, thank you," Maria said, and smiled at her.

"We're good, thanks," Jack agreed. He unscrewed the top of his bottle and took a sip of water.

"Okay, great. I'll be in the other room if you need me," she said. "Enjoy the local news. My favorite politician is on at the moment." She winked at them, then left the waiting area.

Maria turned her attention to the newscast and read the headline banner: "*Senator Clifford in Florida to comfort Chief Billings's widow and grown son.*"

Maria gasped. *Senator Clifford is in town? Mike Clifford?*

She glanced at Jack, who was also watching the news, both eyebrows raised. She looked back at the TV showing an empty stage in an auditorium. She then saw the senator in the audience giving a woman and man, both dressed in black, a long hug before he walked up the steps onto the stage.

Maria plopped down on the couch next to Jack. *That's the wife and son of Chief Billings, the guy who died under mysterious circumstances while speaking with his lawyer? The family of a guy who participated in my kidnapping and somehow covered it up. They're friends with Senator Clifford?*

She watched the senator take the mic. "My fellow Floridians. Today is a sad day for our community. A beloved police chief has passed away, leaving behind his wife and son. We feel with them, we pray for them. His passing is a shock to us all, a tragedy. His death is still being investigated. I can't help but wonder, was it too much for his kind heart to take when he was interrogated, accused of having committed not one but *two* crimes?"

Maria raised her eyebrows. *Too much for his kind heart to take?*

The senator went on, "Such accusations against the former chief strike me as wild and outlandish. Chief Billings did his best to solve the tragic story of the missing girl that has haunted this community for over twenty years. He was an amazing officer who solved many crimes and kept our community safe. Chief Billings's name *must not* be tarnished forever—we all agree he was an excellent police chief. He worked hard, countless hours, and all evidence in the case back then suggested the little toddler had just walked out. A genuine mistake made in the investigation back then. It happens. And we can't forget that the current chief was involved back then also—a young officer who then got taken off the case. Does that have anything to do with why this team focused on our beloved Chief Billings? We can just wonder about it—and we *cannot* forget that Jonathan Sullivan is the real villain of this story, the one who kidnapped a small child off Eglin Air Force Base."

Maria gasped. *That's not true! It wasn't him!*

"Maybe Sullivan's passing was God's will. A punishment for an unthinkable crime committed at our beloved Air Force base, the backbone of our community. Eglin. Our home, our sanctuary."

Maria was taken aback. *God's will? What's he talking about? The guy was killed! Both of them were!*

Maria and Jack heard the audience burst into applause.

"Can't believe this guy," Jack said, frowning. "He came to town to charm all those people, and they're falling for it? He might be a good speaker, but he's a damned politician through and through. Full of it."

Maria nodded, then focused on the senator's speech again.

"And no matter where I go, no matter where I am, I'll always be a part of this community. I feel your pain, I feel your confusion. I feel you. And I hear you! My loyal Floridians, my friends, my voters. You put your trust in me to represent you in the Senate—and I proudly toil to fulfill my sacred duty. But today is a day for me to come home and be with you in these times of turmoil. Cry over what was lost and laugh over what's been found. That little girl was reunited with her family. It's fantastic news."

Maria and Jack tilted their heads in disbelief but continued to listen.

"I plan to meet the little girl—now a grown woman—to welcome her home and apologize for the things that went wrong when her case was investigated."

"What?" Jack stood up. "He wants to meet you?"

Maria felt sick. *He wants to meet me?* She ignored the feeling and kept watching the TV. The cameras zoomed in on the politician on stage. They showed his tan face, his bright blue eyes, his perfectly straight white teeth, his big jaw, his curly beach-blonde hair.

Her eyes widened, then turned completely green. She had a headache, an unbearable headache. *I definitely know this guy. I know him!* She shook her head to get rid of the pain, but it didn't help.

Jack turned to her. "Are you alright, Maria? Don't worry, we won't let him anywhere near you. He doesn't know it yet, but the only people he'll be meeting with are the police."

She nodded slightly, rubbing her temples. "Yeah, that's right. We better let them know he's in town. Or do you think they already know?"

Jack shrugged his shoulders. "No idea. Better safe than sorry. I can't believe smug Senator Clifford has the nerve to show his face in town. So suspicious. What does he want?"

Maria glanced at the TV again, her eyes bright green, her head still pounding. *No kidding, very suspicious. What do you want from me, Senator Clifford?*

CHAPTER 62

"**S**enator Clifford is in town?" Brad repeated back.

His colleague nodded. "Yep. Flew in just this morning. Had his first TV appearance already. Heard he'd love to meet you and your family. He's so excited for you."

The color left Brad's face. *Mike is in town? My enemy. Here and excited for me? Nope, can't be. What does he want? Meeting me and my family? Why?*

Drew, who was sitting next to Brad in the meeting room, put a hand on his shoulder. "You alright, man?"

Brad was ghostly white, his face starkly contrasting with the black leather chair. "I need to talk to Elisabeth. And Chief Parlot," he mumbled.

Drew raised his eyebrows. "What did you say? What's going on, Cave Man?"

But Brad didn't hear him. He was deep in thought. *Mike Clifford is here? Definitely means he's up to no good. He was involved, I know he was. All those years ago, he told me I'd pay. And now he's here? Not good. Need to get to Elisabeth and Maria. Need to tell the police. Now!*

He jumped out of his chair. "Need to go now."

Irritated, the rest of the team in the meeting room watched him pack up his things. They all looked at each other and shrugged their shoulders.

"Is there a problem, General Collins?" one of them finally asked.

Brad briefly looked up. "I gotta go. Have a great day, sirs!" He threw his computer bag over his shoulder and left the room.

"Wait up," he heard Drew yell after him. "Wait! You can't just walk out of a meeting. We haven't even started yet."

But Brad didn't stop. He was determined to get back to his two girls. *Gotta protect them. Need the police on board. They have to arrest Mike. He's dangerous.* That was all he could think as he rode the elevator down. When he stepped out, he almost ran into Drew. "Goodness, Drew! You scared me. How did you get here?"

"I took the stairs—and I guess I beat you, didn't I?" Drew said, and grinned.

"Guess so. But what are you doing here? Why aren't you in the meeting?"

"That was exactly my question!"

"What do you mean?"

"What do *I* mean?" Drew laughed. "Seriously, Cave Man? You're asking me that? *I'm* the one wondering what the heck you're doing down here, walking out of this building in the middle of a workday, even though you committed to attending the rest of our meetings together during our time here. And now you leave, just like that? Without an explanation? You may be a general, but even generals have limits to their privilege. I gotta inform everyone in that meeting room why you left so suddenly. So? What's going on, man?"

Brad sighed and glanced down at his boots, then he put both his hands on Drew's shoulders and looked him directly in the eye. "Listen, Drew, I just realized something: Mike Clifford absolutely loathes me. He hates my guts. Ever since the Academy incident. And now he's here! He's taking revenge again."

"What the heck are you talking about, Brad?"

Brad's now green eyes rested on Drew, who uncomfortably shifted under his friend's grip and stare. "I think he has another evil plan in mind. Think about it. He told me I'd pay for ratting him out, promised he'd destroy me like I destroyed him. And he did. He kidnapped my little girl. He's Cliff. I'm sure that's right. And now he's here? That's not good."

"Gosh, I'm not quite following, Brad, I—"

Brad's grip tightened. "He's here to *take revenge* again. We found her, and now he wants us to lose her again."

Drew couldn't get out of his friend's hold, so instead, he put both his hands on Brad's shoulders and gently shook him. "Cave Man, you gotta wake up. Come back to reality! Even if you're right, how would Mike pull it off? He'd ruin himself if he tried to do something."

Brad let go of Drew's shoulders. "I don't know. All I know is that he threatened me and promised I'd lose it all. And now he's here, claiming he's excited I got my daughter back? I doubt it. Something's not right. He's planning something, something bad."

Drew stared at his friend. "I don't know, man. It's a bit far-fetched—"

"—but worth letting the chief know. They need to arrest him, need to watch him closely."

"Yeah, I guess," Drew whispered. He watched with wide eyes as his friend made for the front door of the building. All of a sudden, he snapped out of his trance and ran after him. "Brad, I'll come with you. If you're right, this is all so freaking messed up. More important than what we were going to discuss upstairs. If Mike had anything to do with Maria's kidnapping, if he's planning something else... we're gonna bring him down. You and me together."

Brad smiled briefly. "You're a good friend, Drew, a very good friend."

Drew grinned. "Yeah, I know. I'm the best. And an excellent colleague—I'll even call the colonel on your behalf to let them know the meeting is postponed due to an urgent personal matter."

Brad gave him a fist bump. "You're awesome, man. I know I can count on you. Let's go talk to the cops. Make sure whatever Mike Clifford has planned won't work out."

CHAPTER 63

"Out there?" Chief Parlot said, and pointed outside the police station window. "You mean to say the senator is right here in Niceville, roaming our neighborhoods?"

"Yes, Chief, we just found out," Sally said, and Tonya nodded.

Chief Parlot stared at them. *Clifford is here already? Holy moly! What's his game plan?*

"Well, I think he's definitely behaving like a guilty man," Tonya said. "He's afraid we're onto him. Otherwise, he wouldn't have come here."

"Agreed," Tom yelled from behind his laptop screen. "He's here to sow confusion and delay our investigation—but he's too late. I've already found one of the last pieces to the puzzle."

"Found what, Tom?" the chief said.

"Where the poisoned chocolates came from. Took me a while, but I got into FedEx's mainframe. Located the shipping label." Sally, Tonya, and the chief all walked over to Tom and his computer. "The box of chocolates was sent from a FedEx close to the Capitol Building in Washington, DC, by one Olivia Dunkin, congressional intern."

"Let me guess," Chief Parlot said. "She interns for Senator Clifford."

Tom grinned. "Bingo!"

"Well, well, well, then," Tonya said. "Now we know who had an interest in shutting up Chief Billings."

"No kidding," Chief Parlot said. "The prime manipulator and mastermind behind the kidnapping. Ladies and gentlemen, congratulations. I believe we just solved the puzzle of the past."

They high-fived each other, but Sally didn't look happy at all. "Unbelievable," she whispered. "Such a criminal is sitting in the Senate? How could nobody know about this?"

Tonya put an arm around Sally. "Girl, I'm afraid you're only now beginning to learn that not everything is as it seems. Unfortunately, there's a lot of people out there who are quite skilled at building a good reputation for themselves, who charm everyone around them while hiding their true selves. And let me tell you, their true selves *ain't pretty*. Our job can feel a bit daunting, Sally, but don't worry. Just gotta grow a thick skin and do your damnedest to bring them to justice."

Sally sighed, her face pale. She nodded, and the color returned to her face. She got out of Tonya's hug and said, "Let's bring that asshole down. Let's arrest him now, before he can run. We have enough to prove what he did beyond a reasonable doubt."

"Absolutely," the chief said. "First order of business will be to confront him over Moana's kidnapping and the chocolates that killed Billings."

"What a creep! What an asshole! Murderer! Kidnapper!" Sally grumbled and started pacing. "Can't wait to arrest him. Luckily, he's not too far. So, let's go!"

Chief Parlot watched his colleague. *Poor youngster. Her innocence gets shattered more and more each day.* "Not so fast, Sally," he said, but Sally was already on her way out the door. Before she could open it, there was a knock. "Come on in," the chief said, and Sally opened the door.

One of the police officers came in. "Hi, Chief, got some important news for ya. We just got a call from Senator Clifford's staff director. He wants to meet with you so you can bring him up to speed on Chief Billings's death and the old kidnapping case."

The chief stared at his colleague. "Senator Clifford called our office just now?"

The policeman nodded. "Well, no, his staff director did. But he wants to meet you. Not the staff director, the senator, I mean."

"Meet me? Senator Clifford wants to meet *me*?" Chief Parlot couldn't believe his ears.

The policeman nodded. "Yes, while he's in town. He already met with the Billings family—"

"—the Billings family? What the heck—" Sally interrupted, but got shushed.

The police officer went on, "He met with the Billings family to show his support and now wants to meet you, Chief, to get an idea of how your investigation is going."

"Of course," the chief said, not bothering to mask his sarcasm.

"He also would like to meet the Collinses to—"

"—*the Collinses*? Is he serious? He's such an a—" Sally interrupted, but got a stern look from both Chief Parlot and Tonya this time.

"Yeah, the senator wants to congratulate the Collins family on their reunion, said he wishes to pledge his support in their pursuit of the truth."

Yeah right! More like bury the truth. Chief Parlot wanted to frown but forced a smile instead. "Sure, please give me the staffer's phone number. My team and I will set something up."

"Great, Chief. Here it is," the policeman said. He handed him a note with a phone number on it, then walked back to the front desk.

Chief Parlot closed the door and the team sat down at the table.

"I can't believe this asshole is in town, pretending to comfort the family of *the guy he killed*, then wants to meet the family of *the girl he kidnapped*, and then—"

Tonya started rubbing Sally's back. "Girl, we gotta stay calm and come up with a plan. Right, Isaac my man?"

374

He nodded. "Yeah, sure. But honestly, Sally's right. The nerve of the guy…"

"Well, at least this way, he saved us a trip to Washington, DC," Tom said.

"But he clearly knows what's up. He'll lawyer up and deny, deny, deny…" Chief Parlot mumbled.

Tonya tilted her head and winked at the chief. "Yeah, he would, if we arrested him. But what if we don't bring him in? What if we agree to meet him on his terms, make him feel safe? Meaning somewhere outside of the police station. Right, Isaac my man?"

He looked at the FBI agent. *Sheesh, she's good. Smart. And knows exactly what I'm thinking. Love working with her.*

He grinned. "Right on. We'll meet with him—but not here at the police station."

CHAPTER 64

"The police station? Sí, you need to go right away—tell them to protect you and Maria. ¡Vamos!" Martina said.

Elisabeth looked at Martina. "You think we all need protection?"

"¡Sí! Maria's kidnapper is in town. He is your enemy. The police need to stay close to you. You never know what he could be planning...."

Lieutenant Martinez gave a slight nod before staring straight ahead again. Drew caught the gesture and grinned. "You know Martina is right when even Lieutenant Martinez is 'voicing' his agreement. Not that he would even admit it, of course, since he's only here to keep an eye on Martina and not share his opinions." Drew winked at him. "But I think we all agree: you have to let Chief Parlot know right away that they need to keep a close eye on Clifford."

Brad and Elisabeth nodded.

Martina's face turned pale. "¡Dios mío, mija! She's out there. Same town as her possible kidnapper. She's in danger."

"What? You think Mo—Maria is in danger?" Elisabeth walked over to Martina and stood nose-to-nose with her.

Tears were fast forming in Martina's eyes. "Don't know, but maybe. We can't let anything happen to her, not again. Quick! ¡Vamos! To the police. Tell them. Tell them to really protect her!"

A big knot formed in Elisabeth's throat. *Martina is right. My baby girl. She's out there, so close to her former kidnapper. Just walking around. We need to protect you, mein Engel.*

She gave Martina a quick hug, then took Brad's hand and pulled him away from the group toward the Air Force Inn's entrance.

"Let's go, Brad. You heard the lady. Let's head to the police station."

As they parked their car in front of the police station, reporters surrounded them. Lights were flashing, cameras clicking, voices babbled all over each other. Elisabeth glanced over to Brad and saw him sigh. She knew he hated reporters, ever since they invaded their privacy twenty years ago, ever since they tore apart their story, their lives, exploited their pain, their feelings.

She took his hand. "Come on, hun. We can do this. Together. For our daughter."

Brad squeezed her hand and turned to her. "Yeah, you're right. We can do this. Have to. For our little one." His now green eyes rested on hers. "Let's go, Elisabeth. Let's go! Push them out of the way, don't comment!"

She nodded, gave his hand one last squeeze, then opened the passenger door. Immediately, there were reporters in her face.

"Mrs. Collins, how do you feel?"

"Mrs. Collins, do you still love your ex-husband?"

"Mrs. Collins, do you hate Martina Sullivan? Or do you actually believe she's innocent?"

"Mrs. Collins, does your daughter remember you?"

"Mrs. Collins, does your daughter love you?"

Elisabeth bit her lip to resist the temptation to scream at the reporters. *Of course my daughter loves me! Leave me alone! Leave us alone! Get lost!*

She carefully made her way through the crowd and joined Brad behind the car. He glanced at her, then took her hand. Together, they made their way through the crowd of reporters, trying to ignore their questions.

"General Collins, I see you're holding your ex-wife's hand. Does that mean you still love her? Are you getting back together?"

"Where will you live?"

"What about your daughter?"

Elisabeth kept her mouth shut, glanced over at Brad, and squeezed his hand. Suddenly, he stopped.

"Listen, everyone. We are *family*. We are the Collinses. And all I can say now is: We *will* stick together forever and take on whatever gets thrown our way. *Nobody* can tear us down. I want *everyone* to know that. No further comment!"

Elisabeth grinned. *Well said, Brad, well said. If Mike is listening, he'll know we won't be brought down by whatever he does or says. We will fight him—and this time, we will stand triumphant. As a family.*

Elisabeth and Brad sat in one of the rooms inside the police station and talked to the officers and agents. Dr. Davies was there as well, but kept quiet and just listened to everyone talk. Elisabeth noticed him, but tried to concentrate on what the officers and agents said. But even as they chatted, Elisabeth found herself preoccupied.

Can't believe Mike Clifford kidnapped my child out of revenge. How could he? He was our friend. Even I knew him at the Academy.

A tear escaped and ran down her nose, dripped onto her hand. More and more tears were forming as the thoughts engrossed her. *Losing our little one caused us so much pain, so much unbearable pain. It broke my heart. It broke us, me and Brad. And now Mike's back in town? Why? What does he want from us? We gotta stop him.*

She felt Brad take her hand and intertwine his fingers with hers. He held it tight and gave it an encouraging squeeze. She felt the warmth of love stream up her arm. At that moment, she found she was strong again—strong and angry. With a flushed face, she looked up directly at Chief Parlot and said, "You have to arrest him. Right away. You have to arrest this fucking asshole, this jerk! Arrest him, now, and make him rot in prison forever."

Irritated, Brad turned to her, and she briefly glanced at him. *I know I usually don't swear, but I can't help it. Not when we're talking about the guy who stole my child, stole the past twenty years of my life from me.*

Elisabeth let go of Brad's hand and stood so that she was face-to-face with the chief. "Arrest him! Now! Go!"

Chief Parlot sighed. "Mrs. Collins, I must ask you to stay calm. Listen, we have a proposition for you—"

"No, you need to go now. He's out there, stalking our daughter. We can't let anything happen to her again."

Agent Anderson put a hand on Elisabeth's shoulder. "Please, Mrs. Collins, your daughter is fine. She's currently being escorted back to the hotel on base." Elisabeth's face softened. "Aaron called us earlier. They ran into reporters while looking at apartments—"

Brad jumped up now, too. "Those damn paparazzi are bothering my daughter again?"

The agent nodded. "Yeah, afraid so, General Collins. But rest assured, the Niceville police are doing everything we can to keep everyone safe from both reporters and bad guys alike."

Elisabeth sighed, tears forming in her eyes again. *Bad guys. Yeah, Mike is definitely a bad guy. Why didn't we think of him sooner? Like twenty years earlier?*

"Mrs. Collins, Agent Anderson is right," Chief Parlot said. "Maria is safe. My colleagues are escorting the Heikinnens and Maria back to Eglin—*away* from the reporters and *away* from Senator Clifford."

Elisabeth snorted. *Senator... What the heck? How can he be a senator? He's not working for the people, he's just doing his own thing. For him. For revenge. A criminal. He's a freaking criminal. And an asshole!*

"Mrs. Collins? Did you hear us? Do you understand? Maria is safe."

Elisabeth snapped out of her thoughts and nodded. "Yeah, thank you, Chief. Thank you, Agent Anderson."

"You're very welcome," the agent said. She smiled and gave Elisabeth one last gentle squeeze, then let go of her shoulder. Elisabeth and Brad sat back down and took each other's hand again. They both let out a sigh.

Brad spoke. "So, what's the plan now then? Will you arrest and charge him? He's still walking around out there, talking to the press, pretending to be a nice guy. Honestly, it's sickening. You gotta arrest him. You already seem to have everything you need to tie him to this and—"

"General Collins," Chief Parlot said, "yes, we have some crucial information, but—"

"So, what the heck are you waiting for then?" Elisabeth yelled, throwing up both hands.

"Well, we were just coming up with a plan on how to extract a confession from him. That's why we were so keen to talk with you. The both of you. And Dr. Davies."

Elisabeth looked up. "Dr. Davies? You mean this guy over there?" She pointed at him. "The psychologist who worked with our daughter?"

Dr. Davies grinned. "Yes, the chief talked about me—child trauma specialist. That's why I'm here. To learn of the plan."

Chief Parlot nodded. "Correct. Both you and he have to give us the okay before we try out this somewhat unusual plan."

Elisabeth raised her eyebrows. *Unusual plan? What are they talking about?* She kept listening to the chief.

"We assume that Mike Clifford will lawyer up, big-time, if we bring him in for questioning. However, it does seem he wants to meet with all of us."

All of us? Elisabeth was irritated and glanced over at Brad, then saw him nod. *This is making sense to him?*

She kept listening as Agent Anderson took over. "Our team was informed about an hour ago that Senator Clifford requested to meet the police officers leading the ongoing investigation. Apparently, he's very interested to learn how much progress we've made on the case. He's also keen on exchanging words with your family, the reunited Collins family. We were thinking about granting both his requests."

Elisabeth couldn't believe her ears. "What? Don't you understand he just wants to manipulate—"

"How exactly will you get him to confess during the meeting?" Brad said.

Irritated, she turned to him. "You're down with this ridiculous idea of meeting with him? The man that caused all our pain, all our misery? Brad, seriously?"

"Let's hear them out," he said, his voice stern.

Elisabeth shook her head. "I *most definitely will not* meet with him."

The room fell silent.

Brad took her hand again, turned her face toward his, and looked deep into her eyes. "Don't you want to make sure he goes to jail for this? That he's locked away for good? Forever, because we have clear-cut evidence that shows he's behind all of this?"

Elisabeth nodded. "Of course, I do. You know that. But don't we already have enough to do that?"

"Maybe. But if there's any doubt about how he was involved, anything at all, he'll use it. His lawyers will exploit it. It's hard to get at people in power. He has a lot of people who work for him, a lot of supporters he can influence and manipulate. We need him to dig his own grave."

Elisabeth sighed. She looked around the room. Officer Johnson, Agent Anderson, Chief Parlot, the young FBI agent Tom Cooper, and even Dr. Davies all nodded. She took a deep breath in. "Okay, fine then, let's hear what this grand plan is. And then we decide."

"Excellent, Mrs. Collins, thank you," Chief Parlot said.

Within the next hour, the police team, Dr. Davies, Elisabeth, and Brad had come up with a plan, a mission on how to get a confession out of Senator Clifford. Everyone walked away happy with the plan.

"Alright then, I'll call the good senator to set it all up," Chief Parlot said, and grinned. "He has no idea what's in store for him." The chief left the room to the sound of everyone's laughter.

"Yep, he has no idea at all, that man. Nice work, team," Agent Anderson said, and walked around the room to high-five everyone.

Elisabeth's high five was weak, but nobody noticed. *I'm still not sure if this is as good an idea as everyone thinks. Somehow, I've got a bad feeling about it. A real bad feeling.*

CHAPTER 65

"A bad feeling? What? Why, Mamá? Why do you have a bad feeling about the apartment we chose?" Maria asked.

They were sitting in the lobby of the Air Force Inn, discussing Aaron's new apartment. Proudly, they had told Martina all about Aaron's new quarters, shown her pictures both on their phones and in the brochure the leasing agent had given them.

But Martina couldn't muster any enthusiasm, even though she knew they were hoping for a better reaction. She knew they wanted her to be just as excited as they were about finding such a nice place, but she couldn't help herself. She just wasn't happy with it, and it didn't take long for Maria to figure that out.

Martina sighed. *Mija. I know she's disappointed with me. But I do have a bad feeling about it.*

"Mamá, ¿qué pasa?"

"It looks beautiful."

"Exactly. So, why aren't you excited about it?"

"Waterfront living, mija?"

"Mamá, what's wrong with that? You love the water. You love the views. Didn't you always want something like that in Miami?"

Martina smirked and couldn't help but laugh. "¡Sí, but too expensive!"

"Still don't get it, Mamá!"

"I'm just worried, mija. Are you sure you can stand it?"

Martina noticed Aaron and Jack had a puzzled look on their faces, and realized no one was taking her hints. She sighed. *Guess I have to be direct.*

"Maria, this is the water you almost drowned in. Twice now. Are you sure you can bear seeing it every day from that pretty balcony?" Martina pointed at the picture on the brochure.

"Oh, Martina," Aaron said, "you don't have to worry. I already checked with Maria about that, and she's okay with it. She assured me she is. And luckily, 'The Cove Apartments' are on Cinco Bayou—a little different than Choctawhatchee Bay."

Martina raised her eyebrows. "Doesn't matter. Same difference. Maria will see water. Maria is afraid of water. She almost drowned. I don't know if she can handle it. I need her to feel comfortable."

"We all do," Jack said, and Aaron nodded.

Maria turned to Martina, looked into her beautiful brown eyes, then gave her a hug. "You really don't have to worry, Mamá. Aaron is right. Really, I'm not afraid. Not afraid anymore. Believe me!"

"¿Estás segura?"

"Sí, Mamá, I'm sure. I'm older now and understand that water doesn't equal drowning. And what happened to me was so unusual, so uncommon. I know that. Chances are very low it will ever happen again."

Martina felt the warmth of her daughter's body in their embrace, Maria's breath in her hair. She felt Maria's heart beating as they hugged each other. Despite the warmth of her embrace, a cold shudder ran down Martina's spine, sending her thoughts spinning.

I'm not sure. The water scares me, scares me for you, Maria. I'm probably being silly, but you almost drowned twice already. Twice in that water. I have such a bad feeling.

She tried to shake off her thoughts and smiled. "Okay, mija, that's good. ¡Muy bien! Glad you like it. It's beautiful. ¡Claro, vistas muy hermosas!"

"¡Exactemente! Beautiful views. I love it. I'm excited." Maria gave her one last squeeze and let go of her mom.

Martina took a deep breath and smiled. "Okay. Good that you like it and feel safe there."

As she watched Maria nod, her false smile faded and her anxious thoughts returned. *Are you sure you'll be safe, mija? I feel so afraid for you.*

CHAPTER 66

"For you, Senator. The Niceville police chief is on the line."

"Oh, okay, good. Thanks. I'll take it," Mike Clifford said, and took the phone from his staff director. "Hello? Chief Parlot?"

"Hi, Senator Clifford," said the chief on the other end of the line. "What a surprise to hear you're in town. I was told you'd like to meet?"

"Yes, I would. You'd honor me by allowing me to drop by to thank you and your team for keeping watch over my old hood. You know I grew up in Niceville, right?"

"Yes, sir, I know you went to school here for a time. Niceville High School."

"Yes, that I did. The old high school. But I do consider Niceville my home. You know, being a military brat sure was hard. But Niceville was a great experience."

"I'm sure, Senator Clifford, glad to hear," Chief Parlot said. "And thank you for your kind words. My team and I are working hard to maintain peace and order in our small little town. We appreciate your support."

"Anytime, Chief, anytime."

"Well... you said you just wanted to meet to thank us? Appears you already did."

"Err, yes, Chief, but not in the right format."

The chief paused. "What do you mean, Senator?"

"I'd like to thank you in person. And hope to get an update on how the investigation is going."

"The investigation?"

"Yes, Chief, I'd like to be kept informed. The old kidnapping case is one thing, but Chief Billings's recent death is something else entirely."

"Yes, Senator, it was a shock to all of us."

"I'll say. Goodness, what a shame. Especially since he was probably crucial for completing your investigation into the kidnapping, right?"

Mike Clifford heard a slight pause on the other end. "Crucial for the investigation? Why do you say so, Senator?"

Now Mike was irritated. "Well, because Chief Billings led the charge on the original kidnapping case, of course. I heard you brought him in for questioning as he seemed to know the poor fool who tried to kill the Collins' daughter?"

"Yes, Senator, you heard right."

Mike laughed out loud. "Of course I heard right, Chief. I'm the *senator*. They brief me well. I've got a good team. I know people, you know."

"We *know*," he heard Chief Parlot say, his voice sharp.

"Well, anyways, Chief Billings seems to have been a crucial witness—or even suspect, right? He probably knew more. Would've said more."

"Said more?" The chief suddenly sounded suspicious.

Mike started pacing, then took a deep breath. *Can't say too much, idiot. Need to keep it together. Make him feel uncomfortable, not feel uncomfortable myself.*

He stopped pacing and spoke clearly. "Yeah, you know, Chief, we all want closure. The death of two crucial witnesses—suspects, even—is such a damned shame. And bad publicity!" He grinned. *Yeah, intimidate him. Let him know he can't mess with me.*

He heard a gasp on the other end. "Excuse me, Senator?"

"Well, like I was saying, I support Niceville and its community. I'm here to help. I don't want any trouble in my home state, let alone in my hometown! Now, two deaths in two days, another kidnapping, and, of course, that bungled case twenty years ago, all happening right under the nose of the same small-town police station.... Doesn't that seem a bit, I dunno, unusual?"

Silence on the other end.

Mike smiled. *Yeah, I know how to press the boot into the neck. People do as I say!*

He heard Chief Parlot clear his throat. "Well, Senator, I can assure you, we've got everything under control."

"Good. Very good then. I want this case closed. I don't like bad news coming out of Florida."

"I understand, Senator," came the small voice of Chief Parlot.

Mike's smile widened into a big grin from ear to ear.

"And *that's* why we have a good idea on where we'd like to meet," he heard the chief say, his voice suddenly crisp and clear. "To help all of us put Florida and Niceville back in a good light."

Mike's grin faded. *What does that mean? What's he planning? Wants to arrange the meeting to save face in front of his department, or something else? Does he know more than he's letting on? Did Billings share something?*

"Senator, I can assure you that, soon, it'll be nothing but good news coming out of Florida," Chief Parlot said. "I'm talking about closure here."

Through the phone, Mike could almost hear the chief grin. Sweat started coating his forehead. *Good news for Florida? Closure?*

This time, it was Mike's turn to clear his throat, but even then, his voice still sounded a bit hoarse. "Closure, Chief? So, you have new leads? New information? From Billings?"

"I cannot comment on that at this time, Senator Clifford. You'll have to wait and see. You know us cops always love keeping people in suspense, letting them wonder if we'll get the bad guy or not. But rest assured, we will. And we'll punish him to the full extent of the law."

Mike's face went pale—luckily, it was only a phone call. He quickly walked over to his table in the fancy hotel room and grabbed a bottle of water standing there. He took a sip, then said, "Yes, Chief, that's good to hear. Finding whoever committed these crimes and punishing him sounds like exactly what Florida needs right now."

"So, Senator, do we have your support?"

Mike took another sip of water. "Of course, Chief."

"Great. So here's what we were thinking. Before we begin, do you want to discuss these matters on your lonesome, or with an aide present?"

Mike sat down in the fancy chair next to the fancy table in his hotel suite. "Well, usually I like having my staff director on the call. Logistics, you know. Please wait a minute. I'll call him in and we can all discuss this together."

"Okay, Senator, sounds great," the chief said.

Mike paged the director and within moments, he was in his suite, equipped with a notepad, pens, a schedule, and a calendar. As his help coordinated with the chief, Mike barely listened, was far away with his thoughts.

They have new information. They'll find the bad guy and punish him?

Find me?

He shuddered. *No, I can't let them find me. Or anyone else. I can't.*

He loosened the tie around his neck as the conversation wore on, not really paying much attention to what was said.

I need to come up with the mother of all fucking plans to defend myself. If they get to me, I need to have a plan. A good plan!

CHAPTER 67

"**A** good plan?" Martina's eyes widened in horror and she violently shook her head. "¡Naguará! No, no, not a good plan at all."

Elisabeth was visiting Martina's room. Lieutenant Martinez was standing in the corner per usual, ensuring everything was in order. She glanced over to him; he was trying to not show any emotion, but she could tell he was having a hard time.

"Martina, it will be alright. The police will be there. Dr. Davies too. They're going to protect her. They won't let anything happen to her," Elisabeth said, trying to sound convincing. She sighed. *At least that's what they said when they were reassuring me.*

Martina stopped shaking her head. "Elisabeth, mi amiga, you're her mom, too. Do you believe this is a good plan?" She cupped Elisabeth's hand in hers and looked her straight in the eye.

Elisabeth had a hard time withstanding her stare. "Well, I guess it's worth a shot...."

"Oh no, that doesn't sound convincing at all. You have your doubts, too, don't you?"

Elisabeth shuddered, her hands cold compared to Martina's. *Of course I do, but I need to convince her to permit Maria to go.* "I'll be there, too. I won't let anything happen to our daughter," she said, and smiled.

"Look at us, Martina. *Our* daughter. Who would've thought the two of us would ever refer to her as *our* daughter."

Martina broke out into a smile as well. "Sí, *our* daughter! Maria has two moms now to worry about her, no?"

The women laughed together, still holding hands. Warmth flooded back into Elisabeth's hand. The warmth of their newly found friendship, the security of knowing that Maria would always be protected.

I hated Martina, but I was wrong to feel that way. She's such a good person. Such a good mom. And such a good friend. She took good care of my baby girl. And now it's my turn.

"Well, Martina, you seem to know me well already," Elisabeth said. "Of course I'm worried. I'm worried I'll blow it by showing my hatred toward that man. Afraid Maria will collapse when she meets with one of her kidnappers. We need her to stay strong so she can identify him. Yes, I'm very worried about her. Worried it will be too much, or something will happen."

Martina nodded. "Sí, me, too. Very worried."

"But we need to stick together, Martina. We need to be strong for her. Both of us. Because we both want that bad guy behind bars, don't we?"

"¡Definitivamente! Yes, we want the bad guy to pay for what he did to our Maria. And to you, and Brad…"

"And you!"

"Me?"

"Yes, you, Martina. He forced Jonathan Sullivan to contact you again, sent him to your new apartment, your safe space, had him intimidate you, tricked you into believing a false story about the baby girl he made you raise. It wasn't fair to you either."

Martina nodded, tears welling in her eyes.

Elisabeth noticed. "What is it, Martina?"

"Well, if it hadn't been that way... I wouldn't have had Maria," she whispered, her face full of shame. "I'm sorry, Elisabeth, so sorry for—"

"Stop, Martina. It's not even worth looking back now, thinking 'what if.' It happened the way it did. We have the chance now to make it better. And while the police's plan is risky, it seems worth it. Worth it to finally finish this... this absurd puzzle of the past. We nearly have all the puzzle pieces assembled—we just need to put one last piece in place and call it done."

Martina nodded, her voice strong and clear now, her brown eyes sparkling. "Sí, we need to get this over and done with. Get the right guy this time, the big enemy. This jerk behind the whole kidnapping plot. Time to catch him and put him in jail!"

"Exactly. Let's expose Senator Clifford in front of the cameras, in front of the whole world."

"¡Sí! Expose and punish!"

The two moms smiled at each other, high-fived, then hugged.

Martina nodded. "Okay. Let's tell Maria she needs to go with you and convince Aaron to stay with me. They don't need to know the whole plan. Thank you, though, for telling me."

Elisabeth let go of Martina and looked at her. "Of course, Martina. You had every right to know. You're her mom, too."

Martina smiled, then linked arms with Elisabeth. "¡Vamos! Let's go see *our* daughter. *Our* Maria."

CHAPTER 68

Maria was sitting in the car with Brad and Elisabeth, sandwiched between a police escort.

"Where exactly are we going?"

"Turkey Creek," Brad said.

"And that's where we'll meet the press? Why there?"

"Well, it's a nice setting," Brad explained in a quiet voice while focusing on the road.

Maria glanced at Elisabeth and saw her mom's face flush as she solemnly stared out of the window. "Mmmh... I feel like you're both keeping something from me. And why is Dr. Davies coming? I see him riding in the backseat of the car with the police officers right in front of us."

Brad had to grin. "You're very perceptive, Maria."

She snorted. "I guess I've kinda had to be that way lately, you know? I feel like I'm always having to watch my back with all the paparazzi around. And then getting attacked that night *really* made me aware of my surroundings."

Brad grinned. "Just like I told you in front of that water fountain at the Air Force Ball—'be aware of your surroundings.'"

Maria laughed. "Yeah. Just wish I'd known you were my dad back then. Would've saved us all a lot of heartache, right?"

Brad's smile faded; sadness washed over his face. "Yeah, it would've. Damn it!" He hit the steering wheel of his car. "That was my fault, all my fault—"

Elisabeth turned to him. "Brad, don't do that. It wasn't your fault. You couldn't have known who she was. For goodness' sake, you didn't even know she was still alive."

He nodded and blinked back tears. They went silent for a while. Maria watched the blinking lights of the silent sirens on the police cars that were herding them along. *A lot of commotion just for me. Gosh, my life is so different now. I hate being the center of attention. A press conference? For me? About me? Unbelievable. And another police escort. I even have my own shrink now....*

"Oh, you were wondering why Dr. Davies is here? He just wants to make sure you're alright, Süße. Just in case something happens that triggers memories or something," Elisabeth said.

"I see," Maria said. *Why are they worried that might happen? Not sure. But I have a feeling my parents know more than they're letting on. What are they hiding?*

They kept driving into the late afternoon sun, along the shoreline of an offshoot of Choctawhatchee Bay. They all looked out their windows. Nobody said a word.

"Here we are," Brad said. He pulled into a dusty parking lot right behind the police car carrying Chief Parlot, Officer Johnson, and Dr. Davies. The car with both the FBI agents came to a stop next to them. Despite the dust cloud kicking up in their wake, Maria could already see the reporters swarming toward them. She sighed. *I just want to be left alone. This is ridiculous.*

She watched as the reporters were stopped in their tracks by a line of police officers and other official-looking men dressed in black. They pushed them back from the parking lot, behind a small wooden fence. Maria grinned. *Much better. That should be far enough away from us. Definitely far enough that they can't pepper us with questions.*

She got out of the car with Brad and Elisabeth. Brad walked over to grab Elisabeth's hand and squeezed it. Maria noticed the gesture. *Why's he doing that? To encourage her or something? What's going on here?*

"How are you feeling, Maria?" came a gentle male voice. She turned and found Dr. Davies standing next to her.

"Pretty good, I guess," she said. She looked around while the doctor studied her face.

"That's good to hear," Dr. Davies said, then gestured her to follow her parents. "Keep walking toward the picnic area, please."

Maria nodded and followed the little group. She saw a picnic area under a big sunroof with a stone fireplace in the middle, set into some wooden planks that looked like the floor of a deck. *Why does this place seem familiar?*

She kept walking, Dr. Davies next to her, her parents, the chief, Officer Johnson, and the FBI agents in front of her. She studied the area around her. The distant din of the reporters had faded away, and she heard the faint sound of water splashing, as if it was running over rocks, moving around, pooling in deeper pockets. *Sounds like a river?*

She noticed a sign now that read "Turkey Creek." *That's right. Turkey Creek. My dad mentioned that in the car. Must be behind the picnic area?* She looked for it, but the manmade structures blocked her view—and that's when she saw a tall man standing in between the picnic tables, waving at them. All she could make out behind him was a trail, like a boardwalk, that apparently led toward the creek. *Is it a big body of water? Turkey Creek. Did I ever come here before? When I was little?*

"Welcome, welcome," a warm, loud voice rang out, snapping her out of her reverie. "Great to see you in person, Chief Parlot. And nice to meet you, Officer Johnson."

Maria remained where she was and watched both police officers approach the unknown man. They shook his hand, then both Agent Anderson and Agent Cooper greeted him as well, then her parents. All Maria could see of him was his tan forehead, wide shoulders, and locks of curly beach-blonde hair.

A shudder ran down her spine. *Who is this guy? Do I know him?*

"Maria, our turn next," Dr. Davies whispered to her, and stepped out in front of her. "Hello, I'm Dr. Davies. A pleasure to meet you."

Maria saw them shake hands. As she studied the man's profile, she heard the clicking of cameras, what sounded like a million voices babbling on about the meeting, the faint swoosh of the water from the creek.

"The pleasure is all mine, doctor," she heard the friendly voice say. "If you don't mind me asking, why exactly are you here?"

"To support Maria," Elijah Davies said.

"Support her?"

"I'm a child psychologist."

The man grinned. "Oh, I see. A *psychologist*. Guess the poor girl requires a lot of emotional support these days."

Dr. Davies ripped his hand out of the man's and grinned back at him. "Yeah, especially when her memories come flooding back."

The tall man's grin vanished; he pressed his lips together.

Dr. Davies turned around. "Come on, Maria. Your turn."

She looked at Dr. Davies and nodded, then stepped closer until she could make out the man's face.

"Hello there," he said, his voice loud and friendly, a smile on his face. "Hello, Maria. Ah, I heard you're going by Maria now, not Moana? Is that correct?"

She stared at him and felt like she couldn't move. The clicking of the cameras suddenly seemed so loud that her ears rang as though her eardrums were about to burst. She saw the man's bright blue eyes smiling coldly from behind his sun-kissed tan face, the curly beach-blonde hair moving slightly in the warm wind, his pearly-white teeth shining brighter than the setting sun. She felt paralyzed.

Oh my gosh, it's him. Senator Clifford!

As he took her hand, all she wanted was to run. But the warmth of his hand, the strength of his grip made her legs go weak. *It's a setup. Not a press conference. It's Cliff. I don't like this guy.* She felt so weak, so small. It all happened so suddenly. She didn't hear the words he was saying, didn't see the others staring at her, didn't notice the reporters capturing every moment of the meeting.

All she felt was nausea and panic rising up inside her. *Don't like him. Bad guy!* His grip was so tight. *I need to get away!*

As if in a trance, she looked up from their handshake and stared at his pearly-white teeth. They shone so bright that she had to close her eyes. When she opened them again, she was lost in a vision from the past.

She was staring at white teeth on a super-tan face. Curly beach-blonde hair framed it. Intense blue eyes stared back at her through the metal poles. Those blue eyes looked down on her, scolded her. They were so close to her, so big, peeking into her little cage. They oozed disgust and anger.

She heard a laugh. A loud, cruel laugh.

"Good job, Sully," he heard. "Good job shutting her up with that tape. That'll keep her quiet."

Her eyes widened. *Don't like him. Bad guy! Worse than other guy!*

She started whimpering, then crying, but the thing over her mouth made her very quiet.

His big hands now came closer, pressed themselves through the metal poles. He tried to poke her, make fun of her.

No, no, no! Don't touch me!

But his big tan hands squeezed through and grabbed her hand, squeezed her hand. She tried to kick, tried to move her arms, but couldn't. She was stuck to the metal poles. She was helpless. So very helpless. And so small. He held her hand, a big grin on his face, firmly gripping her little hand. She closed her eyes to not see him anymore.

When she finally opened them again, the same big, strong hand was still holding hers. He was still there, a grin on his face. *No! I need to get away from him and his scary hands. Now! Make noise, kick to get out!*

She opened her mouth and screamed, a loud scream at the top of her lungs, then ripped her hand out of his, kicked his shin, and took a few steps back while still screaming. *I'm free! Mouth not stuck closed anymore! Not stuck to box!*

Surprised, the man stared at her, then held his ears. "Make her stop screaming!"

She heard cameras clicking, a muddle of voices, then a soft voice next to her. "Maria, it's alright, it's alright. Look at me!"

But she could only focus on the man, the bad guy still standing in front of her, now rubbing his shin.

Her head got turned to the side and she stared directly into the eyes of Elijah Davies. "You're safe, Maria, you're safe," she heard, then saw him raise two fingers and snap loudly.

Irritated, Maria closed her eyes and mouth. When she opened them again, Dr. Davies was right in front of her, smiling, telling her to focus on him alone. He led her away to one of the nearby picnic tables. Maria collapsed onto the wooden bench.

Senator Clifford watched her and Dr. Davies while holding his shin. "What the heck?" he mumbled, then called over to his staffers. "Get her some water. Some bottled water."

Quickly, one of the senator's staffers ran over and handed her a bottle of water. She took it absentmindedly.

"Drink, Maria, please," said Dr. Davies in a calm voice. "Know that you're safe here."

She nodded. With shaky hands, she twisted off the cap and took a sip. She almost spilled it, her hands so shaky. She took a few big gulps, then felt better. Calm but exhausted. Her head pounded. *What just happened?*

She took another few big gulps of water, then looked back over to the senator and shuddered. *Oh my gosh, I know him. He's the bad guy. Sullivan's accomplice. I'm sure of it. I remember him! Cliff. He's the one who ordered Sullivan around. He's the one who held me captive on that boat. On his boat! All that time. He's the one. They need to arrest him. I need to tell them to arrest him!*

She was ready to speak, ready to tell Dr. Davies, who was right there in front of her. But her mouth wouldn't move.

I can't speak?

She tried again, but her mouth just wouldn't do what she wanted it to. *What the heck? What's wrong with me?*

She took another few sips of water and suddenly felt sleepy, so tired. She had no reason to feel this tired, but somehow her body was doing its own thing. She had no control over it. Her eyes just closed as she sat there on that picnic bench.

Dr. Davies noticed that Maria was getting very calm and sleepy. "I know that was exhausting, Maria. I'm sorry we did this to you, but we all saw you recognize him. That's very powerful confirmation. You did your part. And now, you can rest. Yes, good, close your eyes and rest. That's good, Maria. You're safe now. Rest."

Rest? I can't rest! Not here, not with the bad guy right there! Something is happening to me. Please help me!

She tried to open her eyes but couldn't. They were so heavy; her eyelids felt like they weighed one hundred pounds. She was scared, so scared, but couldn't tell anyone. Everything suddenly seemed so surreal, so far away. Dr. Davies was far away, her parents, the police, the senator.

She knew they were right there, she heard them, she heard everything, but somehow their voices were muffled. And when she managed to open her eyes just a little bit, she felt like the people around her were under a thin veil, a veil of fog.

What the heck is happening?

CHAPTER 69

"What the heck is happening here?" Senator Clifford asked the police officers and agents. He was still rubbing his shin. "Why'd she do that? Why in the world would she just attack me? I come all this way to congratulate her, tell her I'm happy she found her parents—"

"Liar, such a damn liar," Elisabeth growled, and started walking toward him, her hands in fists, her face bright red in anger, her bottom lip quivering.

Officer Sally Johnson held her back. "Please, Mrs. Collins, stick to the plan. We have to stick to the plan." Elisabeth started sobbing, and the officer gave her a hug.

"What the heck, Chief? I demand an explanation," Senator Clifford said, and stared at Chief Parlot.

The chief stepped toward him, but then turned around and addressed the crowd of the reporters in a booming voice. "Ladies and gentlemen, you've just witnessed something incredible. Something amazing that only the human mind can do. Because the human mind recognizes danger. Fight or flight, right? You're all familiar with that? Well, ladies and gentlemen, you just saw a young lady recognize her own kidnapper!"

Loud mutters and murmurs arose from the crowd. Mike Clifford just stared at the chief. *I knew they'd use her to get to me. Clever, very clever.* He glanced over his shoulder and saw Maria at the picnic tables. *But you underestimated me. I have my own plan, a good fucking plan that'll save me. For now, though, I need to play along with their plan.*

He focused again on Chief Parlot's speech. "That's right, Maria recognized Senator Mike Clifford as her kidnapper!"

Cameras were clicking, reporters babbling all over one another.

Chief Parlot grinned into the cameras. Senator Clifford made it a point to look stunned. "Excuse me, Chief? Are you out of your mind?"

The reporters pushed against the barrier, keen to be closer to the action.

Then Mike Clifford started laughing. "That's ridiculous, Chief, just absurd. I had *nothing* to do with the kidnapping. Nothing! Why in the world would I kidnap a child? The child of an Air Force captain?"

Cameras clicked and rolled, but every voice went silent to listen.

"Well, Senator Clifford—" Chief Parlot started, but was interrupted by Brad, who pushed past the agents and Officer Johnson.

"Because you hate my guts. You've hated me ever since I told on you, ever since I did the right thing and reported you to the Academy. We all know that. We know you told me I'd pay—and so you took my child, didn't you, Mike?"

The senator shook his head, was all smiles. "Tsk. Brad, Brad, Brad... Don't be silly. That's ridiculous. Why would I be mad at you? You actually helped me—turns out, politics suit me *much* better than military service. I love my life, and I certainly wouldn't risk it for the likes of you."

Brad's face flushed. "We all know you did it. We know you worked with Sullivan, and Agent Borman. You forced your friend Chief Billings to derail the investigation and—"

"*Please*, General Collins, I need you to stay back," Chief Parlot said, and tried to push him away. The two FBI agents stepped forward to help.

The senator burst into laughter again. "That's ridiculous! So far-fetched. You're losing it, Brad."

"Senator Clifford," the chief started again, but before he could say anything more, Brad surged forward, pushed the chief aside, ran up to Mike, and punched him in the face. The crowd *oohed* as everyone watched the senator stumble backward, holding his face.

"Liar! Asshole! You ruined my life! How dare you take my child?"

Mike looked up again, blood trickling from his nose. "How *dare* you attack me? Are you out of your mind, Collins?" Mike stared at him. *Wish I could beat you up right now. Beat you senseless. Smug general. Fucking bastard. I hate you, Collins! But I know better. I've learned. I need to hold back.*

"Get that idiot away from me," the senator said, and the two FBI agents rushed in to restrain him. They pushed Brad back, away from the senator.

"Chief, this is nuts! How dare you let him attack me? It wouldn't be unreasonable for me to sue you for criminal neglect," Senator Clifford said, dabbing at his nose with his hands.

"I apologize, Senator," Chief Parlot mumbled. "But General Collins here has a point. *We know*, Mike Clifford. We know what happened. Got anything to say to that?"

You wish. Another smug asshole. I will certainly not confess. He glanced over at Maria and saw her head hanging down. *Looks like she's asleep. Good, good. Just like I planned. Now to sink the knife.*

"I certainly do not, Chief. If you think I did something wrong, you'll have to bring me in for questioning, treat me like any other citizen. But to pick this moment, this place? That's just *wrong*, Chief. I offered to meet you here, to support my community, and now look at this mess. I've been accused, I've been attacked. It's not right! And to use a young, vulnerable lady to apparently entrap me, make me out as some bad guy, is not only irresponsible, and wrong, but undeniably illegal."

The chief was about to say something when Mike pointed toward Maria. Everyone now looked at her, slumped over the picnic bench, her head hanging low, her eyes closed.

Chief Parlot called over to Dr. Davies. "Elijah, is she okay?"

The senator grinned. "Looks to me like she's either having a psychotic episode or is just plain drunk. What did the doctor give her? Too many psycho drugs? No wonder she was screaming like crazy earlier."

Everyone stared at the senator.

"You know, certainly goes to show she didn't recognize me at all. She's too out of it, totally drugged to the gills," Mike said loudly, expertly playing the crowd of reporters, who scribbled notes and talked into their cameras.

"I can't wake her up! She seems unconscious, Isaac," Dr. Davies called back. "I need help!"

Quickly, the chief turned and ran over to Maria and Dr. Davies.

"Nein, meine Süße," Elisabeth whispered, and made her way to her daughter, Officer Johnson by her side.

"My baby girl," Brad said. The agents released him so he could join the huddle, Agent Cooper in tow.

The senator just stayed where he was and watched from a distance. He had to hide his smile. *Good. All according to plan. They'll focus on her now. And I get to work the press. Feed them the narrative. Tell them my story. It all makes sense. A drugged girl accuses me, then her dad attacks—I'm the victim.*

As he turned to step closer to the press, he almost bumped into Agent Anderson. She grinned at him. "Where are you going, Senator?"

He grinned back. *This lady is so small, her head barely reaches my chest. Easy to nudge out of the way.*

"Well, Agent"—he looked down to read her name tag—"Anderson. I figured we need to let the press know—"

"—that you're under arrest?" She grinned at him, still blocking his way.

He stared at her. *What the fuck? She must be kidding.* He burst into laughter.

"Go ahead, Senator, try your luck." She smiled as she looked up at him, her cornrow bun bobbing in the slight wind.

He grinned. *Silly woman! Ridiculous. Who does she think she is? A nothing, a nobody. The FBI probably just needed to get their diversity numbers up, I bet.*

He shook his head, then stepped around her, but before he could make it far, he felt cold metal slap onto his left wrist.

What the fuck?

He turned and saw the agent's smiling face.

"Senator Michael Clifford, you are under arrest for the kidnapping of Moana Marie Collins, and for being an accessory to the murder of Jonathan Eric Sullivan and Jim Billings. Everything you say can and will be used against you…"

Mike felt the world spinning. *She's reading me my fucking rights? Arresting me, right here, in front of the press? In front of the world? No, no, no, that can't be. This little woman? This wasn't supposed to happen. I can't let it happen.*

Before Agent Anderson could get the other handcuff around his right wrist, he twirled around, used his left leg to sweep her feet out from under her. His handcuffed hand was ripped from her grasp as she stumbled backward, then fell.

He grinned as he watched her hit the ground. *Yeah, don't underestimate the military training, stupid woman.*

"Tonya!" he heard the other female officer yell, and everyone turned now, away from Maria, to see what had happened.

Mike took in the situation quickly. He saw the FBI agent rise to her feet, saw her partner and the younger police officer sprinting over, but he had the advantage. He was faster. He dodged them and ran straight toward the picnic area, where Dr. Davies was focused on reviving Maria.

Only Chief Parlot saw him coming. But Mike saw him. Running flat out, he jumped into the air and karate-kicked the chief, his fancy Italian leather shoe striking him in the face. The chief stumbled backward right into Elisabeth, who fell down onto the floor with him. Dr. Davies was stunned and didn't know what to do; he heard Brad growl, saw the general's fight response kick in. But before Brad could attack, Mike kicked him in the stomach, and all Brad could do was hold onto the picnic table to not keel over.

Mike grinned. *Guess those karate lessons on top of all that military training really do lend an edge. And I was the Academy's best wrestler. Yeah, don't fight me. I'm a big shot. I know how to save my ass.*

He quickly bent down, kicked the chief in the groin, then pushed Chief Parlot's jacket to the side to grab the gun from his holster. He approached the picnic table. Dr. Davies stared at him, his eyes wide, his face white.

"Step away from her, doctor," Mike said, and held the gun to Dr. Davies's face, the handcuff still dangling from his left hand. "Get up and do as I say." The doctor jumped up and raised his hands above his head. Mike grinned. "Good boy. Glad you were trained right."

"No! Mike, stop this," Brad said, still holding his stomach.

Chief Parlot was curled up in pain on the floor, Elisabeth sobbing from beneath his weight.

"Mike, let's talk about this," Brad said. "Come on, man, don't do this. It won't help you. It'll make things worse. You and I both know that."

"You know *nothing*, Collins," Mike said, disgust on his face. "Nothing! And I know what you're doing. You're trying to stall me. But this time, you won't get me. This time, you can't save the girl. Not this time!"

He glanced over his shoulder and saw Agent Anderson approaching him, accompanied by the other agent and police officer. His own security detail and staffers, the policemen doing crowd control all stared, unsure of what to do.

I need to be fast.

Mike was close enough to Dr. Davies to elbow him in the stomach, which made him stumble backward. Out of the corner of his eye, he saw Brad get up, ready to attack, and saw the other three running toward him.

They can't get me.

He darted over to Maria, who was barely conscious, slumped over the picnic table and seemingly unaware of the commotion. He yanked her up. Then, with a *click*, he cocked the hammer back and held the gun to Maria's head.

"Step back, everyone, or she's dead. For good this time!" he growled.

Brad, the FBI agents, and the young police officer all stopped in their tracks.

Elisabeth sobbed loudly. "No, don't take my child. Please. Don't. Not again."

Maria was still out of it, her eyes half open. With a professional hold, Mike dragged her behind the picnic table. "Stay back, everyone. Stay back! Or she's fucking dead!"

"Please, please don't take her. Bitte nicht. Please," Elisabeth begged. "Please don't take my child again."

But Mike Clifford kept going, further and further away from the picnic area, toward the boardwalk on Turkey Creek. "I knew this was a bad idea, just a terrible idea. Oh my gosh, *please don't take my child*," he heard the mother wail.

"Damn straight, Elisabeth," he yelled back at her. "This was a *terrible* idea. Blame the chief. What an idiot."

Chief Parlot moaned in pain.

"Senator Clifford, don't do this. We can make a deal. Come on, man, you don't want to do this," Agent Anderson said.

That fucking lady can't tell me what to do! Especially not her! "Stay back, or I'll shoot," he yelled.

He edged further along toward the boardwalk's entrance, keeping his eyes trained on them. That's when he saw the older FBI agent reach into her jacket. He froze, then cried out, "Drop the gun, bitch! Stop right there. Hands in the air. Same goes for all of you, you hear me?"

He watched them halt and turn to look at each other.

"Do it. Now. Or the girl gets it." He pushed the barrel of the gun harder into Maria's skull.

The female FBI agent slowly raised her arms to comply, then the others followed suit.

He kept going. *Good thing the girl's so light. Turned into a pretty little thing. Those date-rape drugs mix real well into drinks, now don't they?*

"Mike, don't do this. Please, Mike, just let my daughter go. We can make a deal, a good deal!" yelled Brad.

Mike had to laugh. "You're hilarious, Collins, fucking hilarious. A deal? I won't ever make a fucking deal with you! I'd sooner see myself dead. Now shut the fuck up!"

He removed the gun from Maria's temple and shot straight at Brad.

"Everybody down!" he heard the female FBI agent yell, then saw all of them drop to the ground, but Brad was too slow. The bullet grazed his shoulder before embedding inside the picnic table.

Mike heard Brad moan in pain and grinned. *You deserve it, Collins. You deserve it. You ruined my life.*

He saw all of them down on the ground and knew this was his chance. He quickly turned and hustled Maria along—not onto the boardwalk, but below it, into the thicket of swamp surrounding Turkey Creek.

"No, no, my child! Meine Süße." Elisabeth sobbed. "Moana! Maria, please. No, Maria!"

CHAPTER 70

"**N**o, Maria!" Both Aaron and Jack jumped up at the same time, staring in horror as they watched Maria being dragged away on live TV.

Drew threw his hands over his mouth. "My God…"

Martina sobbed. "Mija, no, no, no… He's got her—again. No, mija! I knew this was a terrible idea.…" Tears were streaming down her face.

Aaron stared at her, his eyes suddenly icy cold. "You *knew* about this, Martina? You knew they were meeting this guy who was behind Maria's kidnapping?"

Martina nodded. "Elisabeth told me—"

"And not me?" Aaron interrupted. "Not any one of us?" He pointed at Drew, Jack, and himself.

"No…" Martina whispered, and didn't dare to look up at Aaron. Her tears dripped onto her hands she had folded in her lap, her shoulders sunken in.

Aaron stared at her. *She looks miserable. Probably didn't have a say in any of this.* He sighed. "You told them it wasn't a good idea?"

Martina nodded.

"Yeah, damn it, it sure wasn't!"

"I just don't understand why nobody protected her. There were so many people there armed to the teeth, and nobody did anything?" Jack shook his head.

"People get paralyzed in traumatic situations—even well-trained soldiers," Drew said. "Still, this shouldn't have happened. It's horrible, just horrible. Someone needs to help her."

"You're damn right about that," Aaron said. He grabbed his car keys and stormed off.

"Son, where are you going?" Jack yelled after him.

"To save my fiancée!"

"Aaron, wait—"

But Aaron had already left the hotel lobby, leaving Jack, Drew, and Martina behind. Lieutenant Martinez came over and talked softly to Martina in Spanish while rubbing her shoulder, but that did little to calm her. She was devastated.

Aaron sped off base and was surprised to find no reporters waiting to ambush him or follow him. *Guess they're all busy reporting on the missing toddler who now got abducted, again, by the same guy.*

He hit the steering wheel with both hands. *Damn it! I thought she was safe here. Safe with the police, the FBI, her parents. And me. Except I wasn't there. I let her down.*

He blinked back tears and pushed down on the gas pedal. He knew he was going way too fast, but he didn't care. *I just need to get to her, need to find her. Need to save her. 'Cuz I love her. Can't be without her.*

A tear escaped his eye now. He quickly wiped it away with his bare hands and focused on navigating, sped away down the near-empty road. In no time, he arrived at the parking lot outside the entrance to Turkey Creek's picnic area and boardwalk, but fast realized it was jam-packed with reporters, policemen, emergency medical personnel, and fleeing civilians.

There's no way through them.

He briefly parked on the side of the road and looked at Google Maps on his phone. *I need to find another way in.*

But there was only one entrance, one parking lot to access the boardwalk. He kept studying the map, but it was no use. Only one way in or out—and it was blocked. He closed his eyes and thought for a while.

The creek. I just need to follow the creek! Yes, that's it. I'll just go up the creek.

He studied the map and put a plan together. He turned around onto State Road 85, a three-lane road, then pulled into a parking lot across the street that belonged to a restaurant. "Fresh Greece Pizza & Grill" the signage read. He jumped out of the car without locking it and ran toward the edge of the parking lot.

The creek must pass by right behind these trees here. According to the map, it leads into that big bayou from here. Guess people use Turkey Creek for tubing down into the bayou. So I have to walk upstream to get to the boardwalk.

He made it through the trees and saw Turkey Creek flowing lazily right in front of him. He quickly realized that the riverbank was lined by big trees, and much of it was swampy. *Shoot, might have to swim. Hope the current isn't too bad. What about my phone? What should I do with my shoes?*

He knew he might need his phone later to call for help, and had an idea. He ran back to his car and searched the trunk. Inside was a waterproof phone bag he'd used back at Embry-Riddle. Quickly, he put his phone inside, sealed it, and slid it up his arm. He left the car unlocked, the keys on top of his front tire.

He took off his shirt but left his shoes on. *In case I need to walk through the forest later. Easier on the feet.*

Then, he ran back to the riverbank and waded in. He soon found himself waist-deep and started swimming. He took big, strong strokes. His determination helped him swim faster than ever before.

Don't worry, Maria, I'll find you. I'll save you. Just hold on, Maria! Be strong and hold on.

CHAPTER 71

"Hold on," Maria heard someone say, and opened her heavy eyes.

Where am I? She saw shrubs, bushes, and trees, then heard the faint sound of running water. She tried to keep her eyes open, tried to work her limbs, but it felt like she couldn't move at all. She seemed to have no power over her own body. *What's going on?*

She felt mud and water around her bare feet. *Didn't I have shoes on? What happened to them? Why is the water so muddy?*

Suddenly, she panicked as not only her memories from her early childhood came flooding back, but also more present fears. She felt an arm around her chest, holding her by her armpits. She felt a sharp piece digging into her one armpit, something shiny stuck to the wrist of the arm that held her. She wiggled.

"Waking up, huh?" said a male voice.

Who is that? She glanced up and saw the curly beach-blonde hair and tan neck. *Senator Clifford? Didn't the police get him? Didn't they arrest him?*

She quickly realized the loose handcuff was the sharp piece of metal digging into her armpit. *Oh my gosh, they didn't get him—somehow he got away? With me and only one handcuff on his left wrist?*

Her eyes widened as he was dragging her deeper into the woods, into swampland. There was a little creek beside them. Her feet dragged in the water. Her breathing came faster; she was scared.

I've been kidnapped again? For the third time? What the heck? By the senator? What does he want?

Her heart was pounding, pumping oxygen in her lungs and muscles. She felt her strength coming back, slowly but surely. She tried to stand up.

"What are you doing?" she heard him say, and felt the arm tighten around her chest. "Don't even think about running. I *will* shoot you."

Say what? Then she felt it, the cold metal on her temple. Out of the corner of her eye, she saw a silver pistol gleaming from the dappled sunlight.

"Just like I shot your dad."

What?

"Doubt you remember. Those date-rape drugs are strong."

What? What's he talking about?

"I'm glad you drank so much of that water. I had the whole Fiji six-pack spiked. Ketamine is strong. Used often for medical purposes. Good thing I know plenty of unethical doctors. Sure came in handy. It's odorless, can't be seen mixed in water. Figured I'd get the chance to offer you some water today."

He giggled and dropped the weapon, put it away to better drag her with two hands. "Was going to offer some to your parents and the police chief, too. But I didn't get a chance because, somehow, you recognized me. How is that even possible? How do you remember me? Don't get it. You were so young."

He sighed. "Well, I guess it worked out. I wouldn't have had enough water for everyone anyway. Didn't know they were bringing so many others. Two FBI agents, another police officer, a shrink? Seriously? Who the hell are all those people?"

She tried to speak, tried to ask about her dad. *He shot him? I just found him again. I can't lose him now.*

"I guess they had their own plan—how'd that work out for them? Wanted to arrest me in front of all those people? Seriously? Tarnish my good name like that? No, no. They can't. And this time, I'll make sure fucking Collins loses it all for good."

With all her might, she forced air through her lungs and made her mouth move this time. A slight whisper came out. "My dad?"

"Oh, look at that now. Already talking, huh? The dosage clearly wasn't as strong as I thought. Well, most guys only need ten to fifteen minutes to make use of the drug, so guess that's not too surprising." He laughed out loud. "It's usually not used to sedate someone for a prolonged time. But that's fine. It served its purpose. We're way away of civilization now. And we'll be out of here in no time. Trust me, I know the way out, the only way out. Don't think they'll think of it. No, they won't."

"My dad... okay?"

"Oh, I see. You're afraid your dad got hurt?"

Maria blinked.

"How sweet of you to worry so much about him. Did you know he's the reason I'm not a pilot? Not an Air Force pilot?"

She blinked again.

"'Cuz he ratted me out. Asshole! I was young, just having some fun. The girls always had fun with me, you know? Always. And I was a good driver, no matter how much I had in my system. Always had everything under control. But your dad, your *fucking dad*, he just wouldn't believe me. So he told the Academy. What a dick-move, I'm telling you. Got me kicked out. A month before graduation. Can you believe it?"

Maria shook her head slightly.

"And you know what happened next?"

"No," she whispered. *But I'm sure you're gonna tell me your sob story. Idiot!*

"My family shunned me. All my dad wanted was for me to follow his path, step into his shoes. Just like him, I was supposed to become a fighter pilot, then a general in the Air Force. But when they kicked me out of the Academy, out of the Air Force Academy, I became nothing to my parents. A nobody."

He sighed and stopped walking for a minute. Maria almost felt sad for him. Then, his grip tightened once more, and he kept going, dragging her along.

"It was tough being all alone. I had no one. I was in a deep hole. Started gambling, just wasting my life. But at least I was good with the women. Always have been, you know. Always will be."

Maria saw him grin, his white teeth shining in the dark brush around them. She realized it was growing darker; the sun was setting.

"Yeah, I was a player, I guess is what you'd call it. The ladies loved me. Still love me. I'm very charming, you know? Just the best at the game of love. And something I've always been better at than Collins! Yeah, I was better than him—still am. And better at making and keeping connections. Life-changing connections. Important connections."

All Maria could do was listen and wait until her strength came back, until the effects of the drug wore off. She knew she just had to wait.

"Yeah, those guys represented important connections. Good years with them. Awesome years. Gambling, girls, fun. It was great. They took me in and made me one of them. We were the 'Fearless Four,' including JB and Bill. They lived far away, but visited us on and off. Thanks to all of them, I was introduced to the elites, the powerbrokers, and went into politics. Who knew you'd get to know people like that just visiting casinos?" He laughed again. "And you know what?"

Maria shook her head, indicating she was listening. *Gotta keep him talking. I know that. From previous experience.* She almost had to laugh, but couldn't yet anyway.

"This job suits me better than a pilot position in the Air Force ever would have done. You know, people... the common folk, the voters... they don't mind a leader who's a player. They just don't. And you know why?"

Maria shook her head again.

"Because they respect masculinity. They take it as a sign you can take care of business. And you know how I know that?" This time, he didn't even wait for a reaction from Maria and just kept talking. "Quite a lot about women came out during the elections, after I had climbed high up there, but not once did it ever hurt me or my career. Instead, it somehow boosted my standing."

He laughed. Maria frowned. *Bunch of idiotic voters who'd rather vote for a player and bring back 1950s patriarchal society. Oppress women, immigrants, other races. This sunny Florida boy fits right in.*

"I see you frowning. You disagree with me, girl? You dare disagree with me? Just like your stupid dad?"

She quickly shook her head.

"Good. You better not. You better do as I say! Remember, I'm the one with the gun. Right here!" He pressed it against her temple again.

She shuddered under the cold metal and her thoughts went back to her dad. "My dad okay?"

"Is he *okay*?" He laughed out loud. "Well, I guess so. I got him, I think, but not in the heart. Guess he'll survive. I'm good at a lot of things, but never been a good shot."

Relieved, Maria exhaled. *Gosh, I'm so thankful he's okay. I couldn't stand to lose my dad again.*

"But your dad, your fucking dad, was an excellent marksman. He always got awards for being such a good shot. Every class at the Academy, he always excelled. God, I was jealous. So jealous. Collins was always great. An awesome shooter, an excellent athlete, a model cadet. I didn't mind too much, until he took everything away from me. The chance to be a pilot. He cut me off from my family. Him! His fault. So yeah, I wanted to see him go down. Wanted to hurt him bad, take from him what he took from me."

Maria saw him shake his head, his beach-blonde curls flying all over the place. He grunted. "But I didn't know how. Collins was rising to the top, on track to becoming top brass in the Air Force. I was so mad, so fucking mad at him. I wanted retaliation. Somehow."

Maria now felt them going down the riverbank, further into the water. Her feet were totally submerged now, the water creeping up her body. She tried not to panic and focused on his story.

"You know, I was totally drunk when we came up with the idea. We all were. Looking back, it was a crazy plan. Insane. And yet, I was convinced it would work out. And I knew it would break Collins. I knew losing his daughter would break him. He seems tough, but I knew from my time with him at the Academy, living with him, being his buddy, that he's a hopeless romantic."

He laughed and dragged her deeper into the water, careful to keep her head above the surface.

This dark, murky water... What's his plan? What does he want?

"And you know, I felt super important I'd been chosen to plan this absurd kidnapping. I was eager to please him, my father. He built me up, took me under his wing, helped me become a great Clifford again. My redemption."

Maria was confused. *Wanted to please his father? Thought he didn't have anything to do with him?* But she didn't have much time to think about it any further as he pulled her through the shallow water. Panic rose in her, but she noticed he was going slowly, lifting her head to make sure no water got into her nose or mouth.

"You know, I was so eager to please him—I would've agreed to anything. And this plan happened to give me what I wanted more than anything: to hurt Collins. Get payback for him ruining my life. So, of course I agreed to it. We all did. But I took on the biggest job. I was the one dealing with the middleman, with Sullivan, you know."

Maria nodded.

"And I was the one who then helped Sully out when the plan went wrong. 'Cuz you know you were actually supposed to drown, right?"

She blinked fast, her eyes wide.

"But instead, we kept you alive on that damned yacht. Sully and I. Neither one of us could kill you. Sully was just a coward and refused to finish you. And me? Well, I don't know. I guess it was your damn unique eyes." He laughed and shook his head.

My eyes? What about them?

He kept dragging her through the water, carefully, the loose side of the handcuff hitting the back of her head due to the force of the water. He continued to talk. "I got close once to killing you. Kill you through asphyxiation. You were so little—all I had to do was put my hand on your mouth and nose and push hard. I did, but you fought me. And then stared at me, begged me with your damn unique eyes. Just like your dad. Same big, unique eyes. They just stared at me and reminded me of your dad. Thought I'd be more mad, thought I wouldn't mind, but those eyes just reminded me of all the good things we had. You know, we were good buddies, your dad and I. He was a good friend—we had lots of fun together at the Academy. The two of us and Drew. The BDM Team."

A frown hushed over his face, then sadness washed over it. "You know, those two, Drew and Brad, were the only real friends I've ever had. Brad always listened to me, believed in me, encouraged me, and tried to make me be a better man. He always looked at me with those big, unique eyes of his—just like yours—and often gave me good advice. Too bad he had to throw our friendship away, stab me in the back, just because I had made *one* mistake. Too bad, really too bad."

Maria nodded, indicating she was listening, but making sure she wouldn't swallow any of the water she was dragged through.

Mike went on: "Yeah, I fucking hated him for ratting me out, telling on me. Wanted to take revenge, but every time I tried to lay a hand on you, you stared at me with those fucking exotic eyes, making me feel as if I looked into my friend's eyes. Fuck! Can't believe it got to me—you got to me with those freakin' eyes of yours."

Maria stared at him now, her eyes wide. *Maybe that'll convince him to let me go now also?*

419

But Mike didn't pay attention and kept dragging her through the water, pouring his heart out: "So nobody was able to kill you. I wanted to starve you, but Sully kept feeding you. Behind my back. Fucking idiot! Didn't know what to do, how to get rid of you. But then, Sully had an idea that wasn't too bad. So I arranged it all. The birth certificate, the social security number. I knew my peeps; I knew who to call. 'Cuz I'm a somebody, a big shot."

He sounded triumphant, a smile on his lips. Then, he stopped abruptly and lifted her up out of the water. Maria tried to move her arms and legs, but couldn't. Her face seemed back to normal, though, so she turned her head around and saw a rotten, wooden something.

What's that? A boat? She found she was able to speak again. "What is—"

"Oh, this?" he interrupted her, then lifted her all the way up and pushed her in. She fell sideways into the small wooden thing.

"This is a canoe. An old canoe. I knew it would still be here. When I was a boy, we hid it here and the park rangers apparently thought it looked cool because they never got rid of it. Other people, of course, rent better canoes, the new plastic kind, to float down Turkey Creek. But this will have to do for today."

He hoisted himself up. The canoe rocked, tipped dangerously to one side under his weight, but he managed not to tip it completely and got in. He searched for something on the floorboard, the loose handcuffs scraping along the wood, the sound of it ringing in her ears. "Ha, here they are. The paddles," she heard him say.

Maria watched him inspect them right in front of her. She tried to sit up, but still couldn't. She was lying on the bottom of the canoe, her legs up on the small wooden bench at the front where he was sitting, inspecting the paddles.

Wish I could kick him out. She tried to move her legs, but all she could do was wiggle her toes and move her fingers. *Shoot. The drugs are still in my system. All I can do is hope they'll be gone soon so I can move again. So I can fight.*

She watched the senator move her numb legs beneath the front bench. He then crawled over her, paddles in hand, and sat down behind her on the second bench.

"Alright, off we go," he said, and gave the water a big push with the paddles. The canoe slowly floated down the little creek. Maria watched the trees pass by above, saw the purplish sky. She sighed. *The sun is setting. It'll be dark soon. Harder to find me.*

"Isn't it beautiful here at Turkey Creek?"

She looked up and saw him smile.

"*Isn't it?*" He peered down at her.

Really? He's demanding an answer? As if he were taking me on a sightseeing tour. She nodded, making sure he saw it.

"Good, I'm glad you like it. Used to be my favorite spot as a kid. Many fun memories here on Turkey Creek. Us high schoolers went here often. Was a good dating spot, too."

He grinned, but then frowned. "Been a while since I've been back here. My family. Didn't want me around. Crazy, right? I mean, I have a great career. You know, I'm a senator. The senator of Florida! Seriously, what more can a parent want?"

"Don't know," she managed to say.

"Exactly. Me neither." He paddled on in silence.

"You know, after your kidnapping, I didn't tell anyone you were still alive. Only Sully and I knew. We all had sworn to secrecy anyway and gone our separate ways. We had to, I was told, so that nobody could ever link the job back to us. There was no trace of us as a group anymore. I stayed on the East Coast. Sold that yacht and drove up to Orlando. There, I met the then-mayor of Orlando and we became friends with each other. I started working for him and then worked my way up the political food chain."

Maria saw him break out in a big, proud smile.

"I eventually ran for representative, then governor, now senator. Impressive, huh?" He looked down at Maria, who was still lying beside his feet in the well of the canoe.

"Yeah, impressive," she whispered.

"I know, I know. Father thinks so, too. Thinks highly of me to this day. And that trust, that impression of me can't be destroyed! Can't be. Not now, not ever. I'll do anything to keep that trust, that love, to not disappoint him."

Him? Who's him? His father? They made up? Maria was confused, the drug still clouding her mind.

"Yeah, I won't disappoint my father again."

"Father?" she asked, and saw him nod. All she could think of was her own father. *My daddy. Brad Collins. Why did he shoot him? I really hope he's okay.*

Tears were forming in her eyes. Her tongue felt heavy, but she managed to spit out a few words. "I want. My father. Please. Need to know. If he's okay. Is he okay?"

CHAPTER 72

"**I**s he okay?" Elisabeth's scratched and bruised face was covered in tears, her bloodied lip quivering. She sat next to Brad, who was lying on a stretcher. The paramedics were applying first aid to the bullet wound in his shoulder.

"I'm fine," Brad said. "It's just a grazing wound. Please, I can get up."

"No, sir, we need you to lie down, please," one of the paramedics said. "The bullet hit an artery and you've lost a lot of blood."

Brad heard Elisabeth sob. *I need her to stop crying and worrying about me. I need her to save our daughter! Otherwise, I will do it.*

He ignored the paramedic and sat up. "I need to go. My wife seems fine, no concussion, and I'm fine, too. I need to go now."

Determined, he grabbed her hand with his uninjured arm. "Elisabeth, don't worry about me. I'm fine. Just like you are, even after that tough fall. We're both fine. Most important is that we find her. We need to find our daughter. Let's go."

Elisabeth's eyes grew wide, but she nodded and got up. Brad tried to do the same but was quickly pushed down by two paramedics.

"Sir, please lie down."

"No, I need to go to my daughter! Now!" With the strength of a dad, he sat up again.

The paramedics struggled to keep him on the stretcher. "We'll have to strap you down, sir, if you don't comply!"

Yeah right, just try me. Determined, he broke free of their grasp.

"Chief!" one of the paramedics yelled. "Can someone find Chief Parlot? We need him over here. General Collins won't let us help him."

"No, don't call the chief over, fools," Brad growled, his voice deep and angry. "He's leading the search for my daughter."

"Then I suggest you lie down and let us take you to the hospital. You need emergency care."

"No, I need to stay here. Just use a tourniquet," he said, anger in his voice, tears in his eyes. "Please. I can't lose my daughter again."

He heard Elisabeth sob next to him.

"Sir, this isn't a war zone. You need proper stitches or possibly surgery, not just a tourniquet. I know you're worried, but please leave the search to the authorities. They'll take care of it."

Brad started crying, right there on the stretcher. "I don't trust anyone with my daughter's life. Please, I need to stay here."

It happened again. I failed her. Didn't protect her. Agreed to this stupid plan. Elisabeth was right when she had her doubts. But I convinced her to do the wrong thing. Again. Just like back then with the stupid laundromat. He was lifted off the ground on the stretcher.

Elisabeth stepped closer, remained by his side. "Brad, we'll find her. *I* will find her. Alive. But if... if..." Her voice broke and she started sobbing again. "I need you. I need you to get healthy again. I can't lose both of you again."

"Oh, Elisabeth," he whispered, and took her hand. "Please don't worry. You won't lose me. Ever. Never ever again." Through her tears, she nodded. "I need you to be strong for the both of us, okay, hun?"

She nodded again, squeezing his hand tight. "I promise, Brad. I promise to be strong."

"That's good. Know that we *will* find her! We'll find her and end this once and for all. Tonight. You hear me?" *I need her to be strong, can't let her see my doubts. She needs to help the cops find our daughter.*

"Elisabeth, believe me. You can do this. I'll see you both at the hospital when this is all over, right?"

Elisabeth nodded, her lip quivering.

"Please, you have to believe. You have to think positively. You were right all along. She was alive. Still is. She's a fighter!"

"Okay, Brad, I'll try to believe it will all end well. I'll try."

"Don't just try. Believe. Or I swear to God, I'll stay here."

A faint smile crossed her lips. "You're so stubborn."

He smiled back at her. "Yeah, I know. And so are you. And so is our daughter. The Collins family. Stubborn and strong. You ladies got this."

Elisabeth inhaled deeply and wiped away her tears. She stood taller and squeezed his hand. "Okay, you're right. We got this. We'll find you in the hospital. Get better fast, 'cuz we'll both need you. Maria and I… we need you."

"Trust me, I'm not going anywhere. Now that I'm back, good luck getting rid of me." He winked at her and squeezed her hand one more time before the paramedics carried him away.

She waved at him. "We'll see you soon, Brad. And we will find her. Just look at everyone who's here and ready to help, ready to search all of Turkey Creek. I believe. We *will* find her."

He waved until she disappeared amid the hustle and bustle around him. He saw police officers and FBI agents giving orders to different groups, watched the K-9 unit being readied to search the woods, noticed the SWAT team just arriving, and knew then they'd all do everything in their power to find his daughter. His kidnapped daughter.

Kidnapped again. And again, it's my fault. Oh my gosh, all my fault. All of it. Clifford wanted to get back at me. And my family has suffered because of it. It's all my damn fault.

Tears streamed down his face as his stretcher was lifted into the ambulance.

Please, please, find her.

CHAPTER 73

*F*ind her! I need to find her!

Aaron was swimming for his life upstream. He felt like he hadn't gone very far, yet had no choice but to keep pushing forward. His arms were burning with every stroke, his legs tired, but pure willpower kept him moving, one powerful stroke after the next.

He heard dogs barking, people talking along the bank. *The search team. He'll spot them from a mile away. They're too loud. Even I can hear them.*

He focused on his swimming, tried to calm himself, but both his thoughts and his heart were racing. *I can't lose her. Can't lose Maria. Have to find her. Protect her. End this once and for all. There must be an end to this.*

He kept pushing forward through the cold, clear, calm water. There was no movement on its surface except the ripples of his own strokes. It seemed like hours passed as he swam up that stream; he lost track of time.

He watched the sky turn a deeper purple and gold as the sun began to set. *It'll be dark soon. Gotta find her before it gets too dark. He'll hide her in the darkness of the night, in the swampy shrubs and bushes covering the waterway.*

His head was getting tired from keeping it above water to look around, and he let it sink a little lower. With another strong stroke of his arms, he cut a path forward, but splashed so much water that it flew into his mouth just as he was breathing in, forcing him to swallow involuntarily.

He coughed and flailed. *Shoot. Have to keep quiet.* He cleared his throat until he could breathe again, then began to swim once more. *At least it's not salty. A freshwater creek.*

He saw the purplish-golden sky reflected on the surface of the creek. The disturbance from his arm strokes made the sunset appear fractal, broken. *Like I'm broken without her. I need her. She completes me. Without Maria, I'm just a puzzle with a missing piece.*

He blinked back tears and swam even faster. *I'm coming, Maria. I'm coming. I'll find you, so you can complete me.*

As he pushed forward, his arms numb from swimming but his strokes even, he noticed movement atop the water. Ripples in the stream not of his own making. *Is there a waterfall coming up?* He shook his head. *No, too close to sea level. Maybe a little dip? Some rapids?*

But then he realized there was something else on the water causing those little ripples. A tiny boat—no, a canoe—was headed his way, traveling downstream. He was confused, not sure what to do. *Who is that? Who goes canoeing this time of day? During a major police search?*

And suddenly, it dawned on him. *That could only be Clifford, trying to escape. Trying to get out onto the open bayou, away from the police cordon. Damn it! Smart. So smart.*

He tried to confirm if it was in fact Clifford in the canoe, but couldn't make any detail out. The sunset was too bright. He looked around and found the perfect hiding spot: a low-hanging tree branch, its green leaves dipping right into the water. Quickly, he swam over and hid beneath them.

The canoe drew closer, and Aaron recognized the occupant's beach-blonde curls contrasting with the purple of the sky. Clifford sat in the back of the canoe on a little wooden bench, paddling with both hands, one in a handcuff.

Both hands... No gun? What happened to the gun? Aaron crept to the edge of his cover, making sure he stayed hidden under the safety of the leaves. Then he saw it. The shiny silver gun was resting on the bench beside Clifford, next to his thigh.

Where's Maria? Aaron couldn't see her at all. A shudder ran down his spine. His heart sank, his arm hairs stood up. *Did he leave her in the woods? Did he already kill her?*

Numbed by that thought, his body started sinking, his willpower broken. He felt his legs touch down on sand. It tickled his knees and shins, irritated him, snapped him out of his spiral. He realized this part of the creek was so shallow he could stand up in it. Without thinking, he rose up in a crouch, and his head struck a branch of the low-hanging tree, causing it to shake.

"What was that?" he heard Clifford say.

The canoe came closer and closer to where Aaron was crouching. He lowered himself back down into the water to better hide behind the tree branch.

"Did you hear something?" he heard Clifford ask, and saw him look down into the canoe. "What? Did you shake your head? So you didn't hear anything?"

Aaron's heart jumped in joy. *Maria! She's alive. She must be in the canoe.*

"No," Aaron heard a weak voice.

Tears of joy formed in his eyes; a smile came over his face. *That's definitely her. She's alive. Oh my gosh, she's alive.*

But then, his smile faded, his tears dried up, his blue eyes turned icy cold. A reddish color flushed his face. *He's holding her captive. Trying to escape with her into the bayou. No, no, he can't take her. I won't let him!*

Quickly, Aaron put a plan together in his head. He took the strap off his arm and hung the waterproof bag containing his phone on a small branch of the low-hanging tree. He was trembling, his knuckles white as he bunched his hands into fists; it took everything he had to let the canoe pass by.

I have to wait and attack him from behind. He can't see me coming. The attack needs to be a surprise; he needs to be surprised.

CHAPTER 74

Surprised, Mike watched the gun fall into the bottom of the canoe, right next to Maria's head. *How did that happen? And why is the canoe rocking?*

Before he could ponder it any further, he felt two strong arms grip his waist and pull him backward off the canoe into the water. Shocked, he fell in, still holding onto his paddles. *What the fuck?*

Only when the cold water hit his face, did Mike realize what was happening. *Shit! Someone's attacking me. Fuck!*

He found himself underwater. He had lost hold of one of the paddles but clung to the other. His attacker was still behind him, holding him. The moment they broke the surface, Mike lifted the paddle and, with all his might, swung it behind him, hoping to strike his attacker's head.

"Ahhh—" he heard, then the grip loosened around his waist.

He grinned. *Got him! Great hit!*

In one swift movement, Mike turned around in the water and twisted out of the hold. He realized the creek was shallow enough to stand in, the water just beneath his chin. Paddle still in hand, he found himself face-to-face with his attacker. He recognized him right away. *Aaron Heikinnen. The boyfriend is here to save the love of his life. How cute.*

He grinned at the young guy standing in front of him, rubbing his head, then lifted his paddle again to smash it down on the kid's head. But it only hit the surface of the water. Bewildered, Mike looked around. *Where the heck is he?*

Suddenly, someone was at his legs, pulling them out from under him. Surprised, he lost hold of the paddle and plunged into the water. He felt the young man's strong hands pulling him down, holding him, not letting him back up to the surface. Mike's hands flailed, swung about in search of his attacker, but failed to score a blow. The kid squeezed hard, causing him to swallow a mouthful of water. *What the fuck?*

Mike went into survival mode, his former military training kicking in. Skillfully, he twisted out of Aaron's hold and got his head free. He shot up to the surface, gasping for air. As he filled his strained lungs, he found Aaron floating in front of him.

"Give up, Clifford," he heard him say breathlessly. "You can't take her. I won't allow it. I'll fight you till the end, I swear. And don't forget: the police are here, looking for you. They got you surrounded. You won't make it out. You're going down."

"You're fucking wrong, kid!"

In a rage, Mike pushed himself off the sandy ground and flung himself forward. As he came down, he crossed his elbows and crashed them right into Aaron's neck. Aaron was knocked off his feet and fell sideways into the water. Mike swam over and pushed his knee into Aaron's back while holding his head underwater. Aaron's flailing arms could do nothing to stop him. He kept pushing down, holding him there, until the flailing grew weaker then stopped completely.

Mike grinned and let go. *What a shame. Sucker.*

He swam back over to the canoe and found Maria trying hard to sit up. She hadn't made it far, just upright enough to lean her head against the wooden bench in the back of the canoe—just high enough to have seen the fight in the water.

Mike's grin widened. *Guess the ketamine is still doing its job. She can't move. She can barely speak. But her brain still works. She's able to take in this terrifying moment.* As he drew near, he saw the tears streaming down her pale face, her eyes wide in horror. Big, wide, green eyes lit by the setting sun.

"Well, that was a nice try by your boyfriend. Oh, your fiancé, I guess? Well, doesn't matter now. Too bad he couldn't save you. But he died a heroic death, didn't he? Well, pretty girl, we gotta go. Would you be so kind as to hop to the side so I can climb in?" He smiled maliciously.

She just stared at him, her green eyes flickering in hate, big elephant tears dripping down onto the wooden bench.

"Aw, come on now, come on. It's okay. They'll find him. And bury him."

Maria's weak lungs choked out a sob.

"Shhh… There, there, pretty one. Know that I'm sorry. Truly. It was self-defense. I didn't mean to kill him. Didn't mean to kill Aaron."

CHAPTER 75

*D*idn't *mean to kill Aaron?* She sobbed again and closed her eyes. *He killed Aaron. Oh my gosh, Aaron. No, no, no, Aaron. My Aaron. Why? Why in the world did he have to kill Aaron? He drowned my Aaron!*

Mike Clifford had reached the canoe and was trying to pull himself in, but the craft was rocking sideways under their uneven load.

Maria felt something cold against her hand, cold like metal. *What is that?* Able to move her fingers, she felt the object. *Gun. It's the gun.*

Mike was still trying to pull himself up, the handcuff scraping the side of the canoe, his weight still tipping the boat, and the gun slid further into Maria's hand. She took a firm hold of it. *He killed him. The love of my life. He'll pay for this. Right here, right now!*

In agony, she gathered her strength and forced herself to lift her head off the bench and sat up fully on her bottom. She pushed her hands forward, gripping the gun.

"You'll pay for this," she yelled. "You'll freakin' pay for this."

Surprised, Mike stopped pulling himself up and looked at her while hanging off the side of the canoe.

With all her will and might, she lifted the heavy gun and pointed it right at his forehead. "I will shoot you, Mike Clifford! I *will* shoot you!"

For a second, Mike just stared at her, then burst into laughter. "No, you won't. You don't even fucking know how."

She looked at the gun in her hands. *He's right. I have no clue how to use this.*

Out of nowhere, she heard coughing intermixed with, "You... can... do... this!"

Aaron? Her eyes searched the creek and finally spotted Aaron on the side of the riverbank, standing in shallow water. He was coughing, wheezing, retching. *Oh my gosh! He's alive, he's alive. Thank God he's alive!* Tears welled in her eyes.

"Shoot... him," Aaron said. "Pull... the... little... thing on... on the... the bottom."

She focused on the gun in her hands again, but it was too late. Mike Clifford rocked the canoe so hard that the gun flew out of her weak grasp. She fell backward against the wooden canoe bench and hit her head.

She saw stars all around her, her head spinning, the canoe rocking. Then it tipped over, and she splashed right into the cold water, so much water submerging her, pulling her under.

I can't move. I can't fully move yet. I'll drown. Again. Panic rose in her; it was completely dark around her. *I can't see. Which way is up? Why is it so dark? Did the sun set?*

Then she realized she was under the tipped canoe. It was upside down, right above her. With all her will, she kicked her legs and moved her arms, found that it was hard but doable. She crested the water's surface and took a deep breath in, inside the tipped-over canoe.

She kicked her feet to stay afloat when she noticed sand under her toes. *It's shallow enough to stand here. I can even stand here! But can I stand?* Her legs still felt weak, stable as Jell-O, but she managed to keep her head above the waterline, hidden beneath the canoe. *It must have drifted further toward the riverbank. Thank goodness.*

She tried not to think about water and drowning, tried to breathe calmly to suppress her fears, not let the panic take over. She closed her eyes as she focused on her breaths.

433

Then she heard splashing water, followed by grunts, moans, groans. *Aaron. Oh my gosh, Aaron. Is Clifford fighting him again?*

She felt the water swirl around her, kicked up by the scuffle, wet sand brushing her legs. *They must be right next to me. I have to help Aaron, have to back him up. We need to defeat Clifford.*

Adrenaline coursed through her body and gave her strength. Her willpower worked hand in hand, enhancing the adrenaline so that she was able to control her extremities again. She quickly thought up a plan, then took a deep breath and dove underwater, away from the canoe's shelter.

As she dove, she avoided the two pairs of legs nearby that looked like they were dancing back and forth with one another across the sandy, sunken ground. Just as she was trying to figure out which legs belonged to whom—which pair to attack—one of them lost their footing, and in the next second, she found herself face-to-face with Aaron underwater.

His face was bruised, his lip cut, his eyes wide. A hand grasped his neck from behind. He stared at her in shock. Bubbles were coming out of his mouth.

Oh my gosh, Aaron!

She swam forward. She knew she didn't have the strength to push away the strong hand holding him underwater, so instead, she rose up and bit the hand as hard as she could. She felt blood in her mouth and let go. The hand shot out of the water. Both Aaron and Maria broke above the surface and took deep breaths in.

"Argh, you bitch," they heard Clifford swear. "You bit my hand. What the fuck?" He cradled his hand, then turned toward them. "You'll fucking pay for this!"

He threw himself into the water to get to Maria, but Aaron blocked his way. They started fighting again.

"Maria! Gun!" Aaron yelled, before a blow to the head almost knocked him out.

Maria stared at him in terror and confusion.

434

"Ground!" Aaron said. The air cracked as he landed a fierce counterpunch on Mike's face.

"Argh, you broke my fucking nose," Mike said, blood streaming down his face into the water. Aaron came at him again.

Maria dove down to search the creek bed for the gun, but couldn't see it. The guys' legs were kicking up the silt, causing it to swirl all around her. She had to close her eyes to not get sand in them. She turned and swam to the canoe again. She quickly came up for air, then dove down once more.

I can't find it, I just don't see the gun, I don't—

She was running her hands along the sandy ground, feeling for the pistol, but no luck. A big underwater wave came washing over her as one of the guys crashed down into the water. The turbulence pushed some of the soft sand away, and that's when she saw it: a piece of metal sticking out of the sand, shining dully in the waning light.

There it is! The gun! She swam as hard as she could, picked it up, came up for air. She saw the guys were still fighting hard, punching, kicking, pushing each other under.

"I got it, Aaron, I got it," she yelled.

He looked up and nodded, then got hit again.

"Aaron, here," she yelled, and was about to throw it to him, when she saw him shake his head.

"No, you gotta do it, Maria!"

She stared down at the gun in her hand.

I don't wanna shoot anyone. I can't do it.

Her hand was shaking, her eyes filling with tears. She blinked them back and saw Aaron get elbowed in the neck again. He went down, and before she knew it, Clifford was stalking toward her, covered in blood and raving. "Come on, Maria. You don't want to do this. You don't want to shoot me. I know you don't."

I don't want to. I don't want to kill anyone.

"Come *on*! It doesn't have to end like this. Come on, we can save your fiancé. Your beloved Aaron. We can save him—you and me together."

Aaron? Maria looked over at him. His body was floating face up on the surface.

"Don't worry, he's not dead." Mike bit his lip. "He's just knocked out. You have two options, Maria: you can either try to shoot me, and fail, then I'll wring the life out of him—or you can end it. Right here, right now. Come with me. You're a pretty little thing, I can see myself living with you. We'll stick together, get the hell out of here; nobody will ever find us. We'll run away. Just you and I. And you'll save Aaron."

Her hands were shaking. *I have to save Aaron. That's what's most important.* She slowly lowered the gun.

"There's a good girl. You don't wanna do this. You just want to save poor Aaron."

Yes, I just wanna save him. Tears ran down her face. She glanced over to where Aaron was and then heard him coughing. Retching. "Maria…"

Oh my gosh, he's okay. But he seems unable to fight this guy off. I have to save him. Have to save Aaron.

Clifford came closer to her, smiling, talking to her. "Come on, Maria. Be a good girl. Just come with me. That's the only way Aaron will survive this."

Maria was so confused. *I guess he'll leave Aaron alone if he has me. Right?* Her hands were shaking, her whole body shaking. Clifford drew ever closer. He was now in arms' reach.

She heard more coughing, then Aaron took in a deep breath and yelled, "Don't believe him! Just shoot!"

Shoot… him?

He reached for the gun in her hands. She took a step back.

"Or he'll shoot me," she heard.

He'll shoot Aaron?

"Maria. He's the bad guy. The mean guy! Fight!"

Her mamá's words came to her. *"Mija, fight back when someone is mean to you." Aaron is right—Clifford is the bad guy. He took me once, hurt me, was mean. I cannot let him do this again.*

With newfound determination, she took another step back out of his reach. She lifted the gun, held it in both hands, felt the small bolt handle on the bottom and pulled it back. She knew the gun was loaded now, ready to fire.

"Stop, Clifford! Just stop it!"

He stared at her. "Maria, you don't want to—"

"—do this? Yes, I do. You have to pay for what you've done. You hurt Aaron, you hurt my parents, you hurt me. You've hurt everyone around me, everyone that I love. And this is the end of it."

Silence. Absolute silence. Aaron and Mike were both focused on Maria. She stared at Mike, her eyes bright green, piercing through him.

She heard dogs barking from not too far away, heard movement in the brush. *The police! They're coming. I just have to stall him. Talk to him.*

"You won't get away this time," she said, her voice strong and clear, her eyes resting on the bad guy. "You'll pay for this. Rot in jail for this. For everything. For kidnapping me when I was little, for holding me on that boat, for deciding my fate. For all the other things you've done. You'll rot in jail forever."

He withstood her gaze, his wet curly beach-blonde hair sticking to his tan forehead. His bright blue eyes stared at her. He smirked. "You think I'll end up in jail? What if I told you, I have my ways, my people. I know *everyone*. I can manipulate *anyone* into doing things they'd never otherwise *dream* of doing. A jury would definitely not lock me up. I'm Florida's senator, their sunshine boy! Nobody will lock me up. Just watch."

For a second, Maria was unsure. *Would they really let him go? Does he own the judges? The lawyers? Oh my gosh, he probably does. He'd get away with it?* Her heart sank in doubt, and so did the gun in her hands.

Before she knew it, Mike sprang toward her and grabbed her hands holding the gun. She yelped. *No, no, don't take it, don't hurt me, don't hurt Aaron!*

She was wrestling with him, trying to hold onto the gun, but he was strong, too strong, the loose handcuffs flying all over, hitting her hand. Mike was ready to pry the gun out of her hands. It was now pointing further downward, facing Mike's belly. He twisted her hands so much that she screamed in pain. Out of the corner of her eye, she saw Aaron wading toward them, rushing to help her.

"Just hold on, Maria, hold tight to the gun," Aaron yelled.

But that was easier said than done. Mike was trying to turn the gun around, twisting her fingers off one by one, but she held on, redoubling her grip.

As their hands fumbled about, she accidentally pulled the trigger. *Boom!*

Surprised by the force, Maria's one hand slipped off the gun, the other, still holding the firearm, flew upward, and she flopped backward into the water.

Oh my gosh, what happened?

She came up for air and saw Clifford stumbling toward her. A cloud of blood blossomed in the water around him. He staggered, held his navel. His blue eyes were focused on her, only her, stared directly at her.

He lifted his hands and tried to reach for her, moved his mouth slowly. "You... shot me. Bullet... in... my chest. Just wait... just you wait... *Bullet will get you.*"

Horrified, she watched as his eyes crossed and he splashed down into the water, right in front of her. The creek ran red. The gun dropped out of her hand and sank to the ground. She couldn't move, but her body was shaking, trembling, tears streaming.

"Maria, oh my gosh, Maria. Are you okay?"

She looked up and saw Aaron half-wading, half-swimming over. She slowly nodded, then started sobbing. Clifford's lifeless body floated in front of her.

Aaron reached her and pulled her in for a hug. She cried helplessly on his shoulder. "Oh my gosh, I killed him. I-I... *killed* him. Didn't mean to but... the... the—"

Aaron stroked her back. "It's okay, Maria, it's okay. It was self-defense. You did the right thing."

She sobbed even harder and held him tight, felt his warm body against her, felt the cuts and bruises on his back. His arm was swollen and a big welt was rising on his neck. Blood from his lip trickled into her hair. "Aaron, you… you fought for me. You saved me."

Without letting go of her, he nodded. "But in the end, *you* saved *me*. You saved yourself. You're strong, Maria. I love you."

"I love you, too, Aaron," she whispered between her sobs, and pressed her head closer to his chest, felt his heart beating fast.

They heard the barking dogs getting closer, heard movement in the bushes along the creek, knew the search team would be upon them any minute now.

"The police are coming, Maria. They're here to help. You're safe now," Aaron whispered. "We got the bad guy. You're safe now."

She felt herself nod automatically, but a shudder ran down her spine. *Safe? Am I safe? Did we get the bad guy?*

A dog appeared on the riverbank and barked and barked. A bunch of men dressed in black appeared, accompanied by more baying dogs. She forgot about her fears and focused on the present.

"Chief, we found her," she heard one of them shout into his police radio. "Looks like Clifford is down. Another guy is here, not sure who."

Before they knew it, a bunch of men jumped into the creek, and within seconds, they were surrounded. A bright smile came over Maria. She looked at the guy in charge. "This is Aaron, sir. My fiancé. He saved me."

"Okay, good to know. Come on then, both of you, we've got you."

The SWAT team grasped them and helped them back to the riverbank. Maria glanced over her shoulder and saw one of them flipping Clifford's lifeless body face up. "Suspect dead, sir."

Maria shivered, then decided not to look back anymore. The man with the police radio handed both her and Aaron a warm blanket.

"Here. Stay warm, guys." They nodded, then wrapped themselves immediately.

The man looked them over. "I'm Commander Reed. Glad to see you're both alive. You're both pretty banged up, huh?" Before waiting for an answer, he spoke into his police radio again. "Need two ambulances, Chief. They're hurt."

Hurt? Like my dad? Maria's mind was racing. "Is my dad okay?" she asked.

Commander Reed smiled. "He sure is. Already being treated and waiting at the hospital for you. I'm sure you'll see him soon."

Maria nodded. "And my mother?"

"Which one?" Commander Reed grinned.

"Both."

"I'm sure your whole family is waiting for you. Both your families. Come on, you two, we gotta get back to civilization before it gets pitch-black out here in the swamp."

Aaron and Maria nodded and watched the last glimmers of the setting sun disappear behind the trees.

"Mmm, nice sunset, right, Maria?" Aaron looked at her, his one eye almost swollen shut. "Another day done. Crazy day. But now you're safe, and the puzzle of your past has been solved." He smiled at her, then took her hand and squeezed it gently. "A new day will come with the sunrise. A new day, a new start to a safer life."

A safer life? Another shudder ran down her spine. She couldn't stop thinking about Clifford's last words. *Bullet will get me?*

"Come on, Maria, let's get out of here."

She nodded and, surrounded by the SWAT team and their dogs, started walking along the riverbank with Aaron, the love of her life. She felt the warmth of the blanket, the warmth of his hand in hers, as they followed Commander Reed into the cold, dark night.

DID YOU KNOW?

Reader reviews are very important to an indie author's success. They validate our work and help others find our stories. If you enjoyed "Puzzle of the Past", please leave a review filled with stars. Thank you!

Big thanks for joining me on this author journey. If you'd like to receive a little free gift, please email me (subject: gift) at gpschumacher.author@gmail.com.

Follow me on Facebook: G. P. Schumacher
Follow me on Instagram: author.g.p.schumacher
Find me on Pinterest: gpschumacherauthor

ALSO BY G. P. SCHUMACHER

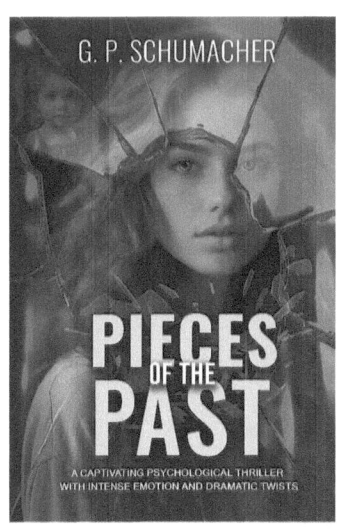

Coming soon:
Puppets of the Past
(Trilogy – Part 3)

ACKNOWLEDGEMENTS

Let me start out by thanking my amazing husband Ben, who is always there for me and encourages me to achieve all of my life goals. Thank you for cheering me on every time I write my stories. Big thanks for giving me the resources, time, and space to write my second novel. And thanks for believing in me!

Huge thanks also to my two kids, Maila and Ayden, who have not only listened to many drafts of my book, but have also given me excellent ideas and even corrected some grammar mistakes. Without you, I couldn't have created the characters of Elisabeth and Martina because I simply wouldn't understand the strength of a mother's love, the worries and the laughs that come with being a mom—an important knowledge to have for writing these two characters. Watching you grow up, I experienced all of the feelings that toddlers have and learned how much little kids already understand about the world. This helped me immensely for creating the character of Moana.

Thanks to all of my former 2Day2s Class students at SSDS! Because of you, I understand the amazing minds of little human beings much better. Thank you to my former colleagues at SSDS for giving me the opportunity to learn more about little children and their development. This experience, on top of having my own kids, really helped me in writing the parts out of a toddler's perspective.

Danke to my parents, Renate and Horst, who have often listened to numerous stories I've written for fun as a child. Thanks for encouraging and supporting me in my author journey. Danke also to my sister Inga and her two kids, Alissa and Marlon, for being interested in my first book. Your interest helped me in writing and finishing my second novel.

Big thanks to my in-laws: Nancy and Charles, Will and Heather and family, Marasie and family. Appreciated your interest in the writing process and thanks for following me on my social media platforms.

Danke also to Gisela and Costa for encouraging me to create a real "author business". Appreciate your ideas for marketing and hope I can soon translate the books into German, so you can enjoy reading them as well.

Thank you to my friends Elise and Melody who didn't only throw me a launch party for book one, but also constantly support me in my author journey! Thanks, Elise, for the native Spanish input for book two. Thanks, Melody, for your unwavering support and encouragement. Appreciate both of you—so glad we've met and become friends!

Special thanks to all of my editors at Motif Edits. Jeff, thank you for the fantastic line edits and the helpful comments that made me re-write paragraphs and clarify the content. And thanks for the supportive comments that often lifted me up. Thank you, Kathy, for proof-reading my novel and making sure it's grammatically correct. Big thanks also to Shavonne for the plot discussion calls that made me realize what I need to write to genre. Appreciate everyone's professional feedback and amazing edits. All of you helped me make this book the best one possible. I'm looking forward to continuing my work with you!

Thanks also to Self-Publishing School (SPS) for teaching me how to be a self-published author—how to write, edit, publish, and market my novel. Thanks to my coach Barbara for the helpful information and thanks to Ramy, Joe, and Brittany, who run the awesome online coaching calls I love to attend.

Last but not least, thank you to Dakota for being my SPS book production team manager, and for everyone else within that team. Thanks to Joice for the beautiful cover art and thank you, Honeylette, for the wonderful interior design. Really appreciate all of you for helping me with the finishing touches of the book.

SPS offers a wonderful and supportive online community with an immense knowledge. Happy to be a part of it!

WANT TO WRITE A BOOK OF YOUR OWN?

Self-Publishing School helped me, and I know they can help you!

Check them out now at: https://self-publishingschool.com/friend/

MEET THE AUTHOR

Greta Schumacher grew up in Bad Nenndorf, Germany. She immigrated to the United States in 2010 and has since lived in numerous states and cities while following her husband's Air Force career. She currently lives in Ohio with her husband and two children.

Due to moving a lot, she's had the opportunity to meet all kinds of people, encounter different lifestyles, and opinions. She believes each place, person, and experience shapes your life in one way or another.

Psychology and the human mind have been an interest of hers since she was a teenager, and she loves exploring these themes in her writing.

As a teacher and mom, she's especially interested in early childhood development, language acquisition, and young children's memories. She believes that toddlers' understanding of situations and feelings are often underestimated. Early childhood memories play an important part in her novels.

AUTHOR CONTACT

Interested in learning more about the author?

Follow me on Facebook: G. P. Schumacher

Follow me on Instagram: author.g.p.schumacher

Find me on Pinterest: gpschumacherauthor

Reach me via email: gpschumacher.author@gmail.com

www.ingramcontent.com/pod-product-compliance
Lightning Source LLC
Chambersburg PA
CBHW031028030726
47497CB00004B/1053